The BARGAIN

The
BARGAIN

PLAIN CITY PEACE

BOOK ONE

STEPHANIE REED

Kregel
Publications

The Bargain: A Novel
© 2013 by Stephanie Reed

Published by Kregel Publications, a division of Kregel, Inc.,
P.O. Box 2607, Grand Rapids, MI 49501.

The persons and events portrayed in this work are the creations
of the author, and any resemblance to persons living or dead is
purely coincidental.

Photography by Steve Gardner, PixelWorks Studios

ISBN 978-0-8254-4215-5

Printed in the United States of America
13 14 15 16 17 / 5 4 3 2

To my husband, Tom, one of the good ones.
Too often, the courage it takes to lovingly support a
wife and family goes unrecognized. Thank you for serving
the good Lord with grace and skill.

CHAPTER 1

"When a great adventure is offered, you don't refuse it."
—AMELIA EARHART, QUOTED IN BETSIE'S JOURNAL

BETSIE TROYER REINED in her horse as she reached the outskirts of Plain City. A tear trickled down her cheek as she tried to pretend she was on a normal errand, but grim reminders were everywhere.

As Judith trotted around the corner of Ohio 42, Betsie was barely aware of her parents on the seat beside her. They were silent as the buggy passed the filling station on State Route 161, where the English paid twenty-nine cents a gallon to fuel their fancy cars. Cookie-cutter English houses on postage-stamp lots rubbed elbows with imposing English churches topped with showy bells and steeples. A row of red-brick storefronts marched proudly along West Main Street. The glare of shop lights was absent, but Betsie could almost hear the evil crackle of electricity as it surged through the ugly wires overhead.

A traffic light commanded a stop. Betsie glanced at the Seth Thomas clock ensconced in the white cupola in the center of town: ten past six on a Monday morning. She gritted her teeth and faced front so that her bonnet served as blinders to block out the English world as much as possible. Common sense reminded her it was much too early for the lazy English to shop for their store-bought goods—the English, who already had everything they would ever desire, anyway. *Ach*, they weren't going to get her parents, too.

S T E P H A N I E   R E E D

"*Dat*, please don't you and *Mem* leave the Amish," she burst out. "How can you ignore what you promised on your knees before the church, long before I was born?"

"Betsie, Betsie." Her father's grizzled beard dragged against his suspenders as he shook his head. "Now that we know the truth and hold it dear in our hearts, *Mem* and I will follow Jesus wherever He leads. He knows how sorry we are that we didn't follow Him sooner." *Dat* sighed. "I pray you and Sadie will follow Him, too. Come with us to Belle Center, *Dechder*."

"Never." The buggy rolled onto Railroad Street. The train depot loomed ahead, and in front of it steamed the black beast that would carry her parents away forever. Fifty miles that might as well be five thousand. If she'd had her way, they would all be at home with her youngest sister. Sadie missed saying good-bye because it would look suspicious if they all went to the depot—maybe *Dat* wasn't so sure of his decision, after all.

She decided to press him. "When I join the church, I will stay here forever." With Charley Yoder, because he thinks a lot of me, and I think a lot of him, too, she added inwardly. She thanked the good Lord for a single ray of sunshine on an awful day. "Besides, you know I made a bargain with Nelson. I promised to mind the harness shop for him while he's away, and you've always taught me to honor my word—up to now."

"Betsie," *Mem* reproved. "You should not speak so to your *Dat*."

"Leave be, Fannie." *Dat* rubbed the back of his neck. "Your cousin never should have asked such a sacrifice of you, Betsie," he said slowly. "I know he didn't choose to be drafted, but it's a shame he agreed to serve in the military hospital instead of keeping that new business of his going."

"*Ach*, it's all settled. Besides, if I didn't help my cousin, what would the bishop say? It took him such a long time to grant me permission to live and work in Hilliard while I learn the trade."

As she spoke, Betsie marveled at how ludicrous her situation was. Why had she, an Amish girl who shunned Englishers, agreed so readily to live among them? She had no explanation apart from her adventurous streak, which cropped up at the oddest times. Of course, *Mem* would say it stemmed from some of the English stories she checked out from the Plain City Library. More than once, her mother had warned that reading about the doings of Amelia Earhart and Tom Sawyer would get Betsie into trouble.

Trouble there had been. Bishop Jonas Gingerich hadn't liked the harness shop idea at all. It helped—a little—that the English family with whom Betsie would live during her apprenticeship included an upstanding father and mother who would look after her welfare. Mr. Sullivan, the former shop owner, had assured Jonas of Mrs. Sullivan's cooperation. They hadn't met the English lady, but Betsie pictured a mother like the one she'd seen in an English newspaper ad for boxed pancake mix. One who wore a starched, knee-length dress and a dainty apron. In one hand, she held a spatula, and she smiled as she poured batter on a smoking griddle.

Maybe the bishop had seen the same ad, for he had ultimately approved Betsie's request to take over Nelson's business while her cousin was stationed at a Chicago hospital for two years. Incredible as it seemed, she was to start her new job this very morning. Mr. Sullivan had promised to pick her up for the week. It wasn't like she'd be with the English the whole time, after all. She'd travel home on the weekends. *Dat's* sister, Lovina, was Nelson's mother, and this very minute she was traveling from Holmes County to stay with the Troyers while Nelson was away.

Only, *Dat* had stopped short of informing Lovina that he wouldn't actually be there. Betsie cherished this uncharacteristic omission as another crumb of proof that he might change his mind.

"Haven't the English intruded on our way of life enough, *Dat?* Whoa, Judith." Betsie pulled up in front of the gingerbread-trimmed station and faced him. "Do they have to take you and *Mem*, too?"

With his rumbly bear voice hardly above a whisper, *Dat* said, "Look around us, child. See the cars, the modern machinery? It's 1971, yet we live as though it's 1841. Do you really think our Lord cares how we dress or how we plow, so long as we give ourselves completely to Him and His care?" He patted her hand. "Come, Betsie. We mustn't miss the train; Pastor Shock's brother is expecting us. Bless his heart for taking us in." He disembarked and gave his hand to *Mem* to help her out of the buggy.

Betsie swallowed tears as she set the brake and hopped down to fasten Judith's neck rope to the hitching rail. When she finished, *Dat* cleared his throat and looked from Betsie to the ticket window and back again. "Look out for the Brewster's dog on the way home, *Dechder*. That fool Prince is liable to rush and snap at the buggy wheels and get Judith all riled up."

"*Jah*, I know." Her throat ached. Always she had heard the same advice every time she drove to and from Plain City, but no more. "*Dat*, please! *Mem!*" She clasped her hands. "Don't sneak away like this. Your place is here."

Mem's face crumpled. "Betsie, you know if we told anyone we were leaving the Amish, we would face unbearable pressure to stay. We must make a clean break. If you children would come with us, our happiness would be complete, but we can't make such an important decision for you. As far as our own faith is concerned, go we must." She embraced Betsie in a rare show of affection and turned away to fumble in her pocket for the train fare.

"Run home and get Sadie. Join us, Betsie." *Dat* nodded encouragingly. "You won't find the good Lord lacking."

His kind blue eyes were filled with such compassion that, for a moment, Betsie wavered. But what about her future with Charley Yoder? If she left the Amish with her parents, it was all over with her and Charley.

She shook her head. "I have never found Him lacking, *Dat*. I don't understand why you have."

He looked at the ground. When he raised his head, his eyes glistened as he rubbed them. "A cinder must have got me." He sniffled and then turned heavily toward the ticket window. "Two for Belle Center, please," Betsie heard him say in his best English.

"Round trip?" The stationmaster's busy hands paused.

"Not this time." *Dat* inclined his head with authority but Betsie saw him clutch *Mem*'s hand beneath the counter. The stationmaster raised his bushy eyebrows, pushed up his spectacles, and issued the tickets. Then he sauntered outside to stow their baggage.

Dat held *Mem's* elbow as she climbed the steps. He paused to look at Betsie one last time. "Be careful out in the world, Betsie." He thrust a paper at her. "Here is the address where we will be. Write to us so we know you and Sadie are safe. Trust in the Lord." The conductor took their tickets and showed them to their seats.

Betsie waved and stumbled toward the buggy as the train chugged. One sob escaped her as she undid her mare's neck rope. She held the harness strap as Judith nudged her and nickered. Betsie rubbed her mare's nose, determined not to let the curious stationmaster see her distress.

Her resolve lasted until the train hooted and crossed the road in front of her to retreat into the distance. Then she mounted the buggy step. Mechanically she sat down, the piece of paper still clutched in her sweaty hand. "Our new address, 211 East Buckeye Street, Belle Center, Ohio," she whispered. She shoved the paper deep in her pocket and dissolved in quiet tears, only dimly aware of her surroundings as she drove through town. She passed a few farms and was nearing her own driveway when a childish voice pierced her grief.

"Betsie! See my kitty!"

Wearily she searched the early morning shadows and spotted her neighbor, Katie Miller. Her pixie face wreathed in smiles, the tiny girl lugged a patient orange cat, its distended belly practically dragging the ground.

"If you come over now, I'll let you play with her!" Katie promised.

"Not today, but soon." Betsie managed a wan smile and a one-fingered wave.

Katie beamed. "You're a *gut* friend, Betsie!"

The sweet words thawed the block of ice in Betsie's middle a fraction, but she needed to get home. She managed to pass a couple more farms before a friend of *Dat's* hailed her. With a sinking heart, Betsie tightened the reins. Judith shook her head and arched her neck but submitted to steady pressure. The mare was just as eager as she was to get home.

Joe Miller, Katie's great-uncle, stood next to a white sign he'd tacked to a fence post. "*Guder mariye*, Betsie. Just who I needed to see. Tell me, can a good reader like you make out my sign all right from the road?"

How was it that most Amish signs looked like they'd been lettered by the same hand? Joe's letters were the usual endearing mix of spidery capitals and lowercase. "'Firewood, split and camp, ask for Sawmill Joe,'" she read aloud. "See? I can make it out fine." She hoped he couldn't make out her tears.

"Such a big help you always are, Betsie. Tell your *Dat* I said hello." Joe raised his index finger and touched his hat brim.

Betsie shuddered and drove home, a very different home than the one she'd left this morning.

She cared for Judith in a fog, turned her out, and wandered inside for some sisterly comfort, but Sadie had already left for her job. Betsie knew she should eat a good breakfast, but a cup of tea and some crackers were all she could manage. When she finished the meager fare, she simply sat, something she'd not done in recent memory. Finally she carried her dishes to the sink. She washed them in the cooling water from the teakettle, and as she swiped her clean teacup with the dish towel, a car horn honked. The fragile cup slipped from her hands and shattered on *Mem*'s spotless linoleum.

Betsie checked the clock. Was it only yesterday that *Mem* had wound it for the last time? She steeled herself and pushed that thought away. Eight o'clock—Mr. Sullivan was here. She sidestepped the broken glass and pulled the black bonnet over her *Kapp*. She hurried to grab her satchel and dashed out the front door.

A car the color of a buzzing yellow jacket idled in the driveway. A black stripe encircled the car's back end. As Betsie approached, the window lowered. Her steps slowed; this was not Mr. Sullivan, her new boss. Instead, a lady with fluffy auburn hair that dragged on her shoulders sat in the driver's seat. She flipped her hair back and revealed brown eyes. Her face was devoid of the paint that English ladies liked. It came to her that the lady had stopped here because she was lost.

"Hey." The lady looked up and down at Betsie's bonnet, apron, violet dress, black stockings, and sensible shoes. The car door opened and two bare feet topped by fringed trouser hems emerged. The trouser material flared wide around each ankle but fit skin-tight above the knee, except for rips that revealed hairy kneecaps.

Betsie sucked in her breath. This long-haired person was a man, and a long-haired English man was properly classified as a hippie. She'd glimpsed his kind in Plain City but had given them a wide berth. He towered a half a foot or more above her, increasing the threat.

Her heart slammed. "Don't come near me!"

"Verrry funny. Okay, joke's over."

The hippie made a grab for her satchel, but Betsie whipped it behind her and backed away. "You English have taken everything I have, but you're not getting me!"

He froze. "Whoa, easy there. My old man sent me to pick you up, but seems to me you're dealing with something pretty heavy."

"My satchel is *not* heavy. I can carry it." Tears welled up. "Please leave me alone!"

"Oh, wow." He held up both palms in a gesture of submission. "Listen, my dad is Gerald Sullivan. Harness shop. Ring a bell?"

Was that sympathy she glimpsed in his eyes? She willed herself to breathe. He was saying the right words, but how did she know if she could trust him? Maybe he only wanted to placate her long enough to force-feed her psychedelic drugs and then abduct her.

Then again, what did it matter? No *Dat* appeared at her side with solid advice; no *Mem* waited in the house with loving arms. The life she knew was over. She hesitantly surrendered her bag and trailed toward the car.

"Cool." The hippie hoisted the satchel. His cuffs were wide and frayed, his green shirt unbuttoned nearly to his navel. His long hair hid his face as he stowed the satchel in the back. Betsie wrapped her dress around her body like a shield and slid backward into the sloped bucket seat.

The hippie settled himself, twisted a key in a flat wooden panel, and touched a wooden knob on top of a silver stick between the seats. He moved the stick, and the car emitted a powerful snarl.

As the car backed up, Betsie caught a glimpse of her empty house, a tall white square graced by a wide front porch. Cottonwood shadows danced across the white siding. Her heart ached as she bid a silent good-bye to the green shingles and the shutterless windows.

She crumpled a fold of her dress and rubbed her thumb over the rough fabric. A dull pain throbbed in her right arm, and she realized she was plastered against the window crank. The tires crunched, and then they were on the road.

"You okay?"

Adrenaline raced. Her survival instinct kicked in and set her nerves on a knife edge. She nodded but kept her eyes peeled for Joe Miller or any other neighbor who might come to her rescue if the hippie tried anything.

"Cool," he repeated. "Kinda touch and go there for a minute."

She needed an escape plan. Her fingers curved over the door handle. She'd nearly worked up the nerve to bail out and roll to the pavement when there was a click. Loud music flooded the car. Betsie clapped her hands over her ears and squealed.

"Oh, sorry." The hippie pointed to the black square display with white numbers above five silver keys. "That's the radio," he shouted.

"I know it's the radio," Betsie snapped, heart racing. She folded her hands in her lap so he wouldn't see them shake.

"I thought music might help you relax. Forgot I had it cranked to wake me up." He lowered the volume and punched a key. The orange line skittered to another number. Horns blared.

"Much better, huh? Just drop all that heavy stuff and unwind, like the song says." He drummed his fingers to the music.

Betsie scrunched down and did her best to ignore his talk. When the music faded, she was relieved, but nearly jumped out of her skin when a man shouted, "All *right!* Keep it tuned to WHOA, baby, where the hits never stop! Great new tune coming up, but first, these messages." Then another man spoke quite solemnly about a buddy dropping a dime.

"Is this station okay?" the hippie asked. He glanced at her dress. "I mean, for your religion? They pretty much play bubble gum. My little sister likes it."

She drew her dress still tighter around her knees. "What was he screeching about?"

The hippie grinned and wiggled his eyebrows. "Well, if you have to ask . . . Hey, wait a sec. Screeching? This station is easy listening."

"Easy? He hurt my ears."

"Huh. No wonder my old man hired you; you think like him." He braked for a bend in the road. "Pretty soon you'll be telling me that all guys should cut their hair above their ears and all chicks should wear dresses." He glanced at Betsie's dress and flushed.

Chickens in dresses? She stifled an almost hysterical urge to giggle. This hippie wasn't so sure of himself now. "You have a funny way of talking, ain't so? What's your name, anyway?"

"Michael Sullivan, comic relief at your behest, ma'am." He stopped for a traffic light.

Betsie stole a look at him, but he caught her in the act and winked.

"Well, what's the verdict? Perfectly harmless . . . ain't so?"

Betsie narrowed her eyes. Was this Michael mocking her?

"Skip it." He held up a couple of fingers, his gaze fixed on the red light. "Peace."

What? Now she was the one off balance. With annoyance came a surge of her adventurous streak, and she punched one of the radio keys. The orange line jumped to another number.

"Listen up, people. I could lose my job for playing this one," the man on the radio said. "Tomorrow, May 4, 1971, marks one year since we lost Jeffrey, Allison, William, and Sandra. Rest in peace, Kent State Four."

Awful twanging filled the car. The twanging lasted a long time. It wasn't a happy sound—even Betsie could tell the difference from the song Michael played before. Angry thumps reverberated beneath the twangs.

The traffic signal changed from red to green. Betsie braced for acceleration, but Michael didn't move. He stared at the road with a lost look while the howling voices mourned about soldiers and dead and O-hi-o. She thought he would break the wheel in two, he gripped it so hard. Droplets of sweat popped out on his forehead. Betsie pointed at the green light, but he flinched.

Quickly Betsie rolled the silver wheel until the music clicked off. *Mem* was right. Nothing good ever came out of a radio.

CHAPTER 2

The English family I live with is very strange.
—BETSIE'S JOURNAL

A CAR HONKED, and Michael jumped. He floored the gas pedal. The tires squealed, and the car shot forward.

Betsie grabbed the bucket seat. "What's the matter?"

Instead of answering, Michael tromped harder on the gas. The ride passed in silence as the car whizzed past farms, a school, and many English homes. After a harrowing ride, she was relieved to glimpse a sign that read, "Welcome to Hilliard."

The car rocketed across a railroad track and slewed into a blacktop driveway that curved in an arch. To one side, a faded wooden sign that read "Sullivan and Son—Harness Shop" swung from a post. Michael pulled up in front of a long, brick house that sported a fine crop of grass and a row of shade trees. The trees lined a fenced pasture full of weeds that enclosed a spotted pony and an open shed. On the other side of the house, Betsie noticed a white building with diamond-shaped window panes. All that was missing from the property was a barn.

Michael moved the stick and turned the key. He got out, leaned to retrieve Betsie's satchel, and stalked inside the house.

Only the pleasant morning breeze remained to welcome Betsie to her new place. She trudged toward the door, alone again.

"Hey, are you our new helper?"

A girl of about eleven peered at Betsie from behind one of the trees. The spotted pony nibbled a carrot from her outstretched hand. The girl's wavy brown bangs fell across brown eyes flecked with gold as she studied Betsie.

"Yes. I'm Betsie Troyer." Her knees trembled; the day's events were taking a toll.

The girl patted the pony's dusty neck and climbed the fence. She ran to Betsie's side. "I'm Sheila Sullivan. I thought you'd be a lot older. How old are you, anyway?"

"Nineteen." Betsie examined the girl's short blue pants and skimpy red shirt that revealed her knobby elbows and knees. "How old are you?"

"Almost twelve. Hey, do you think we can be friends, Betsie?"

The girl seemed harmless enough, but after today, the last thing Betsie wanted to do was make friends with the English. "I will be awfully busy, and you must go to school, ain't so?"

"Yeah, I guess so. But Dad let me stay home from school today so I could show you around." Her shoulders drooped. Long hair escaped in wispy tendrils from her ponytail. "I'm supposed to take you to your room."

Betsie removed her black bonnet as Sheila led the way into a crazy room crammed with English foolishness. A soft, white rug covered the entire floor. Sheila took her shoes off before she walked on it, so Betsie followed suit. She had to admit that it was like walking on a cloud, so cozy under her stockings.

A clear walking path was tacked down over the white rug. Etched lines kept feet steady. Betsie pursed her lips. If Mrs. Sullivan didn't want a rug to show dirt, why buy a white one?

To the right, in front of the window, was a sitting room. Whoever had built this house was certainly a poor craftsman; the floor was not level at all. Two steps led down to a white couch and other furniture. Why anyone would put up with such an uneven floor was beyond her.

Two gold-and-white chairs faced each other under a clock that bristled with shiny golden spikes. It looked like a small child's drawing of the sun, with rays shooting out in every direction.

The couch and the chairs faced a wooden cabinet with a green glass square set inside. All along the top of the cabinet were lumpy vessels made of streaked pottery.

"Come on, Betsie!" Sheila grabbed her hand and dragged her down the hall. Her stockings scratched on the plastic path as they passed closed doors. The girl had shown spunk in shrugging off her disappointment. It would be difficult to keep the relationship all business, as the bishop had advised.

"This is your room." Sheila pushed open a door.

Betsie peeked inside. Her satchel rested on the floor by the bed. Her window revealed a view of the front yard with the pasture to one side. The fat pony grazed there, a clump of grass hanging from his mouth like an Amish beard. Something tight inside Betsie loosened as she watched the peaceful scene.

Following Betsie's gaze, Sheila pushed up the window. "Fledge is my pony." She pursed her lips and whistled at him. "Hey, Fledge!" He ignored her and cropped more grass. "He doesn't mind very well. Dad bought him for me. Fledge seemed like a real bargain until I tried to ride him."

"What do you mean?"

"Well, he won't let me."

"Your dad won't let you ride him?"

"No, *Fledge* won't."

"Oh." Betsie studied the lazy pony with narrowed eyes before she inspected the room, from the white ruffled curtains to the nubbly white bedspread. Against the wall was a dresser with six drawers. Betsie did not own enough clothing to fill even one drawer. She set her satchel on the ladder-back chair in the corner.

"Do you like horses, Betsie? I loaned you my prettiest pictures."

Betsie glimpsed her reflection in the mirror and frowned. Useful horses like Judith, who pulled the buggy at home—that was the kind of horse Betsie preferred. But she nodded. "I like horses."

A bell whirred, and Betsie jumped, her sense of peace broken.

"The phone's ringing!" Sheila scurried to answer it. Betsie heard her speaking to someone in the other room, so she unpacked her satchel.

Finding no pegs on the wall, she hung her bonnet on the ladder-back chair spindle.

As she turned, she caught a whiff of something faintly sweet. On the dresser was a teacup, violets spilling over the rim. Betsie brushed a purple flower with a fingertip; Sheila must have picked them. Her throat tightened. *Mem* grew many flowers in the flowerbeds at home, but who would care for them now?

Mustn't think about that. Where had Sheila gotten to, anyway? Betsie glimpsed an English privy across the hall, but it was empty. *Dat* had talked about putting a bathroom inside someday soon, but this one was even fancier than the one in the public library. The tile floor glistened with many squares of pink. Different hues blocked out a pattern which ran all the way up the wall under the high window at the end of the narrow room. A pink rug lay in front of a white cabinet with a pink bowl set in a counter. Above the bowl was another mirror.

Behind the bowl was a spout with a round clear handle on either side. Betsie cranked one a couple of times, and cold water gushed over her wrists. Ahhh . . . even if she lived to be one hundred, she would never tire of the convenience of running water. She blotted her hands with a fluffy fingertip towel and rearranged it on the silver ring.

Next to the sink stood a pink toilet, lid open, bowl filled with bright blue water. A handy spindle mounted on the side of the sink cabinet held a roll of scratchy paper printed with gold fleur de lis.

Most wonderful of all was the deep pink tub with the shiny spigot. A wicked desire consumed her, a desire to sit in that tub and wash herself off all at once, instead of piecemeal in the metal washtub on Saturday night at home.

Bam! A sound shook the walls, so loud that Betsie felt it in her stomach. Loud angry thumps punctuated wails of pain. Shaken, she darted across the hallway and touched a closed door; it vibrated. She twisted the knob.

What a sight. Heaps of dirty clothes littered the floor, a desk, and a bed. Blood red walls were plastered with bright posters. One of the posters showed black words scrawled in fat letters that marched across mustard-toned paper. Black stems sprawled under what looked like a sunflower. In between the stems, Betsie made out what the poster said: "War is not healthy for children and other living things."

"Woodstock Music and Art Fair" was painted on a red poster. A white bird perched on one foot. White fingers clutched a blue-and-green guitar. Betsie had seen guitars in books, but they weren't this colorful. Wide yellow-and-white letters spelled out, "Three days of peace & music."

A felt pennant drew her attention next. Blue letters on a gold field spelled out "Kent State." Just below, it looked like someone had punched a hole in the red wall.

She rubbed her pounding temples. Words assaulted her—angry words that she recognized as the same wailing song she had heard in the car. The sound screamed out of tall brown boxes with black screens on the front.

And then she spotted Michael, sprawled lengthwise on his stomach amidst a heap of messy bedclothes. His feet hung over the edge of the bed, and he faced away from her as he watched a machine that spun a black disc in a never-ending circle. A bloody cloth was wrapped around the knuckles of his right hand.

She had to get out of there before he saw her. Her knees wobbled as she fled to find Sheila.

CHAPTER 3

I don't know what to make of Michael. He's like Ohio
weather; if you don't like it, wait fifteen minutes for a
change. His little sister, Sheila, is like a perfect summer
day, sunny and warm.

—BETSIE'S JOURNAL

WHEN BETSIE REACHED the far bedroom, Sheila was still chattering
into the pink handle of a telephone that rested on a small table by the
bed. With her back to Betsie, she twined the curly cord around one
finger.

"Okay. Yeah, Dad. I'll tell her. G'bye!" She replaced the phone on
the hanger-up. "Betsie!"

"Here I am."

Sheila jumped. "Gosh, where did you come from? Dad says he'll
show you around the harness shop tomorrow when he's off work. Hey,
I'm starved! Wanna eat? I'll make breakfast."

The girl was already halfway to the kitchen. Betsie sidled past
Michael's room and followed. She sank into a kitchen chair to watch
as Sheila rummaged through cupboards and plinked cold cereal into a
bowl from a yellow box.

"That is breakfast?"

"Mm-hmm, my favorite." She poured milk from a waxy carton and
sprinkled lots of sugar on the brown doughnut shapes. "Want some?"

"I've eaten already. You go ahead." Betsie smoothed her apron and halfway stood to see the prickly clock in the living room. Almost nine—most of the morning was gone. Betsie got up and gingerly poked at the stack of dirty dishes in the sink. "Why didn't you eat breakfast when your *mem* made it?"

Sheila stopped, spoon dripping. "Mom didn't make breakfast. She's too busy."

"Oh." Betsie nodded. "I guess she figures you can fix your own, and besides, it *is* high time to set the wash drying on such a pretty Monday."

"She's not doing laundry, either. She walked down to the library." Sheila dabbed her chin with a paper napkin. "Mom wants to be in a play, so she's reading her lines. She never does housework. She's . . . finding herself." She added her empty bowl to the sink full of crusty dishes.

"Finding herself?" Signs of household neglect were easy to find. The ugly green stovetop with its curly burners was smudged with fingerprints. Betsie wrinkled her nose at a sour smell, like something had boiled over. As she walked to the cupboard, her shoes stuck to linoleum patterned like dull red bricks. She made a face and rummaged for a pan to boil some water. She filled it at the spout.

"What are you doing, Betsie?"

"Why, redding up, of course." Betsie set the pan to boil and cleared the sink. She scoured it with steel wool and plenty of elbow grease, stoppered it, and ran a little cold water to make sure it held.

While she waited for the water to boil, Betsie pawed through helter-skelter cupboards and drawers and set the contents to rights. In much less time than it took with the wood-fired stove at home, the water boiled steamy hot. She dribbled Ivory liquid in the sink and tipped the pan of boiling water into one side, steam rising to warm her face. She poured the rest of the water in the other sink. Once she rolled up her sleeves, she found a clean dishrag and plunged the dirty cups and glasses in the billowy soapsuds.

Sheila edged nearer. "You're washing the dishes by hand!"

"You sound like you've never seen it done before." Betsie chuckled.

"Yes, I have! My grandma used to."

"Your grandma? What does your *mem* do when the dishes are dirty?" she asked with a smile. "Throw them away?" She upended the last clean glass on a towel to dry and scooted the cutlery from the countertop into the suds.

"Only when we use paper plates. But if we use real ones, like at Christmas, Mom uses the dishwasher. Dad bought it for her because he says she isn't too good at all that housewife jazz. But he uses it more than she does."

"Your dad washes the dishes?"

"Yep. Mom says that's the machine that made her a liberated woman." Sheila pointed at a green box under the countertop. Betsie examined the silver and black push buttons and pulled on the silver handle to reveal two big baskets inside.

Sheila reached past Betsie and rolled one of the white baskets toward her. "See? You put the dishes in here, like this. But Dad usually soaks them first." She scraped at a crusted plate with her thumbnail.

What an upside-down family. "Well, now, if ever he had to soak dishes, it'd be these here. So, we'll let them sit awhile and scrub the counters and floors while we wait."

A spark lit Sheila's eyes. "Can I wash the dishes instead? I love playing with bubbles."

"Sure you can." Betsie handed her the dishrag.

Sheila beamed as she lowered the dishes in the warm soapsuds. Betsie smiled, too. Whenever she felt out of sorts, scrubbing a big pan of dishes washed her troubles down the drain.

"Now, then, do you have a machine to clean these countertops? Or will a sponge do?"

"A sponge." Sheila grinned, and Betsie applied hot water and elbow grease to the task.

Soon Betsie was ready to mop the sticky floor, but the new-fangled squeeze mop posed a problem. At the back of the closet, she spied a string mop. She boiled more water and tackled the linoleum, with Sheila scooting chairs out of the way.

"I've never mopped before," she hinted.

Betsie had mopped for her mother since she was just five years old. "You can rinse for me while I open the windows to let the floor dry."

When she finished, Sheila sniffed appreciatively. "Mmm! That was fun, Betsie. And boy, oh boy, am I hungry again. It must be almost lunch time." She glanced at the sun clock and drooped. "I can't believe all that work only took two hours! It's eleven o' clock."

"I had my breakfast very early, so I'll cook us something," Betsie offered.

"Cool!" Sheila raced to the green refrigerator. Betsie peeked over her shoulder to examine the contents. She counted several open bottles of soda pop. One of the bottles had tipped over and dripped to the shelves below. A partial stick of oleomargarine glowed an artificial yellow. No eggs and no pie, much less lard for pie crust. A few sad apples tumbled in the crisper as she closed the door.

"Where do you keep your bread, Sheila?"

"Here." Dust sifted as she pulled a plastic rectangle printed with red, blue, and yellow balloons from the top of the refrigerator with a sneeze.

Betsie fingered the loaf, stale and light as a feather, but it would have to do. She set it on the counter and returned to her room, Sheila hot on her trail. Betsie hardly noticed Michael's music this time. She retrieved the jar of peanut butter spread that she'd brought along in case she got homesick.

With Sheila close by her side, Betsie found two clean saucers and opened the bread. She slathered the thick mixture of peanut butter, corn syrup, and marshmallow crème on two slices of bread. She slapped on two bread lids and cut each sandwich catty-corner. Sheila poured two glasses of milk and joined Betsie for a feast.

"Mmm, so good, Betsie!"

A glob of peanut spread stuck in the corner of Sheila's mouth. Betsie dabbed it away with a paper napkin.

"I'm glad. We take them to church a lot, to eat between services," Betsie told her.

"Lucky—"

Sheila shrank in her chair. Betsie, too, had heard the warning click of an opening door and the crackle of footsteps on the plastic path.

"Hi, Mike." Sheila stared at her plate.

Michael stalked silently to the refrigerator and yanked it open. His lanky hair concealed his face; he flipped the hair out of the way, but it slithered back. Betsie reflected that a good Amish haircut would remedy the problem.

Michael propped the refrigerator door open with one hip. He lifted the carton of milk to his lips and tilted his head. When it was empty, he whacked the carton on the clean counter and poked around in the crisper.

"Hey, Mike, this peanut butter spread is yummy. You want some?"

"Nope." Michael polished a shriveled apple. "Gotta split. Catch you later."

As he crossed the kitchen, he saw Betsie, checked, then stalked out of the house, frays and tatters fluttering. The yellow car growled, and tires squealed.

Betsie patted Sheila's hand as the girl sniffled. "I guess he's having a bad day." She recalled a saying her father was fond of: "The gem cannot be polished without friction, nor the man perfected without trials." She chewed her lip. Surely it would be better to let friction work until Sheila was polished up to a shine.

Impulsively she squeezed Sheila's hand. "I will be your friend."

CHAPTER 4

Two habits of the English are very strange: the way they
do the wash and the way they do the marketing.
—BETSIE'S JOURNAL

WITH THE HELP of the washing machine instruction manual, Sheila
and Betsie finished the wash by early afternoon. Sheila grumbled some
about the unaccustomed chores, but the cure for sadness was plenty of
hard work; at least that was what Betsie's *mem* always said.

The washer was a wonder for sure. The machine was easy to turn
on, and it shut off by itself. No water to boil and no washboard to bust
her knuckles—Betsie nearly pinched herself to make sure she wasn't
dreaming. It was fun to stuff the dirty clothes in the flowing water,
plop in a soap tablet, and click the button. Betsie also enjoyed hanging
the clean clothes out to dry, though Sheila said they never used the old
wire clothesline these days.

"Why use a machine to dry your clothes when the good Lord gave
us all this fresh air?" Betsie pegged the last basket, full of what Sheila
called "blue jeans," to the line. They laughed at the family display.
Sheila's shorter pants, Mr. Sullivan's work overalls, and Michael's tattered trousers flapped in the sunny breeze when Betsie hoisted the
clothes pole to prop the wire.

When the laundry was finished, the girls rested on the back steps
beside a lilac bush covered with fragrant purple blossoms. Betsie

wrapped her arms around her skirts. Sheila rested her chin on her knees for a while and watched Fledge shoo flies with his tail. The sheets she'd washed earlier billowed like sails. Betsie couldn't wait to smell them when she went to bed.

She stretched. "Ready to dust the furniture, Sheila?"

"Dust?"

"Why, yes, seeing as how we got the wash done like lightning, why not begin Friday's work?"

"But Betsie, it's Monday." Sheila's eyebrows puckered.

"Oh, I meant the rhyme my *mem* taught me. 'Wash on Monday, iron on Tuesday, mend on Wednesday, market on Thursday, clean on Friday, bake on Saturday, go to meeting on Sunday.' Since we're saving all this time with your fancy machines, I figure we can do more house-cleaning." Betsie blotted sweat from the back of her neck. "Going to market is awful needful, though. If only I had Judith here."

"Who's Judith?"

Betsie suppressed a smile. Sheila's questions had more to do with delaying work than with curiosity. "She's my mare, the one I hitch to the buggy when I need to go somewhere."

Sheila giggled. "Gosh, Betsie! I can just see you trying to hitch up Fledge." She gestured at the pinto.

Betsie privately decided that no lazy pony would ever get the better of her. It was all a matter of letting Fledge think he was boss.

"Man," Sheila continued, "I didn't know we were going to work, work, work. I thought you were going to help Dad in the harness shop."

"Well, he's not here, is he? What am I supposed to do, sit idle the livelong day?"

"That's what Mike does. It makes Dad blow his top, all right."

Betsie brushed her apron. "What does that mean?"

"It means Dad yells at Michael. A lot."

"Oh." Betsie tucked away the phrase. No one in her school had learned English words faster, and she was going to learn their funny way of speaking just as fast.

"Mike used to be so nice. He still is, sometimes." Sheila picked at a scab on her knee.

Betsie thought back to her car ride with Michael. She had to admit that despite her initial fright, he had been okay until the disturbing song played on the radio.

"It's weird," Sheila sighed, "but I miss Mike, even when he's here. I wish he could be like he was before college. We laughed a lot."

A train whistle mourned. Fledge spooked and cantered toward the shade trees at the far side.

"Do you think Michael would—" Betsie paused to hold her thought until the noisy passenger cars clacked over the adjacent tracks. For an instant, she thought of the next stop, Plain City, where her parents had boarded and left forever, but she squelched her sadness.

"What?" Sheila cupped her hand to her ear and yelled.

"Maybe Michael can drive us to the market later," Betsie hollered. The racket lessened, and she felt foolish for yelling.

"No way. Mike won't drive us anywhere."

"Says who?"

Betsie jumped about a foot. Michael whistled a jaunty tune as he rounded the corner of the house.

Sheila fidgeted. "Don't be mad, Mike. We didn't mean it. You don't have to take us anywhere."

He folded himself up next to his sister and ruffled her hair. "Hey, Squirt, no sweat. Sorry, okay? I'm mellowed out now. So, where do you need to go?"

"We don't have anything Betsie can cook for supper. And . . . and we wanted to go to the market," she finished in a rush.

"The market, huh?" He looked at Betsie. "That right?"

"*Jah*, but we thought if we asked you to drive us, you'd blow your top."

"*Betsie!*" Sheila blushed. "Sorry, Mike."

"It's cool." His mouth quirked. "You learn fast, huh, Betsie?"

Why not admit it? "I like to learn."

Michael appraised her. She felt like a horse up for auction, scrutinized by a wary bidder.

He turned to his sister. "Tell you what, Squirt. You scoot inside and put your shoes on, and while you're at it, get some dough out of the change jar. I'll give Betsie the scoop on how the market works. Betcha it's somewhat different than she's used to. Meet us in about twenty minutes, and I'll spring for ice cream on the way home." He stuck out his hand. "Gimme five."

Betsie watched, puzzled, as Sheila slapped her brother's palm and headed for the house with a big smile.

A few minutes later, Betsie's vocabulary suitably enriched, Michael assured her she would do just fine on her own.

"Oh! Aren't you coming in with me?"

He hesitated a second. "Okay, sure, why wouldn't I come with? I've got some serious munchies—um, that means 'I'm really hungry.' Can't wait for some real chow. I mean 'food.'"

The three of them piled in the yellow car and headed for the market, Sheila talking a mile a minute. Betsie felt a little flutter in her stomach, nervous that she wouldn't remember all the new words and phrases.

"We're going to let her do all the talking, aren't we, Squirt? Don't worry, Betsie." He parked and reached to pat her shoulder, but she flinched. A shadow flitted across his face, the same quick sympathy she'd glimpsed early this morning. When he glanced her way again, his grin looked forced. "Sorry. You'll be fine."

He handed her a few dollars and pointed at a sign on the window. "Looks like they have a deal on apples today—59 cents for four pounds. The ones in the fridge are getting mushy."

Betsie nodded, the phrase reserved for paying compliments to the grocer galloping through her mind.

The market was filled with ladies, some of whom wore blue jeans. Most had fussy *kinner* hanging to their legs. Many gawked at Betsie's clothes; the rudest English always did. She steeled herself and concentrated on her shopping list.

Beside her, Michael rubbed his chin. "Hey, Sheila, this will probably be pretty boring for you. Why don't you go check out the latest *Tiger Beat* mag? Betcha there's some new pix of David Cassidy." He pulled a comical excited face.

"Oh, can I get one if it's the new issue?" Sheila punctuated her question with exuberant hops.

"Don't see why not."

Betsie watched absently as Sheila zeroed in on the magazine display, pleased that Michael took some interest in his sister. But back to business. Chicken and noodles ladled over mashed potatoes, hot buttery biscuits, fried apples, and fresh green beans simmered with bacon and lots of butter—surely a meal like that would please the Sullivans. She loaded the squeaky cart with the fixings.

At the meat counter, Betsie listened politely as the butcher, Archie according to his name tag, explained the cuts of meat despite the fact that she had helped with the butchering all her life. Betsie studied his velvety black skin. Good nature twinkled in his dark eyes. His huge cloud of frizzy black hair floated with each step he took behind the tall counter. On top of the cloud perched a white paper cap.

"So that's what makes this your best grade of beef," he finished. He scooped up the ground chuck and slapped it in a red-and-white-checked paper boat. All in one motion he tore off a heavy sheet of butcher paper and expertly taped Betsie's parcel. He scrawled a price with a black crayon and pushed the package beside the parcel of chicken she'd already selected.

"You have a nice day, now." He wiped his hands on his bloody apron.

Michael wandered past, jostled her arm, and gave her a meaningful look. She gathered her courage, clenched one hand into a fist, and raised it high.

"Power to the people," she told the butcher.

The butcher pursed his lips and studied Betsie thoughtfully. His gaze flickered toward Michael before he raised his fist in return.

"What it is, mama."

Mama? As Betsie wheeled her basket away with wounded dignity, she passed an official-looking man in a white shirt, black trousers, and a red bowtie. He glared at the butcher.

"Napier?"

From the corner of her eye, Betsie saw the butcher straighten. "Yes, Mr. Ayers? Sir?"

"I don't pay you to get all metaphysical with the customers, boy. Get back to work."

"Yes, sir." The butcher scowled at the manager's back before scrubbing the counter with vigor.

What a strange way of talking, to call her *Mama* and a young man like Archie a *boy*. Finished with her selections, Betsie moved toward the checkout lanes, Michael a few steps behind. He coaxed Sheila away from the magazine rack by handing her a couple of quarters.

"You can go through the line ahead of us and pay for that *Tiger Beat* first. How would that be? Sort of show Betsie the ropes?"

"Cool!"

When she saw the conveyor belt, Betsie caught her breath. She maneuvered into a checkout lane crammed with all manner of candy and more shiny magazines. The pictures of the magazine ladies were shameful, what with their short pants practically baring their *Hinnerdales*. Betsie ignored them while she waited for her turn to check out.

"Thanks for shopping at Ayers Market," the cashier told a woman ahead of Sheila.

"Mo-om! You said I could get baseball cards if I cleaned my room." The woman's son plopped a pack on the counter.

"Not this trip. I don't have enough cash." The harried mother returned the cards.

"You promised!" The boy bopped his mom's arm.

"Ouch! All right, get the cards, but just wait until I tell your father."

Betsie shook her head, scandalized, while Michael choked back a laugh.

Now came Sheila's turn to pay for her magazine. Betsie envied her calm efficiency. As the cashier handed over the purchase, Betsie saw a new checkout girl approach the register. She darted glances at Michael with every step.

"Mr. Ayers says it's time for your break, Janet. I'll ring this order up." The new girl practically shouldered Janet out of the way.

Janet's eyes narrowed as she looked from the black-haired checker to Michael and back again. "Sure thing, Peg. Have fun."

Betsie watched her selections glide magically down the belt until she noticed that Michael, lighthearted and smug up to now, had stilled. It was almost like he was trying to hide behind her. The cashier remarked on his presence with exaggerated surprise.

"Well, if it isn't Michael Sullivan! I didn't know *you* were here. What's shakin'?" She fluttered a wink with stiff black eyelashes.

"Oh, uh, hey there, Peg," Michael stammered. "Didn't know you still worked here."

Peggy tossed her head. The black tower of hair didn't budge.

"Where else would I be? Listen, it's been too long. How come you're such a stranger?" She patted her hair. "I mean, Officer Petey is in here just about every day to jaw about old times."

"You mean Petey Schwartz from Hilliard High?" Michael snickered. "He's about your speed."

"Shut up." Peggy frowned and pulled Betsie's selections toward her. She searched for price tags as she punched buttons on the shiny metal cash machine with a vengeance.

"Lighten up, Peg. I was pulling your leg."

Her chin came up, and a red spot appeared on each cheek. "Give me a call sometime and I'll show you how fast I can go."

Michael's eyes widened. "I just might do that."

Peggy winked again and punched the button marked "Total." White-on-black numbers popped up in a little window.

"That'll be $19.27," she informed Betsie. She snapped open a brown paper sack and filled it while Betsie fished in her pocketbook for the money. Peggy flipped up the holders, shoved in the bills, and slapped the correct change in Betsie's open palm.

"Thank you for shopping at Ayers Market, your friendly neighborhood grocer." Peggy scowled. "Please let us know if we can serve you better. At Ayers Market, the customer is always right. Have a nice day!" She dismissed Betsie and fawned on Michael.

"I say it now, right?" Betsie gave Michael an inquiring glance.

Still bemused after his exchange with Peggy, he hesitated a split-second before he understood. "What? No, wait—"

But Betsie was already employing the traditional English good-bye that Michael had patiently taught her. "What a rip-off!" She was careful to add a broad smile and a friendly wave, as coached.

Peggy stared. "What is this, *Candid Camera* or something? Nice going, sis. Your phony getup had me a little suspicious, though. Run along, now." Her words dripped honey. "So, Mikey, like I was saying . . ."

Betsie looked from Peggy to Michael. "Did I say it right, Michael?"

"Hey, wait a sec," Peggy barked. "Is she with you?"

"What's taking you guys so long?" Sheila appeared at the end of the lane, swinging her bag in an arc. "Give me the keys, and I'll pop the trunk."

"Knock yourself out." Michael tossed the keys, and Sheila grinned as she fielded them with one hand.

"Wait, I will come with you." Betsie lifted her bags from the counter and arranged them carefully in the rolling basket.

The door opened magically for her. As Betsie exited, she held up two fingers at Peggy to complete the traditional good-bye. "Gotta split."

Peggy flushed brick red. Fists doubled on hips, she whirled on Michael, who cringed. "What gives, Sullivan? If you prefer Miss Medieval Times to the 1971 model, just say the word," she raged. "Talk about prehistoric . . ."

Unruffled because she'd done exactly as Michael instructed, Betsie spotted Sheila by the yellow-jacket car. Together they loaded the groceries into the trunk.

None the worse for wear after his exchange with Peggy, Michael swaggered up and held out his hand for the keys. "Wow, Betsie, that was super-duper. I guess I'm a pretty good teacher."

Betsie slid into the seat. "No sweat."

"I bet Michael taught you that, right, Betsie?" Sheila piped up. "What was eating Peggy, anyway? She's a weirdo."

"Mind your own beeswax, Squirt." He cranked the key and pressed on the gas, but Betsie thought he looked pretty pleased with himself.

CHAPTER 5

One of the oddest things about the English is that
boys dress like girls and girls dress like boys.
They are also very lazy.
—BETSIE'S JOURNAL

MICHAEL PLOPPED THE sacks on the kitchen counter and immediately retreated to his room, where he cranked the music. Betsie shook her head. "We did not get our ice cream."

"Nah, I knew we wouldn't. One thing you'd better get used to around here—Mike teases everyone all the time. Whatever he told you about how to talk at the store, forget it." Sheila grinned. "Serves Peggy right, though. I wish she'd stay away from Mike."

Betsie preferred not to dwell on it. "What with the wind whipping, everything but the blue jeans must be nearly dry."

"I'll go out and see," Sheila offered.

"Mind you check the waistbands and pockets. They take the longest." Betsie handed her the wash basket. A few minutes later, the girl dropped it at Betsie's feet, clearly pleased with herself.

"Thank you. If you carry it to my room, I'll tend to that after we get supper on."

"Sure!" Her smile warmed Betsie's heart.

She scurried to prepare the chicken and put it to roast. Sheila showed her how to turn on the oven, and Betsie in turn demonstrated how to make homemade noodles.

When they finished mixing the dough, Sheila giggled. "You've got flour on your nose!"

"*Ach*, happens every time I make biscuits." Betsie rubbed her nose absently with the back of a hand and resumed rolling out the dough. She let Sheila roll some while she mixed up biscuits and cut them out.

"Gosh, Betsie, you cook fast."

"This is easy," she scoffed. "At home, I cook on a wood stove."

"You mean like in the olden days?" Sheila goggled at her. "How come?"

"That is just the Amish way. We don't have electricity in our house."

"No electricity?"

Betsie bridled. "What do we need electricity for, when we have our own two hands which the good Lord gave us?"

"But how can you cook with a wood stove? Won't the food catch on fire?"

"Of course not!" Betsie laughed. Her floury hands flew as she cut the noodles with a sharp knife. "If the fire gets too hot in one place, I just move the pot to the back. My father chops wood and kindling for us, now that my brothers have all grown up and moved to Missouri. *Dat* keeps the woodbox full always."

Or at least he did. But Betsie pushed her troubles to the back burner and peeled potatoes while Sheila watched.

"So how do you cook those?"

"Same as your *mem* does, I imagine." Betsie ran cold water in the pan and set it on a burner.

"Mom starts with boiled water," Sheila frowned, "but then she sprinkles instant potato flakes in it."

"Potato flakes?" Betsie made a face.

"They're good! But I like the TV dinner kind best." She pulled a frosty metal tray from the freezer to show what she meant.

Betsie stared at the unappetizing picture on top. The food probably tasted no better than the cardboard. Grayish-brown fried chicken, brittle peas and carrots, crispy mashed potatoes with a smidgen of butter on top, and a sad brownie—this was not supper. "Put this away. Tonight we will surprise everyone."

While Sheila shoved the box back in the freezer, Betsie quartered the potatoes. She slipped them into the cold water and turned on the burner. Then she ransacked the cupboards for a large plastic bowl and dumped the paper sack of string beans.

Sheila fetched yesterday's newspaper while Betsie carried the bowl outside to the back step. She dropped the bean ends on the newspaper as she snapped. Sheila was fascinated, just as Betsie had been whenever she watched her mother snap beans.

"You want to try?" Betsie pressed a handful of beans in Sheila's hand.

"Sure, it looks like fun! Hey, I have another question."

Betsie hid a smile. "What is it you want to know?"

"I don't think my dad would want me to ask, though." The words tumbled out anyway. "Why do you dress like that?"

Surprised, Betsie thought a moment. "You think I dress funny, maybe?"

Sheila blushed. "Not funny, just . . . different, I guess."

"And you don't think it's different for young men to dress like girls? Or for young ladies to dress like boys?" Betsie smiled and pointed at Sheila's shorts.

"I never thought about that before," Sheila mused. "I dress like everyone else does."

"That's how it is where I come from," Betsie said. "It's the Amish way, to dress modestly. And now we are finished with the beans, ain't so?" She rolled up the newspaper and Sheila carried the bowl.

"Betsie?"

"Yes?" She gave the steamy potatoes a stir before starting the string beans.

"It's time for my favorite TV show. Do you want to watch it with me?" Sheila gestured at the brown box with the green square of glass.

"You mean television?" Betsie shuddered. "Oh, no, I can't. I will fetch some mending to keep me busy."

"Can't the Amish watch television?"

"No, indeed." Why would anyone want to? "I'll be right back to check on the beans."

She heard a pop, and a drop of boiling potato water splashed her arm. As she nursed the red spot, Betsie saw Sheila twist a knob on the box. Fascinated, she saw tiny people come to life on the green screen. A big, fat man in a blue shirt pulled off his hat and hit a skinny boy in a red shirt and short white trousers. The next minute the fat man called the skinny boy his "little buddy."

Why would he hit his little buddy? She caught her breath. Just like that, she'd looked at television. How easy it was to slide down the slippery slope of English misdeeds. She fled for the shelter of her room.

Safe once more, Betsie thanked the good Lord that she'd thought to bring along her mending basket. She sorted the pile of spring-fresh blue jeans with a practiced eye and carried most of them back to the kitchen table. She sewed and snipped to her heart's content, very sober and dutiful as she did the mending instead of looking at the wicked images on the screen. A twinge tormented her when she thought of the damage the television was doing to dear Sheila's soul.

When she was finished, Betsie folded the mended clothing and picked up the stack. She plowed her way against a steady stream of loud music.

"Michael," she shouted.

He lowered the volume, the picture of guilt. "Oh, hey. Listen, I hope you aren't mad at—wait, are those my jeans?"

"*Jah*. All clean." Betsie deposited the stack on the bed.

"Wow, thanks, you didn't have to do that," he said slowly. He smoothed the top pair and met her eye. "About the market, are we cool?"

Betsie shrugged. "We are . . . cool."

He picked up the jeans and suddenly froze stiffer than the TV dinner. Betsie smiled modestly as he examined the fruits of her labor. Where there had been fringes before, a neat hem showed. She'd also ripped out the clumsy patches that covered the knees and darned the holes shut. She watched him finger each pair. He flipped the last pair over, and a spasm crossed his face.

Betsie reached in her pocket and flourished a swatch of silky red, white, and blue material at him. "Wasn't so hard, taking out that piece of American flag and those crooked stitches and putting a proper patch on that ripped-out seat," she said. "I figure you sewed it on yourself. Can't say as I blame you. That hole was near bigger than the seat was wide. Must have been terrible drafty. I took some of the extra material out of the legs for the patch. Looked like someone had made your *blue jeans*"—she pronounced the phrase carefully—"much too wide." She dusted her hands. "Well, I must see to dinner."

"Betsie, wait!"

"*Jah?*"

Michael's brown eyes bored into hers before he dropped his gaze with a sigh. "Skip it."

Betsie supposed a thank-you was too much to expect, but at least nobody could say that Michael dressed like a scarecrow while she was on the job.

As she walked back to the kitchen, she successfully averted her gaze from the television. Sheila giggled at whatever it was she saw. Betsie was pleased to see her so happy, but at what cost, *ach*, what cost?

She pierced a potato with a fork; nice and tender, ready for mashing. Quickly she saved some unseasoned potatoes for the morning. To the rest, she added salt with a generous hand. She worked in a big lump of butter and mashed the potatoes fine. Then she added some milk from what she had set to warming. It had taken her a second to find the right knob for the curlicue, but at last it had glowed dull red.

She dribbled the warm milk in, a little at a time, whipping the potatoes until her arm was tired. Then she whipped them some more to make them fluffy. She clapped on the lid and set them aside to keep warm while she tasted the cream gravy. A dash of pepper and it was ready.

The fried apples smelled delicious. All that was left to do was take up the green beans, but they could wait. Nothing was worse than cold beans.

Tires whined on the driveway. Sheila dashed to meet her father, shouting, "Dad! Dad! Betsie cooked dinner for us! Roast chicken!"

Nervously Betsie wiped her hands on her apron and walked to meet her new boss. Through the window, she saw that Mr. Sullivan was pleasant in appearance. He was tall, though not as tall as Michael, and he had close-cropped hair. He wore a dark suit over a white shirt and a striped tie. His shiny black shoes tapped on the asphalt. The raggedy grass caught his attention, and he directed a scowl at Michael's car before smiling at his daughter. He looked like a man used to being in charge.

He shook Betsie's hand. "You must be Miss Troyer. I'm Gerald Sullivan. I hope Squirt here hasn't been too much trouble."

"Oh, no," she said.

"Listen to what we did today!" Sheila rattled off the list of chores.

"Well, haven't you ladies been busy?" Mr. Sullivan's smile was strained. "Where's your mother?" he asked Sheila.

"She's not home from the library yet, but that's okay; we did all the work." Sheila watched him like an anxious puppy.

"Sheila is a good helper," Betsie hastened to assure him.

A genuine smile for his daughter belied his reserve. "She sure is. I apologize for being so late. I had some things to take care of before I take tomorrow off to train you." His face took on a prideful look. "I don't expect you to keep house for us, Miss Troyer. The harness shop will be enough of a chore."

"Oh, it was no trouble." Betsie waved a hand. "I was here plenty early enough to set the house to rights. I like to help."

There came a crackle of footsteps on the plastic path. Mr. Sullivan raised his voice. "Mike picked you up on time, then. Will wonders never cease?"

"Thanks for nothing." Michael elbowed past his father, his face stony.

"Just a minute. Where do you think you're going, young man?"

"I think I'm gonna split," Michael ground out, never breaking stride, "and I don't know what time I'll be back."

Mr. Sullivan grabbed his son's arm. "Stand still while I'm talking to you. I hope you're headed out to mow the lawn. I told you to a week ago."

Michael cocked his head to consider before he shrugged. "Nope, 'fraid not." He jerked away from his father in a huff.

Betsie exhaled. She looked at Mr. Sullivan, whose top was about to blow, and Sheila, who was about to cry. Together they watched Michael's departure through the picture window. As he retreated, his respectably mended blue jeans came into view.

"Dad, quick! Look at Michael's jeans! The flag's gone!" Sheila pointed.

Mr. Sullivan did a double take. He and Sheila stared at Betsie for an uncomfortable moment. Then they collapsed against each other and laughed until Mr. Sullivan wiped tears from his eyes.

Though Betsie still didn't see what was so funny, she had to admit that their laughter cleared the air. The pleasant feeling continued through dinner. Sheila and her father enjoyed every bite, but as Betsie cleared the table, she saw Sheila sneak a glance at the front window.

"What's wrong, Squirt?"

Her spoon clattered to her plate. "Why is Mom so late?"

"Are you talking about little old me?" A lady with flowing blond hair swirled through the back door in a vivid geometric-print skirt. Bare toes peeked from beneath the hem as she floated to the kitchen.

"Hello, family! Did you miss me? Mmmm, those TV dinners sure do smell good . . . Oh!" She stopped short and peered at Betsie over wire-rimmed glasses with blue lenses. "Who are you?"

"My name is Betsie Troyer. I came to work in the harness shop." Oh, how she wished her own sweaty feet were bare.

The lady flipped her hair and tossed a fringed bag on the counter. "I thought that was supposed to be a guy. Norman or something."

And I thought you were supposed to be a respectable mother, Betsie thought, but she held her tongue.

Mr. Sullivan cleared his throat. "Phyllis, I told you there'd been a change. Betsie's cousin Nelson was drafted. He's in Chicago at the army hospital, remember? So she's taking his place. Betsie, this is my wife, Phyllis Sullivan."

"Gerry, puh-lease! I read for a part tomorrow. How can I stay in character if you don't cooperate?" She turned to Betsie. "I'm Sunshine Sullivan. Everything copacetic? Great threads, by the way."

"Mo-om, Betsie's Amish. That's the way they dress."

Sheila's blasé tone contrasted oddly with the blush of pink on her cheeks. To Betsie's eye, it was almost like Sheila was the adult who was embarrassed at her child's behavior.

"Are you hungry?" Betsie dished up a plate for Mrs. Sullivan, who thanked her vaguely and carried it down the hall, nose stuck in a sheaf of papers.

Nonplussed by the woman's odd behavior, Betsie loaded the dishwasher, practically an old hand at it by now. The kitchen floor didn't take long to sweep clean. Betsie felt . . . well, not proud, but certainly content. As long as she worked hard, her troubles seemed remote, and there was room for peace.

What in the world would she do now, though? She tapped her toe. Mr. Sullivan had migrated to the living room, where the television blared. Though she didn't look, Betsie couldn't help hearing, "And that's the way it is, Monday, May 3, 1971."

She decided that a breath of fresh air would do her good. The television voice faded as she strolled out to the pasture. Fledge crowded the fence, eager for a handout. When he saw that Betsie was empty-handed, though, he resumed his grazing. Very peaceful it was, with no wailing or fighting or television talking all the time. The *gut* tiredness from the day's work settled pleasantly, and she was ready to face the English once again.

She found Mrs. Sullivan surveying the kitchen, amazed. "How long did it take you to accomplish this?" She lowered her dirty dinnerware into the sink. "Cook and clean up and all that?"

"Oh, not long," Betsie replied airily. "Sheila is a big help."

For a moment, Mrs. Sullivan's expression was unreadable. Then she laughed. "I guess I must have been behind the door when God was passing out the housewife skills." She dug her elbow into Betsie's ribs and winked.

Momentarily taken aback, Betsie quickly rallied. "Mrs. Sullivan, would you like me to do your regular housework while you study? It would be no trouble for me."

Mrs. Sullivan's answering smile seemed wistful. "You know what? I'm a hopeless mess in the Suzy Homemaker department, so go for it."

Betsie nodded and headed for her room. She passed Michael's room and her own to peek in Sheila's door.

"I'm going to bed. Goodnight, Sheila."

"G'night, Betsie! I had fun today!"

"I did, too." Betsie turned with a smile and glimpsed a handmade sign taped to Sheila's door. "Thou wilt keep him in perfect peace, whose mind is stayed on thee, because he trusteth in thee," she read. The words were homey and comforting, surrounded by doodled hearts and flowers.

Peace filled Betsie's heart. In the privacy of her room, she turned down the dusty bedspread and the sheets. Carefully she unpinned her dress, shook it out, and laid it across the chair. She doffed her *Kapp* and out came the bobby pins. Blissfully she scratched the itchy spots and climbed into bed, free of any worries over what tomorrow might bring.

Just before she fell asleep, her thoughts drifted to Charley. Was he thinking about her, missing her? Wonderful *gut* it would be when one day she didn't have to speculate; Charley would be at her side. She'd fix a fine dinner after a good day's work, and Charley would smile in that special way. After dinner, maybe the pair of them would have time for a walk or a drive to the covered bridge, but if not, what was wrong with caring for the livestock and doing chores together? No shame in that. Finally, to bed . . . Eyes closed, she smiled. Charley, close enough to touch . . . She could almost hear him breathing . . .

CHAPTER 6

I like harness making so far. It is the English
that are difficult to understand.

—BETSIE'S JOURNAL

"CHARLEY?"

Betsie rolled over. Had he called her name? In a rush, she remembered she was far away from Charley and Plain City.

Mr. Sullivan, then? But his room was at the end of the hall. The voice was closer than that. Sheila, next door? Betsie pulled the pillow over her ears. Immediately a muffled thump sounded. She heard a male voice; unmistakably Michael—his room was the one on that side.

She heard a female voice, a few words and a smothered giggle. Was there a strange girl in Michael's room?

Don't be silly, Betsie chided herself. It must be the radio. But how was she supposed to get her sleep with all that racket? She planned to get up early to make breakfast, after all. Hastily, she pinned her dress on over her nightgown and padded down the hallway.

As she raised her hand to knock, Michael's door opened and lamplight flooded the hall. A girl in a skimpy skirt and a tight blouse careened into Betsie and squealed. Michael clapped a hand over the girl's mouth and drew her against his chest. She snuggled there quite contentedly.

Michael winked. "Did we wake you? Sorry." He didn't look one bit sorry. He squeezed the girl and removed his hand from her mouth.

The girl glared at Betsie, eyes smudged with black. "Hey, wait a minute! You're that fresh pilgrim from the store." She pulled away to glare at Michael. "You said she was nobody. What's she doing in your house?"

"Keep it down, will you? It's cool, Peg. She works for my old man." Michael sounded amused. "What's up, Betsie? Besides you, that is."

Betsie yawned. "It is nothing to me if you want to be bundling, except I do have to get up early and my room is next door to yours."

"How convenient." Peggy's voice clinked like ice cubes.

"Can it, Peg." An odd look crossed Michael's face. "What the heck is bundling?"

"Bundling is a bedroom courting custom with some Amish— *Ach,* I am too tired to explain. Just please be quieter," Betsie begged.

"Oh, we will. We're outta here." As they turned the corner, Michael paused. "Nice hair," he mouthed behind Peggy's back.

Betsie clapped her hand to her head. No *Kapp* and hair loose! She blushed and fled to her room.

Before the sun rose on Tuesday morning, Betsie splashed her face with warm water in the pink bathroom. She coiled and twisted her hair and pinned it in place. She settled her *Kapp* and fastened it primly. The memory of Michael's admiring gaze rankled.

Newspaper pieces were scattered in the living room. Betsie crumpled them into the trash. Then she was ready to start breakfast, though she'd missed out on plenty of sleep, thanks to Michael's escapades with Peggy. *Nobody,* he'd called her. She pursed her lips.

Doughnuts would be a nice way to start the morning, she decided. She opened the cupboard where she'd found the roasting pan and discovered a welter of pots. A yank on the handle of a pan with a heavy bottom failed to loosen it. Betsie kept up a steady resistance, like when she helped *Dat* birth a stubborn calf.

Crash! The whole pile clanged and clattered on the clean floor with a most satisfying racket. She set aside the pot she needed and whacked each one back into place. *Thump! Thump!* There was something satisfying about setting the pots and pans firmly in order. It wasn't like she was making any noise anyway, since she was nobody.

She was vigorously mashing the cold potatoes when Betsie heard a low moan. It was Michael, clad in a pair of fringed, blue-jean shorts and a ripped-up gold shirt. Betsie mentally marked both garments for her mending pile.

"Do you know what time it is?"

"Mm-hmm. Quarter past four." She whacked a few more pans for good measure.

"Please stop," Michael groaned. He clutched his head.

"*Ach*, too noisy for you? What a pity there is *nobody* here to tell." Betsie rummaged in the refrigerator for the milk carton and thumped it on the counter. The earthy potato smell wafted. She stuck in a finger and licked it.

"Mmm, cold potatoes. Want some?" She tilted the container enticingly.

Michael's face paled. He dashed from the room.

"I will save you a doughnut," she called cheerfully.

Her good spirits restored, Betsie scooped and measured happily. In went the mashed potatoes. Her mouth watered. There's nothing like doughnuts made with mashed potatoes, so tender, yet so substantial. The good smell made her stomach growl.

By the time the dough was ready, Betsie heard Sheila splashing in the bathroom. She heated lard in the deep, heavy pan. With a practiced hand, she cut out the doughnuts. Into the hot lard they slid, where the rings of dough sizzled and browned until she fished them out to drain.

The doughnuts were ready to glaze when Sheila trailed into the kitchen with one eye shut. She groped in the cupboard for a cereal bowl before her nose awoke the rest of her.

"What's that yummy smell?"

"Doughnuts." Betsie swirled one in the frosting and plopped it on a plate. "I made them special for you."

Sheila stared at the doughnut, which almost covered the dessert plate.

"You made these? Here at home?" She lifted one. "It's still warm! And so heavy." Open went her mouth. She gobbled one doughnut standing up; she sat down to savor the second one.

"Sooo good." Sheila licked glaze from her fingers and drained a glass of milk. "Wish I could stay home today, too."

Betsie wished the same thing. "I expect I'll be awfully busy in the harness shop. But I'll see you when you get home."

A honk sounded from the driveway.

"There's the bus!" Sheila wiped the sugary, milky ring from her mouth and wrapped Betsie in a hug. "Bye!"

Stunned, Betsie watched her go. She wasn't used to such displays of affection, but before she could dwell on it, here came Mr. Sullivan. He wore overalls, old ones with proper patches.

"Good morning, Betsie! All ready to work?" He rubbed his hands together, but he stopped, astonished. "Doughnuts? I haven't had homemade doughnuts since I was a kid." His voice filled with wonder.

"About time you had 'em again, ain't so?" Betsie set a place for him and poured fresh coffee. Then she set to redding up the kitchen. She smiled when Mr. Sullivan attacked a third doughnut with gusto.

"Have you eaten?" He licked his fingers.

"Oh, yes, I tasted the first ones out of the fat," she assured him. "I will set a place for your wife," she began, but Mr. Sullivan stopped her.

"Don't bother. When Phyllis does eat, she'll have chicory coffee, alfalfa sprouts, and brown rice."

Betsie regarded him doubtfully; she decided he must be teasing, like Michael. "Let me get my notebook, then, and I'll be all ready to work."

"Notebook?"

She waved a black, wire-bound notebook. "I am going to write down what you tell me about the business for my cousin Nelson. Then he can read it when he gets back." She stuck a sharpened pencil stub behind her ear. "Now I am ready."

"Miss Troyer, you're really something." He grinned and held the door for her.

Betsie decided that must be good, so she smiled too. If only the English would say exactly what they meant.

The spring breeze rippled her skirts as they stepped outside. A red-winged blackbird welcomed the morning exuberantly, but Betsie yawned.

"Didn't you sleep well, Miss Troyer?"

"*Ach*, fair. Please, call me Betsie."

"Betsie it is." He tucked the newspaper under one arm and plunged his hands deep in his pockets.

When they arrived at the white frame building, Mr. Sullivan produced a set of keys. He looked almost boyish in his excitement. "These are for you. This one's for the house, and here's the one for the shop." He inserted it in the lock, and an old-fashioned shopkeeper's bell dinged as they stepped inside.

Betsie saw a row of tables stocked with worn tools and rolls of leather. A greasy, black stitching machine with a treadle loomed in one corner. Saddles hung on sawhorses, and bridles hung from every available nail, many high overhead. A fancy, silver-studded black harness trimmed with silver buckles took Betsie's breath away. She imagined Judith decked out in something so pretty, and then she chided herself for thinking such prideful thoughts when there was work to do.

Mr. Sullivan scooted a high stool toward her and rubbed his hands together in anticipation. Betsie nudged aside a roll of cowhide to make room for her notebook and retrieved the pencil stub from behind her ear. At last, the real work could begin, except for one detail.

"Who will be working with me when customers come?"

"Well, there won't be too many customers at all, you know, unless there's a horse show," he hedged. "This hasn't been what you'd call a paying business for quite a while. Relocate it where you Amish appreciate the value of a strapping work horse and a well-made harness, and I promise you it'll thrive. But I can show you what to do if anyone happens in today. Don't worry."

"But that is not what I meant," Betsie said slowly. "Didn't Nelson tell you that I may not wait on customers by myself, as he would have?" She settled her skirts modestly. "A girl like me, it just isn't proper. I've sold produce at a stand, but the prices are on a sign and I just point. You see?"

"Let me get this straight. You can do the work; you just can't talk to the customers." He pressed one palm on the crown of his neat crew cut. "Darn cowlick," he muttered. "Tell you what, we'll cross that bridge when we come to it. For right now, Betsie, let's get down to brass tacks. Here's the leather I get from a supplier." He slapped the tawny roll curled up on the table. "All my suppliers' phone numbers are in the index-card file."

Betsie made a note. "The leather doesn't look very supple."

"It softens up as you work it." He moved on. "Now, see this carousel? These are my tools. They belonged to my granddad; he used them to make the harnesses for his work and buggy horses, and I learned the trade from him, just like he learned from his father."

He pointed to a round holder that bristled with sharp implements. The paint on the wooden handles was worn from many years of use.

"Your grandfather kept work horses here in the big city?"

Mr. Sullivan laughed. "The big city? Hilliard used to be mostly farmland back when it was called Hilliard's Station. My great-granddad, my granddad, and my dad all farmed this land in turn, and then I did." A fond, faraway look came into his eyes. "We lived in the original farmhouse up until about five years ago."

Betsie thought about the low modern house. "Where is it?"

"Went up in smoke in '66. A bad electrical storm blew in, lightning hit the roof, and the whole place burned to ashes. It was a blessing that we were at the Ohio State Fair, but the house was a total loss. Not only that, the sparks flew on the wind and set the old barn on fire, too. I'm certainly glad it missed the harness shop, for your cousin's sake."

"Oh, but your house and barn! How awful."

"Yes, but the family was safe. That's the important thing. We're all scared to death of fire now, though." He sighed. "Lots of memories on this old homestead, even if the house and barn are gone. Phyllis and I were married in the front room." His eyes clouded. "Things sure do change. We started over after the fire. Phyllis had said for years that we were sitting on a gold mine, holding on to all this land when there were developers clamoring for it right and left. Don't let her artsy talk fool you. What with the insured value and the sale, we cleared a bundle and I had this modern house built. It was Phyllis's dream house . . . for a while."

"So you were a farmer." Betsie traced a circle on the roll of leather, anxious that maybe she was shirking her duties, but fascinated all the same. "How many acres? What did you produce?"

Mr. Sullivan smiled. "I had a hundred acres in corn and winter wheat. We sold off all but five because I thought I'd always want a vegetable garden and some livestock, but this year I'm not even going to set out any tomatoes; go figure. Our livestock consists of that worthless pony I bought for Sheila when we bought Michael the Super Bee."

"He has a bee?"

Mr. Sullivan pushed up his glasses. "What? No, that's what his car's called. Anyway, we had plenty of money, but I hated having nothing to do. I took a few classes and qualified to be an income tax preparer. That keeps me busy the first part of the year, and I earn good money. Just finished up with the season, as a matter of fact."

"Why did you keep the harness shop?"

"Oh, partly because I hated to let all this equipment go to waste. Every piece is in good working order. Some of it is very old, like that chain stitcher." He pointed to the greasy machine with foot pedals. "It was built in 1862. But partly, too, working with leather gets in your blood. Yes, there are a lot of Sullivan family memories in this shop."

Betsie tapped her pencil on the notebook. "I sure have a lot to learn."

"No flies on you, huh, Betsie? Back to work it is." He grinned and picked up a tool. "This is an edger. You use it like this." He ran it along the edge of a leather strap that looked like the beginnings of reins. He smoothed the rough edge with one sure pass. "Now that edge won't chafe the horse, see?"

Betsie stopped writing to peer at his work.

"Here, now you try it." He handed her the edger and the strap.

"Me?" She took the edger and tried to run it along the other side as easily as he had, but flakes of leather were the result. Betsie looked at her boss in alarm.

"Not bad," he said. "Keep trying."

With a little effort, she did get better. Betsie paused to make a note but Mr. Sullivan picked up another piece of pale leather. To her unpracticed eye, it looked finished.

"Try your hand with this stain," he said, handling a small can. He took out an applicator shaped like a round ball and swabbed it along the leather strap, which turned a nice, brown, horsey color. "Now you," he said, and the brush was in Betsie's hand.

Dopplich described her efforts that morning, clumsy and all thumbs. Mercifully, the stitching machine operated by treadle like the sewing machine at home, but new ideas swirled round and round her brain. Mr. Sullivan's large hands moved with such grace across the leather, Betsie was sure her hands would never catch on.

Mr. Sullivan noticed her distress. "Look, Betsie, we can't hope to cover all the fine points of harness-making in one day. It seems odd, but this is one business that's best learned by actually doing it. The most important part is to get a feel for working with leather, and you show real promise." He grinned. Opening a drawer, he slipped a battered book out of a leather cover and extended it toward her.

As she reached for it, he continued, "In the meantime, let this book be your Bible."

"What do you mean?" Shock tinged her voice as she snatched her hand away.

"Sorry, Betsie. It's only an expression. If you read this book and study the illustrations, you'll get an idea of the process. Do what it says, and you'll be fine."

He pressed the book in her hands, and she read the words on the front: *The Harness Maker's Illustrated Manual*. Mr. Sullivan handed Betsie the leather cover. She slipped the boards back inside and traced the delicate scrollwork.

"This cover is so beautiful. How did you make the leather look this way?" she asked.

"With the embossing machine. We can set it up to stamp all sorts of fancy designs in leather." He stretched. "Let's take a little break, shall we? I'm going to get a drink of water. Can I bring you some?"

Betsie nodded and flopped down on the high stool with her precious notebook and manual. She yawned again and rubbed her watery eyes as Mr. Sullivan watched.

"I'm sorry you slept so poorly, Betsie. Is anything wrong with your room?"

"Oh, no! It's a comfortable room." She yawned. "It's just the bundling that woke me up."

His expression was quizzical. "Bundling?"

"Mm-hmm. I was somewhat surprised. I thought it was an Amish custom. That is, the bishop in my district frowns on it, like most, but a very few less strict districts allow it. Anyway, it kept me awake, with them being on the other side of the wall."

"Betsie, who are you talking about? And what in the world is bundling?"

"I don't really know so much about it," Betsie demurred. It was no kind of subject to discuss with her boss, but he had asked her a direct question. "I hear the courting boy stops by late when the girl's parents are already in bed, but this is customary, just as it is customary to eat pie unchaperoned in the kitchen and stay up late to talk together in the sitting room. Bundling is in bed. Sometimes there's a board to divide the young lady's bed down the middle, sometimes not. Sometimes the girl is under the covers and the boy on the covers beside her. Bundling keeps the courting pair warm and cozy while they . . . talk." Her cheeks felt plenty warm and cozy. She fiddled with her *Kapp* strings and studied the wrought-iron scrollwork that suspended the shop bell. "Some call it 'bed courtship.' Anyway, that is what I supposed Michael and Peggy were doing. Bundling."

A fly buzzed through the open screen door. "Do you mean to say that Michael . . . had a *girl* in his room last night? Peggy?"

"*Jah.*" She squirmed uncomfortably.

"That does it." Dull red flared at the base of Mr. Sullivan's neck and flooded his face. He stiff-armed the door. "Michael!"

CHAPTER 7

The English don't realize what they have right under
their own noses.
—BETSIE'S JOURNAL

MR. SULLIVAN STORMED out of the harness shop. The brass bell leapt from the scrolled hook and clanged to the floor. It rolled in a semicircle and disappeared under the counter.

Stuck in the shop, thirsty, hot, and tired, Betsie folded up a section of the paper and tracked down the doddering fly. As she disposed of it, she noticed a hand-lettered sign: "In God we trust," she read. "All others pay cash." The fat letters were red, white, and blue, and in the corner was one of those peace signs that she saw everywhere these days.

To pass the time, she read what she'd recorded so far. When she finished, she doodled hearts along the edge of the paper. She opened the windows for a cross-breeze and winced when she realized the top-blowing was still going on, with Michael giving as good as he got.

Quite a novelty it was to have spare minutes with no work to fill them; rarely did she have the burden of free time. Why not keep a journal? It might be good to recall her English adventures one day. Hesitantly at first, but with growing confidence, Betsie jotted her impressions of life in an English house, which so far had been a revelation. She described Sheila, the trip to the market, Michael's gaudy clothes and his eternal teasing, and what it was like to ride in a car with him.

Her pencil stilled, and she tapped the eraser against her chin before continuing. It was funny to write about how homely Michael looked when she thought he was a lady. He hadn't been angry when he found out about her mistake. Why, he had even poked fun at himself. Deep down, she suspected he wasn't as bad as his father made him out to be, but what she wrote about Michael in secret and what she wanted him to know were two different things. No, there was no use inviting trouble by keeping these pages where someone might read them. When she got home, she would simply tear them out and hide them in a safe place.

The steady crescendo of yelling pricked Betsie's conscience. Michael might perhaps not be in this mess if only she'd kept her mouth shut about him and Peggy. Silence was an Amish practice that had always stood her in good stead. She made up her mind to hold her tongue from now on, yes, and to apologize to Michael as soon as the argument ended.

She sighed. If anything, the top-blowing sounded worse, so she organized the shop. She rearranged the tools and swept the plywood floor clean. With a dustpan improvised from the newspaper, she tucked away the dust and leather scraps and pitched the paper in the wastebasket. She poked under the counter for the brass bell and replaced it. Then she stepped out of doors to shake the rag rugs, sneezing as the dust flew.

A movement caught her eye. Michael's shirttail fluttered like a white flag of surrender as he strode past.

She waved her arms at him. "Michael, wait."

He ignored her and hopped in the yellow car, which growled and carried him away. He sure has a lot of places to go, she couldn't help thinking.

Mr. Sullivan barreled from the house, and she ducked in the door while he glared at the disappearing Super Bee. He broke into a run, then changed his mind and kicked a stone, which sailed clear across the driveway. He shoved his hands deep in his pockets and trudged toward the shop.

By the time the brass bell announced her boss, Betsie was reviewing her notes for the umpteenth time. He cleared his throat twice before she looked up.

"Sorry about that, Betsie. Michael and I don't always see eye to eye," he said. He ducked his head. "It's been really hard since he . . . since he dropped out of school. Maybe Sheila told you?"

"Some."

Mr. Sullivan took off his glasses and rubbed his eyes. "You know, I keep hoping Michael will improve, but he just seems to get worse. He's so different than he used to be."

She studied him as he picked at a speck of glue on the counter; goodness, how moody. Something *Dat* always said sprang to mind. "Young bucks like to try out their antlers some."

"I wish that was all it was, Betsie. I really do." He pressed on the nonexistent cowlick. "The problem is, I always get mad and say the wrong thing. Phyllis can kid him out of it sometimes." He brightened. "Hey! You swept up in here, put things away."

"Hard work helps when I have trouble." Betsie picked up her notebook and pencil.

A funny glint came into Mr. Sullivan's eyes. "Yes, you're right about that," he answered slowly. "Lots and lots of hard work. Come on, let's call it a morning."

After lunch, Betsie tackled the mending pile she'd assembled. She persevered until Sheila burst on the peaceful scene after school, chattering about her assignments. Betsie enjoyed her company as the girl labored over science homework.

"Did you like science when you were in school, Betsie? I do, but I've heard it will be a lot harder when I get to high school. Was it?"

Betsie thought a moment. "Yes, I guess I did like science, but I don't know if it's harder in high school."

"Why not?" Sheila nibbled her pencil.

"We only go to the eighth grade."

"You are so lucky!"

"Oh, I don't know about that. I wish I could have kept on with school." Betsie peeked in the oven and straightened, satisfied with the casserole's progress. "I like to learn."

Everyone seemed to feel better after Betsie's supper except Michael, who didn't make an appearance. While Betsie finished the dishes, Mr. Sullivan read the newspaper and his wife marked up her ever-present script with a pencil. Sheila had escaped to her parents' bedroom; her voice rose and fell as she talked on the telephone. The atmosphere was almost peaceful until Michael skulked in the door.

Mr. Sullivan rattled the newspaper. "Michael?"

He didn't respond. Betsie watched as he stalked to the kitchen and yanked open the refrigerator door practically under her nose. He selected an apple and made it halfway to his room before his father addressed him again.

"Didn't you hear me, Son? Pay attention when I'm talking to you."

Michael struck an exaggerated pose, hand to his ear.

"Of all the-the disrespectful . . ." Mr. Sullivan sputtered.

Betsie cringed and braced herself for more yelling, but help arrived from an unexpected quarter. Mrs. Sullivan, momentarily distracted from her script, held her place with one finger and looked over her blue glasses.

"Gerry, for gosh sakes, lighten up. Listen, Stringbean, your dad wants to rap with you, dig?" She doubled both legs under her billowy skirt and resumed reading. "Go ahead, Gerry," she murmured, already engrossed.

"For crying out loud, Phyllis! Who do you think you are, the referee?"

The bedroom door opened. "What's the argument?" Sheila's voice was strained.

"It's all right, Sheila. Don't worry," Betsie said. The door closed.

Mr. Sullivan glowered at Michael, who chose that moment to chomp on his apple. Betsie thought for a moment that Mr. Sullivan might be having a heart attack, his face got so red. Mrs. Sullivan patted his arm without losing her place. He choked back what he'd started to say and spoke calmly to his son.

"Miss Troyer has let me know that she can't wait on customers. Since I can only spare one day to teach her harness-making, starting tomorrow you will work side by side in the shop. Between customers, it's your job to teach her what she needs to know, provided you haven't forgotten everything your grandpa and I taught you about the business. After all, it's been quite a while since you've done anything useful."

Michael stiffened. "What's that supposed to mean?"

"What your father means is it's been quite a while since you've worked with leather," Mrs. Sullivan supplied wearily. She thumbed through the script half-heartedly, sighed, and left the room.

Mr. Sullivan snorted. "What I mean is make yourself useful and get your rear end out to the shop at the crack of dawn." He folded the newspaper, brushed past Michael, and headed for the bathroom.

Michael's chin jutted. He hefted the apple behind his father's back. Betsie caught her breath, one quick inhalation. She saw him reconsider, drop his arm, and shoot her a glance of pure misery.

Betsie couldn't help herself. "I'm sorry," she mouthed. She thought she detected a smidgen of gratitude before his guard clanged shut. Then he slammed his door. Betsie was alone.

CHAPTER 8

The problem with the English is that everyone wants to
lead. No one wants to submit to authority.
—BETSIE'S JOURNAL

ON WEDNESDAY MORNING, Betsie stretched to switch on her lamp.
She patted her notebook on the nightstand and tried to cheer herself
up. The wash and mending were done. She hoped Michael would be
pleased to see that she'd trimmed all the fringes on his shirt cuffs and
tightened the loose buttons hanging by threads.

Her mind was not really on breakfast as she prepared it, nor was her
heart in her perfunctory response to Sheila's good-bye as she dashed for
the bus. Mr. Sullivan left for work with a polite nod. Mrs. Sullivan had
left before sunrise; Betsie hoped she had enjoyed her alfalfa sprouts.

She emptied the dishwasher with vigor, the dishes clattering as she
stacked them in the cupboard. If only she could get the family together
over a good meal. Michael was the prime offender. Not once had he
eaten with the rest of them. For the past couple of nights, she'd prepared
food enough to feed a barn-raising full of folk. Back home, Amish
men like Charley wolfed down hearty meals, but Michael apparently
existed on apples. He was scrawnier than a plucked chicken.

When the kitchen was in apple-pie order, she headed for the shop.
She found it just as she'd left it yesterday, clean as a whistle. Well,
almost. She huffed at a smudge on the window and polished it with a

corner of her apron, but she wasn't satisfied with the result. With a purposeful stride, she returned to the house for a bucket and some rags.

As she passed the hallway, she glanced toward Michael's bedroom. His door was pulled to, not quite closed. Was he in there? Betsie changed course, tiptoed to the door, and nudged. She spotted a crumpled bath towel but no sign of Michael, the one who was supposed to teach her the harness business. She shrugged and headed for the shop.

By the time she'd scrubbed both sides of every window in the shop with vinegar and old newspapers, Betsie was sweaty and resigned. Michael wasn't coming at all. Well, that was not her fault. If he didn't want to work with her, she would teach herself the best she could.

An early lunch would leave the afternoon for uninterrupted reading, she decided. She ate quickly, seasoned some hamburger patties to broil for dinner later, and returned to the shop. She settled into a webbed lawn chair in one corner and prepared to learn about leather and harness-making. The scrollwork on the cover proved more interesting than the dry-as-dust text, but Betsie found it helpful to follow the process in a logical order.

Toward the end of the afternoon, Betsie stretched and slapped the book shut. She caught a glimpse of the glorious May day outside the sparkling window. Springtime beckoned. Betsie heeded the call and stepped into the sunshine.

She heard a snort from Sheila's pony, Fledge. He was named after a flying horse in an outlandish schoolbook, Sheila had said. As Betsie watched, he bobbed his head and coaxed for her attention with a friendly nicker.

She chirruped and waved a carrot that she'd tucked in her pocket. Fledge trotted down the fence line to meet her. She scratched behind his ears and flattened her hand to offer the treat. He crunched it and licked a stray fragment from his lip while Betsie examined him.

"Poor Stubby-Legs, you will never fly, that's for sure," she laughed. Fledge bobbed his head. How sweet it was to spend time with somebody who didn't talk back!

As she rubbed Fledge's nose, an idea took root. Back home, horses were for pulling the buggy or the plow, good solid work. Boys rode horses to their jobs sometimes, but Betsie didn't know many girls who rode horseback.

She'd always wanted to ride a horse. Why not have an adventure? The Sullivans were gone, and they wouldn't be back for a while— maybe not at all, in Michael's case. It was the perfect opportunity.

Besides, that's what *Rumspringa* was for, the running around time where she could be as wicked as she dared, if she was to believe some people. She scoffed. There was nothing remotely *veesht* in riding a pony bareback, was there? Betsie couldn't even bring herself to believe it was *loppich*, though maybe her bishop would deem it plenty naughty to push up her skirts and bare her stockinged legs for all the world to see. But which was worse, bare legs or leaving the Amish?

Fledge dozed, hind leg flexed, as she mustered her nerve. His non-chalance did the trick. One quick jog around the pasture on a sleepy old pony and she could say she'd ridden bareback. Maybe the Sullivans couldn't handle him, but Betsie knew her way around a horse. With that thought, she swung the gate open. Fledge followed her progress with friendly curiosity.

She caught his mane at the crest and rested her other hand on his nose, improvising a halter. With gentle pressure, she led him to the shade trees near the back of the lot, away from passing cars and prying eyes. Fledge enjoyed her company. He snuffled at her apron pockets for the other carrot she had hidden there, seemingly unaware of her intent.

Now! She rested both hands on Fledge's back, elbows bent. With a hop and an awkward scramble she hoisted herself up on his broad back.

The startled pony tossed his head some, but he didn't otherwise object. Betsie fussed with her skirts while she waited for the fun to begin.

And waited. How did she make him go? *Ach*, she recalled her favorite book character, Laura Ingalls, a spunky girl who understood the value of good hard work, even if she was English. *She'd* ridden a pony bareback, once upon a time. Let's see, she kicked the pony in the ribs . . .

Betsie kicked. Fledge squealed with rage and charged like a horsefly had chomped on him. Instinctively she grasped his mane in both hands as he thundered down the pasture. For good measure, he bucked like the *loppich* pony he was, and she slid every which way on his slippery back.

By the third trip across the pasture, Betsie's *Kapp* loosened. With every jounce, bobby pins surrendered. Betsie let go with one hand and snatched at her *Kapp*, and that's when Fledge made his move. He skyrocketed up and plummeted to land on all four hooves. Betsie chomped hard on her tongue and wondered if her head might jar loose.

When he realized Betsie was still aboard, Fledge grew downright *veesht*. If crow hops wouldn't get rid of the nuisance on his back, maybe brushing her off under low-hanging branches would do the trick. When he hunched his back so he could lie down and roll, Betsie's sharp kick in his well-padded ribs convinced him not to try it.

Fledge tossed his head and careened toward the wire fence that ran along the road. Betsie yanked on his mane and hollered, but she may as well have tried to stop a circus elephant.

At the last second, he veered and slowed. With her leg pinned between his side and the fence, he rubbed against the wire grid to scratch an itch. The rusty metal shredded Betsie's black stocking and raked her skin from knee to ankle. "Ouch!" Desperate, she pummeled him with her free heel. It was no use; she was nothing more than an annoying gnat. "Stop, stop, you *loppich* pony!"

In mid-howl, she spotted Michael leaning against the Super Bee with his hands in his pockets and his long legs crossed at the ankles, apparently enjoying the show.

Betsie gritted her teeth and hung on as Fledge plowed through a honeysuckle thicket that grew along the fence. Limber green switches snapped her face and legs. She tried to break one off, but shreds of green leaves slipped through her fingers. Instead, she smacked Fledge's rump and hollered, "Whoa!"

Up went Fledge's head and rat-a-tat went his hooves. Betsie's skirts rippled like the library's American flag during a gale. Partway down the field, she heard a long *creak* and a blast of air as Sheila's bus stopped. The obstinate pony spooked. He planted his forelegs and pitched his hindquarters forward in one fluid motion. Betsie's legs came unhooked from his slippery barrel. She soared like an ungainly heron, limbs sprawled.

Hop right back on, she thought as she hurtled toward a tuft of green grass. A split second later, she blacked out.

CHAPTER 9

It turns out there's worse things than falling off a horse.
—BETSIE'S JOURNAL

THE GRASS WAS much softer than Betsie expected. It must have been covered with dew, too, for her face was wet. She opened her eyes. A vague shape hovered nearby—Fledge. Would he kick? She gasped and struggled to get out of his way.

"Thank God you're okay." Strong hands restrained her, but gently. "Come on, lie down."

Betsie blinked, very woozy. Had she been drugged? She squirmed. "No—"

"Please lie still, Betsie. You're hurt."

Something icy bathed her forehead. Slowly her vision cleared—she was lying in bed and Michael sat beside her. He held a sopping pink washcloth splotched with red. She hoped it was water that dribbled toward one of her ears. She shifted to avoid it, but the slight movement made her head throb. Every muscle ached, and her swollen tongue practically filled her mouth.

"Water," she croaked.

Michael stayed put. "Get her some, will you, Squirt?"

"I already did." Sheila offered the glass.

Sheila—why wasn't she at school? Betsie half-raised herself while

Michael supported her and held the glass to her lips. The water tasted rusty, but it soothed her parched throat.

Michael lowered her to the pillow, and she closed her eyes for a second. "*Denki.*"

"Oh, Betsie," Sheila whispered. "We were so scared! Everyone on the bus saw Fledge throw you, and then you were so still. I thought you were dead."

"Shut up, Squirt." Michael was chalk white.

"Mike picked you up and carried you to the house, and your head rolled, just like you were . . ." She glanced at her brother's bloodless face. "I mean, I held the door, and Mike was really careful. We got you into bed all right, but that's when we noticed your mouth was bleeding."

Michael drew a shaky breath. Groggy though Betsie was, it dawned on her that he couldn't stand the sight of blood.

"Sheila, will you get some iced tea for your brother, please? I sugared it well when I made it. He shouldn't have carried me all that way on such a warm afternoon."

"Sure, be right back."

After she left, Michael stared at the floor. "When I saw you lying so still, your mouth all bloody, it was like . . . like—"

"Don't speak of it anymore. That rascal Fledge! I bit my tongue, that's all. It feels better after the water." She smiled with more spirit than she felt. "You would never make a good Amishman, Michael, what with doctoring animals and people and butchering, even."

He responded to her ribbing with a sickly grin. "Duly noted."

Ice clinked as Sheila minced toward her brother. Michael drained the glass and placed it carefully on the lacy runner that covered the dresser. Soon his breathing slowed and his color improved.

"I guess you got really tired, huh, Mike? Carrying Betsie like that . . . I mean, not that she's fat, but it's a long way from the pasture, and it's pretty hot for May, you know, like the weatherman said, and—"

"Squirt?"

"Yeah?"

"Can it."

"Make me." She stuck out her tongue.

Michael lunged at her, and off she sprinted. Betsie closed her eyes and smiled as Michael chased the girl through the house and Sheila squealed.

In a bit, she must get up to start dinner. The whole family would all be here, and at last they would gather at the table, just as it should be. Then maybe they would appreciate all that they had. She smoothed the bedspread. Ah, it felt so good to rest . . .

When Betsie awoke for the second time, the room was dark. She hobbled out of bed, confused. One leg throbbed, and she clutched her head, it ached so. Her adventure with Fledge came flooding back. Ruefully she stripped off her shredded stockings and swabbed her scratches with the wringing-wet pink washcloth that she found on the floor. She slipped on another pair of stockings and found her *Kapp* hung carefully on the ladder-back chair.

How her head ached. She would give anything for a cup of soothing chamomile tea. As she steadied herself against the nightstand, she noticed a piece of paper sticking out of her notebook. Squinting to read in the dim light, she made out, "Glad you're okay. PS You weren't that heavy." The handwriting was precise, not at all what she would have expected. She hoped Michael hadn't paged through the notebook and seen what she'd written about him earlier. Worrying about it was too much of an effort; she put it out of her mind.

She crossed the hall to the pink bathroom and splashed her face with cool water before she glanced in the mirror. Sure enough, there was a lump above her left eye and a painful gash on her tongue. She sniffed; a smell of burnt meat hung in the air. Had she started dinner and forgotten about it? Befuddled, she limped to the kitchen.

Chaos greeted her. Smoke billowed from the oven to the ceiling. A distraught Mrs. Sullivan, face framed by straggles of hair, frantically fanned at hunks of charred meat. She stared at Betsie, her eyes as wide as saucers.

Betsie coughed and stumbled to the sink, soaked a dishtowel, and squeezed it out. "Turn off the oven and open the back door," she directed. Then she whirled the damp dishcloth above her head to drive out the smoke.

"I don't know what happened!" Mrs. Sullivan waved a sheaf of paper that Betsie recognized as the dog-eared script. "You weren't around when I got home, so I put your hamburger patties under the broiler and I sat on the steps to read my lines. Next time I checked my watch, it was a quarter to six. Then I smelled smoke and ran inside and, oh, is Gerry ever going to freak out!"

Betsie headed for the hallway to tell the others what happened, but she found Michael already hammering frantically on Sheila's door. "Mom, Betsie, fire! Everybody outside! Sheila, fire!"

She popped out of her room. "Fire? How can it—"

He grabbed Sheila's wrist and dragged her. "No time for questions, Squirt! Be quiet and move!"

"But, Michael—"

"Hurry, Betsie!" Michael propelled Sheila forward, where she promptly tromped on Betsie's heels.

"I smell smoke! Our house is going to burn down again! We have to call the fire department," Sheila sobbed.

"No time! Keep moving!" Michael bellowed.

"Please listen to me, Michael!" Betsie begged. She yanked Mrs. Sullivan's sleeve. "You have to tell them!"

But Mrs. Sullivan was soaking up the atmosphere. She muttered, "What wonderful energy. I can use this. This is happening. This is real . . ."

Betsie stared at her. "Mrs. Sullivan!"

"No time for jawing, Betsie, we need to get out of here!" Michael shoved them through the door, but now they met an immovable force. Mr. Sullivan, home from work, blocked their way.

"What in Sam Hill is going on?" Mr. Sullivan's eyes were wild.

"Oh, Gerry!" Mrs. Sullivan pasted on a brave smile. "There's been a fire—"

"Fire? Get out of the house, quick!" He hauled his wife down the steps and grabbed Betsie's arm next.

With another incredulous glance at Mrs. Sullivan, Betsie broke free of her employer's grip, pushed past Sheila and Michael, and raced to the kitchen. She snatched up a pan lid and banged on it with a spoon until the family got quiet.

"There is no fire," she said firmly. "Something cooked for too long, that is all. We need to air out these rooms."

Three blank faces and one guilty one stared at her. They walked inside, staring at the cloud of smoke that issued from the kitchen.

Mr. Sullivan recovered his poise first. "You burned dinner, Betsie?" He frowned. "Why not own up to it instead of giving us all a heart attack?"

Betsie's mouth dropped open. Before she could defend herself, Mrs. Sullivan walked like a queen to the kitchen, slipped on a pair of oven mitts, retrieved the smoking pan, and dropped a gallant curtsey.

"*I* did the cooking. Ladies and gentlemen, may I present tonight's burnt offering?" She proffered the sacrifice.

"You mean . . . there wasn't a real fire? It was just Mom's cooking?" Sheila erupted into nervous giggles.

"Way to go, Sunshine," Michael managed to say.

Mrs. Sullivan responded with a sheepish grin. "I put dinner on when I got home from the library. I figured Mike and Betsie were busy in the shop."

Betsie glanced at Michael, who reddened.

Mr. Sullivan did not smile. "Then I owe you an apology, Betsie. I'm sorry—I should have known someone as diligent as you would never let dinner burn." He turned to his wife. "So what was it this time, Phyllis?" His gaze fell to the script on the countertop. "Oh, I see. Off in la-la land with your imaginary friends again."

She flushed. "Fight fair, Gerry. The theater is my life."

"No, it isn't. *We* are your life," he snapped. He snatched up the script and waved it under her nose. "This is some other poor sap's life, a dreamer who thinks putting a bunch of words on paper is going to make him rich." He pitched the script in the trash can and included Michael in his angry glare.

"Dad, please don't." Sheila struggled to hold back tears. "Everything will be okay."

"The only way everything will be okay," Mr. Sullivan replied evenly, "is if your mother gets it through her head that she will never be an actress." He addressed his wife. "Stop gallivanting off to the library every day, Phyllis, and take care of your family and this house you wanted. Starting tomorrow, I expect you to stay home and be a housewife."

"But, Gerry!" Tears pooled and spilled down Mrs. Sullivan's cheeks. Her face looked like melted wax, all the life gone.

"No buts. Do I make myself clear?"

Instead of answering, Mrs. Sullivan covered her face with both hands and fled to her bedroom. Michael and Sheila stared at the floor while Mr. Sullivan practically threw off sparks.

Had the whole Sullivan family gone crazy? Of course Mrs. Sullivan should stay at home and take care of her family; that's what Betsie's mother and grandmother had done, and all the women before them. It was what Betsie herself planned to do someday.

But surely Mr. Sullivan should not speak so to his wife. She checked for Michael's reaction and flinched; he'd gone brick red.

"Michael, will you take me home, please? I—I don't feel well," she faltered. "I will come back tomorrow," she said to Mr. Sullivan.

"Certainly you can go. I don't blame you for wanting to get out of this madhouse." Mr. Sullivan turned. "Michael, make yourself useful and get Betsie's things for her." He switched on the television, effectively shutting them out.

Betsie didn't wait for Michael but hurried to her room, head pounding. When her satchel was packed, she tried to pick it up, but her hands trembled. Michael reached around her to grab it.

"Ready?" Vivid splotches of red showed on his cheeks.

"I—I think so."

"Then let's split." He pointed at the nightstand. "Don't forget your notebook."

Betsie fetched it and tucked it under her arm. She hurried to follow him out, but she couldn't keep up with Michael's long strides.

Sheila hugged Betsie before she retreated to her room. A grim Mr. Sullivan sat on the couch, parked in front of the TV.

"I'm very sorry you aren't feeling well, Betsie. I hope you feel better in the morning."

Betsie managed a nod, grateful that in the commotion he'd missed the lump on her forehead. "I'm sure I will."

The flash of the television screen commanded her attention. Uncle Walter, as Sheila called the talking newsman, was saying, "Good evening. I'm Walter Cronkite. It happened one year ago this week at Kent State University in Ohio."

His voice was a steady anchor in a sea of chaos. As she lingered, the reassuring face faded and the newsman's words described black-and-white pictures of young people who dressed as Michael did, to her surprise. Some of them doubled angry fists. Another picture showed a flower sticking out of the barrel of a shotgun.

The pictures changed to reveal English police with wicked guns. The police walked shoulder to shoulder up a hill. Puffs of smoke dotted the air as sad music played. Betsie saw a picture of a person lying on the ground, and then a picture of another person in a pool of what looked like blood at butchering time. Slowly it dawned on Betsie that the people lying on the ground were dead. Other pictures showed living people, frozen with horror, crowded around the dead.

The worst picture of all stayed on the screen the longest; Betsie would remember it always. It showed a face-down person; whether it was a boy or girl, she couldn't tell. Beside the dead person, a young girl crouched, horrified. Her mouth was open, and her heart cried, "Why?"

The music stopped. The pictures faded. Betsie forced herself to breathe.

Mr. Sullivan rose abruptly and snapped off the television. "Michael's waiting for you in his car," he told Betsie. "He'll be back for you tomorrow morning."

She nodded again and left the house. With all her heart, she wished she didn't have to return.

CHAPTER 10

I don't know where "home" is anymore.
—BETSIE'S JOURNAL

THE WARMTH OF the May afternoon had given way to an early evening chill. A blast of warm air met Betsie as she opened the car door. She stowed her satchel and the notebook at her feet and braced herself for what Michael would say after his father's angry outburst, but his first comment unnerved her.

"I guess we should have warned you not to ride the devil pony. At least that's what I call Fledge."

Betsie shivered; Michael's moods changed faster than Ohio weather in May. Though her head still hurt, the last thing on her mind was Sheila's pony.

"Hey, are you okay?"

How could he be so casual? The fire, the fight, and the awful television pictures replayed in her mind and locked her tongue.

"Betsie?" Michael slowed the car and pulled over in front of a church. "Look, maybe we should go to the hospital. You could have a concussion or something."

She held up her hand. "Please, no. I'll take something for my headache when I get home. It's just that I do not like fighting. Also I . . . I saw pictures on the television, and they upset me. Guys like you, dead, somewhere called Kent. It was awful." She dug a hankie out of her pocket and applied it to her nose. "I'm fine, really. I just want to get home."

But now it was Michael who shivered. "Kent State."

Betsie remembered the yellow triangle on Michael's wall. "Yes, that was it."

Michael's knuckles whitened on the wheel. His breath came in short gasps.

"What's wrong, Michael?"

"Argh!" He pounded the dashboard. "I was there at Kent State that day. I saw . . . all that."

Betsie clutched her throat. "You were there? So *arig*, Michael! Bad, I mean."

He watched a black cat slink into the forsythia bushes in front of the church building. "Bad doesn't begin to describe it. It's been a year since those students . . . died. Plenty long enough to move on, right? Only I can't move on, no matter how hard my old man pushes. It's like I'm stuck in time. Everywhere I turn, I see their faces. One minute they're alive, and the next, *pow*, gone forever into the great unknown."

"Had they done something wrong?"

"Nothing bad enough to die for. A couple were on their way to class, like me." Michael gritted out the words. "But die they did, and that is the supreme irony, because we were protesting the Vietnam War. Unless we can get the government to stop this thing pronto, I could be sent to my death in Vietnam, and that's a fact. Can you beat that?" He stared at her. "I didn't even have a cap gun as a kid. I hate guns."

"We don't believe in guns or wars where I come from. We don't even have police."

His smile was sarcastic. "Well, glory hallelujah, maybe I should join the Amish. But just so you know, that wasn't the fuzz shooting people at Kent State, Betsie. Governor Rhodes called out five hundred National Guard troops on us, on American *citizens*, if you can believe that, like we were the enemy. That action was way over the top for what was going down. The worst I saw that day was people calling names and throwing rocks. We shouldn't have done that, I guess, but some of us did," he admitted. "The Friday before, some drunks got pretty rowdy, too. They smashed windows and set the ROTC building on fire to protest military presence on campus. They even cut the fire department's hoses with machetes so the firemen couldn't keep the building from burning down."

Betsie made no attempt to hide her shock. "That was wrong, Michael."

Michael frowned. "Okay, but come on. Did those four students deserve to die for mere hooliganism? That begs another question: who killed them in the first place? No one will admit to giving the order to open fire, and no one will own up to firing that first shot—we may never know. The fact remains that the Kent State Four got up that morning, ate breakfast, and went to class, same as I did. It was just another day, except those four students didn't make it home. They died, but I'm still here. And I don't understand why. Because apparently I escaped death solely so I could be drafted and sent to Vietnam to die."

He looked at Betsie like he expected an answer. The only answer that sprang to mind was that his friends weren't in the great unknown—they were in the horrible place reserved for the non-Amish—but she was not encouraged to share her beliefs with any English person. Joining the Amish church and keeping every rule in the *Ordnung*, that was the surest way to maybe go to heaven someday, and not the other place. But even the Amish couldn't know which place they were going to end up in until they stood in front of the good Lord Himself and He revealed it. It was prideful to believe otherwise.

She decided those didn't seem like very good answers for Michael, not the way he was hurting. Betsie pressed her lips together and kept silent.

"Hey, thanks for not telling me to lighten up and everything will be all right. I get that all the time." He fixed his gaze on the road ahead. "Maybe I just needed to talk about Kent State with somebody who listens. Someone like you. But I've kept you here long enough. Let's get you home." He twisted the key and the engine roared.

It was dusk when the Super Bee pulled up at Betsie's house. Her heart sank. In the hubbub of the day, the fact that *Mem* and *Dat* were gone had somehow slipped her mind. A fresh wave of grief welled up. Then, from the corner of her eye, she glimpsed a buggy drawn by a fast-stepping horse. Betsie spied her sister Sadie in the passenger seat. Her stomach fluttered when she recognized the driver.

Towheaded, sunburned, and strapping in his plain Amish clothes, Charley Yoder smiled at Betsie and raised his forefinger. He vaulted from his buggy and sauntered to the other side to help Sadie alight.

Before she knew it, Betsie was out of the car and running. She flung herself into Sadie's arms. The sisters cried a little, full of exclamations about their separation. When Sadie left her and turned toward the house, Betsie met Charlie's warm gaze.

"Welcome home."

Her cheeks flamed with a pleasant heat. She wiggled her fingers at him and smiled at her toes, at the same time uncomfortably aware that Michael stood beside her. He walked around to the passenger side of his car to retrieve her satchel.

"I'll get that for you, Miss." Charley, always polite, spoke English for Michael's benefit as he reached for it.

Betsie wiped away tears and giddy laughter bubbled. "Miss? Why so formal, Charley? I've only been gone a couple of days. I'm the same Betsie you've known since we were *kinner*."

Charley laughed, too. "*Ach*, Betsie, such a *Schnickelfritz* you are. I wasn't talking to you, but to this young lady here." He jerked a thumb at Michael.

Michael flashed a wintry smile as he relinquished the satchel. "Here you go, pal. The name's Michael Sullivan, by the way."

Shock registered. Charley and Sadie took stock of Michael's long hair and girly clothes, noses wrinkled and lips curled. Michael didn't help matters any. He pasted on a sardonic smile. Betsie decided her two worlds had collided plenty long enough.

"*Denki* for bringing me home, Michael. Good-bye!"

His mouth quirked with wry humor, like he knew perfectly well she was trying to get rid of him. For a moment, she recalled the awful experiences he'd gone through at Kent State and blushed with shame.

Sadie had no such qualms. She linked elbows with Betsie and

practically dragged her away from the hippie in the car. Charley walked protectively on her other side.

A sudden honk of the car horn startled them all. Betsie turned to see Michael brandishing her notebook.

"Don't forget this—unless maybe you wanted me to read it?"

"Oh, no." She brushed past Sadie and snatched it. "I'm sorry," she said, but she wasn't talking about leaving the notebook.

He winked so only she could see. "I'll be back to pick you up in the morning," he said, just loud enough for Sadie and Charley to hear, too. "Plan on spending the whole day together." He clicked the radio and thumbed the wheel until Betsie was sure the loud music was audible all over Plain City. "Gotta split."

Michael was irrepressible. She scrambled for the right response. "Catch you later." She grinned in triumph and turned around.

Was in der welt? The hurt and surprise on Charley's face stopped Betsie in her tracks. "Oh, Charley, it isn't a bit like it sounds." She crooked her finger and nodded at the porch swing. "Can you sit for a minute with me?"

"I shouldn't stay. It's the middle of the week."

"It will be all right for a little. Just let me ask *Dat*—" Her heart squeezed. *Dat* wasn't here. Did Charley know why?

Sadie darted a sympathetic glance. "It's all right, Betsie. He knows *Mem* and *Dat* are visiting"—her sister placed the slightest emphasis on the word—"in Belle Center."

"*Denki*, Sadie." Betsie favored her with a look of pure gratitude.

She sat on the wood swing and the chains popped as Charley eased next to her. With a push of her toes she set the swing in motion, eyes downcast, and tapped her fingers on the wood slats between them. There was so much she wanted to say, but so little that she could really share.

Charley broke the silence. "I missed you."

Oh, he was so sweet. "I missed you, too, Charley. It's nice to be . . . back." Not home, not anymore. She was grateful the swing was in the shadows so he couldn't see her tears.

"Does your job go well?"

"*Jah*, I have a lot to learn, but it seems good." She drew a deep breath.

"Mr. Sullivan has a new job, so that boy, Michael, will be teaching me. He used to work in the shop, too. Sullivan and Son, it was called."

Charley grunted and shifted his weight. "It's all right, Betsie, I . . . trust you."

"Oh." Tears smarted and her throat ached. "That means a lot, Charley."

"It seems to me that harnesses and horses and such don't make proper work for a girl like you, though. You could get hurt."

She was glad the darkness hid the knot on her forehead, too. "I . . . I'll be all right. How does planting go?"

Her relief was palpable as Charley launched into a detailed account of his farming to date. She listened with half an ear, jumbled thoughts of the day competing for her attention. *Charley trusts me. The good Lord knows I've been faithful to my upbringing. Except for riding bareback. And watching television. And listening to worldly music.* She came back to Charley's conversation with a start.

"But I don't know what the bishop is thinking, letting you work with a wild-looking English boy who may try to lead you into the ways of the world. The less you have to do with him, the better. That's what I say." He planted both boots to stop the swing, and the chain rattled.

"But, Charley! How can I have less to do with Michael when he must work with me every second in the shop? You know I can't wait on customers."

"It's really not so difficult, Betsie. Decide to do what's right, and do it, why don't you?"

"I am trying to do what's right, but how do I know what to do when there is more than one right choice? I do my best. You said you trusted me, Charley." She rested her hand briefly on his shoulder and felt his muscles tense.

"I do trust you to do what's right." He pulled away and held her gaze. "But also I want to look out for you until your parents return, and I don't intend to fall down on the job."

A sparkle of tears blurred her vision. She jumped up to retreat to the doorway, her back to him. "I know you won't. *Denki*, Charley. Good night."

"*Gut nacht*, Betsie," Charley whispered. "It's good to have someone to take care of." His boots thumped on the porch steps.

Betsie closed the door and leaned against it, flushed and out of breath. When she was here in Plain City with Charley, it was all cut and dried, but now that she knew an English family, knew their heartaches, it was not so easy.

"There you are," Sadie greeted. "Good to have you home."

"Where's Lovina? Has she gone to bed already?"

"No, a letter from her arrived the day *Mem* and *Dat*—I mean the day you left. Lovina said she's not coming until tomorrow. That's why Mattie Yoder sent me home, so I can pick Lovina up at the station in the morning. It will be good to have our aunt to take care of us." She rolled the ends of her *Kapp* strings between her forefinger and thumb. "What did Charley have to say?"

Betsie's face warmed. "He warned me about the English again. But listen, Sadie, they're not all bad. Why, the little girl, Sheila—"

Sadie covered her ears. "Don't tell me about the English. I don't want to know. Don't let them fool you, Betsie. They are so deep in the ways of the world that they can never get out. Have nothing to do with them outside of your work."

Exasperation threatened to choke Betsie. "But it's not that easy!" she wanted to shout. Instead she took a deep breath, pulled Sadie's hands away from her ears, and changed the subject. "He also said he would take care of things around here for us. You know what a hard worker he is." She mustered a grin. "Oh, it is good to see you, and only think, Friday night I'll be ho—*here* for the whole weekend."

"*Ach*, I'm glad. Are you hungry? Eat with me while I tell you what I overheard in the bakery."

The sisters giggled over Sadie's account of Sawmill Joe's chickens flying the coop every night to roost in Ada Gingerich's buckeye tree. The supper dishes took much longer to redd up than at the Sullivan home, what with filling the woodbox, kindling the fire, boiling water, and washing and rinsing every dish by hand. But what did it matter as long as they were together? Betsie wrung out the dishcloth and hung it on the drying rack before she refreshed herself with another sip of chamomile tea. Laughing with Sadie made doing chores as much fun as a frolic.

When their work was done, Betsie and Sadie threw on their shawls against the chill, lighted a lantern, and headed to the pasture to visit Judith. Betsie's heart swelled with gladness at how happy her horse was to see her. She knew it wasn't only because of the carrot she brought, as Sadie teased. She limped back to the house, forever content to drive Judith rather than ride her.

As the sisters got ready for bed, Betsie shivered. No more nudging the thermostat to get the heater to run, like at the Sullivan house. They'd banked the kitchen fire for the night, so she layered quilts on her bed.

"*Ach*, Betsie, did the calendar turn to February, maybe, while I wasn't looking?"

Betsie looked from her bed to Sadie and burst into gales of laughter. Sadie giggled with her as they peeled off a couple of quilts together. Love and laughter was better than blankets.

She snuggled into bed. "Ahh. Good night, *Schweschder*."

"Betsie?" Her younger sister paused with her hand on the door frame. "I wish I'd gone to the station with you. I followed *Dat* out and told him while he hitched up that if he was going to the English, I didn't ever want to see him again. But now I miss *Mem* and *Dat*," she finished in a small voice.

"So do I." Betsie sat up again and dashed away a tear. "We had such a happy home, one where we all worked hard together toward going to heaven someday, maybe. But they will never go to heaven now."

Sadie sniffled. "Maybe they will come back home before it's too late. If they don't, oh, Betsie!" Her face was white. "Think of writing to all our older brothers and sisters and their families in Missouri to tell them. Think of Abijah, out there to help Eli and his family until Eli's broken leg heals. I don't want to tell our little brother that *Mem* and *Dat* are gone forever. Oh, so sad! They have to come back."

"Hoping won't bring them back, ain't so, Sadie? We must pray to the good Lord." The tears Betsie had been choking back overflowed. She moved over to make room for her sister and patted the bed. Sadie stumbled forward and clung to her, weeping.

CHAPTER 11

The surest way to get Michael talking is to
give him work to do.
—Betsie's journal

THE NEXT THING Betsie knew, the rooster down the road announced the new morning; if only today and Friday would fly by, too. She and Sadie, spent from their uncharacteristic outpouring of emotion the night before, said little as they built up the fire, drew water, made eggs and toast, and set tea to steep. By the time they'd washed the dishes and swept the kitchen, the Super Bee was rumbling into the driveway. With a peck on her sister's cheek and an encouraging squeeze, Betsie was out the door before Michael honked. A hobble was all she could manage. Michael hopped out of the car to assist her.

"Wow, you're all crippled up. Need help?"

"I will be all right," she said briefly, mindful of Charley's advice to have as little as possible to do with the English.

But Michael proved hard to ignore. His sleeveless cowhide vest, for example, cried out for her surreptitious attention. The bottom edge of the cowhide was fringed, with tiny beads knotted at the ends. Betsie supposed the beads were a stopgap measure to keep the vest from fraying further. There were no proud buttons to keep this flimsy covering shut against the morning chill, and no shirt underneath, either, to her consternation. Betsie looked away and decided to add the sad garment to her mending pile.

It was a quiet drive until Michael said, "So this Charley guy. You're kinda hung up on him, ain't so?"

"Hung up?" Betsie pictured clean wash flapping on the clothesline.

"Yeah, you like him, am I right?" Michael slouched with one hand on the wood wheel, the picture of bored indifference.

Betsie felt her color rise. Compared to her best friend, Rachel, she was quite reserved about her feelings. As far as Betsie was concerned, the identity of her special friend was a private matter, but to maintain silence would confirm Michael's suspicions. She half-turned to rest her cheek against the cool window. "I'm not . . . hung up on him."

"Huh."

She tried again. "I—*we've* known him, Charley, I mean, for a long time."

"So I gathered. 'I'm the same Betsie you've known since we were *kinner*,'" he mimicked.

She stiffened. "Tell me, Michael, how long have you known Peggy?"

"W-what?" The car rocketed into the Sullivan's driveway with a careless bump.

"Yes. Maybe *you* are hung up on *her*."

Michael laughed and brought the car to a stop. "Nice comeback, Betsie. Meet you in the shop in a few." He grabbed her satchel and carried it inside, whistling a tune.

She'd handled that well. Betsie practically skipped to the harness shop, eager to get to work. As she unlocked the door, a flash of blue where there should have been only greenery caught her eye. She ducked inside the shop to peer at the weedy verge beside the road. *Was in der welt?* She spotted the top of Mrs. Sullivan's head above the tall grass, craning as she watched the house behind her blue glasses.

A battered VW bus rumbled into view. Mrs. Sullivan stood, slung a faded blue tote bag over one shoulder, and signaled the driver. She took another long look at the house, her aqua granny dress fluttering. Then she squared her shoulders and climbed aboard. The bus belched exhaust as it chugged out of sight.

Betsie shuddered—was it wise to defy Mr. Sullivan's order to stay at home? She hoped Mrs. Sullivan would find herself while she studied her lines at the library, and that it would be worth the trouble later.

"*Ach*, it is no use, Michael." Betsie tossed the single-crease tool on the work table and massaged her temples. Early afternoon sunlight reflected off the Super Bee in the driveway. Had she known how demanding harness-making would be, she would have refused to strike a bargain with her cousin. Now she was trapped. "We've been working on this part for some time, but I will never learn."

Michael scoffed. "Lighten up. Creasing leather is tricky. Hang on a sec, try this." He fumbled in the match safe that hung by the door, struck a sulfur match, and lit a candle stub he found in a drawer. "Heating up the metal helps sometimes. There . . . that should do it."

He stood beside Betsie as she gripped the wooden handle. Before she could object, he grasped her hand and guided the tip of the creaser down the leather strap, a fraction of an inch from the edge. "See? We're sealing the fibers and sort of outlining where you'll be stitching." He poked her arm. "All right! I knew you could do it."

Betsie didn't know whether to laugh or cry. "That was you, not me. I'm a *Nixnootzich*."

"What's that?"

"A good-for-nothing." She flushed and slipped her hand from his grasp.

"Man, are you ever down on yourself. It takes years to learn this business—I don't know the half of it. I was always a *Nixnoodle* at the stitching part." He wiggled his eyebrows.

Betsie smiled wanly. "It's *Nixnootzich*." She traced the newly creased leather. "Why don't you help your *dat* in the shop anymore?"

Michael stretched. His vest rode up before Betsie could avert her gaze, and he slapped his bare belly. "I used to help out all the time, even after I started high school. We got along pretty good, I guess. Did you hear about the fire that burned our house and barn down?"

She nodded.

Michael hitched up on a stool and rested a bare toe on the floor. "Somehow that brought our family closer for a while. We had almost nothing left; this shop was about it. Me and Da—my old man were bound and determined it wasn't the end, though. We had to live in here until the new house was finished, but as long as we had each other, we could make it work. The business was still Sullivan and Son, just like it had been for a hundred years, one generation teaching the next." He shifted. "The situation changed when my old man sold off the farmland. For the first time, we had bread to spare."

"Well, it is good to have plenty of bread to eat," Betsie ventured.

"I mean money," Michael translated. "So they built a modern house where the old farmhouse used to stand. Spare no expense—that was my old man's motto. All the latest status symbols. You name it; we had it."

"Like a Super Bee?"

"Ouch, Betsie." He fiddled with the creaser. "Yep, I do love my car. Guess you've heard that part."

"Yes, but I still don't know why you stopped helping your *dat*," she reminded. Reluctant to sit idly, Betsie fetched the broom and tidied the floor. "Go on, I am listening."

He sighed. "My old man would tell you it's because I'm a *Nixnootzich* dreamer. See, I had this high school English teacher who turned me on to journalism. Newspaper writing, you know? That did it; I wanted to be a journalist, but Dad wasn't buying it. We had one huge hairy fight after another about my chosen profession." He looked down his nose and mimicked, "'Writing for a newspaper is not going to put food on the table, Michael.' 'Journalism isn't going to pay the bills; sticking with the family business is the way to go.' You get the drift."

She nodded.

"But here's the part that blew my mind, Betsie. Every evening at dinner, my dad is reading me the riot act about my wanting to be a journalist, but every day in journalism class, Mr. Dugan is raving about the articles I wrote for the school paper. 'Sullivan, you've got a gift. It would be a crying shame to waste it.'" Michael rounded on Betsie with palms upraised. "So which voice was I supposed to listen to? How do you decide when there are two right choices?"

Betsie drew in her breath sharply. Hot tears welled; her face crumpled. She hid her face in her hands and the broom clattered to the floor. "*Ach*, I am so clumsy."

Michael was beside her in an instant. "Hey, you're shaking! Are you okay?"

"*Jah*. It's just—everything's so tumbled around, Michael."

"Really heavy, huh? Let it all hang out, Betsie." He patted the other stool. "Talk to me," he amended when she didn't respond.

"But that's it exactly," she cried. "I shouldn't be talking to you at all, much less working unchaperoned with you in this shop. But if I don't . . . Oh, I am so tired of trying to figure it out." She took a deep breath and tried to explain. "Once, in the pet shop at the five-and-dime, I saw a . . . hamlet? No, a guinea pig."

Michael's expression was politely vacant. Oh, what a muddle she was making. "Ginger-and-white fur it had," she rushed on, "very pretty, with wee folded ears. The poor thing was in a cage filled with smelly wood shavings. It scrambled up on a wire wheel and ran in place while the wheel turned. No matter how hard it tried, though, that guinea pig didn't get anywhere. And I feel the same."

"You're kidding. The way you tackle stuff head-on, I really thought you had it together. So what's the problem? Come on, I won't bite," he reassured. "Besides, how is anyone back home going to find out if you talk to me, or that we're here alone?" He held up one hand to stop her from answering. "Wait, let me guess; does this have to do with that Charley guy?"

Crestfallen, Betsie held her tongue.

"Whoa. I could understand if you were worried that your parents would find out. I mean, most parents would flip if I arrived to escort their daughters to work. I think it's my threads or something." He winked.

"My parents left the Amish," Betsie blurted.

"Left? What do you mean?"

"They don't want to be Amish anymore." She blew her nose. "They've left the church."

"Oh. Is that all? I mean, I haven't been to church in a while, myself."

His attitude said he didn't miss it. "I don't get it. Why is leaving the Amish such a big deal?"

"Leaving the church means *Mem* and *Dat* don't want to be a part of the Amish life anymore." It hurt to say the words aloud.

Michael frowned. "Why would they want to leave a life where you live off the land and everyone helps each other? Why leave Utopia?"

"Never mind. I can't explain." Betsie scrambled to her feet and shuffled work orders on the already spic-and-span worktable.

"Betsie. Come off it."

Reluctantly she faced him. "I don't mean leaving the way of life only." A vivid memory surfaced, edged with *Dat*'s rumbly voice. "*Mem and Dat* got different about God than they used to be, almost desperate. *Dat* always read to us from the Luther Bible, like this: 'Listen once to the Word, *kinner. Roemer 10:9: 'Denn so du mit deinem Munde bekennst Jesum, daß er der HERR sei, und glaubst in deinem Herzen, daß ihn Gott von den Toten auferweckt hat, so wirst du selig.'*"

"Have a heart," Michael protested.

"You don't understand it? It was the same way always for me. Our Bible was in High German. That's not the same as what we speak at home. But lately, *Dat* patiently translated for us what verses meant. *Dat* is very good with German, and maybe I'm a little like him when it comes to English."

"You don't make too many mistakes," Michael admitted.

"I like English. Anyway, *Dat* asked what good is it to hear the Word and not understand it? So he taught us Romans 10:9 in *Deitsh*, our own language, and maybe you know it like this, in English: 'If you confess with your mouth Jesus, that he is Lord, and believe in your heart that God raised Him from the dead, thou shalt be saved.' And *Dat* would repeat, 'Thou shalt be saved! There's no muddle about that, no waiting until we get to heaven to be sure. We know *now*.'" Her eyes misted. "I've never told anyone else about his Bible translating before; the bishop wouldn't approve. The *Biewel* reading we hear in our meetings is in High German. And Michael," she confided, "I understand almost none of it."

He spread his fingers, palms up. "I don't understand much about religion, myself, so let's move on. My parents said a Nelson Miller bought this shop. So how come you're working here and not him?"

"*Jah*, Nelson is my cousin, and I am trying to tell you, but it's hard." Betsie kneaded the tender place on her forehead. "He's kind of like you, not wanting to fight in Vietnam, that is. The Amish don't believe in war, but Nelson got his draft notice all the same, the one that said he must serve his military time regardless of his beliefs. He argued with the army about it, but he still had to serve in Chicago at some military hospital for the wounded. It made no difference that he had already bought this harness shop from your *dat* and was to be trained by him."

Michael stared. "Wait, back up. You mean to tell me that he doesn't have to go to Nam simply because the Amish don't believe in war? Man, what a crazy, mixed-up world this is. Your parents left the Amish, and I'd like to—"

The last thing she wanted to hear was more talk about her parents. "I'm hungry and it's long past time for lunch," she broke in.

He looked surprised but shrugged. "I could go for some chow. Come on." He headed for the house, and Betsie trailed behind, drained.

"Hey, Phyllis?" Michael called and shrugged. "Guess she's out again."

With a start, Betsie remembered the VW bus. "I saw her leave right after we got here."

"Score one for women's lib." He rummaged in the storage bin and emerged with his old standby. "Apple?"

"*Denki*, no. How about I fix us some bread soup?"

Michael made a face and chomped the apple instead.

"Bread soup is what I am having. Food and drink at the same time, you'll see."

Michael displayed the apple with a flourish. "Ever hear of apple juice?"

"Yes. I've helped make it, too," she shot back. If only he knew the gallons and gallons of apple cider her happy family had pressed over the years. She crumbled bread slowly into a bowl of milk and sprinkled it with sugar.

He wiped his mouth with the back of his hand and waved the apple. "That's what's so cool about you, Betsie. You live off the land. No rat race for you. If you need threads, you sew 'em. If you need food, you grow it or raise it. I've done a little farm work, but I can't imagine how groovy it would feel to go whole hog like that."

"It would feel like a lot of hard work," Betsie replied wryly. "I wonder how you know so much about what we do."

"I'm a journalist, remember? I ferret out what I want to know. So," he said as he stood, "chop-chop with the bread soup. I've gotta hear the rest of the story."

"All right, I am hurrying."

True to her word, Betsie followed Michael back to the shop a few minutes later, where they sat cross-legged on the clean, plywood floor. He brushed back his hair for the umpteenth time and fiddled with some unfinished strips of leather he'd pulled from the counter.

"So I still don't get why you're here at the harness shop and why your parents moved and all." As he talked, his fingers worked the six strands into a narrow braid.

She didn't get it, either, but she plunged ahead. "Like I said, my cousin tried to get out of being drafted, but it was no use. Then Nelson got his wonderful idea. Why shouldn't I, his cousin Betsie, take an apprenticeship as a hired-out girl to Mr. Sullivan while he, Nelson, served out his time? He reasoned with my *dat* that I would hold on to the clients that Mr. Sullivan had built up, and then I could train Nelson to make harnesses when he came back. That way, the shop could continue even though Nelson was not here." Betsie watched Michael's fingers, fascinated by his skill.

"So this was your cousin's bright idea."

"Well, *jah*, he went to my *dat* to make a bargain about me, but the funny part is I *wanted* to do it. It just sounded right, like an adventure. *Dat* said harness-making wasn't a job for a girl, maybe, but after some talk, he and Nelson shook hands on it and Nelson left for Chicago. *Dat* spoke to Bishop Gingerich, who after a long wait approved my hiring out to an English family. There are rules I must follow, lots of them; I can't wait on customers, for one." Betsie colored. "That rule I was glad to follow. I was afraid of you when you showed up to drive me that day," she confessed. "And that is all, I guess."

"Whoa, whoa, whoa, you're nowhere near done. Let me read between the lines, Betsie. You wanted adventure. Everyone was giving you grief about doing men's work, but you stuck to your guns until you got what you wanted. You showed your parents what's what, and now you call the shots. Looks like Phyllis isn't the only feminist around here." His eyes twinkled. "I'm impressed."

"It was not like that at all." She faced Michael, clenching and unclenching her fists. "I want my parents at home. *Dat* and *Mem* made up their minds, told me and Sadie good-bye, and left for Belle Center. Dat's sister Lovina, Nelson's *mem*, is arriving today to stay at our house, so Sadie and I won't be on our own. But, oh, Michael"— Betsie drew a shuddery breath—"I'm so afraid."

"Come on, Betsie, it can't be that bad. Spill it."

Betsie winked back tears. "I don't think I will ever see *Mem* and *Dat* again. Not even in heaven."

CHAPTER 12

One thing is for sure, life is never dull with
Michael around.

—BETSIE'S JOURNAL

TO BETSIE'S SURPRISE, Michael groaned. "Oh, come off it, Betsie. Your parents had the perfect life. Of course they'll come back—they don't have to go to church to do that, do they? Why all this fuss about God? What's He got to do with anything? The truth is . . . no, skip it. It's too heavy for you." He placed the braid against his forehead and tied the long strips at each end of the braided part behind his head. "Ta-dah."

Oh, he was infuriating. "So you make me talk about what's troubling me, but now you will not do the same? I'm plenty strong for anything you want me to carry."

"What a spitfire. All right, you asked for it." He crossed his arms. "I don't believe in God anymore."

"*What?* Oh, Michael," she whispered, "you shouldn't say such things. The good Lord, He's everywhere. He'll hear you."

"Nope. No one can hear me but you, Betsie. You might as well get used to it. It'll make your life a heck of a lot easier." He picked at a hangnail.

"Then why do you look like life is so hard?" She almost touched his arm. "You said you don't believe in God *anymore*. So you did—once?"

"I guess," he mumbled. "When I was a kid." He fingered the scarred edge of the table in front of him.

"What made you stop believing, Michael?"

"Lots of things." He spit the reasons. "Too little proof. Too much education. Too many unanswered prayers at Kent State."

When she didn't answer, Michael shifted and frowned. "Look, I've been to church, Betsie. I've heard believing only takes faith as small as a mustard seed. Once I thought I had that much. But when I begged God to stop the shooting, He didn't. If God doesn't answer a prayer like that, I don't want anything to do with Him." He gritted his teeth and glared at Betsie. "That was the last time I prayed."

"You're wrong." Betsie lifted her chin.

He stared. "Excuse me?"

"That wasn't the last time you prayed. You've talked to God since. I heard you."

"I beg to differ." A condescending smile played on his lips.

Betsie was undeterred. "When I revived after I fell off Fledge, you prayed. I heard you." She cocked her head and looked him in the eye.

Dazed, Michael dropped his gaze and didn't speak for a full minute. "'Thank God you're okay,'" he muttered at last. "Son of a gun. All I can say is I must have been in shock. There was blood everywhere and you looked . . . come to think of it, I didn't flake out on you. Maybe I'm getting better. It's sure been a long time coming." He tightened his braided headband. "Oh, man! Come to a rap session with me and my friends. You would really blow their minds. Everyone would be all impassioned, griping about the rat race, crazy for peace, and then you would shoot them down and bring them back to earth. You work your tail off, but you radiate peace like a hundred-watt bulb. Unreal."

Peace? Her life was in shambles. Melancholy threatened, but she tried to match his mood. "I don't always understand your fancy talk, but I know one thing: I do not have a tail under my dress, Michael."

He laughed. "Guess I'll have to take your word for it."

He checked his wristwatch, one with a black leather band. On its face, Betsie spied a funny mouse with red shorts, yellow gloves, fat yellow shoes, and a tail. The mouse's gloved hands showed the time, twenty past two.

"Listen, it's been a rough day. You could use a break, and we have some time before Sheila gets home. Go for a ride with me, and I'll buy you some ice cream to make up for the tail remark." He quirked a smile.

His moods shifted like lightning. Nevertheless, Betsie's mouth watered. Ice cream, sweet and cold. She wavered. Right now was work time, not play time. She must not go, especially not for a joyride alone in a car with an English boy. The bishop had told *Dat* she could ride to and from work only. More importantly, what would Charley say?

"Well? Are you coming?"

Tom Sawyer would never turn down ice cream, she reasoned. She retrieved her bonnet from the peg by the door and settled it primly over her *Kapp*, ready for adventure, as much of an adventure as she could have with a person dependent upon a mouse to tell him the time, anyway. She peered at Michael from the depths of her bonnet while he fidgeted with impatience to be gone. Truth be told, he reminded her of a gangly puppy, loyal and true. Betsie imagined throwing a stick for him to fetch and struggled to keep her expression sober. "I will go. Should I lock up the shop?"

"Good idea. I locked the house. I don't need to give the old man another excuse to blow a gasket."

Soon the Super Bee pulled into a crowded parking lot. A shooting-star sign read Milky Way Ice Cream Shoppe. Several customers stared as Betsie and Michael got out of the car. Betsie supposed they did make a funny pair.

Michael clapped his hands together. "Ye olde hangout," he announced. "I used to work here part time the summer before last." He shepherded Betsie through the door and pointed to the menu. "What'll you have?"

"So many flavors!" She scanned the selections twice before one item caught her attention. "Ice-cream sandwich? Whatever kind of bread do they use?"

Michael grinned. "Oh, it's a kind you'll like." He placed their order and flipped a dollar bill at the cashier, pocketed the change, and grabbed the white paper bag. "You don't want to eat inside, do you? Pretty packed-out—crowded," he clarified. "Looks like a school field trip or something."

Betsie eyed the crowd. No one in the room looked as though they'd ever stepped foot in a field. Bareheaded boys in loud shirts clambered all over the furnishings. The adults—were they teachers?—ignored the children and gabbed. Most of the boys wore chocolate beards. Girls in colorful short skirts sported rivulets of ice cream to their elbows. Oh, for a washcloth and a bucket of soapy water so she could scrub their messy faces clean.

Michael was already halfway to the door. Betsie's shoes stuck slightly to the tile as she followed. They passed a record machine that played songs so loud she could almost see the people singing, "Baby, baby, baby." Another minute and her ears would melt.

She breathed easier once they were outside, where concrete tables were circled in a fenced corral off the street. Betsie was shocked to see young boys standing on top of the tables, smeared faces gleeful. When a car approached, the boys pumped their arms. Most drivers obliged by honking the car horns. With every blast, a loud cheer erupted from the children. Hands over her ears, Betsie didn't know Michael was talking to her until he nudged her to come along. By the time they got in the car, she had forgotten all about the ice-cream sandwich.

"*Ach*, how my head pounds."

"Pretty rowdy, for sure." He dug in the bag. "Groove on that."

"Oh!" Betsie tore off the white wrapper, suddenly curious. "How can they wrap something melty in paper? Oh, it's like a whoopie pie." She took a cold, sweet bite. "Ice cream between two chocolate cookies!" She took a bigger bite. "I like it. Thank you, Michael."

"You're welcome." He spooned up vanilla ice cream drowned in glossy brown. "Want a bite of my sundae?"

Betsie had watched the worker ladle the topping out of a steamy bucket of molten chocolate. She tasted it. "It's very good, but why doesn't the heat melt the ice cream to soup?"

"It's one of the mysteries of the universe." He offered another scoop. "Cherry?"

"*Denki*, no. I see you do eat." Betsie wiped her sticky fingers on a paper napkin. "Must be that you don't like my cooking, I guess."

He started the car and rested his arm on the back of the seat as he eased out of the space. "What makes you say that?"

"You have not eaten with us once."

Briefly he looked startled. "Nope," he admitted. "But you're wrong. I dig your cooking—I sample it when I raid the refrigerator late at night."

"So that is what happens to the leftovers." Betsie watched a flock of swifts swirl like smoke from a nearby chimney. "Will you eat dinner with us tomorrow?"

"No can do, Bets." He reclined lazily, one hand on the wheel. "Okay if I call you Bets?"

"No."

"Cold." He glanced sidewise at her and smiled.

As they drove, Betsie noticed a hand-lettered sign tacked to a fence. "Horse Show, Franklin County Fairgrounds, Saturday," she read. "I didn't know the fairgrounds were so close."

"Good thing for the harness shop. We would have never had any business otherwise. Er, I hope my old man clued you in about that." He looked guilty.

"Don't worry," Betsie said airily. "When he moves the business one day, Nelson will be very busy. There will always be Amish in Plain City, and they will always drive horses."

He glanced at the radio and reached to punch a button. "Well, I hope you're right—"

"Michael, look out!"

CHAPTER 13

The good Lord will never forgive me for the
wicked things I've done.

—BETSIE'S JOURNAL

"HANG ON!" MICHAEL hit the brakes. The car lurched to a stop a few yards from where a farm wagon was towing an Amish buggy onto the road. A team of muscular horses strained to draw the double load.

"Trapped like rats. Crud." Michael tapped on the wood wheel for a second. Then he rolled down the window and craned to see.

Betsie followed suit. "*Ach*, someone's cut a flat place in the wheel, poor things." She pointed to show Michael. "You can't drive a buggy with a wheel like that very easy."

"How'd they drive all the way out here, then?"

"Likely they didn't. It's those wild English from Dublin. They sneak out to where our horses and buggies are tied, while we are visiting friends or on meeting Sundays, usually. Then the rowdies steal the horse and buggy and drive it to some outlandish place. They cut the rubber tire and slink away like the *Nixnootzich* they are. Once we found a buggy on top of the school. We don't fight back, but it's very mean."

"And definitely not my bag," Michael said. "I feel sorry for them, but man, they're moving like molasses. Better back 'er down." He tapped the brakes a couple of times to leave some distance between his car and the buggy.

Betsie twisted in her seat to view a parade of cars stretched behind them. Drivers honked their horns. "Hurry-up English." She smirked as she faced front. "I know you are anxious to pass, too."

"Feisty, huh? Hang on to your bonnet when I buzz around them."

With a defiant sweep of her hand, Betsie pushed her bonnet back. Her airy *Kapp* was the only barrier between her hair and the wicked world. She fussed with her skirts and hid a smile. "No need to hang on to my bonnet at this rate."

"Oh, yeah?" Michael yanked the wheel hard left and tromped down on the gas pedal.

Betsie's right shoulder slammed against the door. Why had she teased him? She gripped the edge of her seat and watched in dismay as the orange speed needle skyrocketed to forty dizzying miles per hour.

Air streamed through the car as they gained on the crippled buggy. As they drew even with the wagon and the unfortunate driver, Betsie couldn't resist taking a peek.

Charley Yoder stared back at her in open-mouthed amazement. Betsie shielded her face with her hands, but she knew it was hopeless. Charley had seen her for sure, and there was no mistaking who she was with, thanks to the showy Super Bee.

Michael zoomed past unaware and neatly angled back to the right side of the road. Betsie's fingers trembled as she pulled up and retied her bonnet. Oh, was she ever in *Hase-Wasser*. Boiling hot water.

"What's up? You're white as a sheet. Ice cream didn't agree with you?"

She gulped. "That was Charley."

"*The* Charley? Wait, he saw you, didn't he?" He grinned. "With yours truly."

Betsie sketched a miserable nod. "I am in trouble."

"But he knows I drive you to and from work, right? Come on, it's not so bad."

"He is not dumb. He knows it is not going-to-work time." She raised both hands in a futile gesture and let them fall to her lap. "I only hope his *mem* wasn't with him."

"What gives? I thought you weren't hung up on him, anyway." He scowled. "Lighten up, it's just a car ride. It's not like he caught us making out or anything."

What Michael meant, Betsie didn't know or care. For Charley, there was no such thing as going for ice cream with a friend. He'd caught her keeping company with the very English boy he'd asked her to avoid. Without meaning to, she'd hurt Charley. Worse yet, if Mattie Yoder was with her son, she would tell the whole community what she'd seen, but she would make it sound like it was for Betsie's edification. Briefly Betsie wondered why the bishop had never taken Mattie to task for her tale-bearing. But what was she thinking? Was not her own sin a hundred times worse? Would Charley ever forgive her?

Her heart sank and passed her stomach along the way. "Let's go back to the harness shop."

"WHOA, baby!" the radio hollered. "It's the top of the hour and time for your local news. The Hilliard Stalker strikes again! Hilliard police warn of another attack on a solitary woman—"

"What a sicko." Michael punched a button. A loud English ditty played, and for a moment Michael hummed along. "What good would more work do? Talking about what's bringing you down is the cure. How'd you like to go to a rap session at my buddy's house? Tons of people hang out there. You'll feel better, and you'll sure as heck be a breath of fresh air for them." He glanced at her. "You game?"

She kneaded her sore stomach. "Won't Sheila be home soon?"

"Ooh, I forgot." He checked his mouse watch. "Phyllis left pretty early, so she should be back home any time. She can let her in, right?"

Betsie scrambled for a way out but came up empty. "I suppose," she sighed.

"Cool." He stuck up one thumb. "It's not far; we'll be there in a sec. Trust me."

Slowly Betsie cranked the window shut. Disappointing Charley hurt terribly, but another thought was almost worse. The good Lord wanted her to follow the *Ordnung*; that much she had been taught ever since she could remember, but she hadn't done it.

A tear splashed her apron. She'd behaved poorly, and she desperately wanted to make amends with the good Lord, but she knew He must be angry with her. Her eternal fate would be uncertain until she faced Him one day, when she was dead and out of the sinful world, and then—maybe—it would be too late.

She simply could not think about it anymore. She pretended to be interested in the passing scenery until they arrived in a decrepit part of town.

"This is it." The house where Michael stopped was plain, like Amish houses. Peace crept back into Betsie's heart, and she pushed away her misgivings. Maybe Michael was right and talking would help, after all.

He parked along the street. Coarse weeds caught at her skirts as she got out; she sidestepped and nearly tripped on the broken sidewalk. Michael caught her elbow. Betsie flinched and gently pulled her arm out of his grip. Despite her resolve to put her troubles out of her mind and trust Michael, she could almost feel the bishop and Charley—especially Charley—watching.

As Michael knocked, the door opened. Dark curtains shut out the daylight. Betsie tried to hide her dismay at how gloomy the house was. It may as well have been midnight, save for the flickers of light from a fat drippy candle on a dish in the center of the floor. Several people sat in a circle around the glow. There were no chairs or couches, just dirty linoleum to sit on. A music machine turned a record; Betsie heard scratchy clicks.

Betsie blinked as her eyes adjusted. A dozen or so mangy cats prowled the edges of the room, so that accounted for some of the smell. Most of it emanated from a smudge of smoke such as she'd never smelled before. She cowered behind Michael.

"Hey, where's Steve?" he asked no one in particular.

A point of red light glowed and faded in reply. The peculiar smell strengthened as the red light bobbed around the circle. Betsie heard somebody inhale noisily and was repulsed. Why people smoked nasty cigarettes was beyond her. She didn't know too many Amish who used tobacco, and she avoided the ones who did. This sickening sweet smell must be from a new brand.

It certainly seemed to be affecting the people in a strange way. They barely moved and didn't speak. Where was all the wonderful talk she was supposed to hear?

She tugged on Michael's sleeve. "I want to leave."

It was too late. A girl who looked vaguely familiar reeled across the floor in Michael's direction.

"Mike! Hey, babe, am I glad t'see you!"

"Hey, Peg," he said flatly.

Peggy pushed past Betsie and pulled Michael down to plant a kiss on his mouth that made Betsie blush. He swiped it off with the back of his hand as Peggy tried to focus on him. The whites of her eyes were all bloodshot, like she hadn't slept well.

"Whassamatta? You're all uptight." She pawed for his hand. "Mellow out. C'mere."

Michael dodged her. "Come on, Betsie."

"Betsie? Why'dja bring the Pilgrim?" she whined. "Send her away. Party with me."

"No can do, Peg," Michael said lightly.

Peggy collapsed against him. He caught hold of her arm and the small of her back and held her at arm's length.

"Well, let her stay, then. Just don't bring me down, man." She swayed to the rhythmic clicks of the record machine.

"I don't think that will happen anytime soon. Excuse us a minute, Bets." Michael steered Peggy through a doorway off the big room.

Betsie clung to Michael's sleeve like a burr. Peggy whimpered as he lowered her to a lumpy mattress on the floor.

"I miss you, Michael. Why'ncha stay and keep me company?"

Betsie held her breath.

"No way. You're stoned. Stay in here and sleep it off."

She heard the click of a lock as Michael pulled the door shut. Then he led Betsie past the people who sat like blind statues.

When they emerged, she gulped fresh air until they were in the car. Then she realized that her hair and clothes reeked of the funny cigarette smoke. Disgusted, she rolled down the window.

"Not much talking in there," she observed tartly.

Michael was shamefaced. "Don't rub it in. I shouldn't have taken you there, all right? Mea culpa."

"They must have gotten hold of some bad tobacco." She fanned herself. "I've never smelled anything so awful."

Michael shook his head. "Um, yeah. It may come as a shock to you, Betsie, what with your Amish upbringing and all, but some people are pretty heavy into drugs. They weren't smoking tobacco. It's called marijuana."

"Marijuana?" Betsie sat bolt upright. "You took me to a *pot* party, Michael?" Whiffs of the cloying smell of sin rolled up in waves, and she nearly gagged.

His jaw dropped. "How . . . what . . . where did you hear about pot?"

She rounded on him. "There are few vices unfamiliar to Amish youth, and what's more, a few have bragged to me about what they've done, at least before they married."

Michael narrowed his eyes. "Does that include Charley, your honey?"

"I will tell you one thing," Betsie flashed. "*Charley* would never take me to a pot party, that's for certain. We would do respectable things together, like . . . like go to singings with the church youth groups, or go for a drive to the covered bridge, or—"

"Or bundling?" Michael cut in with a smirk.

Betsie clamped her lips shut and refused to take the bait, even though her insides seethed. Why had she thought she could trust him?

He cranked the ignition and the engine turned over. "Well, excuse me for trying to help you forget your troubles. I guess it's a lost cause."

It was an unpleasant ride to the Sullivan house. Once in the driveway, Michael turned to her. "Listen, Betsie, I said I was sorry. Can't you forgive me?" he said. "We do have to work together tomorrow, you know."

"No." Her clenched jaw ached.

"Man, talk about stubborn."

"I am no more *schtaerkeppich* than you." How it hurt to have him point out the fault that *Dat* had most often warned of. She exploded out of the car but stopped short. Sheila huddled on the front steps, crying as though her heart would break.

CHAPTER 14

Why is it that just when things start going well,
they get worse?
—BETSIE'S JOURNAL

BETSIE RACED TO Sheila's side. "What's wrong, dear heart?"

"I'm locked out! The bus dropped me off ages ago, and no one was home to let me in. I tried the shop, but it was locked, too. I thought everyone left me, and I'm thirsty and hungry, and worst of all, I really have to go to the bathroom. Oh, Betsie!" She flung herself into Betsie's arms.

Michael's shadow fell across them both. "That's quite a performance, Squirt. I nominate you for best actress at the next Academy Awards." He consulted his mouse watch. "Especially since Mickey says you've only been out here fifteen minutes."

Sheila glared at her brother through angry tears. "Why weren't you here to let me in?" She sniffed. "And what's that funny smell?"

"Mind your own beeswax." He nudged her toward the door. "Come on, you're fine. I thought Phyllis would let you in, anyway."

"Well, she didn't. I was awful worried, Mike. I imagined somebody kidnapped you guys and left me here alone, and I was going to have to do all the cooking and cleaning and—"

Michael tugged her ponytail. "Good grief, Cinderella, it wasn't that bad." He put the key in the lock. "Let's rustle up some grub, what do you say?"

"Sounds good, I'm starved!" Sheila shot through the door ahead of them, ponytail flying, and Betsie followed, shoulders stiff.

"Hey, Betsie, wait up," Michael said.

"Yes?" She didn't turn around.

"I meant it when I said I was sorry." He held the door. "Look, it's such a beautiful day. I was thinking maybe you guys could help me wash and polish my car. Before you say no, we'll work in front of the shop in case any customers happen by. We can get some work done, catch some rays, and make up for this afternoon all in one. What do you say?"

"Well—" Betsie wavered. "I've never washed a car before."

He sniffed audibly and peeked over her shoulder. "Soap and water and fresh air will be a great way to get rid of this stink."

She flinched at his nearness but smiled at the idea of an afternoon outside. What harm could there be in honest work? She shrugged. "All right, I will help."

It didn't take Betsie long to rustle up cookies, fruit, and glasses of milk while Michael and Sheila changed. She served cookies and milk on the steps. Sheila wore a skimpy, two-piece green-and-blue bathing suit. Michael was worse; he wore cut-off denim shorts with long white hem straggles and no shirt at all. Betsie blushed and focused on the tree line behind the harness shop as she nibbled, but she could hardly help but compare poor Michael's skeletal frame with Charley's robust good health.

Michael cranked the squeaky spigot while Sheila squeezed the trigger of the garden hose and squirted the yellow car. "This is fun! We haven't done this together in a long time, Mike!"

"Not my fault," Michael informed her. "I wash my car every week, and you always *used* to help me." He watched as Betsie dipped a sponge in the cold suds and took some tentative swipes at the car's yellow sides. "Mind starting on the roof, ladies? By the way, Sheila's car-washing style is how she got her nickname."

"It is not!" Sheila dropped the hose and retrieved a sponge. "Dad started calling me Squirt because I was so short, but I'm lots taller now," she told Betsie. She stuck out her tongue at Michael, flounced toward the car, and tiptoed to reach the roof, her bare midriff an enticing target.

"That's not why we called you Squirt. This is!" In one swift motion, Michael scooped up the hose and directed an icy jet of water at his little sister. The stream smacked the small of her back, and she squealed.

"M-Mike, you big ape," she chattered, arms stuck at awkward angles from her sides. "I'll get you for that!"

"Gotta catch me first," Michael taunted. He danced backward on the balls of his feet, pulling horrible grimaces at Sheila as she lunged at him with the bucket full of sudsy water. The water sloshed over the sides as she chased her brother, liberally soaking herself in the process. She plopped the bucket on the ground and another wave of water cascaded over her before she fished out a sponge and waved it menacingly.

Betsie paused her car-washing to watch, smiling indulgently as brother and sister feinted and dodged. She chuckled as Sheila cocked her arm to hurl the dripping sponge. Michael shielded his face and backtracked rapidly toward Betsie, momentarily blocking her line of sight as she daydreamed about happy times with Sadie and—

Sploosh! The loaded sponge smacked Betsie full in the face and blinded her. She sputtered and coughed as she rubbed her smarting eyes.

"Oh, Betsie, I'm so sorry!" Sheila sounded suspiciously like she was trying not to giggle. "Michael ducked."

"Look on the bright side, Bets," Michael whispered, his voice brimming with fun. "At least you don't smell anymore."

Betsie bent over slightly as she coughed and snorted, still unable to answer.

"Hey, are you okay?" she heard Michael ask. He patted her back helpfully.

Splat! Betsie planted the sopping sponge directly in his face.

He fell to his knees, spluttered, and blindly snatched up the hose to aim it at Betsie. "All right. You asked for it, so stand still and take your medicine. Oh, so you can dish it out, but you can't take it, huh?" he needled as Betsie backed away with hands clasped.

"Michael, please don't," she implored. "I am already soaked!"

"Too late for—" he broke off with a drowned gasp as Sheila crept up behind him and dumped the bucket of dirty water over his head.

"I surrender!" Michael yelped as Betsie and Sheila congratulated each other.

Betsie excused herself from the buffing part of waxing the car to start dinner. Her dress had nearly dried in the strong afternoon sunlight. As she cooked, she scratched her itchy nose and discovered to her chagrin that it was sunburned. She decided it was worth it to feel so lighthearted and refreshed.

Deep in dinner preparations later, she was startled to find Mr. Sullivan at her elbow. His smile was quizzical.

"Working hard, as usual," he said. "I hope Phyllis has been helping you?"

She felt her face redden and fanned the steam that curled from the bubbling pot of chili. "*Ach*, this stove gives off good heat. I started early, and I don't know where she is right now," she apologized.

Mr. Sullivan smiled wryly. "Don't worry about it, Betsie. You shouldn't have to keep tabs on a grown woman." He stepped toward the hallway and raised his voice. "Phyllis! She's probably off in her own little dream world," he added. He cupped one hand to his mouth. "Phyl-lis!"

Sheila and Michael, hair bedraggled, trooped into the house, distress over their father's yelling evident as they edged by him to change clothes. Betsie stirred the simmering pot. Should she tell him that Mrs. Sullivan had boarded the Volkswagen bus hours ago?

There was no need. Sheila streaked into the kitchen then, damp and grimy, a crumpled piece of notebook paper clutched to her chest. Her eyes were enormous as she thrust the paper at her father with shaking hands.

"I found it on your dresser. It's from Mom," she said. "She's run away."

Mr. Sullivan stared at the note. "What?"

Sheila rattled the paper as tears rolled down her cheeks. "Read it!" Her voice was shrill. "We have to do something!"

"About what?" Michael cruised into the room and took the paper.

"Whoa, heavy. Looks like Mom's following her dream and auditioning for an off-Broadway production of *Hair*," he said. "I didn't know she had it in her. Good for Phyllis." A sprinkle of freckles stood out against his chalky skin, and he sounded hollow.

"What are we going to do, Dad? She says she's not coming back until she hits the big time." Sheila pulled her father's arm. He opened his mouth once or twice, but no sound came out.

Gently Betsie disengaged Sheila's hand and encircled her shoulder with one arm. "Sheila, honey, let's leave your *dat* alone for a little. He's had a shock. Mr. Sullivan, maybe you should sit down." Betsie gestured at the couch. "I'll take care of Sheila."

"That won't be necessary, Miss Troyer," Mr. Sullivan said. A muscle in his cheek twitched. "I'll take care of Sheila. Under the circumstances, I believe it would be best if you went home a day early. We need to get this mess straightened out, pronto. If you'll get your things together, Michael will drive you home." Mr. Sullivan draped an arm over Sheila's shoulder, and they retreated down the hallway. Betsie could hear the soft sobs of the young girl and an answering heavy sigh from her father.

Michael took a couple of steps after them. "What a cold son-of-a—"

"Michael, don't." Betsie blocked him. "He's hurt. It's like when my parents told me they were leaving the Amish."

"It's not at all like that. I'm ecstatic Phyllis showed that much spunk. He crushes the life out of us, Betsie. No," he said at her protest, "I'm done with him. Pack your bag and let's get out of here. Come Monday, I'll be long gone."

CHAPTER 15

Today was the worst day of my life.
—BETSIE'S JOURNAL

BETSIE COLLAPSED ON the car seat and resigned herself to more top-blowing as Michael climbed in beside her.

"This is good-bye, Betsie. I mean it. I've had it up to here"—he slashed at his forehead—"with my old man, okay? Phyllis was exactly right to leave, and when I split, too, that'll teach him."

"But, Michael, where will you go?"

"Who cares? I may join this commune I've heard about. It's called the Farm; there's no government. Everyone works together and lives in peace by choice, kind of like you guys. Man, that must be cosmic." A faraway look came into his eyes.

"What about Sheila? If you go, she will lose her brother, too."

"Umm." Michael fiddled with his car keys. "Low blow, Betsie, playing the little-sister card like that."

"I am only telling the truth. She would miss you terribly."

"What about you?" He colored and turned away. "What I meant was how will you get back and forth? Oh, crud, that's what talking to my old man does to me."

Tears smarted. "I wish I could talk to my *dat*."

Michael stopped jingling his car keys and snapped to attention. "What did you say?"

"I said I wish—"

"I heard. Just let me ponder for a sec," he begged. "Where did your folks go? Do you have an address?"

As if she would ever forget it. "Two hundred eleven East Buckeye Street, Belle Center, Ohio." She rattled it off.

"What, no zip code?" He winked at her. "Relax, I'm kidding. How would you like to go there?"

The thought of it took her breath away. "But I can't drive Judith that far, and I don't have enough for train fare."

He scoffed. "Like, what are we sitting in, Cinderella, a pumpkin? Belle Center is a hop, skip, and a jump from Indian Lake, and I've driven up there lots of times. It's only about an hour from here, so it's no sweat. So what's the verdict? Are you up for a road trip?"

"You would do this for me?" She massaged the sore spot on her forehead, overwhelmed. "How would we manage it? It's getting late, and your *dat* sent me home for the weekend."

"But that's the beauty of it. My old man thinks you'll be home in Plain City for the next three days, and your sister thinks you're here in good old Hilliard until tomorrow night." He snapped his fingers. "Presto. A day off and a free ride."

"Where will I sleep tonight? I will not hide in your room like that awful Peggy."

"Details, details." He scratched his chin with a key. "Got it—you can sleep in the harness shop. And look, you're already packed." He pointed to her satchel with a pleased smile. "Come on, Betsie, I can tell you're dying to see your folks. Let me drive you up there to make up for everything."

She fingered the ends of her *Kapp*. What she wouldn't give to see *Mem* and *Dat*, to show them the error of their ways, entreat them to come home with her. Surely by now they'd had their fill of English life. And how happy Sadie would be when she walked in with *Mem* and *Dat!*

"How do I get inside the shop without anyone seeing me?" she asked.

Michael flashed a huge grin. "Atta girl! We'll leave right now, only we'll head for Dublin instead of Plain City. We'll grab a couple of sandwiches someplace and hide my car behind the 1919 Building on Post Road. It's just a short hike to Indian Run Falls from there, and that's where we'll eat." He checked her shoes. "It's rough going in some spots, but those'll do the trick. Not that many people know about the falls, so we can hang out there. Then when it's dark, we'll drive back here, park behind the shop, and sneak around front to unlock the door and get you settled in for the night."

"Where will you sleep?" Betsie was fascinated at how easily she assimilated into a life of crime.

He slapped the car seat. "Right here."

She considered for a moment. Surely, surely the good Lord had provided this opportunity so she could persuade her parents to come back to the Amish. Their eternal destination was certainly worth fudging a few simple details. "Let's go," she said.

"At your service, Cinderella." With a bow, Michael peeled out for Dublin.

The plan went off without a hitch. When they finished dinner, he guided her over a treacherous path to a clearing secluded by an impervious screen of honeysuckle. The trees that towered overhead were only faintly green, but Betsie easily imagined the leafy cathedral that the arched branches would form in the summertime. She sat on a dry rock, arms wrapped around her knees, mesmerized by the blue-green waters of Indian Run as they cascaded over the falls and crashed on the mossy rocks below. Oh, so beautiful, so peaceful. She laughed as Michael tossed sticks into the current and raced them downstream as they rocketed in the swift current.

Had she ever seen Charley this lighthearted? But that wasn't fair. Charley had lost his father very young. He'd become the man of the family. Combine that with having Mattie Yoder for a mother and it was plain to see why frivolity was all but smothered. She smiled and shook her head as Michael larked. The English and their tomfoolery. She didn't blame Charley one bit for being scandalized when he saw her cavorting in an English car with Michael. Maybe he wasn't one to frolic, but Charley was steady and dependable, a real man. She would have to do better by him, that was all, even if Michael was pretty harmless.

At last the cool evening air and hungry mosquitoes forced them to surrender the peaceful paradise. As Betsie stood up on a wet rock, it teetered. Michael encircled her waist with one arm and offered his hand to assist her.

"*Denki* for bringing me here, Michael," she said. "It's very pretty, but we need to get back." She gently extricated herself from Michael's grip and picked her way up the riverbank.

"I'm glad you liked it." He gathered their things and led the way back to the car.

Michael didn't turn the radio on for the drive home, and that was fine with Betsie. She soaked up the peaceful stillness, strangely content, as one by one the silver stars twinkled into view.

Her conscience revived and pricked a bit when Michael killed the engine and coasted to a stop behind the shop. She felt lowdown and mean to deceive not just her Amish family, but her adopted English family, too. Charley's dear face filled her thoughts. Surely he would take her to see her parents if he had the time and if Belle Center wasn't too long of a journey for a horse. He would understand that Michael was simply the driver, a necessity.

She fished her key from her pocket and they stole through the shadows. She fumbled with the lock in the dark, but at last they were inside. Michael located the horse blankets and spread one on the floor for Betsie. He gave her a thumbs up, slung another blanket over his shoulder, and headed for the car.

"*Gut nacht,*" she whispered. She locked the door and rolled up in the earthy-smelling blanket with her arm doubled up for a pillow. In her mind's eye, she saw the waterfall as it hurtled over the gorge to splinter into a million droplets. Faster than she would have believed possible, she was asleep.

She was awakened by an insistent tapping. Woodpecker? She squinted as bright sunlight streamed into the unfamiliar, stuffy room. She twisted to see the window behind her, where Michael tapped again.

Flustered, Betsie hurried to let him in, glad she'd slept in her *Kapp*.

"Good morning, starshine. Man, were you ever zonked out. Sheila's bus just left, so we can get in the house and uh, freshen up. Grab a bite to eat, too, so let's make tracks." He groaned when Betsie, ever fastidious, retrieved the horse blanket to fold and hang it neatly.

"Are you sure your *mem* isn't inside?" She smoothed the wrinkles from her dress.

His eyes clouded for a moment, but then he shook his head. "I've been awake for a while, and I've got it scouted out. Let's just say it's not the first time I've done this."

Fifteen minutes later, the road trip was underway. "I can't believe I will see *Mem* and *Dat* in just one hour." She patted the Super Bee's dashboard with affection.

"Belle Center or bust," Michael agreed.

He lapsed into silence, but by now Betsie knew he wasn't angry, just pensive. Still drowsy, she whiled away the hour planning her reunion with her parents. She smiled dreamily at the plowed fields they passed, some newly planted. But eventually an unpleasant thought intruded on her reverie. What if, after she'd said her piece, *Mem* and *Dat* simply refused to come home? But that was impossible. Surely the good Lord had gifted Betsie with this opportunity. Surely it was God's will that she should succeed. She leaned forward, hands clasped, as they entered Belle Center.

The town was small, and it didn't take long to find Buckeye Street. They passed a few houses before Michael slowed the car. "Is that it?"

Betsie peered at a weathered gray house in the shadow of twin buckeye trees that grew on either side of the porch. Her gaze skipped past the elderly English couple who sat idly reading on the front porch as she searched for a glimpse of her parents.

"I don't know." She wiped her sweaty palms on the hem of her dress. "I've never met the people my folks are staying with."

"Well, the address matches, at least. So are you getting out? This is what you've been waiting for." Michael stretched and turned off the car.

"*Ach*, you are like all of the hurry-up English. Can you let me think a moment only?"

As she pondered her next move, the man spotted the car and helped the woman to her feet, like they thought Michael and Betsie were lost, she decided. The pair of them headed to the curb, speaking in low tones to one another as they darted cautious glances her way.

Betsie watched them warily. The man was clean-shaven and hatless, older than she'd guessed at first. He moved with all the authority he could muster while clothed in denim overalls and a blue checked shirt. The woman wore a fawn-colored dress sprinkled with tiny red flowers that only came to her knees. The dress had buttons all down the front. Soft wings of hair swooped on either side of her face, and the rest was smoothed back in an uncovered bun. Oh, it was easy to guess that these were the people responsible for her parents' corruption.

She twisted to face Michael. "I don't want to talk to these people. Take me home before they try to change me—"

"Betsie! Is that you?"

She whipped around to stare at the smiling stranger who had spoken her language and called her by name. "*Dat?*" she whispered.

"Betsie! Betsie!" *Mem* leaned in the window to kiss her cheek. "Where is Sadie? Have you come to join us?" Her eyes shone.

"*Ach, Mem!* I can't believe this is you!"

Michael coughed politely. "So, I take it these are your parents?"

Betsie didn't know how to answer. They talked like *Mem* and *Dat*, but oh, what a change a few days had wrought, and not just in their appearance. Her heart quailed at her resolve to bring them home.

"Here's an idea," Michael went on. "I'll drive around while you visit with your folks. Looks like you've got a lot of catching up to do." He flashed a wicked grin and mimicked her accent. "Ain't so?"

"That sounds like a wonderful *gut* idea, young man," *Dat* said in English. "*Denki* for driving our Betsie."

Michael's eyes widened but he quickly recovered his aplomb. "You're welcome, sir." As *Dat* backed up to let Betsie out, Michael whispered, "Keep your chin up."

She joined her parents on the sidewalk and watched until he turned the corner, unsure of how to proceed.

"What a nice young man. Unusual, but nice. Come meet our hosts,

Betsie." *Mem* grabbed Betsie's hand, unrestrained as a child. "*Ach*, I can hardly believe you are here!"

She followed her parents on rubbery legs. This wasn't how she'd planned their reunion at all.

"Sadie did not make the decision yet, I see." *Dat* rubbed his unfamiliar smooth chin and broke into a beatific smile. "Well, we will continue in prayer for her. Pastor Shock's brother Jimmy says it is our privilege to pray to the good Lord every day for the salvation of our family and friends. I'm thankful it didn't take long for you."

Betsie stopped in her tracks. "But I am not staying here. I came to take you home for good."

Her parents stared at Betsie in dismay. "Oh, surely not! We will never turn back." *7* gave a sad shake of her head. "Come along, now, and we will talk."

Betsie didn't budge. "I am not stepping foot inside this house. The English won't get me, and they don't have you yet, either, fancy clothes or no. Don't worry; in time, your beard will grow back, *Dat*. And *Mem*, I am ashamed to see you dressed so," she scolded. "Change back into your plain dress at once and let's be gone from this wicked place."

A sorrowful look came over *Dat*. "Betsie, do you want to know what true wickedness is? It's teaching people that they can't be sure of their salvation before their time on this earth is up. That's the most wicked, unspeakable lie I can think of. Please don't speak so about the decision *Mem* and I have made. We want our people to know the truth about Jesus Christ."

"Betsie, if only you understood this: we are free now." *Mem* reached to caress her cheek, but Betsie drew away from her touch. "Come up and sit on the porch. We were just reading from the Word, *ach*, so *gut* to be able to drink it up, to know for sure what the good Lord offers! Wouldn't you like to eat a dish of ice cream and listen while your *Dat* reads to us? It would be how it always has been with our family. We miss you and Sadie so."

Betsie's lips trembled. "Then come home, *Mem!* Come home to us. We are waiting. We haven't told anyone what you've done. No one would ever need to know." She caught *Mem*'s hand. "Come with me, you and *Dat*, before it's too late."

Instead of answering, *Dat* bowed his head. A fresh breeze set the buckeye leaves above to rustling. Betsie heard a measured tread and the squeak of floorboards from inside the house.

"Noah? Fannie? Is everything okay?" A man appeared in the doorway. He looked curiously at Betsie, and then he smiled. "Why, this must be your daughter. We've been praying for you, you know. I'm so happy you've joined your parents!" He held out his hand in a gesture of welcome.

Wordlessly Betsie stared at her father, pleading with him to set the stranger straight, but he didn't. Slowly Betsie turned her back on her parents and stumbled toward the road.

"Betsie, please stay . . ." The rest of *Dat*'s words were drowned as *Mem* laid her head on his shoulder and sobbed.

Betsie covered her face with shaky hands. She couldn't lose *Mem* and *Dat* twice—she must stay.

As she lifted her chin to tell her parents, she saw the yellow car flash through the intersection at the end of Buckeye Street.

"Michael, wait!" Betsie sprinted for the corner, her shoes pounding the pavement.

"No! Betsie!"

Pain edged *Dat*'s voice, but Betsie had gained the corner. She heard the welcome screech of tires as the yellow car backed into view.

"Hop in," Michael said.

Shaken to the core, Betsie crawled onto the seat, covered her face with her apron, and wept.

CHAPTER 16

Will I ever be happy again?
—BETSIE'S JOURNAL

HOURS LATER, BETSIE'S feet dragged as she climbed her porch steps. If she could just avoid Sadie and make it to bed, she wouldn't have to share the awful news about *Mem* and *Dat*. A squeaky hinge dashed her hopes. Her sister scurried forward in the dim light, hands wound in her apron.

"*Ach*, Betsie, what are you doing home so early?"

"Early?" It seemed like Michael had driven her around for days until her bitter tears dried up. He hadn't said much, yet he appeared to share her grief as he doled out awkward hand pats that were oddly comforting. She felt hunched over and a hundred years old, exhausted body and soul.

Sadie poked Betsie and whispered in her ear. "There is trouble. Mattie and Charley are here; they parked around back. And what's more—"

So her horrible day wasn't over yet. Sure enough, Mattie Yoder sat bolt upright in *Mem*'s favorite rocker in the front room. Her grin was as smug as a possum's.

"Evening, Betsie. *Wie geht's?*"

"*Gut, denki. Und dir?*"

"*Gut*, but come, you have not greeted your guest. I've been taking care of her today for you and Sadie."

"My guest?" Listlessly she scanned the couch, where a sprightly older woman with smooth pink cheeks sat.

Sadie wound her hands tighter still in her apron. "Did you forget that *Dat*'s sister Lovina would stay with us while Nelson is in the army? She's going to help out while *Mem* and *Dat* are visiting, isn't that nice?" Her sister's voice was shrill with tension.

Betsie fought an urge to clutch her head. "*Ach*, of course I know that."

"*Jah*, Charley and I were on the way back from the buggy shop. Our buggy wheel was cut, so we borrowed another to use until it was repaired," Mattie explained. "We just dropped the other one off and picked up ours, and we stopped here because Charley insisted on doing your chores, even though he is very tired. When I saw Lovina working on the porch, I was happy to visit with her. We've been having a nice chat, haven't we, Lovina, dear?"

"Yes, but who's that you're talking to, Mattie? Come here so I can see better."

"It's me, your brother Noah's Betsie, all grown up. So *gut* to see you, Lovina!" Her hand was like a limp dishrag as she shook hands with her aunt.

"Betsie? Speak up once, you're a-whisperin'." She squeezed Betsie's hand and drew her closer. "How are you, child? Mattie Yoder says you're with the English now. Tell me this is not true!"

"Ouch, my hand! So strong you are yet, Lovina!" Betsie massaged her bones back into place, but she was glad the pain snapped her out of her misery enough to match wits with sly Mattie. "Of course I'm not *with* the English, only hired out. Let me put my satchel down. Sadie, can you put on some water for tea? Then I'll tell you all about making harnesses."

And, oh, what a nosy talk it would be if Mattie *Wonnernaus* stuck around. Nervous as a cat, Betsie jumped at a noise from the yard and stood on tiptoe to peer sideways out the window. Charley was sluicing the dirt off his hands at the pump. In a minute she would be face-to-face with him at long last. How would he react?

She summoned up her last shred of energy and clucked her tongue.

"*Ach*, what a shame, Mattie, here is Charley, just when I am ready to talk about my job, but it will keep." Betsie grasped Mattie's elbow. "You are good to keep Lovina company. Now I will walk you to the buggy."

Mattie pinned Betsie with the hungry gleam of a barn cat stalking a mouse. "But I want to hear how it is going, working with the English."

"Don't you worry about me, Mattie." Betsie shepherded her through the door. "Making harnesses is exacting work, but I am learning more every day."

They paused beside the buggy. Would Charley mention her indiscretion, riding in the car with Michael? A long steady look passed between them. She thought she glimpsed sorrow in Charley's eyes. If only she could fall to her knees and beg for his forgiveness. She couldn't bear his disappointment. "Charley, I—"

"I'll see you soon." Charley did not smile as he handed his mother into the buggy. "*Gut nacht* to you, Betsie." He nodded, climbed aboard, and drove away.

"*Gut nacht*, Charley," Betsie whispered as the buggy drove out of sight.

After a few minutes, she regained her spirits enough to join Lovina over a plate of Sadie's crusty buttered bread smeared with golden apple jelly. Betsie heard the sadiron sizzle as her sister guided it over a dampened dress. Two more irons waited on the stove to use when the first one cooled down. Comforted by the homey scene, Betsie found that she'd revived enough to pour three fragrant cups of tea while Lovina recounted her grand journey.

"That train ride—oh so wonderful, to travel so far, so fast! No bumps and jerks like a buggy. I had a very good trip. I do miss my Nelson, though."

Sadie glanced up from the board. "We are glad to have you here with us, Lovina. I guess Nelson's situation is kind of like *Mem*'s and *Dat*'s—" She broke off, flustered. "I mean, *jah*, praise the good Lord for your safe trip, and that reminds me of another blessing." Sadie whacked the sadiron on the stove top and darted into the sitting room.

Betsie held her breath. She peeked at her aunt, but Sadie's near slip-up apparently hadn't registered.

"These came yesterday." Sadie waved two envelopes, one addressed in *Mem*'s clear handwriting. "Charley fetches the mail to the bakery for me every day, so I can read it right away."

"So thoughtful he always is." Betsie accepted the letter and refused to pay heed to the stab of jealousy she felt at Sadie seeing so much of Charley. "From *Mem* and *Dat?*" she managed to say. "How are they doing?" As if she didn't know.

"Read it for yourself, why don't you?"

Barely able to prop her eyes open, Betsie sighed. "'Dear daughters, I trust by now Lovina is with you. *Dat* says to remind you he is concerned . . .'" She darted a glance at Sadie, who grimaced and put a stealthy finger to her lips. She read on rapidly to herself: "—about Lovina's health; it is not what it once was. Please watch out for her, and if you get the chance, write back once and let us know how she is doing. She is having a time of it what with Nelson going off to the army hospital—"

"Well, what does Fannie say, Betsie?" Lovina prompted. "Aren't you going to read it to me?"

"*Ach*, I am sorry, Lovina," Betsie glossed over her lapse. She skipped ahead. "'Lovina is so good, so willing to help *youens* as you work in your new jobs so we are free to start our new life here. We are grateful to her. We are very busy getting settled yet. We have not heard from your little brother Abijah for a while. We trust he is a help to your brother Eli out in Missouri and not a hindrance. Well, I must go. There is so much to do, so much to learn, but we rest in the grace of our loving Savior, Jesus Christ our Lord, and all that He has planned for us. Love from your *dat* and from your *mem*, Fannie Troyer.'"

"That was an awful short letter," Lovina fretted. "She hardly talked about Noah. And what did she mean, 'our new life here'? She makes it sound like they're not comin' back."

Betsie gulped back tears. "Of course they are coming back, dear. I imagine she means there are so many new things to see that it seems like a new life." She stared at the page absently. Deliberate *Mem* had never been in a hurry in her life, but a new undercurrent of excitement and urgency pulsed through her mother's writing, as though she couldn't finish with the pen and paper soon enough to get back to the good Lord's plans.

Sadie intruded on her thoughts. "Read the other letter, Betsie. It's from Abijah."

Betsie mustered a smile and withdrew the letter. "Let's see what that *Schnickelfritz* has to say. 'Deer Betsie and Sadie, I am riting to you becos *Mem* and *Dat* will not lissen. I do not liek it here. I miss my frind Levi Yutzy and my rat snake I keep in the barn but nobody nos I have it, it kills the rats in the grane.'"

She gasped and deciphered some more. "'Out here in Mizuree, Eli makes me do things I don't wunt to do, hard work and no one to help me. I want to come back to Plain City. Yore brother, Abijah PS pleas don't tell *Mem* and *Dat* about my rat snake.'"

Lovina's gentle laugh startled Betsie. "Abijah is just like his *dat* when he was young," she told them. "There wasn't a critter Noah couldn't tame, or if it was injured, he would bind up its wounds until it healed or died."

"That's Abijah for you, always trying to get out of chores, and I don't even want to think about his 'pet' in the barn." Little good it would do to share about the snake with her parents. Oh, how sore her heart over her meeting with *Mem* and *Dat!* She sought a topic that would cheer her. Maybe she would see more of Charley this weekend.

"What are you smiling at? A snake is no laughing matter," Sadie groused.

"I . . . it's just so good to hear from *Mem* and *Dat*," Betsie stammered. "And Abijah, how can I help smiling?" Betsie looked at his messy writing with affection. "When will he ever learn to spell? But I miss him terribly."

Sadie shook out a freshly ironed pillowcase. "*Jah*, so do I, but the best way to get over *that*," she said with a snap of crisp cotton, "is to get to work, ain't so?"

"You are right, Sadie," Lovina chimed in. She nibbled her jelly bread and closed her eyes as she sipped her tea. "Oh, that is so *gut*. Now tell me, girls, *was in der welt* does Noah think he is doing, leaving for the back of beyond when he knows I am coming?"

"He certainly should be here, shouldn't he? But you know *Dat* always likes to look at land for sale. He'd love to find a place with more land."

Lovina primmed her mouth. "Seems to me he could find plenty of hired hands around here. Why go to Belle Center, Betsie?"

"Not hired hands. Land." So far she'd seen no sign of the health problems *Dat* mentioned, save that Lovina was certainly hard of hearing.

"Gracious, child, no need to bawl like a heifer birthing her first calf. My ears are a bit stopped up from riding on the train, that's all. Always happens when I have a touch of cold." She yawned an ear-popping yawn. "That's better. I will be able to hear you all right now."

Weariness rolled over Betsie in waves. "Lovina, dear, I'm tired. Shall we go to bed?"

"A cold in the head? *Ach*, you poor dear, I hope you're not taking sick like me, but misery loves company, that's what your sweet *mem* always says, ain't so? Tomorrow first thing I will mix up some of my special cold powders for you. You'll be better before you know it." Lovina drained the dregs of her teacup and smothered another yawn. "Now, you really must show me to my bed, girls. I'm an old lady, and I'm ready to drop after such a long trip."

Sadie giggled under her breath. Laughter with a rising note of hysteria bubbled up from deep inside Betsie, too. If there ever were two sisters who needed a laugh more than they . . . even so, she shushed Sadie. "If you'll do the dishes, Sadie, I will see to Lovina."

"*Jah*, sure." Sadie raised her eyebrows and glanced at the envelope sticking out of Betsie's dress pocket. Betsie understood; Lovina must not read the letter for herself. She pushed down the letter, poured clean water in a plain white ewer, and picked up the lantern. Then she and Lovina made their way upstairs.

Betsie gave Lovina some privacy while she set the ewer in the matching basin on the nightstand. Her aunt rustled into her nightgown with a tired sigh as Betsie arranged a clean towel and washcloth for the morning. She turned down one corner of the pinwheel quilt that *Mem* and Sadie had helped her piece and fluffed the feather pillow.

Finally finished, she patted the clean sheets and beckoned to Lovina. Every bone in Betsie's body ached as she raised the window to let air circulate in the smothery room. Content that even in her distress she'd taken the very best care of her aunt, she turned to go, but Lovina clutched her sleeve with fingers strengthened by years of hard work.

"Betsie, is my brother still strong in his faith?" She searched Betsie's face.

The letter in Betsie's pocket crackled as she murmured in Lovina's ear. "Yes, Lovina dear, *Dat* is very strong in his faith." Betsie caressed her cheek, feeling like Judas. "I'm glad you're here with Sadie and me. See you in the morning."

Before she'd gone two steps, Lovina's gentle snore met her ears. She burrowed into her own bed, thankful that this awful day was over.

Betsie slept until nearly half past five the next morning and awoke wonderfully refreshed. She strolled to check on Lovina and found the pinwheel quilt smooth on the bed. The ewer was gone, the used cloths draped neatly to dry over the towel bar on the side. Remembering *Mem*'s letter of warning, she flew down the stairs, frightened that her aunt had come to some harm, but she found Lovina already hard at work in the kitchen.

"*Ach*, Betsie, so good I slept! One thing I know: there is nothing like having a family to care for. Sit down here, and I will have your breakfast pretty soon."

Her good nature heartened Betsie. Lovina stepped from the icebox to the cook stove with a dish of brown eggs. Betsie caught a whiff of banana muffins baking. Tears of gratitude welled. Oh, so good to be in a home once again. Her aunt's presence dulled her pain over *Mem* and *Dat* somewhat.

Lovina handed a teacup to Betsie. "Now, I been thinking. You girls just put me to work, and we'll soon have this house ready for when my brother comes home." She bustled back to the stove and turned the bacon with a fork, so she didn't see Betsie's hollow eyes.

She shook off her sadness. "Oh, so kind you are, Lovina. Tell you what; maybe today we can do some spring cleaning. You know we have a week's work to finish today, after being gone so much," she reminded her aunt. "It's a good thing church is at Mattie Yoder's this Sunday and not here. I'm sure Sadie's been helping them prepare all week whenever she had a minute to spare."

Sadie breezed into the kitchen with a bucket of water fresh from the pump. "Yes, and now it's time you got to work, lazybones. Take the broom; you can sweep this dusty kitchen while your breakfast cooks."

Her sister had the right attitude, she decided. Work and more work was what she needed; there would be time enough to tell Sadie about her brief visit with *Mem* and *Dat*. With a sense of reprieve, Betsie poked the broom into a dark corner to knock down a cobweb. The three of them working together made doing the chores a pleasure.

The pleasant feeling of accomplishment lasted into Saturday afternoon. Betsie thanked the good Lord that by the second weekend of May in Ohio, there was no more danger of frost. No, it was hot enough in the vegetable garden plot to melt her clean away like a pat of butter in a frying pan. She blotted her moist forehead and knelt in the crumbly furrows of earth. How kind and thoughtful Charley was. He'd tilled the garden; he knew she was eager to transplant her starts.

Gently Betsie untangled the roots of a seedling and pressed the good dirt around the fuzzy stem of a sturdy tomato plant. Juicy red slices on a bacon sandwich crisp with lettuce would taste wonderful good, and she knew how Charley relished tomatoes. She'd seen him eat one like an apple. She smiled tenderly as she slipped a makeshift cardboard barrier around the stem to discourage cutworms before moving on to the next plant.

She lost track of time as she marked where she sowed seeds with stakes and string. Dirt caked her fingernails, but it was dirt from honest, hard work.

A sudden shadow blocked the bright sunshine. Betsie jerked to see who had sneaked up on her.

"*Guder mariye,* Betsie. Sadie told me you were setting out plants. It's a good day for it, ain't so?"

Betsie stood up to greet Charley's mother, acutely aware of the sweat that trickled down the middle of her back under her dress and cape. Two muddy spots on her dress slapped against her knees, reminders that she'd knelt in damp earth for most of the morning.

"*Guder mariye* to you, Mattie," she said. "Yes, I must finish up before I go back to the harness shop tomorrow evening." She winced—mention of her job might lead to questions about Michael and the car ride.

Mattie rested her linked hands on her belly. "It's wonderful that Lovina is here to keep an eye on you while Noah and Fannie are gone and all, though I don't suppose there's much need for that with a good girl like you." She sniffed like she smelled a skunk.

"Don't worry about me. Anyway, I know you must be terrible busy getting ready for church at your house, with just you and Charley at home," Betsie hinted.

"There is a lot of preparation to hosting the service," Mattie said, "but it's awful rewarding. *Jah,* at times like this, though, I miss Henry. It's hard to believe he's been dead for going on twenty years."

"Maybe you need some help?"

"Matter of fact, we're having a work frolic later." She looked at Betsie like sharp needles poking. "Figure on coming, then?"

"*Ach,* of course." Betsie moved to go. "Well, don't let me keep you—"

"Charley mentioned you heard from your folks. When are they coming back?"

"Why, they just left, Mattie." She dug under her fingernail at a speck of dirt. "We don't expect them back for a while."

"If they are looking for land," Mattie probed, "they will sell this farm, maybe?" She gestured at the distant smudge of dust that Charley's dutiful plow raised.

When Betsie thought of Charley, her heart fluttered. How she hoped she could make things right with him! "No, of course they won't sell," she said firmly. "You know *Dat,* always looking! Besides, Nelson's coming back to Plain City in a couple of years, and he will move the harness shop here from Hilliard. He and Lovina will live with us. We have plenty of room since the older children married and moved away." She faced Mattie, a mere silhouette against the strong sunlight. "You can write and ask Nelson about his intentions yourself, if you've a mind to."

Mattie pursed her lips. "Don't squint at me with your sauce. I asked a question only."

"*Ach*, Mattie, I know! It's just the sun is so bright today." She shaded her eyes with her forearm. "See? I didn't mean to upruffle you. I'm sure *Dat* is right grateful you and Charley"—his name lingered on her lips—"are nearby until he gets back, and so am I."

"Yes, Charley is a good boy and no mistake. You would never catch him riding in the front seat of a car."

Betsie's cheeks burned hotter than a cookstove as she watched Mattie go. So they'd both seen her with Michael. Had they told anyone? Glumly she resigned herself to being a scapegoat if it would keep attention off her parents' doings. But oh, the damage Mattie's wagging tongue could do. Why had the bishop never taken that woman to task? She had no heart for the Yoder frolic now.

Despite her misgivings, the frolic was wonderful fun. With other neighbors from the district, happy families swept and scrubbed until the Yoder place sparkled like dew in the morning sun. During the evening meal, the strain began to tell. Betsie toyed with her food and finally gave up. She volunteered to rock Katie Miller's baby brother, with Katie chattering a mile a minute at Betsie's elbow about how her orange cat was now a mother. Betsie admitted to Katie that yes, it would be awfully nice to have a kitten at her house one day. The baby's downy head nestled under Betsie's chin as though he belonged there. She couldn't wait until she and Charley had some *bopplin* of their own.

In the middle of her rosy daydreams, she noticed Charley himself round the corner, his broad shoulders rippling as he hefted an unwieldy bench into place and unfolded the legs. Betsie let her admiring gaze rest on him a second too long, and he caught her looking. He didn't try to interrupt Katie's excited promise of a kitten, but instead gave that special wave and nod that she knew he reserved for her alone. She dropped a shy kiss on the baby's hair, a kiss she would have liked to share with Charley.

She heard Sadie's distinctive titter and bit her lip. Had her sister guessed her thoughts? But no, Sadie was not looking at Betsie. Before Charley ducked outside to get another bench from the church wagon, Sadie waved at him.

Betsie smiled. No doubt about it, people liked Charley. *Ach*, but he would make a happy addition to the family one day.

CHAPTER 17

Now I know why the English talk so much about peace.
—BETSIE'S JOURNAL

JUDITH TROTTED STEADILY, unfazed by the English cars that rocketed around her. Her sensitive mouth telegraphed pride through the reins to Betsie's hands as she drove. Pride was maybe all right for a good Amish *gaul* like Judith.

Lovina chattered about the frolic while Betsie thought about Sadie. She did her share and more, never shirked at chores like some Betsie had heard about. Sadie was smart as a whip, too. Only tell her something one time, and it stuck forever.

And oh, the cakes and pies and cookies she made! Her hands fairly flew when she braided dough or sprinkled flour, sugar, and cinnamon on an apple crumb pie. At the frolic, Sadie had received many compliments from Yoder's bakery customers about her baking. Though Sadie was only seventeen, Betsie believed her sister made the best desserts in the district, although it wouldn't do to tell her so. For certain Betsie didn't want to tell Mattie Yoder that her new baker was better than Mattie, her boss. Mattie was touchy enough already.

She glanced sidewise at Sadie's rosy cheeks and innocent blue eyes. Tucked under her sister's *Kapp* was a wealth of golden hair. *Dat* and Lovina said she took after their side, while Betsie took after *Mem*'s side, with eyes more gray than blue and lank hair, though it was the color

121

of a wheat field in the setting sun. Oh, how she longed for five minutes alone with her sister to tell her that *Mem* and *Dat* hadn't altered their decision in the least.

"Betsie!" Sadie tapped her arm. "Lovina was talking to you, but you sure were thinking hard about something. A penny for your thoughts."

"They are not worth a penny," she said quickly. Her news would keep until Lovina wasn't around. "I sure am looking forward to church tomorrow. You don't know how I've missed all of you."

Sadie's dimples showed. "Have you missed me enough to let me bathe first? After all, you must yearn to spend some time with your horse."

Betsie pretended to sulk. Since childhood, they had joked about which of them would take a bath first. Sadie had won this round fair and square, but Betsie didn't intend to let her off easy. "Sure, you may bathe first. I know you are scared that Abijah's rat snake will bite you when you scoop out the feed."

"Yes, I'm scared, and so are you. You hate snakes."

Lovina laughed. "It does me good to be around you girls. I must thank Noah for inviting me." She folded her hands and smiled as Judith trotted up the lane.

The next morning, Betsie sought an opportunity to speak to Sadie alone, but Lovina was always underfoot. When they arrived at the Yoder house, she gave up and took her place. It was a comfort to see the People enter for worship in a familiar order: fathers with young boys, mothers with young girls, older boys and then older girls, older men and then older women, the few unmarried young men who were in classes prior to joining the church, and lastly the deacons and Jonas Gingerich, the bishop. One side of the house was dotted with the *Kapps* of women friends. On the other side of the large front room, Charley sat with the men.

There wasn't a person in sight whom Betsie hadn't known her whole life, though some dear faces were missing. She sat very still with Sadie and Lovina and waited for her heart to fill with the familiar sense of peace as the gathering prepared to worship the good Lord.

The slow somber tune of the first hymn stretched each word into so many notes that Betsie lost track of the meaning. When it was over, the men doffed their hats as one, and it was time for the second hymn, "*Lob Lied*." Idly Betsie wondered what the songs would sound like if they were played on a piano.

She blushed behind the *Ausbund*, her songbook. Such a wicked thought, musical instruments in the church service! Betsie hoped she hadn't made the good Lord awfully angry, to imagine such a thing. During the silent kneeling prayer, she asked His forgiveness.

Throughout the rest of the service, Betsie was an outward model of good behavior, even though she had trouble understanding High German and what the verses had to do with her. With one verse, there was no such trouble. The text that Deacon Milo read was *Matthaeus 13:22: "Das aber unter die Dornen gesät ist, das ist, wenn jemand das Wort hört, und die Sorge dieser Welt und der Betrug des Reichtums erstickt das Wort, und er bringt nicht Frucht."* Thanks to *Dat*'s patient translation, she recognized the familiar passage from the book of Matthew. Without a doubt, Betsie knew *she* was the seed choked by the cares of this world and deceitful riches, so now she would be unfruitful. She trembled.

When at long last it was time to file outside for dinner, how *gut* it felt to stretch her tired legs. The men carried the benches into the soft afternoon air of *Moi*, the very nicest month in springtime. When the men resourcefully pushed a few benches together to make big tables, the ladies brought out the fixings for the fellowship meal. Conversation ceased while everyone said a silent grace. At last a semblance of peace filled Betsie, peace she hadn't felt for a week. Before the prayer ended, she wiped away a tear, and she and Sadie escorted Lovina to the table.

"Well, well, the stranger returns!"

The familiar voice gladdened Betsie's heart. "Rachel Yutzy!" The pair exchanged a hearty handshake. Rachel held Betsie at arm's length.

"Ah, yes," she said, "now I plainly see the mark of the world on you."

Several older women glanced their way, curious. Betsie caught the twinkle in Rachel's eyes and wondered if Mattie had gotten hold of her.

She sniffed. "Then I guess you wouldn't want to cut in line next to somebody as *loppich* as me." Betsie crossed her arms. "So you must go to the end and wait your turn."

"*Ach*, Betsie, let me in line before I starve!"

Roly-poly Rachel was in little danger of wasting away, but Betsie laughed and drew her to stand with them. Never had she met a truer friend; besides, Rachel had no way of knowing that her smart remark about the world had rubbed salt into Betsie's sore conscience.

"It's so good to see you! Where's your *Bo?*" Betsie craned to see Rachel's special friend, Sam. "Did he find someone better?" she teased.

"I have no one." Rachel held her flaming cheeks. "Shh," she whispered in private. "What's the matter with you? We're not yet published!"

Betsie felt her color rise. How easy to forget, after a week out in the world, what she knew as well as her own name. Everyone could see what was going on with Sam and Rachel, but few spoke of it. Their courtship was supposedly secret, just like Betsie's and Charley's. Though she sorely wanted to talk with Charley right now, there were too many prying eyes here. It didn't make sense to deny such a wonderful thing, but she crammed the corner of an apple-butter sandwich into her mouth to keep quiet.

Soon enough, she found herself surrounded by an excited throng of girls and women eager to visit. When Betsie's neighbors learned of her new position in the harness shop, several families agreed to send work orders and measurements along with Betsie.

They lingered over schnitz pie until it was time for more silent prayer. The familiar surroundings lulled Betsie into thinking that nothing had changed until she recalled with a start that *Mem*, *Dat*, and even Abijah were not here. And suddenly, with all her heart she longed to be back at the Sullivan house, away from the constant reminders that her own family was broken in pieces.

CHAPTER 18

I like waterfalls best of anything in nature. The English
are lucky to have them inside.

—BETSIE'S JOURNAL

BETSIE SLUMPED AGAINST the car door. Only last Thursday, Michael
had been kind and considerate after her horrible meeting with her parents. This morning, he hunched over the steering wheel and drove like
a speed demon, barely acknowledging her presence. Hesitantly, Betsie
asked after his mother, whether she had returned, but thorny silence
shut her out, and she easily guessed the answer.

Peace and quiet was fine with her. Betsie could be quite stubborn,
too, when her dander was up. She brooded about her own troubles until
Michael dropped her off, squealed his tires, and disappeared down the
road. At least he'd picked her up and left her at work in one piece.

She headed straight for the harness shop, pitifully eager to sort the
orders that her Amish friends had sent along with her. A mocking-
bird trilled from the top of the hickory tree as she unlocked the shop.
His cheerful repertoire of songs was pleasant after Michael's spiteful
behavior. At least she hadn't broken her "Don't fraternize with the
English" promise to Charley this time.

Determined to make the best of things, she plunked her satchel
on the lawn chair. She would work hard until Sheila got home from
school and then the two of them would have a good visit.

Once behind the counter, Betsie leafed briskly through the orders she brought back from Plain City, slowing as she studied each one. Soon she frowned. Swept away in the excitement of bringing in new work for the shop, she'd failed to notice that there was not one job she could finish on her own.

She tapped a pencil on the counter and gazed toward the house with a speculative look. Surely the Sullivan house was littered with piles of dirty clothes. Eight o'clock on a Monday morning meant high time to start the laundry. Sheila had shown her how to use the electric washer the other day. It was pretty simple, really.

She put up the Closed sign. Then Betsie strode purposefully toward the house to begin her battle with dirt.

She stowed her satchel in her room and padded shoeless to the kitchen, where a whiff of charred beef patties greeted her. The memory of Sheila's devastation over her mother's good-bye note saddened Betsie. But wait a minute. Bishop Jonas had given her conditional permission to board with the Sullivan family: the English mother was to act as her chaperone. Now what? Betsie chewed the inside of her cheek.

Resolutely, she pushed her troubles out of her mind and arranged the heap of crusty dishes in orderly rows in the dishwasher rack. Sheila had shown Betsie how to sprinkle soap in the dispenser and snap it shut. Betsie turned the machine on and marveled at how the water swished the dishes clean. Then she made a quick pass through the bedrooms, opening windows to air out the stale house as she gathered and sorted the dirty wash.

She lugged a full laundry basket to the washroom and opened the washer. How had Sheila started the machine? Oh, yes, she'd twisted a knob until a jet of clean warm water spurted into the tub; Betsie did the same. She tossed in a soap tablet from the box on the counter and scooped up a heap of stiff and smelly bath towels. How could one little tablet cut through that much soil? She dropped the towels and popped in a handful of tablets. When the soapy water lapped near the top of the tub, she drowned the towels in rich fragrant soapsuds. Satisfied, she closed the lid and headed for her room.

As she passed the pink bathroom, Betsie paused. She flipped the light switch and her feet carried her to the pink bathtub, where she looked longingly at the showerhead. Think of it, a shower in the middle of the morning. Oh, what a sinful waste of time, but then it came to her—no drawing, hauling, or heating water. Just turn the knob and a steamy waterfall streamed out. Back in Plain City, getting clean took forever, but here she could be finished in a jiffy and no one would be the wiser. Thanks to electricity, free time stretched unlimited, a commodity Betsie rarely had at home. It would be wonderful to clean off all at once in such a pretty bathroom.

The temptation was too much. Betsie squelched her conscience and locked the door. Stealthily, she drew back the curtain and peeked into the pink tub. With shaking fingers she doffed her *Kapp*, hung it on the doorknob, and unpinned her hair. From the linen closet she selected a fluffy pink towel and washcloth, which she rubbed against her cheek—oh, so soft! She forgot her troubles and grinned.

She checked to make sure there was plenty of soap and English shampoo. "Golden Bubbles," the bottle read. Next, she frowned at the faucet and then up at the showerhead. How in the world could she make the water flow from up there instead of into the tub? Three knobs bristled at her. She twisted the one on the right to experiment.

A rush of water gurgled through the pipes in the walls and needles of icy water pelted her back. She gasped and danced out of reach of the cold spray, panting. Drenched and freezing, she twisted the knob on the left and slapped at the water until steam billowed. She shucked off her wet clothes, left them in a heap on the fuzzy pink bath mat next to the tub, and stepped into the heavenly warm waterfall.

With a blissful sigh, Betsie lathered her scalp with luxurious suds that smelled like lemonade. How easy it was to rinse her waist-long hair, the streams of water pulsating clear to her scalp. By the time she'd scrubbed herself and rinsed the soapsuds down the drain, her skin tingled. If only she could clean up her life so easily.

The soft bath towel blotted her pink skin drier than last August. She ripped aside the shower curtain and her discarded pile of Amish clothes accused her. Moreover, the clothing was decidedly damp from the blast of cold water on her back. Fortunately she had a dry set in her satchel.

Betsie wrapped the pink towel around her, picked up her clothes, and peeped out the door to make sure that no one had returned. She slunk to her room, locked the door, and unfolded her other clothes. She was thankful that today was good and windy; her dress would soon dry.

She heard a funny sloshing sound as she headed to the clothesline. Betsie peeped in the wash room and clapped her hands to her head. Creamy soap suds streamed from under the washer lid and cascaded across the floor. "Stop, stop! Oh, what in the world?"

In a flash, Betsie shucked off her stockings and waded through slippery suds to slam the washer lid tight, but fragrant bubbles foamed through the cracks and soaked her fresh apron and dress down the front. What little Betsie knew about the washer clean left her head. She pushed, twisted, and dialed all the controls in turn. The washer belched a few more suds and stopped.

An hour later, the floors were mopped shiny clean. She sluiced down the soapy wash tub with a couple of pans of water.

Ruefully Betsie surveyed her second wet dress of the day. She had only packed one spare dress in case of an accident like this, not really expecting to stay over without a proper chaperone. She squelched down the hallway and sorted through Mrs. Sullivan's closet to find something that could serve as a modest covering. Her hand hovered above one silky garment that shimmered with dazzling colors, now blue, now green, with crazy swirls of pink, gold, and darker green splashed across the background.

Mesmerized, she pulled the garment from the hanger and examined the cloth-covered buttons with distaste before deciding she could fasten the front shut with her own straight pins. Yes, this outfit, roomy and long, would do just fine. She donned it and pinned it together, pleased that the dress hem grazed her toes, plenty modest enough, if not very Plain.

The wind blustered as she pegged her wet dresses and stockings to the line. As soon they dried, she'd nip into her room and change back to her Plain clothes. She congratulated herself on the way she'd solved a knotty problem.

Safely ensconced in her room, Betsie combed out and pinned up her damp hair. Then, eager for a chance to do some writing, she sat on the bed, ready to bring her harness notebook up to date for her cousin Nelson. Not much to report there, she realized, so she resorted to the instruction book. The clock tick-tocked as she outlined in the plainest language possible the use of the stitching machine and cutting tools, the dyes, and buckles. She jotted tips on how to keep the shop neat for greatest efficiency.

After a while, she stretched to rest her back. Pensive, she doodled in the margin until a rhyme emanated from her pencil. *Want your business/ To be good?/Keep it tidy/As you should.* Perhaps humor would better make her point than if she nagged her cousin. She grinned. Little hope untidy Nelson would improve.

How restful to work at a pleasant task after such a mixed-up weekend. Thoughts of home naturally turned to Charley. I will see him again in only—her shoulders slumped—four long days. She pressed above her left eye to stop a headache that threatened and doodled hearts with CY + BT printed in the middle. Oh, much better to think on. In a flash she saw it all: the home she and Charley would build one day, clean wash for their children drying in the sunshine.

Another poem issued from her pencil in fits and starts:

> White is the color of Queen Anne's lace
> Newly spun
> White is the color of my love's clean shirts
> Drying in the sun
> White is the color of the fields
> Harvest has begun
> White is the color of my robe
> The battle won.

Where did that come from? She'd written not just a rhyme, but a real poem, all by herself. Often she'd wanted to try her hand at poetry, but there was never enough time for such foolishness at home, especially for poems with such a mushy word as *love*. Amish "thought a lot" about each other. *Ach,* well, if she wanted to eat, she must work; that was the way *Mem* always put it, and that reminded Betsie that she hadn't eaten lunch, though noon had come and gone quite a while ago.

When she finally returned to the harness shop after a brief meal and reversed the sign to Open, Betsie had an inspiration. The treadle-operated stitching machine worked much the same way as *Mem*'s sewing machine, she reasoned. If she practiced with a piece of scrap leather, Betsie felt sure she could get the feel for how stitching worked. She passed the scrap through the roller for a guideline, determined to stitch as straight a seam as possible.

Stitching was harder than she'd expected, but she stuck with it. She was so engrossed that she was startled to hear the school bus squeal to a stop.

The brass bell jangled a few seconds later. "Betsie, I'm so glad you're back!" Sheila wrapped Betsie in a sideways hug. "You're wearing my mom's robe!" she exclaimed. "Is she home?"

Betsie raised her feet from the treadle and the stitching machine sputtered to a halt. "Not yet." She was getting used to Sheila's exuberant displays of affection. A hug felt good. She imagined Sheila at home all weekend with the likes of Mr. Sullivan and the moody Michael. Her weekend had been awful, too. "I'm glad to see you. I am wearing this because I got wet, cleaning. I hope you don't mind. But what's this?" She inspected Sheila closely. "Your eyes are all red, ain't so?"

Sheila swiped her cheeks with her sleeve. "I'm okay. Just some dust in my eye from the stupid bus." She plopped her books on the work table and studied her shoes.

"You are sure that's all?" Betsie prodded.

"No." Sheila choked back a heart-broken sob and sniffled. "Last Friday w-we had to write a poem for our mothers because Mother's Day was coming up. It was yesterday." She gritted her teeth. "Miss Yoho made us go around the class and read them today. And that jerk, Kevin—you don't know him, Betsie, but he's a boy who has green eyes and freckles, and he sits beside me in class," she rushed on. "Anyway, Kevin raised his hand and said, 'Miss Yoho, what if some of us have a mother who's never at home?' And then he smiled right at me." Her lips quivered.

Betsie was shocked. "But how did he know already that your *mem* had run off?"

She shrugged, listless. "He didn't. When Miss Yoho scolded him, he said he was just kidding."

"What happened then?"

"Oh, she sent him to the office like always, but he'd already messed everything up. Everyone stared at me. I can't believe I had to read my rough draft to the class, anyway. It was awful, Betsie." She dug a crumpled piece of paper out of one of her schoolbooks. "Worst of all, I couldn't even *mail* my poem to my mom Friday night, because I don't know where she is. I wish . . ."

She didn't finish, but Betsie knew her wish.

"I like poems. May I read yours?"

"I guess so," Sheila mumbled. "But it's not very good because I felt like crying the whole time I was writing it."

Betsie smoothed out the paper. "'To Mom, by Sheila Sullivan.' Good beginning," she encouraged. Sheila rolled her red eyes. Betsie continued:

> Mom, you are far away,
> I wonder where you are,
> I hope you get in the play,
> And one day you'll be a star.
>
> But what I hope most of all
> Is that you come home to me
> Because I don't want to grow up without you
> And to my heart you hold the key.
>
> Happy Mother's Day.
> Love, Sheila.

Betsie swallowed. Sheila's poem fit her wishes, too.

"I told you it's not any good . . ." Her voice trailed off.

"I like it," Betsie said firmly.

"Then you can have it," Sheila spat as she snatched her books, "because my mom already missed Mother's Day." She stormed out of the harness shop.

CHAPTER 19

A change of clothes doesn't mean a change of heart.
—Betsie's journal

"Sheila, wait!" Betsie caught her by the sleeve. "Let's you and me have a snack together, how's that sound? I brought you some of my sister's snickerdoodles just because you like cinnamon so much."

"Cross your heart, Betsie?" The girl traced an X over her heart.

"What does that mean?"

"It means, 'You did that for me, honest?'"

"Come and see." She was gratified to see the hint of a sparkle.

A half hour later, Betsie and Sheila leaned back in their chairs with happy sighs. Sheila had snickerdoodle crumbs on her shirt that fell off and sprinkled the floor, but Betsie didn't mind, because the crumbs were dislodged by smiles. She brushed crumbs from her own apron as she sipped from a glass of milk.

"Thanks, Betsie. I'm glad you're here."

Silence seemed best, so Betsie patted Sheila's arm.

"I want Mom to come back so bad that I slept in her fuzzy bathrobe last night." She mustered a grin. "It's the old one she used to wear between costume changes in the plays she was in." She hopped up from her chair. "Do you want to see it?"

Betsie held out her hand. "Show me."

Sheila led Betsie down the hallway to her parents' room. It wasn't

133

too hard for Betsie to pretend she'd never been inside; there was a large oval mirror standing in one corner that she hadn't noticed before, and across another corner extended a red folding screen edged with gold. If you stood behind it, no one could see you. Clothes were draped over one panel as though somebody might still be changing back there. Sheila disappeared and emerged wrapped in a dingy white robe. She snuggled the shawl collar under her chin. "In my mom's housecoat, I look like I'm playing dress-up, don't I? Did you ever do that when you were little, Betsie?"

Betsie smiled. All her dresses looked about the same, except for the color. She'd seen her *Mem's* wedding dress; the shade of icy blue set her yearning for pretty clothes. Perhaps she should have been ashamed, but she was not. "Can't say as I did."

Sheila rooted in the closet and emerged with her hands full of colorful material. "Mom left all her 'old-lady' clothes in here. At least that's what she called them, but they're my favorites. Here, try one on!"

"Oh, Sheila, I don't know—"

Her face fell. "It's okay if you don't want to."

Ach, how she hurts my heart. Betsie and her *mem* hadn't played dress-up, but they'd cooked and worked and laughed together. Betsie had never seen Sheila and Mrs. Sullivan laugh together. Wearing fancy clothes to soothe a child couldn't be that bad.

"Well, once won't hurt, maybe," she ventured. She reached into the pile and pulled out the first dress she touched.

Sheila beamed and propelled Betsie behind the screen. At least this dress, a pretty pink one with no sleeves, didn't have buttons. It did have a zipper in the back, which presented a problem. Sheila reached behind the screen without looking and fumbled the zipper shut for Betsie.

"And now, wearing my dad's most favoritest dress that my mom ever wore . . . presenting . . . Miss Betsie Troyer!" Sheila flung out her hand as Betsie peeped around the screen. Then she gasped. "Gosh, Betsie! You look beautiful!"

The dress fit like it was her own. The soft shade of pink was like wild June roses. The neckline crisscrossed without a collar, not low-cut like some English styles. It was much shorter than Betsie's dresses. Though she felt gawky with her bare arms sticking out, she stroked the beautiful fabric with a timid finger.

Sheila grabbed Betsie's hand and dragged her to the mirror. "Look at yourself!"

Betsie spied her cheeks, softly pink like the pretty dress. Her eyes sparkled as she admired herself in that English dress. If only Charley could see how she looked.

No. She could never tell him. A good man like Charley would never court an Amish girl who yearned for English dresses. This was another secret to keep from him, just like riding bareback with her skirts pushed high. *Mem's* words echoed: "One lie brings the next one with it." Oh, so true.

She wouldn't admire herself any longer, but neither would she spoil Sheila's fun. Instead, she plopped on the edge of the bed. "Now, *you* dress up."

Sheila rummaged through the heap of dresses and chose what looked like a bright orange shirt, but when she emerged, her legs showed to mid-thigh. Then Betsie realized that it was a very short dress. Even though the dress looked baggy, orange was certainly her color, or maybe it was that Sheila felt close to her *mem* again. Whichever it was, Sheila was transfigured by joy.

She gave Betsie a speculative glance. "I bet your hair is so pretty," she wheedled. "Please, will you take it down?"

"In for a penny, in for a pound," *Mem* would have said. Resigned to her fate, Betsie removed her *Kapp* and loosened her still-damp hair.

"Your hair is such a cool color!"

"I don't know about that, but at least my head feels better. All that hair is heavy."

"I wish my mom were here with us," Sheila said slowly.

Betsie needed another distraction, fast as lightning. "Tell me more about her."

Sheila's face lit up. "Keen!" She dashed to her room and returned with a battered book. "This is my scrapbook. I put important stuff in here." She snuggled up to Betsie and they faced the light from the window.

A whole book of prideful photographs. *Ach,* how often she had heard *Mem* say, "Why should we look on the outer man, when the inner man is what's important?"

But now this book of scraps was the only way Sheila could spend time with her mother. For a sinful moment, Betsie wished she had such a book of her own family.

So she looked. In picture after picture, she could scarcely look away from Sheila's mother. This woman was very different from the lady who left on the VW bus. Laughing with her head thrown back, hand on one hip, and toes pointed just so in high heels, Mrs. Sullivan was vibrant and full of life. Betsie could hardly wait for Sheila to turn the page to show the next pictures.

"You can see why she wants to be called Sunshine; she's always so happy, at least she used to be. That's why she bleached her hair, too, so she would look like 'Sunshine Sullivan, star of stage and screen!' She said that a bunch after she found out about the musical *Hair*. Dad says she's too old and ought to know better than to try out for it, though."

She flipped another page and Betsie gasped. Here was Mrs. Sullivan in the same pink dress Betsie wore, long hair amassed under a wide-brimmed hat made of peach-colored straw. She clutched a small black purse and flowers were pinned to her dress. Michael and Sheila stood with her, smiling.

"That was Easter last year," Sheila said wistfully. "Mom wore Dad's favorite dress to church, the one you have on right now." She raced to the closet and stretched to retrieve the lovely peach hat from the shelf. Pink ribbon tied in a bow streamed down the back. "Try it on for me?"

The straw hat looked an awful lot like Amish hats, except for the color and the ribbon. She swept her hair up and Sheila perched it atop the thick coil.

"Do you like it?"

A tear splattered Sheila's bare leg and Betsie pulled her close. Time slowed and almost it seemed that the broad brim of the peach straw hat shut out everything.

Behind them, the door squeaked and someone else walked into the room.

"Phyllis, you're back!" exclaimed Mr. Sullivan.

CHAPTER 20

I never know which Michael to expect—the exasperating
one or the considerate one.
—Betsie's journal

Sheila screamed and stumbled to the door. She pushed her dad
aside and bolted past him. Betsie composed herself to welcome Mrs.
Sullivan home.

Sheila burst back into the room. "Dad, where's Mom? I can't find her!"

Instead of answering, Mr. Sullivan glared at Betsie. "Is this some
kind of sick joke?"

Too late, Betsie realized that in the Easter dress and hat, *she* was
Mrs. Sullivan. She stood up to deny his accusation, but no words came
from her numb lips. Sheila looked back and forth between the two of
them, buried her head against her dad's shirtfront, and bawled.

Quick steps crackled on the plastic mat. Michael poked his head
in the room, plainly registered his dad's anger and Sheila's distress,
saw Betsie, and froze. "Betsie, whoa! You're . . . you're . . . okay, I give.
What's going on here?"

Mr. Sullivan's eyes glittered. "What do you care? You take off for
parts unknown at the first hint of trouble."

Betsie winced, but Michael surprised her. "Cool it, Dad." He knelt
and rested his hands on his sister's shoulders. "Hey, what's shaking,
Squirt? Playing dress-up?"

Sheila hiccupped against her dad's chest. "It's all my fault! Betsie tried on Mom's dress because I asked her to, but then Dad came home early and h-he thought Betsie was Mom."

"It's not like you did it on purpose. You're just missing Mom." Michael gently disentangled her from Mr. Sullivan's arms and folded her close. "Come on, now, don't make yourself sick. Let's go to the bathroom and get you spiffed up." With a final unreadable glance at Betsie, he gathered Sheila's clothes and led her away.

Betsie snatched the long robe from behind the screen and edged toward her room. "My dresses got wet while I was working and I needed something to wear until they dried. Then Sheila was missing her mother, and we—"

"No, don't apologize, Betsie," Mr. Sullivan cut in, his voice strained. "I overreacted. Besides, it's nobody's fault but mine that Phyllis left." He collapsed against the wall and buried his face in his hands.

Soberly Betsie brought her dry dresses in from the clothesline, changed into one, and fixed supper. Nobody ate much.

Nobody turned on the television, either. As Mr. Sullivan predicted, Michael had peeled out minutes after making sure Sheila had settled down. Father and daughter retired to their individual rooms well before Betsie had finished in the kitchen.

After she draped the dishcloth to dry, she retrieved her notebook from her room and crossed the driveway to work some more in the harness shop. She pulled the string to light the bare, overhead bulb and sat down at the scarred counter. It was good to be alone with her thoughts after that dismal dinner.

If only she could gather Mr. Sullivan, Sheila, and Michael at the dining-room table. She planned to serve them a wonderful *gut* meal such as they'd never eaten before, and they would enjoy it together in harmony. With the good Lord to help her, Betsie planned to splice the broken Sullivan family as neatly as a mended stirrup.

Of course it would be difficult, with Mr. Sullivan and Michael always at each other's throats. Then, too, Sheila was so sad since her mother left that Betsie despaired of cheering her up. In the end, she decided the chance for failure would be worth the risk. Let Michael say she was *schtaerkeppich* as a mule, if he liked.

Twenty minutes later the shop bell jingled. Betsie looked up from her writing and saw a frazzled lady rush to the counter. "My daughter broke a stirrup on her English saddle."

Here was a pickle for sure, a customer and no Michael to do the talking. Betsie cast a wary glance as the lady fidgeted with her car keys.

"She's entered in the horse show at the Franklin County fairgrounds in a couple of days. Please, do you think you can repair it in time?"

What possible harm would it do to wait on this woman, a mother like her own *Mem?* Still, rules were rules, so Betsie kept mum.

"My daughter, Debbie Keith, is a friend of Sheila's. Sheila told Debbie at school this afternoon that their new helper's name is Betsie and you could maybe mend the stirrup. That must be you," the customer babbled. A desperate gleam showed. "If you can do it, I'll pay you double."

Inspiration dawned. Betsie stared pointedly at the lady's empty hands.

The woman blinked. "Oh, for goodness' sake, I'd forget my head if it wasn't attached! Be right back."

While she waited, Betsie snatched her notebook and scribbled, "Any sort of delay makes the English anxious and ill at ease. Don't be in a hurry to seal a bargain. The less you say/the more they pay." Betsie slapped the cover shut as the woman dropped a heap of leather on the countertop.

Such a saddle! The seat was a flattened curve with no pommel, and the stirrups were silver arches with slender straps looped through. The saddle on display in the shop was a cumbersome, tooled leather affair that curled up behind and in front to hold a rider in, far more substantial. Betsie glanced to where it had been slung across a sawhorse covered with a red-striped horse blanket. It was gone. She fingered the broken strap and nodded to indicate she could do the repair.

"By Friday?"

Betsie tipped her head to one side as she considered and nodded again.

"Gee, thanks! I don't know what I'd have done without you."

Before she headed for the door, Betsie held up a finger, took a lined card from a file box, and handed the woman a pen.

"Oh, where is my head today?" Mrs. Keith dashed off her name. "Address and phone number, too, there you go," she said, smiling for the first time. "You're a lifesaver, Betsie. God bless you. Listen, if there's ever anything I can do for you, or if you need somebody to talk to, ring me up." She left Betsie breathless.

Talking to the English was the worst part of being hired out, that's what *Family Life* magazine warned, but Mrs. Keith had talked so much that Betsie didn't have to break her promise to Charley. Betsie had to admit the lady was quite nice, and she hadn't looked at Betsie's Amish dress once.

She'd done it! Betsie recorded the repair order and tagged the saddle with a big number one. Preoccupied with her success, she filed the card in the order box with a satisfied smile and took up the saddle to hang it over the empty sawhorse.

As she turned, she glanced behind the worktable and her heart nearly stopped. There was Michael, stretched out on a red-and-black striped blanket, head resting on the missing Western saddle. He applauded with three slow claps.

"Michael! What are you doing here? I thought you left."

"Never mind me," he grinned. "I've just witnessed the performance of a lifetime. The way you handled that transaction was nothing short of amazing, Betsie! 'She spoke not a word but went straight to her work . . .' Man, I am blown away."

"Why didn't you come out and help me like you're supposed to?" she scolded. "Besides, we heard you leave."

"Hey, lighten up, one question at a time. I couldn't stand listening to my old man's rants, so I doubled back and coasted behind the shop to park and sneak in. Any port in a storm. I didn't expect you to come out here again tonight, anyway." He clapped his hands together. "Let me at that English saddle. I'll show you how to fix it."

Mollified by his helpful change of heart, she watched and jotted notes while Michael spliced the broken stirrup. At length she itched to be working, too, so she wandered back to her stitching practice. At last, satisfied with her progress, she flexed her shoulders and looked around. Where had Michael gone?

It didn't take her long to find him; he was stretched out on the floor again, head again resting on the Western saddle and one ankle propped comfortably on his knee. He chuckled and turned a page of a notebook . . . her notebook.

Betsie quailed. Definitely there were some comments in there that she didn't want him to see. She stuck out her hand. "That is private, Michael, and it is mine."

He snickered.

"What is so funny?"

He raked aside his bangs. "*You* are. This is great stuff. Your jerk cousin doesn't know how lucky he is to have your notes. You're a natural writer, poems or prose, Bets. Or should I call you . . . Pippa?"

"No, you should not. That's not my name." Betsie wiggled her fingers.

"No, it's something better—your nickname. Know what that is?"

She scowled. "We have nicknames where I live. That's how we know which Levi or Rachel we're talking about. Your *mem* has a nickname for you—it's Stringbean, and it's a good one because you are long and skinny, but I know a better one: Lazy Michael. How do you like that?"

He refused to take the bait. "Pippa the Poet. Ever read 'Pippa Passes'?" He stood up, placed one hand over his heart, and declaimed:

> "The year's at the spring,
> And day's at the morn;
> Morning's at seven;
> The hill-side's dew-pearled;
> The lark's on the wing;
> The snail's on the thorn;
> God's in His heaven—
> All's right with the world!"

He bowed. "By Mr. Robert Browning."

"I like that, Michael. Go ahead and call me Pippa."

Michael snorted. "You'd be insulted if you read the rest of the poem. As it is, you'll never know how much like her you are, Pippa. Promise you'll stay innocent and unspoiled."

She doubled both hands on her hips. "You are exasperating, *and* you are trying to make me forget about the notebook. Now give it back."

"Ooh, see Pippa pout." He hid the notebook behind his back.

"*Schnickelfritz!* You shall not read another word. Hand over my notebook."

"Make me." He danced toward the door. Betsie dashed around the table and grabbed his arm before he could escape. She held on and hopped to reach her notebook, but he waved it impossibly high above her outstretched hands.

"You can't get it," he taunted. He bopped her head twice with the notebook and pretended to read it above her head. "Oh, this is wonderful!"

Betsie was frantic; she had to keep Michael from reading what she had written about him and his family . . . and Charley. She tried a different strategy—guilt.

"Stop! You're hurting me!"

The screen door burst open. *"Freeze!"*

Betsie screamed. Two police officers barreled in the door, waving guns at her and Michael.

CHAPTER   21

Michael doesn't like the police too much,
and the feeling is mutual.
—BETSIE'S JOURNAL

THE BRASS BELL popped off the hook and rolled in a noisy arc on the floor.

"I said freeze!" the young white policeman repeated. Short hair stuck straight up from his head. "Put your hands in the air, hippie! You're busted!"

Completely unnerved, Betsie put her hands up. She sought reassurance from Michael, but his breath came in short puffs as his hands inched upward.

"Turn around nice and slow," the other officer said. "Keep your hands where we can see them."

At the same time Michael revolved, Betsie did, too.

"You can put your hands down, ma'am. Just stay put. Let's see who we got here . . . uh-huh." The younger officer nodded. "Thought that was you, Sullivan."

Michael looked like he smelled something bad. "Gee, what tipped you off, Petey? The fact that you watched Ed, the school bus driver, pick me up and drop me off right here every day when we were in grade school?" he said. "Or the fact that you never forgot the face of the first-grader you shook down for lunch money every week?"

"Shut your trap!" He stuck his gun perilously close to Michael's left cheek.

Betsie dreaded the gun's bite as the second officer moved toward her. He was black like the butcher in the market, only with gray hair shaved close to his head.

"You okay, ma'am?" he asked solemnly.

She nodded slowly, eyes never leaving the gun.

"We got an anonymous phone tip that a man we've been looking for was seen in the vicinity of the fairgrounds. Maybe you've heard about the Hilliard Stalker. The suspect has been importuning, more or less talking nasty to women he finds alone, taking advantage of the situation. We want to nab him before his behavior escalates." The officer noted Betsie's Plain clothing. "We were patrolling the area, noted the car hidden in the weeds, heard a ruckus, and came in to check it out."

Michael cut in, furious. "Do I look like that kind of sicko type? Come on, man, this is my house. I live here. Ask Petey there. He's known me forever."

"Shut up, Sullivan! I'll ask the questions," the younger officer blustered.

"*I* will ask the questions, Schwartz," the older officer reprimanded. "You're still on probation, remember?" He flipped open a notebook and turned to Michael. "I'm Sergeant Deacon. So what's the story?"

"Look, Gerald Sullivan is my old man. He owns this harness shop. This young lady and I are doing some repair work. We were, uh . . ." He met Betsie's frightened gaze. "I guess you could say we were letting off a little steam after a rough weekend."

"Oh, sure," Schwartz sneered. "You've got your paws all over this young lady, she says you're hurting her, but you're innocent. A likely story." He pointed his gun. "You're our man, all right."

"Schwartz," the black officer barked. "Can you tell me what happened, ma'am?"

"*Jah*," Betsie whispered. As she explained, the officer's fierce expression relaxed.

To Michael he said, "I'm gonna need to see some ID, sir. Just a formality."

Despite Michael's show of bravado, Betsie noticed he was trembling. "Back pocket," he said.

"I'm on it, Sarge." Schwartz took a threatening step toward Michael. "I've had my eye on you for a long time, Sullivan. Don't try any funny stuff, or I'll splatter your guts on that wall and no one will care."

"Gun, Schwartz. Hand it over." Sergeant Deacon kept his gun trained on Michael and motioned for the weapon. "Plus I'm gonna write you up for insubordination if you say another word. You get my drift? One more word."

Schwartz glowered, but he gave up his gun. Deacon stuck it on the counter behind him. Then he dug Michael's wallet from his pocket and flipped it open. His lips moved as he read a plastic card, which he flashed at Schwartz.

The white officer sneered. "So, yeah, he lives here. Big deal. Dollars to doughnuts he's done something we could bust him for."

Deacon slammed the wallet on the counter. "That does it, Schwartz; head for the squad car and monitor the scanner for activity."

"But, Sarge!"

"Have a nice day, Petey," Michael said.

Schwartz muttered words that sounded like *dumb* and *bigger* as he stomped out of the shop. Through the window, Betsie noticed that he paused behind the shop where Michael's car was parked. He wrote something on his pad and stormed off.

"Very sorry for the inconvenience, Mr. Sullivan," Deacon was saying. "I'm sure you can appreciate that we were just concerned for this young lady's safety." He spoke politely while he surveyed every inch of the harness shop. "Oh, er, you can put your hands down, too. Before we go, mind if I ask a personal question?"

Michael tossed Betsie's notebook on the table and massaged his biceps. "Sure, knock yourself out."

"What's got Schwartz so agitated? You boys have some bad blood between you?"

"You might say that. Petey's always had the hots for Peggy Marciuliano, down at Ayers Market." Michael smiled thinly. "But she doesn't have the hots for him."

"In fact, she's got the hots for you? That explains it; it's always a woman. Listen, ma'am," Deacon addressed Betsie as he tapped the pad against his leg. "Consider this a warning. Be on your guard, and try not to work alone if that's at all possible. The Hilliard Stalker hasn't tried anything violent yet, but that doesn't mean he won't. All he needs is an opportunity. Don't be the one to give it to him, you get my drift?"

Betsie nodded again, feeling like one of those bobble-headed fuzzy toy dogs she'd seen for sale at the five-and-dime.

"Don't worry, Sergeant. I'll keep an eye on her." Michael walked Deacon to the door. "Keep an eye on Petey. I don't need a rogue cop gunning for me."

His dark eyes narrowed. "You leave Officer Schwartz to me." He smiled toward Betsie. "Good evening, ma'am."

Deacon tipped his cap and strode into the twilight. Betsie and Michael listened as the police car sped down the road. Michael stepped to the window to make sure they were gone. Then he paced the floor, agitated. "This place is one hundred percent cracked. We've got to get out of here or I am going to lose it. C'mon, let's go."

But Betsie had had enough. "No. It's nighttime, Michael, and anyway, if that man, the Stalker they talked about—"

"Hey, you'll be with me and it's barely twilight," he protested. "How about some ice cream? You almost got me arrested, so it's the least you can do." He dug his car keys out of his pocket and dangled them in Betsie's face. "You can drive."

"Very generous of you, since you know I can't."

"Say, that's an idea. Tell you what, I'll teach you to drive tomorrow if you go for ice cream with me." He stuck out his hand. "Deal?"

Betsie was scandalized. "I drive a horse, not a car!"

"Hey, you could learn, but I was talking about the lawnmower. It's pretty easy, and my old man has been on my case to get the lawn mown. You'll be safe on the mower, and it's pretty fun, besides. "

Betsie folded her arms. "I have read about Tom Sawyer, Michael. I know you want me to do your work while you loaf."

"Maybe," he grinned appreciatively. "But I know you'll love driving, and you love chores, too."

Betsie recalled Charley asking her to stay away from the English. But somehow his request lost the battle against the sugary temptation, and she relented. "We will come straight home after ice cream? No visits to pot parties?"

"You cut me to the core, Pippa. No way, all right? Straight home."

Twenty minutes later, Betsie licked her fingertips with a happy sigh. "I believe I like drumsticks even more than ice-cream sandwiches. And now, home. It has been a long day."

"Crud," was his inelegant response. He nodded at the gas gauge. The needle was on E. "My car's running on fumes. Say, Pippa, I know I said we'd go straight home, but if you want to ride instead of walk, I need gas. You have to feed your horse, right? Well, I have to feed my car. Think of it as part of your driving lesson."

He took what he called a shortcut and soon pulled into a service station. The car ran over a black hose that stretched across the pavement. *Ding, ding* sounded a bell inside, and a man in a white uniform hustled to the car as Michael rolled down his window.

"Fill 'er up with ethyl?"

"Nope, five gallons of regular will do it." The man looked down his nose at Michael, his gaze shifting between Michael's long hair and Betsie's *Kapp*. The question in his eyes lingered long enough that Betsie felt her foot tapping on the floor of the car.

Michael waited until the man walked away before grumbling, "They've really jacked up their prices since last week."

The gas station attendant hooked up the car to the gas pump. Betsie watched as he dipped a scraper in a reservoir of scummy liquid and scrubbed the windshield. Then with quick, sure strokes, he swiped the liquid from the glass and left it somewhat cleaner.

"Nice car," he commented as polished the glass with a handful of blue paper towels. He unhooked the nozzle. "That'll be $1.50, please."

Michael frowned and paid him. "Thanks."

"Come back again, sir." Betsie winced at his tone.

"Not at these prices," Michael told Betsie as he flicked on his head-lights. "I'll go broke."

"The grass I feed my horse is free," Betsie remarked. A sign announced that they were entering Hilliard's Station. Old brick shops rubbed elbows with aluminum-sided houses. "I thought this town was called Hilliard."

"It is now, but some of the old-timers still say they live in 'Hilliard's.' My grandpa always—hang on, Pippa!" Michael jammed on the brakes, and the tires shrieked.

Betsie braced herself. "*Was in der welt?* Why are all those people blocking the street? What is going on?"

"Looks like a demonstration or something. Let's hang loose and see what this is all about." He leaned out his window for a better look.

The street certainly did resemble the pictures of Kent State that Betsie had seen on the television. Long-haired young people dressed in ripped blue jeans or long floral skirts linked elbows to stretch across the intersection, effectively blocking the road. Car horns honked as impatient drivers came upon the obstruction. The barricade of hippies remained eerily serene as they faced the cars and refused to budge. A growing mob behind the front line waved signs that bore messages like "Give peace a chance," "End the War in Vietnam Now," and "Flower Power." Some of the hippies chanted songs and swayed back and forth slowly in the mellow glow from the streetlights.

A police siren sliced across the hippie chatter and honking horns. To her relief, Betsie glimpsed Sergeant Deacon emerging from a police car. He calmly approached the hippies and began a dialogue, which he punctuated by indicating the sidewalk with his nightstick.

"Man, that guy is like Big Brother—he's everywhere," Michael muttered. He stuck his head out the window and joined his voice to those of the protesters. "Want us to move along? Fat chance, Pig!" His head swiveled as he followed Officer Deacon's movements, eyes alight with contempt. "Who do you think you are, denying us our First Amendment rights?"

Betsie shifted uneasily. "What are you doing, Michael? You are not part of that group. We are trying to get home, and these people are blocking our way. Officer Deacon is here to help."

But Michael was not listening. He thumped on the side of his car and emitted a piercing whistle that caught the attention of a hippie on the sidewalk. "Hey, Steve, what's going down?"

The barefooted hippie drained the last of a can of baked beans into his mouth, tossed the can on the street, and sauntered toward the car. "Sullivan! How's it goin', man?" He favored Michael with a cheesy grin and imitated the television newsman Betsie had glimpsed on the evil box at Michael's house. He held his fist to his mouth and spoke in a serious tone. "Rumor has it that the lieutenant governor of Ohio is in town tonight and he's going to officiate at the opening of the horse show tomorrow." He relaxed his pose. "I don't know how much truth is in it because nothing like that's ever happened before, dig? But word is spreading like wildfire, man, and people want to show him what Hilliard's all about. The guys are going to carry signs printed with their draft numbers, crazy stuff like that. Want to get in on the action? Looks like things are going to heat up pretty fast. We could use you and your lady friend." He leered at Betsie.

Betsie was already shaking her head no when a rotten apple splatted on the clean windshield. "Michael, we have to leave."

"Sorry, Steve, maybe later." He looked at Betsie with a lopsided grin. "You want to leave? Sure thing." He laughed in a way that was not nice and jammed his foot on the brake and gas pedals at the same time. The engine revved and the crowd looked in his general vicinity. Michael tapped the horn and gestured to the right. When they saw who was driving, the hippies raised fists high in the air and cheered. A knot of them parted obligingly.

"We're outta here!" Michael crowed. He zipped through the opening, mere inches from Officer Deacon's car. The Super Bee roared down a side street, and Michael rejoined the main road a couple of minutes later.

Betsie stole a look at Michael; he whooped and pumped his fist a couple of times as he navigated the railroad tracks and entered the driveway. He hopped out of the car, scraped apple splatters from the windshield with the side of his hand, and was seated again before Betsie fully opened the car door.

"Catch you later, Pippa," he said, backing as soon as she exited. "Don't wait up."

"Michael, don't go back there!" she begged, but he was gone faster than the flicker of lightning that split the ominous sky.

CHAPTER 22

I have a good feeling about this week.
—Betsie's journal

WHEN SHE THREW back the covers Tuesday morning, Betsie had a single purpose in mind—today was Family Meal Day. Now more than ever, the Sullivans needed to gather as one to appreciate their blessings.

Betsie kept her scheme a secret, but menus paraded through her mind as she served breakfast. Already her cooking was doing some good—Mr. Sullivan and Sheila dug in to the pancakes with gusto. Full to bursting with plans, Betsie idly clinked her spoon in her tea-cup, the way *Mem* had never liked.

"Um, Betsie?"

She allowed the menu to parade along without her and noticed dark circles under the girl's eyes. "Mm-hmm, are you feeling all right, dear heart?"

Sheila giggled. "Sure, but you put *bread* in your *tea.*"

Betsie blinked at the mess in her cup and blushed. "Will you look once what I did? I fixed coffee soup for my *dat* often enough. I guess I forgot that I was drinking tea." Thoughts of her father sobered her. *If only I could gather my own family for a meal.*

She dumped the mess in the sink, ran some water, and flicked on the garbage-chewer. Then she filled her cup with milk, broke in some more bread, and sprinkled it with sugar and cinnamon. "There, bread soup. That's more like it; I can eat and drink at the same time."

"Gross!" Sheila pretended to gag.

Mr. Sullivan smiled. "Hey, Squirt, how many times have I seen you put ketchup on your scrambled eggs? Betcha Betsie would think that was pretty gross."

"But, Dad, ketchup on eggs is so good!"

Betsie and Mr. Sullivan laughed.

"Quite a *Donnerwetter* went through in the night," she commented. "I thought the house would blow away in the storm." For the merest instant, she wondered if Michael had slept in the shop when he came home from the demonstration.

"Yes, it's chilly this morning, so bundle up, Sheila," Mr. Sullivan said. "Time to head for the bus stop, pronto."

"When is summer coming?" she grumbled as she shouldered into her jacket.

"Oh, soon enough you'll be complaining about the heat and begging to go swimming," her dad joshed. "See you later, alligator." Mr. Sullivan headed to brush his teeth.

Ach, Mr. Sullivan and Michael were so much alike, the way they spoke and teased Sheila—that is, when they were apart. Betsie thought of her dinner plan and smiled. Surely they could appreciate their similarities when they gathered at the table. It would take some fast talking to lasso Michael, but she had all day.

Mr. Sullivan returned but paused in the middle of donning his overcoat. "What are your plans, Betsie?"

"Michael promised he would teach me to drive," she said, before she thought how it would sound. At Mr. Sullivan's double take, she hurried to add, "The lawn tractor, I mean, if there are no customers, of course. He said it wouldn't be too hard to learn."

"Well, isn't that dandy? Michael loafs while you mow." He thrust his other arm through the sleeve with great energy.

"Oh, I know he is like that *Schnickelfritz* Tom Sawyer, but I think it will be fun. Of course, we will work in the shop when we are finished."

His features softened into a smile. "Betsie, I don't doubt you would enjoy whatever task you put your hand to, but your plan won't work for two reasons: number one, the grass is too wet to mow today after the thunderstorm that rolled through last night. And number two, Michael isn't here, as usual, when there's real work to be done. Better bone up on that harness book I gave you, because unless I miss my guess, Michael won't be back today, especially if he had anything to do with last night's hippie fracas that's all over the newspaper."

Betsie's heart sank as all her plans threatened to fizzle. "Don't worry. I will find plenty to do."

As she entered the shop, she kicked over a crumpled Milky Way Ice Cream Shoppe bag that smelled of fried meat, proof that Michael had spent at least part of Monday night here. She pursed her lips and crammed the bag into the trash can before she retrieved the harness book. The dry instructions provided a few simple exercises that she practiced diligently, but soon Betsie tired of make-work. She sprinted to the house between thundershowers and tackled some much-needed spring cleaning.

Later that evening, after weathering Sheila and Mr. Sullivan's initial disappointment at finding neither Mrs. Sullivan nor Michael at home, Betsie smiled as they admired the spanking-clean house and enjoyed their homemade dinner. The mood was one of forced good cheer, however, not what she was going for at all. She missed Michael's good-natured wisecracks, and of course, her plan for a reunion had failed. Sheila helped with the dishes, did her homework, and went to bed, with Mr. Sullivan retiring to his room soon afterward.

As she climbed into bed that night, Betsie punched her pillow. She hadn't seen Michael at all today, but maybe it was for the best that he was gone tonight. Except now she was unchaperoned in a house with only one English man instead of two. She cringed and wondered what Bishop Jonas . . . or Charley would say. Better they not know.

The house was dark except for vivid flashes of lightning. Betsie snuggled beneath the covers and listened to the rain as it pelted against her window. No driving lesson tomorrow either, she supposed. Her mind wandered over the mostly senseless activities she'd engaged in since she'd returned to the Sullivan house yesterday, and remorse weighed heavily. Why was she here? She was certainly getting little help in learning the harness-making business.

Thunder boomed like the voice of God at Judgment Day. Though Betsie had never been afraid of storms, she pulled the covers over her head.

Seconds later, she heard the stealthy grating of her bedroom door-knob. Paralyzed with fear, she recalled the policeman's warning about the Hilliard Stalker. Before she could protect herself, someone grabbed her shoulder and Betsie stifled a scream.

"Betsie? Betsie?"

Limp with relief at hearing Sheila's voice, she uncovered her head. "What is it, dear heart?"

"I'm scared of thunderstorms," Sheila whimpered, ashamed. "I was scared last night, too, and I can't take it anymore. Mom always used to get in bed with me for really bad ones."

So that was the reason for the dark circles at breakfast. Betsie flipped her covers back. "Want to share?" she invited.

"Honest? Keen, thanks!"

As Sheila burrowed under the covers with a contented sigh, Betsie realized that her question had been answered. Surely if he knew of the situation, Bishop Jonas would understand how much a motherless girl like Sheila needed Betsie around and would allow her to continue to stay here on weeknights. Betsie made up her mind to stick to her side of the bargain for a while longer.

Wednesday and Thursday passed, gloomy but dry, with Betsie working hard on her own to learn harness-making. On Friday morning, brilliant sunlight graced the bedroom window to greet Betsie and Sheila. Though the peals of thunder were long gone, the two of them had cottoned to the idea of sharing a bed like sisters, "just until Mom comes back," as Sheila had put it. Mr. Sullivan had given them his okay.

If there was a cloud remaining, it was that Michael hadn't returned. Betsie wondered at Mr. Sullivan's stoic acceptance, but she didn't question him. For all she knew, Michael might be sneaking in the house late at night. She admitted to herself that the atmosphere was much pleasanter with only one Sullivan man; perhaps getting everyone together for a family meal wasn't such a good idea. She'd have to mull it over. All in all, it had been a pretty peaceful week, much better than the last. *Ach,* maybe she was getting used to English life, like *Mem* and *Dat.* She shuddered.

Betsie saw Sheila off to school and opened the shop alone once again. She'd simply have to wait on any customers herself. Now that the weather had improved, she must expect some business, seeing as how there was another horse event at the fairgrounds this weekend. Michael wasn't here . . . or was he? She checked behind the counter where she'd found him stretched on the blanket, but the shop was empty. On tiptoe, she peeked out the window at the rear of the shop. Satisfied that the Super Bee was not around, she found her notebook and added some fine points for Nelson, and even some notes about her life with the English.

Engrossed in her writing, Betsie forgot all about customers until a blue jay screamed a warning. Through the screen, she glimpsed some-body blond and broad-shouldered. Her heart fluttered—had Charley come to visit her here? What a comfort it would be to see his warm smile and steadfast presence after working alone.

When the man came through the door, she saw he wasn't Charley at all, but a customer. The man seemed pleasant enough. To top it off, he sported an outlandish red riding jacket. She closed her notebook.

"Saw your sign. See, my coat ripped." He lifted his arm to reveal a hole. "Right there. I know this is a harness shop, but sewing's sewing, right? Can you fix it?"

Betsie gave a slow shake of her head. "I shouldn't—"

He shifted from one foot to the other. "C'mon, if you help me out, I'll make a deal with you. I'll spread the word at the horse show about the filly who works here. Betcha your business will double." He ogled Betsie's Plain dress. "So, do we have a deal?"

Betsie let her shoulders rise and fall. "The sewing will not be too hard, but I must ask my boss if it will be okay."

He frowned. "I'm kinda in a hurry. Can't you whip it together, and I'll come back for it later this afternoon?"

Hurry-up English; won't take no for an answer. "If you return before five. After that we are closed."

"You're a lifesaver, babe." He doffed the jacket while Betsie wrote down his name, Mr. Benner. He took a couple of steps but doubled back. "You must get mighty lonely, working here by yourself." He licked his lips and glanced around the shop. "You are alone, right?"

The back of her neck prickled. "No," she lied. "Mr. Sullivan will be right back."

"That's good." He scratched the odd-shaped scar on his nose. "Have a nice day, sweetness."

The bell jangled. Betsie watched Mr. Benner drive off in a black pickup truck. She shivered and hurried to the house for a short break, figuring no customers would come again so soon, but when she returned five minutes later, another car rolled up.

Ach, but this day in the harness shop was different from the ones that had gone before. One after another, customers brought work to Betsie, all of them in a hurry. Each mentioned the weekend horse show at the fairgrounds. Most mentioned Sheila; many of her friends kept horses. Betsie's fingers ached from printing telephone numbers and names.

When Mr. Benner came back less than an hour later, Betsie looked up from stitching his red jacket, annoyed. Did he think she was done with his sewing already? She waited for him to speak, but he only stared—and not at her face. Another warning prickle made her thankful the counter was between them.

The silence stretched out until it was uncomfortable even for Betsie. "Mr. Benner, I am not finished with your repair yet. May I help you with something else, maybe?"

"Well, now, little lady, that ain't for me to say. Maybe you can't, but maybe you can."

What he said was so much like how Betsie felt when she faced anyone English that she almost smiled, but she refrained. There was something unpleasant about Mr. Benner, something more than just the medicine smell that rolled out when he spoke.

"Sullivan come back yet?"

"H-he will be here s-shortly," Betsie stammered. If only it were true.

"Then I'll wait," Mr. Benner said.

He did wait for a minute or so, but when no one appeared, he licked his lips. "Looks like it's just you and me." He fumbled with his leather belt, cold eyes menacing.

Betsie shot backward and stumbled over the English saddle. She caught herself against the stitching machine, a good solid bulk that supported her shaky legs.

"Hold on there, missy," he barked. Betsie watched in horrified fascination as he drew the whole length of the loosened belt very slowly from his waist. "No need to get your knickers in a knot. I'm not going to hurt you." He held the belt out toward her. "See? First my riding habit, and now this loop's busted. Take a look and see if you can fix it."

Betsie gnawed the inside of her cheek. Outside, the blue jay screamed again. Reaching toward him was the last thing she wanted to do, but this man was a customer and Betsie was the shopkeeper. She put out her hand for the belt. He smirked and dropped it behind the counter. It landed beside her shoes and Betsie stooped to retrieve it. Customer or no, she was finished with his games. "Mr. Benner, I don't have time for this kind of—"

Her breath sagged. Mr. Benner leveled a gun at her. Light played along the blue-gray metal as goosebumps prickled her arms.

"Don't scream." His right hand shot out and gripped her wrist with crushing force. "Got you," he slurred. He lowered his gun to the floor and nudged it toward the stitching machine, the grate of the metal over plywood like a shriek.

He dragged Betsie around the counter. She twisted her wrist and dug in her heels, but her resistance only served to enrage him.

"Please don't!" Her begging was drowned out by the mournful hoot of the train as it barreled toward the crossing.

Benner dragged her to the floor. With his left hand he scrabbled at the front of her dress. Angry swear words tumbled from his mouth when a straight pin stabbed his finger. He pinned Betsie's shoulders to the plywood. He grunted as she kicked and struggled beneath him.

The white scar on his nose looked like a skull. His foul breath gagged her. She turned her head. Her desperate gasps stirred a nest of dust bunnies under the counter.

No one could save her now.

CHAPTER 23

The good Lord sends help from unlikely places.

—BETSIE'S JOURNAL

BETSIE THRASHED FROM side to side as she struggled for breath. Her eyes glazed over and fixed on the missing horse blanket behind the worktable. The next instant the red stripes erupted to violent motion and bare feet slapped the plywood floor.

"Let go of her, you slimeball!" Michael grabbed Benner by the shoulders and yanked him off of Betsie. In a split second, the harness shop erupted in a blur of flying fists and muffled grunts. Betsie clawed her way free of the melee. A glint caught her eye; it was the metal buckle of the belt. She snatched it up and flailed at her attacker.

"Betsie!" Michael bellowed. "Get out of here and go for help!"

At Michael's yells, Benner broke free and fled, eyes wild. Betsie began to shake.

"Did he hurt you?" Michael asked gently.

She collapsed in the webbed chair and rubbed her wrist. "I ache all over, but he didn't . . . Oh, Michael, it was awful!"

Remorse tinged his voice. "I had to wait for my chance, Betsie. He was so much heavier than me. I had to wait. I was so scared he would hurt you—" He broke off, shamefaced. "The second I saw you leave, I ducked in here to hide. I thought I would surprise you like the other day, but I was too beat to stay awake."

159

"But how could you sleep with all the noise? Customers were in and out—"

He stared at the floor. "I guess I'm a sound sleeper. I'm really sorry, Pippa. The first thing I heard was when he said, 'Don't scream.'"

She shivered. "Michael, I am finished. I don't want to learn how to make harnesses. I want to go back to Plain City where there is no Hilliard Stalker. Take me home right now."

He draped the horse blanket around her shoulders. "You're shaking like a leaf. Do you want something hot to drink?" A swollen lip thickened his talk.

She gritted her teeth to keep them from chattering. "No. I want to go home."

Michael touched his lip and winced. "Look, you'll be okay with me around. I'll take you home later, but I am not letting you out of my sight for a while." He looked at the floor again. "Maybe we should call Sergeant Deacon."

"No! I can't talk to the police! I—it's not allowed. I want to go home. Now." She clasped her hands together hard to still the shaking.

"Betsie?"

"Y-yes?"

"I forget. What's the Amish word for *stubborn?*"

"*Schtaerkeppich,*" she supplied automatically before she noticed the wry twist to his mouth. "I am *not* stubborn."

"Okay, you win. Can you make some coffee for *me*, then, or cook me something before I take you home? I'm beat."

"I . . . I guess. You will stay with me the whole time?" She blew her nose.

"Cross my heart," Michael promised. He clasped her icy hand with one equally icy and led her to the kitchen, where he boiled water for some tea. By the time she'd taken a few sips and felt the good warmth return, Michael had devoured some warmed-over chicken and noodles. "Do you want to talk about it?" He fiddled with his fork.

Betsie stiffened. Talk, talk, talk, the English answer to every problem. If this near-rape had happened in Plain City, her family and friends would give thanks to the good Lord that she hadn't been harmed physically and go on about their business. Her emotional well-being didn't really enter the picture. She was alive, wasn't she? Thank God and go on, then. Some in her community would even feel that the attack was a judgment on her for living among the English. What did she expect to happen to her when she ventured out into the wicked world? This was God's will, and we're not going to interfere, they would say. She never wanted to think about the attack again, much less tell anyone else.

To her relief, the telephone bell interrupted.

Michael picked up the receiver. "Y'ello." He propped his long frame against the counter and crossed his ankles. "Yup, if I answer the phone, that means I'm back." He covered the mouthpiece. "It's *der Führer*," he stage-whispered. "What's shakin', Pops?" he asked into the phone. A burst of noise made him pull the phone a couple of inches from his ear. The irritable squawks sounded a lot like Mr. Sullivan. "Nope, not yet," Michael droned.

Betsie left Michael to his private conversation and walked to splash her face in the pink bathroom. She straightened her *Kapp*, askew from the attack, and smoothed her disheveled dress and hair. If Michael hadn't been in the harness shop . . . The hot tea threatened to surface. She gripped the vanity until the queasy feeling passed, and then she rejoined Michael, who stared at the telephone.

"How do you like that? My old man called to see if Phyllis had come home, and I told him she hadn't yet. Then I tried to tell him what happened to you in the shop, but he yammered over me the whole time. Finally I just said I took care of it and hung up." He banged his fist on the countertop. "What is his problem?" Suddenly his anger changed to concern. "Hey, are you all right? You look kind of green."

Betsie rubbed the goosebumps on her arms. "I was thinking that we left the shop unlocked, and I-I'm afraid to go back to lock it."

Michael checked the mouse on his wrist. "It's only a quarter to twelve, but we are closing up shop for the day. I'm sticking with you just in case that creep comes back. Not that I think he will."

"Thank you, Michael." Relief flooded through her. Together, she and Michael swished through the long grass to the shop. The day had warmed enough that it felt like April, maybe, but not like May.

Michael insisted on looking in first to give Betsie what he called the *all clear*. They quickly set the shop to rights. Betsie turned the Open sign over to read Closed, and Michael locked the door.

A breeze stirred the shaggy grass into a shimmer of silvery green. As Betsie watched, peace stole into her heart and shut out everything else until Michael waved his hand in front of her nose.

"Earth to Pippa; you're like a million miles away. I said how about that lawn-mowing lesson? The grass is plenty dry."

Betsie pondered. "Sure could use cutting. It's gone to seed. But after . . . what happened, Michael, I need to get home."

He rumpled his hair. "I wish you would stick with me, where I know you're safe." He looked into Betsie's eyes and chewed his lip. "Besides, I think operating a powerful machine would be . . . liberating for you. Come on, you've watched me drive my car plenty of times. All you gotta do is turn the key, shift gears, give 'er some gas, and *bang*. Driving the lawn tractor will be cinchy, I promise. Also monotonous—I mean soothing." As Michael gabbed, he led Betsie around back to the green-striped aluminum shed. He opened the door, and there it was: a shiny green lawn tractor with a lemon-yellow seat. The machine was named Deere.

Michael removed the key from the starter and pressed it into Betsie's hand. She stared at it. At home, she used a push mower; the cylinder of sharp blades whirled, and the long grass was shorn, easy as pie. Here in the shed, the smell of moldy grass mingled with gasoline fumes and nearly overcame her. Still wobbly from the attack, she fanned herself and tried to hand the key back to Michael, but he ignored her.

"Help me push it outside, where we have more room to work, okay?"

Somehow it was comforting to discover that the gas mower must be pushed, too. She threw her weight into the task, shoes slipping in the oily gravel until the Deere sparkled in the sunshine.

"Raring to go! Hop on, Pippa." Michael patted the seat.

Maybe it was being in the wide open daylight, or maybe it was the prospect of useful work, but Betsie threw back her shoulders and drew a grateful breath. She was strong and healthy, and Benner hadn't gotten the best of her, thanks to Michael. With a shy glance at him, she gathered her dress and climbed aboard. She gripped the wheel until her knuckles whitened.

"Hey," Michael said. "You know you don't have to do this. I thought staying busy might help you, but—"

"No." She lifted her chin. "I want to try. How does the key go?"

He showed her the ignition. "When you hear the engine start, keep your foot on that pedal—that's the brake—until you're ready to move. Got it?"

"*Jah*." Moisture beaded on Betsie's upper lip as she cranked the key. The resulting roar of the engine made her dizzy, but she imagined she was Amelia Earhart, poised for adventuresome takeoff. She gritted her teeth and operated the levers and pedals that Michael indicated and finally lifted her foot from the brake. The tractor surged forward.

How wonderful it was to watch the powerful lawn tractor chop the long grass, knowing she was in control. Betsie twisted to admire the neat swath of clippings that magically stretched behind the Deere. She turned to grin at Michael.

He yelled and pointed. "Look out, Pippa! Turn the wheel in the direction you want to go! Turn the wheel!" he bellowed.

Betsie whipped around to see the corner of the house looming. She noted tiny orange speckles in the red bricks before she yanked the wheel and missed the wall with a couple of inches to spare.

Michael jogged to her side, puffing. "Man, that was close. Okay, Plan B. You're going to mow the lawn in a big circle around the house, you dig? Just follow the edge of the short grass, keep steering to the left, and you can't go wrong." He paused when Betsie's eyebrows scrunched. "On second thought, sit for a sec and observe."

She watched as Michael expertly guided the Deere to the ditch by the road. He drove along the edge until he reached the property line to the east. He rounded the corner in a sweeping arc and mowed along Fledge's pasture fence. He waved and Betsie waved back. When he reappeared near the harness shop on the other side, she stood up, and Michael drove to the steps and let the engine idle.

"Think you've got the hang of it now?"

Betsie wrung her hands. "*Ach*, Michael, I don't know. Can you go around another time?"

"Sure," he said after a pause. "I guess it is a little overwhelming . . . Hey, why the grin?"

"I see Tom Sawyer's trick would work on you," she answered. "I am ready to drive now."

Michael pretended to pout. "No way, if that's how you repay me. I'll do it myself. It's pretty cool, you know?" But he was already vacating the seat of honor as he spoke.

To Betsie's surprise, driving the tractor was easy. Apart from her narrow miss of the house and later the mailbox, Betsie enjoyed mowing; it commanded just enough of her attention to shove down memories of the attack. She drove in ever-narrowing circles, grass blades falling like toy soldiers to lie in long green rows.

She noticed that Michael had moved the Super Bee to the driveway, and now he was hosing the sun-baked remnants of the mushy apple from the windshield. Once when she drove by, he flicked the hose to shower her with an arc of droplets. She maneuvered to avoid getting wet and the mower responded by beheading a bed of Mr. Sullivan's freshly planted striped petunias. Betsie straightened the wheel, mindful of Michael's laughter.

When she finally mowed the last narrow strip in the middle of the back yard, it was late afternoon. She drove around front so Michael could help her stop.

"Nice work! I'll park that in the shed after it cools off. I'm going to get an old towel so I can dry off my car—don't want water spots." He hesitated. "Will you be okay alone? Maybe you could get the towel instead."

"*Ach*, I am too hot to go inside. I'll wait out here, but hurry." Betsie mopped her face with her handkerchief and then rested her head on her knees, eyes closed. Her hands were stiff and her seat seemed to vibrate from bouncing over the uneven lawn. She was worn out, plain and simple.

A train whistle sounded, far and wee; Betsie heard Fledge answer with a plaintive whinny. Vaguely she wondered what could be keeping Michael for so long, but the pleasant spring sunshine pressed against her dress with palpable weight. The whistle hooted noisily as the train chugged and clattered over the crossing down the road and faded into the distance. Betsie drowsed until she heard the crunch of boots on gravel.

"Well, well, well, so we meet again."

CHAPTER 24

Love helps us do for others what we would never have the
courage to do on our own.

—Betsie's journal

Betsie gasped and scrambled to her feet. "What are you doing
here?"

"Easy, ma'am." Officer Deacon nodded at his over-eager partner.
"Schwartz thinks we're the Mod Squad." He clenched his jaw as he
turned to his young partner. "Keep sneaking up on people like that,
Schwartz, and you're going to get your fool head blown off one of these
days." He turned back to Betsie. "We got a phone call that there was
an assault, possibly by the Hilliard Stalker, on the young woman who
works here, a Miss Betsie Troyer. That's you, correct?"

Betsie nodded, thinking *Mem* was right when she said telephones
were nothing but trouble. She heard the door open. "Michael—"

"Sorry I was gone so long, Pippa. I thought you could use some
water, but the ice-cube tray was frozen solid, and ice flew all over when
I yanked the handle." Michael backed through the doorway, a glass
of water in each hand. He turned around, saw the police officers, and
slipped into full cop-hating mode. "What the . . . what's going on? Why
are you harassing us?"

"Michael, don't," Betsie warned. "They say somebody called them
about the Hilliard Stalker."

Michael scowled. "Well, it wasn't me."

Deacon said, "The call came from a Mr. Gerald Sullivan."

"Oh, for the love of—" Michael handed Betsie a glass and took a long drink from his own, ice cubes clinking as his hand shook. "Listen, that's my old man, remember? But what he doesn't know is . . ." His voice trailed off as his father's station wagon roared into the driveway. The door opened before the car was fully stopped, and Michael groaned. "Speak of the devil."

"Betsie! Are you all right?" Mr. Sullivan trotted up to Betsie and searched her face. "I would have been here sooner, but it took me a while to read between the lines after I talked to *him*." He jerked a thumb over his shoulder at Michael and rounded on him for good measure. "Can't you understand how serious this is? You should have called the police right away."

Michael's jaw dropped. "But that's what I was trying to tell you. Betsie can't—"

Mr. Sullivan put up a hand. "I don't want to hear your excuses. These officers are here to protect our rights as American citizens."

Officer Schwartz practically saluted. "That's very true, sir."

"Oh, yeah?" Michael snarled at his father. "Why didn't they protect us American citizens at Kent State, then? And it may interest you to know that Citizen Petey here shook me down for my school lunch money every day of grade school. Why do you think I'm so skinny? Go ahead, ask him."

Schwartz glowered at Michael and opened his mouth, but Mr. Sullivan threw up his hands in disgust. "I don't believe it. You're still wallowing in the past. Get on with your life! Right now, it's Betsie I'm concerned about." He turned back to her. "Don't let Michael's hippie talk fool you. Tell the officers what happened so they can catch this criminal."

Officer Deacon whipped out the pad of paper and a pen. "That's right, ma'am, I'm ready to take your statement. Don't be nervous. Just describe what happened in your own words."

The four men stared at Betsie, and she backed up a step. "I do not wish to make a report." She clamped her mouth shut.

Deacon stared. "Ma'am?"

"She can't talk to the police because of her religion." Michael glared at his father. "That's what I was trying to tell you on the phone, but you wouldn't listen. She's Amish, remember? The Amish don't want to deal with the police, and I'd say that's pretty astute of them."

A blast of air sounded from the school bus brakes, and Sheila emerged at her usual headlong run, eyes big as saucers when she spotted the policemen and her dad.

Mr. Sullivan removed his glasses and rubbed his eyes. "I would never ask you to go against your faith, Betsie, but I hope you know what you're doing." He stalked off to intercept Sheila.

Betsie watched as Mr. Sullivan waved his arms to stop his daughter's headlong rush. His voice rose and fell as he darted glances at the police.

"So what if this man attacks somebody else, Miss Troyer?" Deacon jerked his thumb at Sheila. "Like the girl? How will you feel then?"

Betsie chewed the inside of her cheek. In all the years of buggy vandalism, accounts unpaid, and other minor infractions of the law, not once had her district enlisted the aid of the police that she could recall. An attack like this was unprecedented. She watched Sheila with tenderness, but she shook her head.

"Fighting dirty, huh? Don't fall for that, Betsie. Stand your ground," Michael said, but his eyes were troubled as he watched Sheila wave good-bye to her dad before she raced to join them. "You're welcome to check out the shop, Officer," Michael said with a shade more respect. "Here's the key."

"Thank you. Schwartz?"

Officer Schwartz popped up from behind the Super Bee. "Coming, sir."

As soon as the door closed, Sheila squeezed Betsie with a rib-crunching hug. "I'm so glad you're okay!"

There was nothing the girl could have said or done that meant more. "Dear heart."

Officer Deacon opened the shop door. "Could you come here for a moment, please?"

Michael said, "Yes, sir," with exaggerated politeness and a toothy grin. Betsie followed him and collapsed in the webbed chair while Deacon squatted to point underneath the stitching machine.

"Mind if I collect that gun for evidence?"

"The only guns that have been inside this shop are yours and the one your partner was going to splatter my guts with." Mottled red spots covered Michael's cheeks.

"Not Schwartz's gun. The one Miss Troyer's attacker must have used." Deacon raised his eyebrows at her. "He had a gun, right?"

"No," Michael shot back.

"Yes," Betsie whispered.

Michael rounded on her. "That guy did not have a gun."

"Someone sure did." Deacon took out a handkerchief and retrieved the forgotten gun.

Sheila's eyes bugged. Sweat beaded up on Michael's forehead. His gaze flicked from the gun to Betsie. He crossed his arms and beat a nervous tattoo with one toe. "So what? She has nothing to say to you."

"The fact that this guy was armed takes this assault to a whole new level. His threatening behavior has definitely escalated." Deacon tossed his pen on the counter as Schwartz watched for her decision.

Betsie cupped her chin in her hand, partly covering her mouth. Up to now, it had been relatively easy to obey the rules of the *Ordnung*. When a person could be publicly disciplined and possibly even shunned for breaking a rule, the choice was obvious: obey the rule. True, she hadn't formally joined the church yet, so technically there was some leeway about bending a rule—pushing up her skirts and riding bareback, for instance. Much depended on how her district interpreted and enforced the *Ordnung*. She was fairly certain they'd rule that she'd brought the near-rape on herself when she took up with the English. So why tempt fate? She had emerged from the attack just fine; it was best to put it behind her and move on. By far the easiest solution would be to look the other way and let the English take care of their own problems.

She opened her mouth to refuse cooperation, but the scrape of aluminum on plywood stopped her cold. *Sheila.* The dear girl sat on the other lawn chair, one leg doubled up awkwardly as she picked at a scab. Betsie imagined Benner crouched in the bushes as Sheila ran headlong from the bus, short skirt flying. The Amish sensibilities that had long been her guide didn't measure up now that she actually knew some English people, cared for them.

Despite his hatred toward the police, surely Michael would appreciate that she wanted to protect his sister. Sheila had lost her mother, a keen pain that also haunted Betsie. How horrible if she lost her innocence, too.

She bowed her head. "Sergeant, I will make that report."

"You're doing the right thing, Miss Troyer." Schwartz gripped her hand and nodded wisely. "Now we can protect you the way you deserve to be protected."

Betsie tugged her hand free from his moist grip. "I hope so."

"I don't believe it." Michael slammed his fist on the counter. "You're expecting help from the pigs? They're hopeless! They didn't help us at Kent State, and they can't help you. Let's go, Squirt."

Sheila bolted for the door like a frightened rabbit. Michael kicked over the lawn chair and stalked out of the shop without a backward glance.

For the next half hour, Betsie described her attacker, what he said, and the scar on his nose, plus all the other details she preferred to forget. She retrieved the belt and turned it in for evidence. Sergeant Deacon's pen scratched even faster when she produced the note card with Benner's name and phone number. Then she told about the part she would never forget, how Michael had rescued her, even though it seemed like he hated her now.

With the police officers keeping watch, Betsie walked to the house. Despite Michael's outburst, she felt light, clean, at peace. Why did the Amish keep their troubles so much to themselves? She'd made the right choice to talk to the police; she was sure of it. If only she could talk things over with Sadie.

Her optimism was short-lived. She found her satchel beside the front door when she walked in the house.

"I packed your stuff for you," Sheila said. "Michael said he has some places to go, so we're going to drive you home early." Her smile was forlorn. "At least I get to see your house."

"Don't worry; your brother will be all right, Sheila. You know he doesn't like guns, or policemen." And a lot of other things, she reminded herself.

"Michael's not the one I'm worried about." The girl caught Betsie's hand. "Are you sure you're okay, Betsie?"

Quick tears stung at her eyelids, but she kept her emotions in check and nodded.

Sheila was silent for a rare moment. "Anyway, something good happened today. I got invited to spend the weekend at my friend Debbie Keith's house. She's going to a youth rally and a lock-in at her church, and she invited me to go, too." Sheila tightened her hold on Betsie. "It won't be as much fun as our sleepovers, though."

"*Jah*, sure it will, dear heart. You'll see."

Michael strode into view and glared at them. "Let's get this show on the road."

"Are you all right, Michael?" Betsie eyed him. "Do you want to . . . talk about anything?"

"Oh, I'm sure the cops have everything under control. Schwartz to the rescue! You wanted to go home, so I'm taking you home—that is, if you think I can handle it."

His words stung worse than a slap. She waited a moment for him to look at her, and when he wouldn't, Betsie held her head high and hurried to the car with Sheila.

It was a wretched car ride, with Michael rebuffing every attempt at conversation. Finally even Sheila gave up, and they completed the trip in miserable silence.

"Bye, Betsie. See you Monday." Sheila's lips quivered as Betsie leaned in the window to take her hand.

"Don't worry. Your brother can't get rid of me just by ignoring me." Michael flicked a razor glance at her, but Betsie ignored him. "I will be there."

"Sadie, Lovina! I'm home," she called as she undid her bonnet and hung it on the peg. She crossed the sitting room to the kitchen and was surprised to find it empty before recalling that she was home early. Her aunt and sister must still be at the bakery; no, that wasn't right. Lovina had mentioned something about spending Friday with an ill friend who lived near the Yoder house; that must be it.

Alone. After the attack and Michael's animosity, Betsie's nerves were raw. She pulled the curtains aside and looked for signs of life. No one was out, not even the perpetual Katie Miller. "I'm scared," Betsie whispered to no one.

A wave of exhaustion broke over her and threatened to drag her under. She kept her eyes open long enough to inform Sadie in a note that she wasn't feeling well and had already gone to bed. She'd just grabbed hold of the banister when she heard a rustle out back.

Fear turned her insides to ice water. Had Benner followed her here? Surely not, since the Hilliard police were on the job. She recalled Michael's scorn over their ineptitude and quickly locked the doors. Then she crept stealthily to the kitchen and peeked through the sheers that hung at the window on the back door. Her heart almost stopped—somebody was looking back at her.

The next instant she laughed with shaky relief. "Charley! I'm so glad to see you!" She held up one finger at him and twisted the lock. "What are you doing here?" She tiptoed to peer over his shoulder. Sure enough, his horse was hitched behind the house. "You were almost the death of me, hiding your buggy like that."

"*Ach*, I-I didn't know you'd come back this early," he stammered. "I hope I didn't scare you too much. I dropped up a while ago to see to the chores." He stared at a bruise on her wrist. "What's the matter? Are you hurt?"

Betsie slid her hands into her pockets and stared at the floor. She searched for an answer, but when she met his troubled gaze, a movement startled her. "Am I dreaming? Your shirt just moved!"

"No, it didn't. *Ouch!*" Sheepish, he forgot his question and stared at his midsection, where the movement increased. "Well, maybe you're right." He reached in his shirt and withdrew a bundle of calico fur with tiny sharp claws. "I've been to Katie Miller's house and picked out a kitten for you, if you'll have her. I was going to surprise you somehow, but I guess I already did."

"Charley!" Tears of gratitude spilled over as Betsie held the kitten to her cheek. "Listen to her purr, the dear little kitty. But surely she's too young to leave her mother. Katie showed the mama to me the other day and—"

"Do you know how many mama cats the Millers have in their barn?" Charley smiled. "No, this one is weaned, and Katie promised me she's the prettiest. All she needs is a good name and a good home. I had an idea you could give her both."

"Oh, I will. She will be good company." Betsie had read about shining eyes before, and she suspected hers were shining now. The kitten mewed as she cuddled it. "You are so thoughtful. I was lonesome when I got home and no one was here."

"Once you join the church, maybe you won't be so lonesome anymore." Charley shuffled his feet. "Well, I better go pick up Sadie so you have some human company, too. Oh, and by the way, Lovina sends word that she's staying over with her sick friend. Miriam took a turn for the worse. 'Night, Betsie."

"*Denki*, Charley." Betsie's heart thundered in her ears as she waved good-bye and stroked the kitten's wee head. The kitten was beautiful, her fur a rich mix of ginger and black over cream. She mewed again. "Give me a minute," Betsie said, and then giggled at herself for talking to a kitten. She deposited her pet in her roomy apron pocket and poked around for a couple of boxes and some old newspapers. It took a bit to shred the papers and fluff them into a bed. When she finished, she spread a thick pad of folded newspapers in the other box. She located a couple of chipped saucers and filled one with milk from the ice box.

"Here you go," she crooned as she set the kitten before it. True to Charley's word, the kitten lapped up the milk. When she finished, she licked her snub nose twice and scooted under the table in an exploratory foray, but Betsie foiled her.

"No more adventures for you. I'm tired, and you must keep me company tonight, Amelia." She laughed. "Why, already you have a good name. Now I must do as Charley says and give you a good home." She sobered. "I had one once."

The clang of the brass bell startled Betsie, alone again in the harness shop. Before she could react, Benner elbowed his way inside, gun trained between her eyes. Horror filled her; he'd returned even though she'd talked to the police. Why hadn't they helped her? She tried to move, to cry out, but Benner's cruel fingers dug into her shoulders, and he dragged her down as the brass bell jangled across the floor in wild circles. This time there was no one to help her . . .

"Betsie," he said. He shook her roughly, his hot breath smothering her.

"Betsie?" Another shake. "Betsie! High time you woke up, ain't so? It's ten past five."

She opened her eyes as Sadie flicked the lever of the wind-up alarm to still the hammer and leaned to shake her again. Betsie sat bolt upright, and her head smacked her sister in the mouth.

"Ow! Oh, that hurts." Sadie rubbed her lip. "We must cultivate the garden if you want fresh vegetables this year. Tomorrow's opposite Sunday, don't forget. If we don't finish today, we don't go a-visiting tomorrow." She held her mouth and left the room with smart clomps of her work shoes.

Betsie flopped on her pillow. Was there any feeling more serene than discovering that a desperate situation was only a nightmare? If only the police could catch the Hilliard Stalker soon. She dreaded going to the harness shop until they had.

Far back in Betsie's mind, though, she knew that the Sullivans needed her, especially Sheila. Michael had become very withdrawn on that nightmare drive home. She thanked the good Lord that Sheila would be out of that crazy house this weekend, locked in her church and safe with her friend Debbie and a church full of people.

A plaintive mew reached her ears. Amelia! She tumbled out of bed and raised the quilt's edge to search underneath, but it was too dark to see. Betsie wiggled the end of her hair flirtatiously, and the green-eyed sprite pounced on it. She caught the kitty and snuggled her close. She settled Amelia in the middle of her bed, keeping a close eye on her antics while she quickly readied herself. Then she skipped down the stairs two at a time, Amelia curled in her pocket.

When Betsie bragged about Amelia to Sadie, she was surprised that her sister was not immediately charmed.

"You say Charley gave her to you?" Sadie whacked the skillet on the hot stove and flipped in a scoop of bacon fat from the coffee can.

"He brought her over from Katie Miller's. Katie knows I like cats, and Amelia is much cuter than Abijah's snake." Betsie broke up a hot dog into tiny pieces and watched her miniature tiger devour it.

Sadie deftly cracked four eggs into the skillet and sloshed the melted fat over the golden yolks with the spatula. "Well, I guess it will be okay to keep her. Maybe she can be of some use in the barn, catching mice."

Betsie eyed Sadie's back, rigid as she fried the eggs. Someone surely had gotten up on the wrong side of the bed this morning. She shook her head and sighed. Maybe all the work they had to do would help the sisters forget their troubles.

They scrubbed and scoured inside. It was afternoon when they met in the garden. They chatted some as they weeded and watered, but Sadie chewed her lip the way she did when she had something on her mind.

"Out with it, Sadie," Betsie said at last. Sweat stung her eyes as she cultivated the soil around a waxy pepper plant.

"What do you mean?" Sadie, crabby in the heat, had a smear of dirt on her cheek.

"*Ach*, I know you are a *Wonnernaus*, always wondering. Ask me your question and get it over with."

Sadie threw down her trowel and faced Betsie. "You want to know who's a *Wonnernaus*, Betsie? Just you try working with Mattie Yoder for five minutes. 'When are your parents coming home next, Sadie? How much are they asking for their land if they sell it?' That's bother enough.

"But the question she asked me yesterday was the worst. She backed me into a corner and asked, 'What was your sister thinking, riding up front with an Englisher?' And that right there is a question I would like answered, too." She fiddled with the trowel, only to stab it into the ground. "So what have you got to say for yourself?"

CHAPTER 25

*It's difficult to teach children right from wrong, but it's
even more difficult to teach parents.*

—BETSIE'S JOURNAL

BETSIE FELT HER cheeks flame redder than sweet peppers. No two
ways about it, she was in a pickle. But how ludicrous! She knew from
experience that there were worse fates for a woman who lived among
the English than sitting in the front seat of a car. She longed to tell
Sadie about the attack, wished for words of comfort and acceptance,
but it was no use.

"*Ach*, that? We worked hard all day, and we went to get some ice
cream. That's all." Betsie avoided Sadie's gaze. "Here's what you don't
know. I wasn't sitting *with* Michael. The seats are separated."

"Huh. I still think it's pretty strange, keeping company with that
long-haired English boy when you don't have to."

"The English are pretty strange. Be *donkbawr* for every day you get
to stay here in Plain City, very thankful. But listen, Sadie. I have to
confess that I did make another trip in Michael's car." Her words tumbled one on top of the other. "He drove me up to visit *Mem* and *Dat*."

She watched the blood drain from her sister's face. "You saw *Mem*
and *Dat*? When? Did you convince them to come back?"

"Shh!" Betsie scanned their surroundings. "Listen once, Sadie,
and be strong. Michael drove me to Belle Center a week ago this past

Friday. It's not good news I have. *Mem* and *Dat* said they are not coming back." She struggled to hold back tears as Sadie stared.

Always Betsie had believed that her parents were pillars of the Amish church. They obeyed the *Ordnung* and brought their children up as they should, and they shared with them about God. Every evening her father read to the family from the Luther *Biewel*. The difference was, when he read the big book, *Dat* made it come alive. She did not hear, "Don't do this! Don't do that!" when he read, as she did in church. She heard of God's love.

Peace filled Betsie's heart; surely her gentle parents were not doomed. When she looked at Sadie, however, and saw the revulsion and shame that threatened to overcome her sister, fear crowded peace from the safe place deep inside.

"I can't bear to hear this. Oh, what shall we do?" Sadie moaned. "Betsie, if they come under the *Meidung* . . ."

"Don't say that!" But the thought lingered: shunning. Impossible to take in that their parents had both chosen to break their baptismal vows.

"But how can they turn their backs on the church like this, Betsie?" Sadie's breath came in short gasps. "The bishop will say *Dat* and *Mem* have turned their backs on the good Lord!"

A still, small voice comforted her. How absurd to think that *Dat* would turn his back on the good Lord. Her father would never do such a thing, she knew, but she acknowledged reluctantly that there would be no reasoning with the *Ordnung*. Once a person made a vow to the church, a rule was a rule and that was that. Shunning must be the sure result—if it were true that her *Dat*'s mind was made up.

But was it? Betsie clutched her sister's arm. "Sadie! We must write to them. Maybe I got it wrong. When they thought I wanted to leave the Amish too, I was so upset that I panicked and ran away."

Sadie sniffled. "Do you really think you got it wrong, Betsie?"

"We must pray that I did, that's all. The good Lord wants our parents to obey Him, ain't so? And until we find out otherwise, we must believe He will bring us all back together." She blew her nose. "Now let's get back to work, and while we're at it, tell me, what have you heard about Sol and Ellie Beiler's little boy? Is he well from the croup yet?"

If there was one thing Sadie loved, it was talking. She dried her tears and gladly took the bait. Betsie didn't mind; it was much better to hear that Sol and Ellie's croupy baby was improving. And wonderful *gut*, too, to hear of the new house that Sam Hochstetler, Rachel Yutzy's *Bo*, was building. All the neighbors were speculating about who Sam was building the house for, Sadie said, just as if they didn't suspect Rachel was the one for him.

By the time Betsie and Sadie lugged the last bucket of water to give each plant a drink, they were plenty tired, but good honest work meant they'd earned a rest. Betsie kneaded the small of her back as she latched the gate that kept the rabbits out of the garden. She spotted one under the blue spruce. He rose to his haunches with front paws suspended and twitched his nose. Betsie's father had built the *gut* mesh fence plenty strong and high, though, so she ignored the thieving pest and headed inside.

"Did you remember to order new milk from the bakery?" She wiped her brow.

Sadie made a rueful mouth. "I forgot to bring it."

"Oh, that's all right. I hoped to make some cold bread soup for supper, but I fed Amelia the last drops from the bottle," Betsie called over her shoulder as she walked to the screen door. "I'll go check the mail while you cut the bread and soften the butter. Anyway, I'm glad Lovina's not back yet. This way we don't need to tell anyone the bad news."

A floorboard creaked on the front porch. "What bad news?" asked Charley Yoder.

If a lightning bolt had struck Betsie, she couldn't have been more shocked. There he stood, smiling at her through the screen door.

"Charley! How you startled me!" She scrambled for an answer. "What I meant was *Mem* and *Dat* have extended their visit. We were hoping they'd come home soon." Her words were truer than he knew.

"Oh, what a shame. I brought Lovina home from her nursing at

178

Bontragers' special to see them. She got it into her head that her brother would be waiting." He held the door open for the older lady, her face wan with worry over her childhood friend.

"Betsie, dear," she said, "I'm so thirsty."

"There's water in the bucket, Lovina. The dipper hangs on the nail by the sink, you know. Is it well with Miriam?"

"She is little changed, and I am worn to a frazzle. I'm getting a drink and going straight to bed. Good night, girls."

They watched her climb the stairs. With a guilty start, Betsie recalled that *Dat* had asked her to monitor her aunt's health. As if she knew Betsie needed a distraction from her failure, Amelia streaked from a nook beside the fireplace to disappear behind the curtains. Betsie and Charley laughed at her antics.

"I also brought this." Charley held up a milk bottle clotted with an inch of golden cream under the cap. "Sadie forgot it."

"*Ach*, and I thought I was the *fergesslich* one." Betsie smiled. "You are so thoughtful, Charley."

"Figured you'd need some with a new kitten around." He smiled at Sadie as she hurried into the room.

"I was fixing supper and I thought I heard voices." Sadie smiled. "You fetched the milk, Charley."

Charley handed it over. "Guess I better go. I had my supper already. Betsie, can I see you a moment?"

"Surely." She left the oak door open so the lamplight would chase away the gathering shadows. Moths fluttered about the screen. They echoed the flutters in her heart.

"Sit down, why don't you?" He scooted to make room. The lilac's fragrance sweetened the May night, but Charley did not appear to notice. The space between his eyebrows puckered. "Betsie, I don't like that I saw you riding in the English boy's car at night. Tell me, do you think a lot of him?" Pain flickered in his eyes.

"Why, Charley!" Gratitude that he hadn't asked about her parents mingled with consternation that he asked nearly the same question of her as Michael had. Dear Charley: thoughtful, dependable, safe harbor in a storm. "I think a lot of *you*," she whispered.

The change in his expression was subtle, but Betsie detected a hint of manly pride at being the victor.

"That's as it should be, then." He scooted closer and offered an olive branch. "What did you name your kitten?"

"Amelia." Oh, but she was warm all of a sudden. She stood. "I-it's getting late. I should go inside."

Charley propped a foot on the porch rail to block her way. "Wait," he begged in a low voice. He got up and flicked a glance at the open door. "I have a question to ask you before you do. May I drive you home from the singing next Sunday evening?" His blue eyes blazed.

No two ways about it—standing this close to him made her knees weak. "I'd like that." Reluctantly, Betsie backed away from him. "*Gut nacht*, Charley." She stepped inside and gently shut the door. It was good to rest against its solid bulk, and she closed her eyes.

"What did Charley say?"

"Sadie!" Betsie jumped, hand over her heart. "You startled me."

"Didn't mean to. I was cleaning up after your kitten." She pointed to the overturned flowerpot which held *Mem*'s Christmas cactus. Clumps of potting soil dotted the otherwise spotless floor below. The culprit was nowhere to be seen. "What did Charley want?"

"*Ach*, he asked if I liked the kitten. I said yes, but Amelia *Schnickelfritz* is what her name should be." Betsie stooped to help Sadie. "Is the cactus all right? *Mem* won't like it . . . Oh, that's right." Somberly she held the dustpan while Sadie swept up the dirt. "Charley didn't ask about *Mem* and *Dat*."

"That's good." Sadie briskly dusted her hands, but then she drooped. "I don't think I can keep this up, Betsie."

Betsie laid a comforting hand on her sister's arm. "Let's go wash up and eat supper. Then after we finish chores, we will write that letter we talked about. Oh, I am hungry."

To Betsie's surprise, she did feel better after she'd eaten. Sadie perked up, too. At least the thought of writing the letter didn't fill them with dread.

"It's a blessing Lovina was so exhausted, that's what," Betsie said when they climbed the stairs at last.

Sadie carried letter paper and a pen. The girls tiptoed past Lovina's room and hurried to huddle on Betsie's bed. The curtains at the window rippled in the breeze in a way that augured more rain later.

"What if *Dat* says they have decided for good to follow Jesus, as he puts it?" Sadie's eyes filled with tears. "What if they never return to the church?"

Betsie's heart was troubled as she contemplated a future without her parents. That picture was gloomy enough, but to have them barred from heaven permanently because they left the church was even worse. Their only hope: confess their sin and return to the fold, but even then it wasn't a foregone conclusion where *Mem* and *Dat*, or indeed any of them, would land. Slim comfort it was to think that if she stuck to her Amish roots, *maybe* she could go to heaven someday. And oh, the long weary road full of trouble that stretched ahead before she reached her uncertain final destination.

The ache in her heart dulled as she imagined a more positive scenario between now and the day she died—a sweet life with Charley as they worked side by side to provide for the dear children they would raise in the Amish faith. Yes, asking her to ride home from the singing with him was a fine start.

She closed her eyes and pictured it all: arriving with Sadie in a bustle of anticipation, exchanging knowing looks with Charley across the room as she sang along with Rachel, the quick, exciting tempo of the songs and the sweet soaring voices, the joking and the laughter as she and Charley shared a piece of raisin pie, the thrill of leaving friends behind and riding home together on a soft spring night, and then . . .

A pang shot through her. Had not her parents once had thoughts like these? She and Sadie and the other siblings, such a good childhood they'd had! No matter the task, be it churning butter, whitewashing the barn walls, or fishing in the creek for supper, it was good, for the family shared the work. Every day ended with some sweet treat that *Mem* had baked. The children stretched out in front of the fire to munch happily as *Dat* read from the great leather *Biewel*, his rumbly bear voice strong and sure as he shared the Truth. How could our parents leave that all behind?

Anger sparked. What right had Pastor Shock and his brother to lead *Dat* and *Mem* astray? How Betsie yearned for five minutes to set straight those wicked men, the ones who had ruined her sweet home life forever.

"They have to come back." Her voice was flat. "It's up to us to show our parents where they have erred so we can lead them back to Plain City."

Sadie's clasped her hands. "*Jah*, you're right. We must try."

Determined though they were, the task ahead was daunting. How in the world could two girls tell their parents what they should do? Parents were to be obeyed, not admonished. Betsie's heart ached, but her duty was clear.

She grasped the pen. "Dear *Dat* and *Mem* . . ."

CHAPTER 26

"Tom," whispered Huckleberry, "does this keep us from
ever telling—always?"
"Of course it does. It don't make any difference what
happens, we got to keep mum."
—QUOTATION FROM TOM SAWYER RECORDED IN
BETSIE'S JOURNAL

"BETSIE! *DUMMEL DICH!*"

"I *am* hurrying. Don't be so lippy."

Goodness, but both of them were grouchy this morning after their
late night. Betsie was in no mood for a Sunday of visiting, but the sisters had decided that to stay home would only invite suspicion. Sadie
had a long mental list of people who had invited her to drop up and
visit when they saw her working at Yoder's bakery. A good night's rest
worked wonders for Lovina, but she said she had decided to stay with
her ill friend, Miriam Bontrager, once more instead of visiting.

"If you girls don't need me, that is." Lovina hesitated.

Betsie exchanged glances with Sadie. "What's the matter, Lovina? If
you're not feeling well, maybe you should go with us."

Lovina leveled a look at them. "It's time to tell me the truth, girls.
Noah has left the church and he's taken Fannie with him. Ain't so?"

Sadie turned whiter than pretzel dough. Betsie groped behind her
for a kitchen chair and collapsed into it.

"Then I'm right. I may not have such good ears, but I know the sound of crying yet, and crying was not all I heard. My window was open and so was yours." Lovina draped one arm over Betsie's shoulders and the other over Sadie's. "It was a good idea to write a letter, but after Miriam recovers, I will take the train to visit my brother and bring him and Fannie home. We'll see then what an old lady can still do."

"Oh, Lovina!" Sadie burst into tears. "It's so hard!"

Betsie's eyes were moist as she regarded her aunt with affection. "How good you are. I can't think of anyone better to go to *Dat*. He will listen to you, I know it." She held up a finger. "I have a couple of concerns. First, you must take care that you don't overtire yourself. And second, we must tell no one what has happened, no matter what they say. Sadie, this goes for you and me, too. If we can manage to bring *Mem* and *Dat* back here without letting anyone know what they did, no one need be the wiser. You know they would be viewed with suspicion if everyone knew they left and then came back. People would wonder when they were going to try again. So let's agree to keep quiet, and soon enough we'll all be together again, ain't so?"

"Brace up, Betsie." Lovina gave her a shake. "We have the truth on our side, and it will all work out. Now we'd best be going. Miriam needs me."

"I hope she will remember," Betsie worried a few minutes later as she watched Lovina circumnavigate the mud puddles on Miriam's front walk. Why hadn't she recalled that Miriam lived next to Yoder's bakery? She shivered.

"I hope *I* remember." Dark circles shadowed Sadie's eyes. "*Ach*, Betsie, your hands, so *dreckich!* Didn't you wash up this morning?"

Betsie wiped them on the underside of her apron. "It's just horse hair, anyway," she said. "We have a much bigger problem, ain't so?"

"*Jah, jah!* But as *Mem* always says, what we don't know for certain, we shouldn't repeat. That will get us through this ordeal, Betsie."

The buggy wheels hummed on the wet road. "What do you mean?"

"I mean you don't know Mattie Yoder like I do. Trust me, she will ask something awkward when we see her later." Sadie sniffed. "If she weren't Charley's mother—" Sadie checked herself and blushed redder than a geranium. "It's awful to work with Mattie, but she isn't so . . . *Mattie* with Charley around, that's all."

Betsie sobered. She imagined Mattie as her future *Mem*-in-law, telling Betsie she must learn to cook better for Charley, and Betsie with her head bowed, saying, "Yes, Mattie . . ."

No. Like as not, she and Mattie Yoder would grow to be good friends. That is, if she doesn't disown my family for leaving the Amish.

Betsie had done plenty of musing on the situation before she finally slept last night. Scenes of the bishop announcing the *Meidung* had tormented her dreams, with the People in church watching as they wondered, "*Was in der welt?* What's gotten into Noah Troyer that he should turn his back on the good Lord?"

"Betsie! You're passing Sol Beiler's!" Sadie started to saw at the reins, but trustworthy Judith trotted into the drive of her own accord.

Never was there a better cure for trouble than to hold that downy baby boy of Ellie Miller's, Betsie thought. Oh, what a sweet bundle! She nuzzled his neck and smiled as he cooed. How *gut* that he was well, with not even a croupy rattle in his little lungs. She dropped a fond kiss on the top of his head.

A foolish grin softened his mother's features. "Oh, Betsie, he likes you! It's not everyone little Jakob will tolerate."

Sol chimed in. "What do you hear from your folks, Betsie? Coming home soon? It would have been nice to see them today." He rubbed the back of his neck. "Never was a doctoring woman better than Fannie, and I got a crick something awful. Must have slept wrong on it."

"Oh, Sol, you and your neck," Ellie scolded. "I'd rather hear about Noah and Fannie."

Betsie thought fast. "Tsk, tsk, Sol, maybe I can help. Here, Sadie, will you hold Jakob?" She passed the sleeping baby to her sister. "Here, now, stick out your arms," Betsie instructed. "That's right, straight out from your shoulders. Now which side does it hurt on, this one?" She poked his neck.

"Ow, not so rough! *Jah*, that's it."

"As I suspected, it's a little twisted there, maybe."

Sol pulled a mournful face and gazed at his wife. "Is that so?"

Ellie tossed her head.

"Sol, look this way, now. Turn your head as far as you can toward the hurting side." Gently Betsie nudged his chin in that direction.

"Ow, that smarts!"

Betsie ignored him. "Now slowly nod your head up and down, that's right."

"Maybe now I should ask for that new rocking chair, Sol. You are already saying yes." Ellie simpered.

"Have some respect, *Frau*," Sol grunted, nodding all the while. "I am in pain."

"If you do this a few times each day, the pain will be less," Betsie encouraged. "Stop, now. How does it feel?"

Sol flexed carefully. "Do you know, Betsie, it does feel some better. How about that, now?" He beamed at his wife.

"Come, Betsie, we have many friends to visit," Sadie reminded. She handed Jakob back to Ellie. "We must be going now."

The Beilers followed them to the porch. Sol flexed his neck as Ellie waved baby Jakob's chubby hand in a good-bye.

"Already they are asking about *Mem* and *Dat*." Sadie barely moved her lips.

"I did my best to steer the talk another way," Betsie murmured with a nod and a wave.

Betsie encouraged Judith to step up her pace. Come noon, the English would zoom from their church parking lots all at once, and Route 42 would be dangerous indeed. Betsie breathed a grateful sigh when Judith pulled into Rachel Yutzy's drive. A few cockerels scratched near the barn, iridescent black feathers overlaid with bronze. Betsie spied Abijah's friend Levi hiding around the corner of the barn with a slingshot, aiming at the biggest rooster. She'd have to warn Rachel about her little brother.

Rachel's mother had prettied the yard with a rainbow of flower beds that ringed the vegetable garden to one side of the white, salt-box house. The riot of colors on a warm *Moi* morning lifted Betsie's heart.

"I hope no one asks us about *Mem* and *Dat*. There's a lot of buggies here."

Betsie shrugged, determined to be cheerful. "Never too many visitors to suit Rachel." She stretched to pull down a cluster of early honey-locust blossoms and inhaled the sweet perfume before she released the branch. Last night's raindrops sprinkled her upturned face as the branch whipped into place.

"Betsie, you're here!"

"Rachel!" It was near impossible to contain her joy. Here was one person who would always be true, no matter what trouble Betsie's family caused. "I have missed you!" She held her friend at arm's length. "You're twice as smiley as last time I saw you."

"*Ach*, I've missed you, too! It goes well with you at the harness shop, I hope?" She examined Betsie as she drew her into the house, Sadie trailing behind. "Dark smudges under your eyes. There is trouble?"

"No, Rachel, I . . . I'm fine." She made a general greeting, overwhelmed to see so many friends in one place, and hoped Rachel didn't notice her hesitation.

A scratchy voice grated from the crowd. "You are so thin, Betsie. Who cooks for you at the English house?"

She flinched. "Mattie Yoder, I didn't see you lurk—standing there by the stairs. I am doing the cooking for the family."

"Never you mind, Betsie. One day maybe you will cook well enough to fill out some." Mattie leaned against the wall, almost insolent.

Betsie's gaze grew fixed, but she decided not to let Mattie Yoder spoil her happiness.

"Betsie!" Rachel tugged insistently at her sleeve and hauled Betsie upstairs to her room, where she deposited her on the neat bed.

"*Ach*, what's got into you? You nearly pulled my arm off!"

Rachel's cheeks glowed with excitement. "I must warn you that Mattie Yoder has been telling *Mem* such terrible untrue things about you."

"What has she been saying? Tell me."

"I tried to stop her, Betsie, but her tongue sparks worse than a bonfire at the edge of a dry weedy field." Rachel smoothed her apron.

"Rachel! Please tell me what Mattie says."

"It doesn't matter to me *what* she says, because I know it can't be true." Loyal Rachel polished her steamy spectacles on an apron corner and plunged ahead eagerly. "But if you must know, she told everyone you were keeping company with an English boy who looks like a girl. She said you rode up front in his car." She held up a solemn finger. "Alone."

Here it was again, the same report Betsie had heard from her sister and from Mattie herself. She did some quick figuring. The lesser of two evils by far was to allow Mattie Yoder to spread gossip about her and Michael. Objecting would only fuel the fire and set her digging for some other dirt, and it wouldn't be long before she discovered that *Mem* and *Dat* had left.

Rachel eyed Betsie with interest and primed the pump some more. "But I told her you would *never*—"

Betsie put a finger to Rachel's lips and nodded.

Rachel's gray eyes rounded. She pulled Betsie's hand down. "It's true, then?" she whispered.

"Please don't tell anyone, Rachel. Yes, partly true. But Michael—" Betsie swallowed the painful lump in her throat. Michael had been so animated and kind that day when he took her to Indian Run Falls, compared with how he was when she told the police about the attack— *ach*, if Rachel ever knew the half of what she was really thinking about!

She steadied herself. "Michael took me to buy some ice cream because I was feeling bad about a mistake I made. Listen and I'll tell you about the car ride."

For the next fifteen minutes, Rachel proved insatiable, her mouth dropping open when Betsie described what it was like to pass Charley Yoder and his team at forty dizzying miles per hour. Only after Betsie begged for a drink of water did Rachel relent and head for her door.

"Best be careful with that English boy, Betsie. You have gotten so wild," she warned as they exited.

A nervous laugh bubbled up inside Betsie. *Ach*, how Rachel's *blabbermaul* did carry! She darted around the corner to the stairs, where she bumped smack into the back of Mattie Yoder.

CHAPTER 27

"You can't run away from your troubles."

—FANNIE TROYER, QUOTED IN BETSIE'S JOURNAL

BETSIE WILLED HERSELF to stay calm. "Are you all right, Mattie?"

"Don't you worry about me, Betsie. With that fast English boy around, you'd best be lookin' out for yourself, ain't so?" Mattie's mouth curved, but it did not much resemble a smile. She did not explain her presence but descended the stairs.

The sound of an approaching horse and buggy broke into Betsie's frenzied thoughts. She forced herself to follow Rachel to the porch to greet the bishop, Jonas Gingerich, and his family as they arrived.

Her mind roved to a time when she was seven years old. She'd carried a smooth pebble to the old well at her grandparents' house. Of course, *Mem* and *Dat* always warned her to keep away from the dangerous well house. She was never to climb the steps, lower the bucket, or worst of all, to lean over to see the water. At least she didn't lower the bucket that time, but she did climb the steps to look down, down, down. With her thumb and forefinger she flipped the stone and watched the dark, smooth circle of water far below until she heard the sepulchral *plunk* that had resulted in wavering ripples.

Her stomach *plunked* as Rachel welcomed Jonas and his family. Paralyzed, she watched Mattie dislodge herself from her corner by the stairs to neatly intercept Jonas and command his attention.

"I must find Sadie." Betsie backed up rapidly and rammed into a wall. Rachel started to ask a question, but Betsie tore away to find her sister talking to friends in the kitchen.

"Wh-what's the matter, Betsie?" she sputtered as Betsie grabbed her sleeve and guided her through the screen door.

"Mattie Yoder, that's what. She is talking with the bishop right now."

Sadie gave Betsie a lofty smile and lowered her voice to whisper, "What did I tell you? But she can't possibly know about . . . you know."

"She knows enough," Betsie hissed. "Don't forget, she's spreading the story of my car ride far and wide. That's better than gossiping about *Mem* and *Dat*, I know, but I'd rather not discuss my job with Jonas when we have so much else on our plates. Besides, don't you think he's liable to ask us about *Mem* and *Dat*?"

Sadie blinked. "That's so."

"Who knows if Lovina talked to Mattie this morning? But I know this: she was *next door*. All Mattie had to do was drop up to ask how Miriam was doing, a perfectly natural question. I don't know what we were thinking; it's like setting a cat to guard the goldfish bowl. We must pick up Lovina in a jiffy and find out. Come, we've been outside long enough. Mattie may miss us, and we don't need her to be any more suspicious than she already is."

Betsie held the door for Sadie, and they strolled casually into the front room. From this vantage point, they faced Jonas; he took on a glazed, patient look as he listened to Mattie's incessant yammering. Served him right; he should have taken Mattie to task ages ago about her gossip and the trouble she caused.

"Looks all right. Let that teach us not to let our imagination run away with us," Sadie said. "Surely, the good Lord, in His mercy, will not let Lovina reveal what *Mem* and *Dat* have done. She will deliver our letter on Monday as we discussed, and then she will persuade them to see the light, and we will be reunited very soon. Mattie is here and Lovina is not. Let's allow our aunt to minister to Miriam and pick her up later as we planned. Now I am going back to see my friends, so try to enjoy yourself."

Could Sadie be right? Betsie trudged through the rest of the visits like she had a forty-pound sack of grain over her shoulders. When they finally did leave to pick up Lovina, another shock awaited. They found the house locked up tight with a note pinned to the front door to say that Miriam had taken a turn for the worse and Lovina had accompanied the Bontragers to the local clinic.

"Now we may not find out whether Lovina talked to Mattie until tomorrow morning." Betsie chewed the inside of her cheek.

"*Ach*, Betsie! Don't be such a worrywart always!"

Betsie wished she could be as sure as Sadie. She spent the remainder of the drive praying that the good Lord would keep Mattie from discovering the truth about her parents.

At length she sighed. "You're right, Sadie. I will check with Lovina in the morning, and I'm sure everything will turn out for the best." Betsie smiled at her sister.

But Sadie vacillated. "That's what *Dat* always says, and you know how he ended up."

All through breakfast the next morning, Betsie eyed Lovina. When it was time to hitch up, she took a deep breath. "You are so good to take care of Miriam. I wish we could have helped, but maybe some of the neighbors dropped up, ain't so?"

Lovina sighed. "Well, I'm awful tired, but I've known Miriam since we were girls, so I was happy to help out. A couple of the neighbors spelled me when I needed a rest, so don't worry your head about me." She sipped her tea.

"Well, that was nice of the neighbors." Betsie exchanged glances with Sadie. "Tell me, did Mattie Yoder stop by?"

"Now, Betsie." Lovina wagged her head. "I didn't say anything about your *mem* and *dat*, if that's what you're worried about. I have to say Mattie was awful curious to know why they were gone before I got here."

"What did you say?" Betsie held her breath.

"I said I wondered the same thing myself, and I'd ask when I visited them in Belle Center. Now stop worrying."

An uneasy flutter tickled Betsie's stomach. She wished Lovina hadn't tried to be so arch with Mattie. Nothing would intrigue that woman more. "Well, I'm glad your friend is doing better. Hurry back to us, Lovina. We will miss you."

"You'll see! When I return, I'll have your parents with me." Lovina patted her cheek fondly and bustled to help Sadie with the dishes.

Betsie watched them for a moment, sorry that she'd suspected a good-hearted soul like Lovina of divulging their secret. Betsie made up her mind to trust that the good Lord had answered her prayers.

"I'll see to the buggy. Come on out, you and Sadie, when you are ready to leave for the train."

Judith nosed Betsie's pocket for the apple she smelled, and her head bobbed as she crunched the treat. Already the sun beat down on Betsie's black bonnet. Sweat dampened her back as she surveyed the drooping garden while Amelia scampered down the rows, overjoyed to be an outside Amish cat. She pinned a note for Charley to the barn door, asking him to please feed the cat while she was gone. Likely Sadie, a good nurse, would be asked to stay at Miriam Bontrager's this week until poor Miriam was up and around again. It lifted another burden from Betsie; Sadie wouldn't be alone after Lovina left.

Judith snorted at Amelia as Betsie worked the pump handle and drew a bucket of water. As she doled it out amongst the thirsty plants, she wondered whether Michael would behave better than he had last Friday.

Sadie and Lovina, somewhat subdued, appeared on the long front porch, usually so cool and inviting. Today, though the sun was barely up, the temperature promised to be hotter than an oven, and Lovina was already wilting. Betsie hurried to tend to Judith while they climbed in the buggy.

"I have your letter with me, Betsie." Lovina waved the envelope. "And don't worry, I will ask my *Schnickelfritz* of a brother what he means by keeping me down here so I won't know what he's done." She shook her fist in mock anger.

Betsie and Sadie had been solemn as they remembered another

departure, but they burst into genuine laughter at their aunt's gesture. Betsie waved good-bye; it was a merry beginning to the morning.

To keep herself from sad thoughts, Betsie finished watering and pulled a few weeds until even that effort was too much in the heat. She dampened her hanky and cooled her face. With one ear tuned for the rumble of the Super Bee's motor, she pumped the bucket full again, pushed her sleeves high, and drank from cupped hands. Refreshed, Betsie slowly made her way to the thin shade by the pasture. Michael had never been this late before.

She bit her lip. All weekend, her troubles had pushed aside thoughts of Michael and his problems. Maybe he had an accident on the way here. Maybe he's . . . dead.

"No!" Betsie startled a squirrel with her outburst.

At that moment, Michael's yellow car roared into view. She dusted her hands and walked to meet him.

"Let's go," he said.

Betsie got in, stowed her satchel, and rolled down the window. Unless she missed her guess, Michael had tumbled out of bed and headed straight for the car. His hair was all *stroobly*, and his shirt was wrinkled. He did not say another word. Betsie wished Charley could see them together so he would know how wrong he was to be jealous.

She scrutinized every roadside weed and speck of litter between Plain City and Hilliard. Her spirits rose when she thought of the work that waited, until she remembered that Michael would have to show her how to do most of it. The day promised to be difficult, like every day lately.

When they headed east into Hilliard, the morning sun shone in her eyes like a beacon. Betsie squinted to block the glare, glad that the road was nearly deserted.

As the car crested a hill, Betsie savored the exciting feeling of flying before they descended. She enjoyed this hilly part of the drive, though the ups and downs made it difficult to see.

They bumped across the railroad tracks and up another hill. Sure enough, she glimpsed the red taillights of the postman's truck where it was stopped up ahead. Betsie didn't mind waiting, but impatience marked this new, silent Michael, just as it marked all the rest of the hurry-up English. He craned his neck, though she doubted he could see around the postman. Besides, even Betsie knew that the double yellow line painted on the road meant no passing.

Michael tromped on the gas anyway. The Super Bee thrust Betsie back as it rocketed forward.

Crack! A gunshot shattered the silence. The report shocked Betsie, but it completely unhinged Michael. He dodged and windmilled the steering wheel, slewing the tires hard left.

A large bulk blocked the rising sun's rays—clouds? The car narrowly missed the mail truck, but to her horror, Betsie saw that the shadow was from a semitruck that topped the rise just ahead. Michael blasted his horn frantically as the immense truck barreled toward them.

Betsie shut her eyes. She felt the car veer in a long swoop, as though strong hands shoved it out of danger. Her head hit something hard, and bright sunlight momentarily reddened her eyelids. The insistent blare of the horn changed tone, and she realized with gratitude that the truck was behind them and they were still alive.

The first thing she saw when she opened her eyes were the flashing lights from the mail truck ahead. Then she saw the postman as he emerged from a swirl of dust, headed at a dead run for the Super Bee. The postman's blue shirt and eagle patch were all Betsie saw as he hammered on the glass.

"You okay in there?"

No. Even blinking hurt, and there was something about the arch of blue sky that puzzled her. Where had the sun gone?

"Miss, are you all right?"

"*Jah, ferhoodled* a bit is all."

"Better help your friend, then. He's pretty shaken up. That semi missed you by no more'n a gnat's whisker. Worst blowout I ever did see; sounded like a rifle. Blown tire spun you clear around to face the other way. The Man Upstairs sure was watching out for you, that's all I got to say." He shot a glance behind him. "Not safe to stay here on this hill. Want me to help you get the car out of the road?"

THE BARGAIN

Betsie glanced at Michael; his face was ashen. He spouted nonsense that sounded like "This I know, this I know, this I know."

"Michael." She shook his arm. "You are safe."

He panicked, fought her like he was going down for the last time. "This . . . I . . . know." He gulped air and struggled. His damp shirt squeaked against the seat.

"Michael, it was the car—the tire. We are okay, Michael!"

His lips moved. ". . . shot at me," he mumbled.

"No, Michael. No gun."

His pupils were huge, unfocused. His labored breath slowed, but suddenly he shivered.

"Miss? I think he's in shock."

It was good to seize a practical way to help. She rifled through her satchel for the granny-square afghan she'd packed to ward off the chill in her air-conditioned room. When she draped it around Michael's shoulders, he closed his eyes and rested his head against the seat.

"I think I can help you move the car now," Betsie murmured, her eyes on Michael. "We need to move it over there." She motioned to the Sullivan's driveway.

The postman put her in position. Then he stood on Michael's side of the car, one hand on the wheel and one on the frame of the open window. Betsie pushed from the other side. With their encouragement, Michael moved the lever of the still-running car to what the postman called "neutral." Working together, Betsie and the postman rolled the car the few feet into the drive of the Sullivans' house, in full view of the neighbor ladies and children, who watched the show from their windows. Betsie thanked the postman profusely.

"Not a problem. Say, your friend hasn't been in the military, has he?" The man glanced into the car. "I guess not, with that hair."

"No." Betsie hesitated, aware that Michael was listening now. She smiled and stretched through her window to turn the radio on, dialing it to WHOA. Music filled the air, and Michael relaxed.

"He's just"—she searched for the proper hunting term—"gun-shy, I guess."

The postman jabbed his glasses snug to the bridge of his sweaty

195

nose. "Say no more. I was stationed in Korea, and I had a buddy who was what they call shell-shocked. He acted the same way whenever he heard a sharp noise. Poor guy had a rough time of it until he finally . . . uh, forget it." He looked shaken.

"Until he what?" Betsie pressed.

He glanced at Michael, who had upped the radio until the music blared. "My buddy got so he couldn't stand it." He swiped his finger across his throat. "Sat down on the train tracks one night. Never stood a chance."

Betsie gasped, frozen with fear. "What if Michael—"

"Don't think about that right now. If I were in your shoes, I'd get him to a doctor right away." He glanced at Michael. "But even before that? I'd pray."

Once Betsie finally coaxed Michael out of the crippled car, she decided to keep him in sight while she worked. The short walk to the shop wore him out, so she parked him in the webbed chair until she arranged the saddle and the horse blanket between the back window and the counter. She propped open the window.

"Michael? Why don't you stretch out and rest some?"

He trailed toward her like his arms and legs were too heavy. When he was reasonably comfortable, she spread her afghan to keep him warm. Almost before she walked away, he was asleep.

Betsie picked at a curl of dried skin on her lip. Difficult as using the phone would be, should she try to call Mr. Sullivan at work and let him know what had happened? He'd been so angry when Michael didn't call anyone after she was attacked. Or what about calling a doctor, as the postman had advised?

At length she decided that, as he was sleeping so well, she would wait. She smiled at his peaceful face. If only it could always be so.

Pray, the postman had said. She knew the English were prideful enough to think that the good Lord listened to their prayers like some servant in the sky. But the very idea of speaking to God like that was *hochmut* beyond belief. Betsie glanced at Michael one more time, then picked up the harness book and immersed herself in work, tacking together odd pieces of leather for practice. As soon as she mastered one stitch, she moved on to the next. The simple tasks restored a sense of peace that she hadn't known all weekend.

As first the morning and then the afternoon wore on, Betsie's stomach grumbled. She stretched and did her neck exercises before she darted a glance at Michael, who was still sound asleep. Sheila would be home before too long, and maybe she could fetch a snack then.

Betsie's stomach growled again, making up her mind for her. She silenced the clapper of the jangly bell with a wadded-up rag, but now she was faced with a new worry. What if the Hilliard Stalker was out there? She searched the shop and came up with the long, stout hickory stick with the nail head in one end that Mr. Sullivan's grandfather had fashioned to coax bridles from the hooks overhead. She hefted it and scouted the yard before stepping outside. Quickly she retrieved her satchel from the car and stashed it in her room.

Soon she returned to the shop, the stick still in one hand. With the other she balanced a cookie sheet weighted down with a stack of thick, peanut-butter-spread sandwiches and two cold glasses of milk, just in case Michael woke up hungry, too. She managed to set the improvised tray down without making a sound and then peeked over the counter.

Michael was gone.

CHAPTER 28

Sometimes I think the whole world has
turned upside down.
—BETSIE'S JOURNAL

IT TOOK LESS than two minutes to search the tiny shop. No Michael. Betsie's first thought was that Benner had indeed returned, but she pushed that nauseating possibility aside. Michael had helped her when she needed it most, and now she must help him. She steeled herself and tried to think.

The train whistle hooted. Instantly the postman's warning popped into her mind and conjured horrible images of Michael sitting on the railroad tracks as the afternoon train bore down on him. Betsie bolted for the tracks, her soul filled with an unspoken prayer.

Sunshine blazed, and the day was as still as a cemetery. Sheila's bus lumbered up the hill and screeched to a stop at the end of the drive, not far from the disabled Super Bee. From the corner of her eye, Betsie spotted Michael's bare legs sprawled lifelessly near the back of his car. She changed direction and raced to intercept Sheila before she saw her brother, but it was too late.

"Hi, Betsie! Hi, Mike!"

They reached him at the same time, Betsie with tears flowing. Michael's head and most of his shoulders were stuck under the car near the shredded rear tire.

"*Ach*, Sheila, dear heart . . ."

The bare legs twitched and a muffled voice said, "Hey, Squirt, can you hand me the jack? It's by my foot. Gotta get this tire off and put on the spare."

Sheila rushed to help, leaving Betsie standing at the front of the car, hand over heaving chest.

"Oh, wow, it's heavy! Here you go, Mike." The metal clanked.

"Thanks." Michael rolled out from under the car and put the lever in place. While he cranked the car higher, Sheila chattered a mile a minute about the approaching last-day-of-school party.

Had the accident and Michael's distress even happened? Betsie wiped her eyes and blew her nose.

"Gosh, Betsie, what's wrong?" Sheila chirped.

Michael looked at her then. "Uh, I'll handle this, Squirt. Hey, about this morning," he began. He eyed Betsie's damp cheeks and reddened. "Sorry I weirded out on you, man. We cool?"

"Don't worry about me." Betsie sniffed as she tweaked Sheila's ponytail. "As for you, Sheila dear, I made some sandwiches with that peanut butter spread you like. Come along, let's eat them in the shop."

"Goody, I'm starved!"

"Oh, you." Betsie squeezed her affectionately. "You are always starved. I bet you ate a candy bar on the bus."

"Nuh-uh!" she flashed, but her face fell. "Betsie? I didn't have a candy bar, but Debbie gave me a cookie and I ate it on the bus." She licked golden crumbs from the corner of her mouth.

Betsie threw back her head and laughed. She held the door for Sheila and snuck a glance at Michael. He rested his elbows on his knees as he gazed after them. Their eyes met; he immediately looked away and fiddled with the tire iron.

Betsie followed Sheila. "Bring those stools here for us, would you?"

"Sure."

The wooden legs screeched on the plywood. Betsie flinched before remembering that Michael didn't need her to keep the shop quiet for him any longer. She swigged milk and swallowed a bite of sandwich that was far too big.

"Betsie?"

"Mm?"

Sheila twisted the stray hairs that forever escaped her ponytail. "Do you notice anything different? About me, I mean?"

Sheila's heart face glowed with a secret.

"You have a new freckle, maybe?" Betsie teased.

A bit of the light dimmed. "No, it's something better."

Back to the plate went Betsie's sandwich as she scrutinized Sheila. Her hair, was it shorter? English ladies were forever visiting the beauty parlor to have their hair trimmed or cut for outrageous prices. Betsie's own hair had never been cut, save for the time she fell asleep with pilfered taffy in her mouth. Next morning, *Mem* cut the sticky mess out of her hair. "You see? No good ever comes of snitching sweets," she'd admonished. Oh, how glad Betsie had been to hide her shorn guilty head beneath her *Kapp*.

She grasped Sheila's chin to swivel her neck from side to side. The point of her thick ponytail brushed the middle of her back, as always.

Betsie pondered. Whenever Abijah said, "Guess what, Betsie?" she knew he didn't really want her to guess right. She said, "I give up, Squirt."

"Hey, don't call me that!" Sheila pretended to be annoyed, but then she grew solemn. "Maybe it's not fair to ask if you noticed when it's something on the inside, but I thought since you go to church and all, you might be able to tell. Like, didn't it remind you of anything when I admitted I really *did* have a cookie on the way home?"

Betsie frowned and spread her fingers.

Sheila took a deep breath. "That's okay. I got saved." Her smile widened like it was good news, the best news in the world. Gradually Betsie realized she was supposed to feel happy for her and pasted on a smile.

"Saved from what?"

Sheila giggled. "I went to church with my friend Debbie last night, and I got, you know, saved. Like 'Jesus loves me, this I know,'" she sang. "It means Jesus died for my sins but came back to life at Easter, you know? And now I'm going to heaven to live with Him when I die someday. For sure. You're saved, right, Betsie?"

Outside a squirrel scolded and a faraway dog barked. Sheila watched her with the beginnings of a question forming. "Some churches call it 'born again,'" she prompted.

The hair at the back of her neck stood up. Sheila was talking about the same belief that *Dat* and *Mem* now had. "We don't say that at mine." Betsie gulped milk and wished Sheila would drop the subject.

Sheila put down her sandwich and wiped her fingers carefully on her napkin, earnestly considering what Betsie said. "You mean you call it something different from 'saved' or 'born again'?"

Betsie's swallow of milk stopped halfway down. Milk spattered her apron as she coughed and strangled. Sheila slid from her stool and whacked her on the back.

"I guess my church teaches it different than *yourn, jah.*" Betsie dabbed tears.

Sheila's palm stopped in mid-whack. "Like what? I don't get it."

Betsie squirmed. With all her heart she wished to rejoice with her dear friend, to celebrate what obviously meant so much to her, but she could not. It was proud to believe you were saved.

How many times had she been warned not to try to win the English over to the Amish church, or even to share her beliefs? As *she* was raised, so *she* was to remain. That's what *Mem* always said, anyway. What *Mem* would say now that she and *Dat* had left the church, Betsie wasn't so sure anymore. "*Ach*, my English is not good enough to explain, I guess. Best leave the matter be for now, ain't so?"

Sheila's brow puckered. "I'm sorry, Betsie. If Debbie were here, *she* could explain it so you could understand. She's been a Christian for a long time. I'm just starting out, but I'll get better at it. Wait, I know!" She unstrapped her book bag and fished for a book. "See? *Good News for Modern Man.* It's my own Bible. My Sunday school teacher gave it to me after I went up front to get saved."

Betsie didn't want to hurt Sheila's feelings, so she looked. The front showed a cartoon of newspapers from around the world. What did cartoons have to do with the Bible? Inside were odd stick drawings of people; Abijah could have drawn better ones. Images of *Dat*'s worn leather *Biewel* filled her mind. Poor Sheila.

"My Sunday school teacher, Mrs. Cripps, said if I read a little bit every day, Jesus will help me understand and do what He asks me to." She laid her hand on the Good News like she wanted to start reading it right away. "Anyway, I bet pretty soon I'll at least be able to talk to you about it without getting so mixed up. Sorry about that." She wrapped Betsie's middle in a hug. "I love you, Betsie!"

Betsie felt guilty. "*Ach*, I am just an old *Glutzkupp*, not very smart. It's not your fault. Don't trouble yourself."

Sheila drew back to look her full in the face. "But, Betsie, I want you to understand when I talk about Jesus. Don't worry, I'll learn. I'm going to call Debbie right now."

She stiff-armed the screen door and darted outside, ponytail flying.

Betsie removed the wadded-up rag from the bell and nibbled a hangnail until Sheila got safely to the house. No matter that she had hemmed and hawed. Somehow Sheila had seen clean through Betsie's charade. She was pretty sure Sheila knew that *saved* was the last thing Betsie could ever be.

CHAPTER 29

Be careful what you pray for . . .
——BETSIE'S JOURNAL

WHEN BETSIE HEARD a car rumble a few minutes later, she was not really surprised that Michael had left again. Rarely was he home at the same time as his father. Her idea of serving a family meal, one where she and all three remaining Sullivans would sit and enjoy pleasant conversation, would take some doing.

She roamed the shop without lighting on any one task and finally justified shirking her duties with the idea of putting together a good supper for Sheila and her father. She checked the refrigerator, pleased to see that someone had taken her grocery list to Ayers. She decided a pie for dessert was just the thing. Even Sadie, baker extraordinaire, could not make flakier piecrust than Betsie's.

She cut lard into the flour and salt and concentrated on pushing anxious thoughts of Michael aside. With great energy, she rolled out the dough, alternating roll direction by the points of a compass. When the dough was wide enough, she flipped the round over a pie plate, which she had scavenged from the back of a cupboard. She slid the crust into the oven to brown and scalded milk for the vanilla custard. While the milk cooled, she browned ground beef, pushed it aside and sautéed chopped onions and bell peppers before adding a can of tomato soup and simmering the sloppy joe sauce. She doctored up a can of baked beans, too, and put them in the hot oven when the pie crust came out. While she worked, her smile returned.

As she sliced the bananas and arranged them prettily around the bottom of the pie crust, Betsie heard a car. It didn't sound like Michael's. Whoever it was had not pulled far enough forward to be visible from the kitchen. Hastily she poured the custard over the bananas to keep them from browning, covered the pie with an upside-down plate, and popped it into the refrigerator to chill. She hotfooted it to the front window, leaned over the television cabinet, brushed back the curtains, and peeped.

A faded blue car with holes rusted through the paint idled in the driveway. Thoughts of the Hilliard Stalker intruded, and in a panic, she bolted the front door. The windows of the car were rolled down a little. Betsie heard the driver, a lady, yell as she waved her arms and wiped her face with both hands. Probably some English lady who had stopped to bawl out her kids, Betsie thought disinterestedly.

As she started back to the kitchen, the car door crunched open in a shower of rust. Peggy emerged, dressed in her Ayers Market clothes. Betsie strained to see the passenger seat. Wonder of wonders, the other person in the car was Michael.

Though the air-conditioning was on in the house, Betsie eased the window open wide enough to catch what Peggy was saying.

"I *love* you. Don't you understand that, Michael? Of course you don't." She answered her own question bitterly. "Lately, you only come around when you need my help." She made an ugly face. "'Peg, my dad kicked me out. Can I crash here?' Or how about, 'Peg, my spare tire went flat. Can you give me a ride home?' Or, 'Peg, my number's about to come up—'" She swallowed her words as tears spilled. "But no matter what I do for you, you never show me any affection or even ask me how I'm doing. Well, I'm sick of it. Get out of my car. Out!"

Betsie couldn't tear herself away. She saw Peggy storm to Michael's half-open door. She grabbed him by his hair, hoisted him to his feet, and shoved. As he sprawled toward the house, Betsie ducked below the sill. She peeked again just as Peggy grabbed Michael's arm and spun him around to face her. Her voice rose.

"So that's it? I come running every time you call, and you pitch me aside?" Peggy's piled-up hair tilted askew. Her eyes were ringed with heavy black smudges of makeup. "What's the deal? Is there someone else, Michael? That's it, isn't it?"

Michael must have heard a noise by the harness shop, because his glance flicked that way before he scuffed the toe of his sandal. "Maybe."

Peggy threw up her hands and let them slap her thighs. "Well, that's just great. You're not even *sure*?"

It got so quiet that Betsie could almost hear Michael's mouse watch as it ticked off the seconds. "Can't you cut me some slack?" he finally said. "I mean, I'm dealing with some pretty heavy stuff right now, and I can't wrap my head around it all. I need some space."

"Un. Real. Well, I know who you're hung up over, even if you don't. News flash, Mr. Cub Reporter. Take this down." Peggy stuck her face right in his and thumped his chest with each word. "You are majorly messed up, and I am through with you."

"Peg." Michael grabbed her arm, but she jerked it away and strode to the car. "Peg, wait. Please don't leave like this."

"Too late, Michael."

The car door slammed and showered rust. Tires spun. The blue car lurched onto the road.

Michael watched Peggy go with a hangdog hunch to his back. He stuck his hands in his pockets and headed for the house.

The curtain fluttered as Betsie took giant steps to reach the kitchen before he came inside. She planned to ignore Michael, but though she casually stirred the sloppy joe mixture, he did not appear. In a way, she sympathized with Peggy; rarely did he do as expected.

Sheila's faraway voice rose and fell as she gabbed on the phone in Mr. Sullivan's room. "Oh, Deb!" Then more giggles and chatter. Betsie's heart remained soft enough to be grateful that Sheila had not heard Peggy giving her beloved brother what-for.

She got back to work and slid buttered hamburger buns into the oven to toast on a cookie sheet beside the baked beans. She dumped a bag of Sheila's favorite potato chips in a bowl and munched one. A picnic supper took shape with the addition of carrot and celery sticks.

Betsie rummaged in the refrigerator and found just enough leftover macaroni salad so they could each have a spoonful or two. And of course, there was the banana cream pie, soon to be smothered with whipped cream.

When Betsie nearly had beaten the whipping cream into stiff peaks, Mr. Sullivan got home. He waved to get her attention. Then his mouth moved, but the whir of the beaters drowned out his words. He pushed aside the curtains and slammed the window she'd left open. Betsie bit her lip. She knew she should have shooed Sheila off the phone, too. She'd already far exceeded the daily half-hour her dad allowed. Being the lady of the house was a complicated business.

Uneasiness disappeared as she mounded the whipped cream. In the nick of time she nipped a feeling of pride. Much better to dwell on how much money she saved Mr. Sullivan by making a pie at home instead of buying a frozen one at Ayers. Besides, she had once tasted a frozen pie, and it couldn't hold a candle to hers. She stashed it behind the wax milk carton and the ketchup in the refrigerator.

"Supper's ready!" Betsie washed her hands as Sheila followed her father to the table, a bit subdued, but she perked up quick when she saw the indoor picnic. Betsie ladled sloppy joe sauce on the toasted buns and passed the baked beans.

Mr. Sullivan unbent enough to smile. "What's the occasion?"

"Wanted to make a good meal, is all." Betsie humbly took her place and bowed her head to ask a silent blessing on the meal.

"Betsie? Why do you have dirty squares on the tip of your nose?" Sheila stared at her and smothered a smile.

With a guilty start, Betsie remembered the dusty window screen and tried to brush off the dirt. "Did I get it?"

Sheila inspected her and nodded. Then she said, "Dad, may I ask the blessing?" Hope shone in her eyes.

Mr. Sullivan nodded. Betsie shifted and bowed her head again. *Ach,* how embarrassing, to hear somebody pray aloud to the good Lord. But Sheila wasn't shy at all. She joined hands with them and began.

"Dear Lord, we thank You for our food. Take care of Mom and

please bring her home. God bless her and Dad and Betsie . . . and Michael."

Mr. Sullivan cleared his throat. "A—"

"And, dear Lord, please let Michael eat this good dinner with us. Amen."

"Amen." Mr. Sullivan shot his daughter a wry look, which she missed.

Sheila was certainly full of surprises. Betsie didn't recall mentioning that she wanted the family to eat together. She finished her quick, silent prayer to the good Lord, lest He should think she had forgotten the proper way to pray. Then everybody dug in.

Sheila and her dad chatted about church the night before. He seemed pleased that she had been "saved." "You take after your Grandma Sullivan," he said. "She was a Christian."

Sheila grew thoughtful. "I didn't know that. I wish I'd gotten to know her better." She munched a carrot stick and followed it with another bite of her sloppy joe. "But Brother Burchett said we have to decide on our own whether to follow Jesus. Betsie, everything is so good!"

The door opened. Betsie couldn't decide who was more surprised to see Michael—she or Mr. Sullivan. Even from so far away, she could see red rims to his eyes. He looked like a stray dog that had been kicked in the ribs.

Sheila patted the chair next to hers. "Hi, Mike! Betsie made us a picnic. Eat with us?"

If she hadn't spoken up, Michael would have passed them by, Betsie knew. He hesitated as his dad loaded a spoon with baked beans and chomped them. He sought Betsie's gaze, and her heart melted. She hurried to retrieve another plate from the cupboard, scooped a sandwich for him, and set a place between herself and Sheila. "I made plenty. Come and eat."

Michael shot a glance at Mr. Sullivan, who concentrated on his plate like someone might steal his food. He bypassed the kitchen and Betsie heard water running in the pink bathroom. The distinctive squeak of his closet door came next. When he sat down cross-legged on his chair opposite his dad, Michael was no longer bare-chested, sweaty, and *stroobly-Haar*. He wore a clean T-shirt, white except for sunburst splotches of blue, yellow, and green, like there had been a color accident in the washing machine. Betsie made a mental note to add bleach to the grocery list.

Sheila passed the bowls in a soothing way, as though Michael were a wild animal ready to bolt, but there was no need to fear. He liked Betsie's cooking. He sampled some of everything and accepted a second sandwich and another helping of baked beans.

The family meal was a lot more silent than Betsie had imagined, but at least they were all together. By his last bite of sloppy joe, Michael had more than made amends for his behavior of the past few days. *Maybe he's been hungry and tired, after all.* Betsie was pleased to see that every plate and serving bowl had been scraped clean.

"Keep cooking like this, Betsie, and I'll be at the table every night. Thanks." Michael patted his stomach and glanced warily at his dad. He half-rose.

"I always cook like this. *Ach*, but you are not having dessert? Suit yourself. That leaves more for us, Sheila, ain't so?"

Sheila smirked at her brother. "Yup. See ya, Mike."

"Who says I was leaving, Squirt? *I'm* doing the dishes for Betsie." He smirked back, and she laughed.

Betsie smiled with delight. Her plan was working. Father, brother, and sister, all eating together like a real family. She knew it was wrong, but her heart filled with pride.

Then Mr. Sullivan ruined it. "Well, I'll be. It's a miracle."

Betsie jumped. Sheila bowed her head.

"Okay, I'll bite," Michael said. "What do you mean?"

"When you do a chore without being asked, it's a bona fide miracle." Mr. Sullivan dabbed his mouth and threw his napkin on the table like a gauntlet.

CHAPTER 30

. . . because you just may get it.
—Betsie's journal

Betsie sprang from her chair. "The dishes can wait, Michael. We have my dessert yet to eat, and I need your help."

Michael regarded his father impassively. "All right," he said. He unfolded from his chair and sauntered past his dad. He winked at Sheila, whose lips trembled into a smile. He held the refrigerator door for Betsie while she retrieved the pie. His mouth dropped open when he saw it, and he rose to the occasion with flowery dessert plates, forks, and a pie server. When she reached for the server, he didn't let go. She tugged harder as she gave him a questioning glance.

"I'm sorry," he mouthed.

Shocked but mollified, she managed a tiny nod. Michael released the pie server and carried the plates and silverware to the table as if nothing had happened. Betsie followed with the pie, which she set down in the center of the table with a triumphant smile. She'd done it.

Mr. Sullivan let out a long whistle. "Say, Sheila, let's you and I clear the table and load the dishwasher, seeing as how Betsie has made such a spectacular-looking dessert for us." He followed words with deeds. Sheila's cheeks must have hurt from the wide smile she wore while they scraped the dishes and loaded them up together.

Betsie sat and admired her wonderful pie, even though she knew she should not be prideful about her baking. Michael set the plates around and started to cut the pie, but Betsie laid a hand on his arm. "Let's wait for your father and Sheila."

He shrugged and sat beside her. She caught him watching her in much the same way she'd watched him and Peggy earlier—sneaky—and a question popped into her head. "Michael, where is your car?"

He made a shushing motion with his hand and nodded toward his father, but it was too late.

"Let me guess," Mr. Sullivan said. "Impounded?"

Michael blew out a resigned breath and drummed his fingertips. "Sorry to disappoint you, Pops. I had a blowout today. I put on the spare, but it went flat, too, when I was near the market, so Peggy gave me a ride home. If you let me borrow your car, I'll get a patch and repair my tire."

"Where are you going to get the money for a patch kit, seeing as how you don't have that newspaper job you're always spouting off about?" Mr. Sullivan smiled grimly. "Here's an idea." He strolled to the coffee table, picked up the paper, and plopped it in front of Michael. "There you go. The only way you'll ever get a job with a newspaper is by reading the classifieds in one. If you're not going back to school, start looking."

Michael's face flamed, but a front-page photo arrested his attention; he stared at it so hard that Betsie forgot it was a graven image and looked, too. She saw English men in a suit and one English lady in a dress. Each of them soberly examined a large jar filled with capsules that looked like jelly beans. The lady had opened one of the jelly beans and handed the enclosed paper slip to a man who stood beside a board on the wall. That man stuck the paper slip, which had a date on it, next to the number 001. Above the picture in block letters were the words "The Draft."

Cousin Nelson had been drafted but allowed to serve in Chicago because of his religion, she recalled. It looked like many young men weren't so lucky, judging by all those capsules in the big jar. They were going to war.

Michael, pinched and green, made a retching sound like he was going to *vommix*. He gulped a couple of times and pushed the newspaper away. "It'll be difficult to get to work if I can't get my car fixed."

"Car? *No one* had his own car in my day. Getting to work by Shank's mare was good enough for us."

Betsie saw her chance. "Oh, did you have a mare, Mr. Sullivan? I have one; Judith is her name. What did you call yours?"

He ignored her and jabbed at Michael. "You think you know all about the English language. Explain that phrase to Betsie, wordsmith."

Michael, still pale, patted his calf. "Some people call this a shank, like the cut of meat," he said. "He means he walked to work uphill both ways, with his brother on his back."

"That's enough," Mr. Sullivan roared. He glared at his son.

"Who wants pie?" Betsie asked brightly. She nudged the pie plate to dead center on the table.

"I do," Mr. Sullivan said, his face almost purple. "I, for one, worked hard today, and I would love to have a piece of Betsie's delicious pie, because I know she worked hard, too." He surveyed the rest of them. "How about you, Sheila?"

"No, Dad. I'm not hungry anymore."

"Oh, that's a shame. Maybe you'll have room for a piece later. What kind of pie is it, Betsie?"

"Banana cream."

"My favorite!" Mr. Sullivan rubbed his hands together.

Betsie reached for the pie server but Michael beat her to it. "Allow me, sir, since you worked so hard today," he said, his voice husky. He cut the pie like an expert and chivvied a perfect, glistening wedge onto the plate without spilling a crumb. He balanced the plate on his thumb and forefinger and offered it to his father with a flourish.

Astonishment registered on Mr. Sullivan's face, but he quickly recovered his poise. "Now, that's more like it. Thank y—"

Michael whisked the plate out of reach. With a savage flick of his wrist, he winged the pie past his father's ear.

"*Ach*, my pie!" Betsie clapped her hands to her head.

She heard a gooey smack and crash as the plate shattered against the wall. Gobs of pie oozed down the drywall and puddled on the floor as broken crockery plunked.

Mr. Sullivan launched from his chair and knocked it over. Veins stood out in his forehead. "Out of my house!"

Michael licked banana cream from his fingers and smacked his lips. "Already gone."

"Mike! You don't have your car," Sheila sobbed.

He patted his hip. "Going Shank's mare. Catch you later, Squirt."

As he went out the door, Michael noticed Betsie's quiet tears and flinched. "Sorry, Pippa." And for the second time that day, he was gone.

CHAPTER 31

"My story has a moral; I have a missing friend—"
—EMILY DICKINSON, QUOTED IN BETSIE'S JOURNAL

THE LIGHT THE next morning had a late look when Betsie awoke. She rolled over to check the alarm clock and gasped.

"Sheila, honey." Betsie shook her. "You're going to miss the bus."

A groan issued from under the covers. "I don't want to go to school today. I don't feel good."

Outside, school bus brakes shrieked. The horn sounded once before the bus trundled past the house.

"It's too late now." Betsie patted a foot that stuck out. "Sleep a while. I'll check on you later."

"I love you, Betsie."

She dressed hurriedly and rushed to the shop, mindful of last night's disaster. With a stout tree limb in one hand, she opened the door, but the shop was empty. She snapped the lock and poked around. The funny thing was, she couldn't find her notebook. She'd left it in the cubbyhole under the cash register. She clawed beneath the countertop but came up empty. Dusting her hands, she frowned. She longed to be in Plain City, where belongings stayed put and nobody threw freshly baked pie. Before long, *Mem* and *Dat* would be back home, and already Charley waited with the promise of a ride home from the singing next Sunday.

She seized the broom and poked under the work tables to unearth the notebook, raising nothing except dust bunnies. She whacked her way around the shop and set dust motes dancing. A violent sneeze caused her to grab the counter for support. As Betsie blew her nose, she spotted her notebook lying open on the striped horse blanket.

Was in der welt? As Betsie stepped forward, she kicked the flashlight and the metal tube rolled. She picked it up and reached for the notebook, which lay open at her white poem, the one about the wash on the line and the flowers:

> White is the color of Queen Anne's Lace
> Newly spun
> White is the color of my love's clean shirts
> Drying in the sun
> White is the color of the fields
> Harvest has begun
> White is the color of my robe
> The battle won

As she read those last lines, she recalled where she'd heard something like them before. She could almost hear *Dat* as he read the *Biewel*: "These verses are in the book of Revelation. Oh, what a day that will be, *kinner!* Listen: 'And they cried with a loud voice, saying, "How long, O Lord, holy and true, dost thou not judge and avenge our blood on them that dwell on the earth?" And white robes were given unto every one of them; and it was said unto them, that they should rest yet for a little season . . .'"

Ever patient and kind, *Dat* translated the passage from the formal High German so his children could understand. Why these particular verses made him so happy, she couldn't tell, yet the beauty of the language had stayed with her, hidden deep in her heart. A white robe and a rest from all our hard work! It sounded *gut* indeed.

Yet her eye caught a difference on the notebook page, neat spare handwriting beneath her own. Someone had added lines to the poem, and she knew who. Michael had slept out here again.

She read the lines he'd added:

White is the color of a daisy
In the barrel of a gun

Betsie slapped the notebook shut. The postman's warning nudged. Something about Michael was not right. Fear nibbled at her thoughts, but how could she help her friend when she didn't know what was wrong? He wouldn't share his troubles. Peggy seemed the closest to figuring him out, but even she had given up and written Michael off.

Work. Honest, hard work—that's what she needed. She leafed through the order box and thumbed through several receipts, alphabetizing as she went. She chose the simplest repairs and was happy to make a dent in the orders. It was nearly time for lunch when she heard a rap on the door above the whirr of the stitching machine.

"Hi, Betsie." Sheila shaded her eyes. "Can I come in? I promise not to bother you. I just wanted to let you know I was up." There was a hopeful pause.

Betsie unlocked the door. "You are no bother. I know you can't be hungry, since you are ill. I will mix up some medicine to settle your stomach." She hid a smile.

Sheila gave her a sidelong glance. "Aw, I didn't really feel sick," she mumbled. "I'm sorry."

It came to Betsie that for the second time, Sheila had confessed after keeping the truth from her. It sounded to her as though being saved was quite a humbling experience. Truth be told, Sheila's new desire for honesty reminded Betsie of all the half truths she'd told to protect her parents. She shuddered and hoped God understood.

She patted Sheila's back. "*Ach*, I shouldn't tease you, dear heart. I don't feel so well myself, what with all the yelling last night." She finished her seam and snipped the strong, waxed thread. "Come, let's eat."

Sheila dragged Betsie to the door. She stopped by the webbed chair. "What's this?" She picked up a slim blue book. The cover spelled out what looked like a lady's name in fancy gold letters.

"Maybe a customer left it. Although I don't remember taking an order from"—Betsie deciphered the gold letters—"Emily Dickinson."

Sheila doubled over with laughter. Her glad laugh was good to hear, even though Betsie suspected it meant she had blundered somehow.

"Oh, Betsie! Emily Dickinson is a poet. She's Mike's favorite, and I bet that's his book. Open it up and see if his name's written in there."

Sure enough, Michael's signature graced the inside cover. Betsie turned the pretty book toward the light to admire it before handing it back to Sheila.

"Hey, there's something else written here. Oh! I guess it's for you." She pressed the book into Betsie's hands.

"It says 'To Betsie.' He even spelled my name right. But why would he give his favorite book to me?"

The merest glimmer of understanding touched Sheila's expression. "Maybe he was sorry he threw your pie?"

"Oh, it was just a pie," Betsie scoffed. "Guess I got what I deserved, ain't so? *Mem* always said to me, 'Pride goeth before a fall, Betsie,' whenever I put too much stock in my own worth." She thought a moment. "Maybe now she would say, 'Pie goeth before a fall.'"

They giggled at Betsie's joke. Before long, laughter mixed with tears, the happy kind. Betsie felt as free as a draft horse unhitched from the plow after a long day in the fields. She hoped the laughter did as much good for Sheila as it did for her.

The good feelings lasted through lunch. Sheila and Betsie devoured huge wedges of banana cream pie for dessert. Sure enough, it was just a pie, albeit a delicious one. Betsie felt very virtuous for placing her handiwork in the proper order of things.

"Oh, I think I'm gonna burst," Sheila moaned.

"Not getting sick again, are you?"

Sheila grinned, and Betsie changed the subject. "I am going to collect Michael's wash. Do you want to help me?"

"I guess. Hey, you want to look at some of Michael's other books? We can look at his newspaper articles, too, if you want. I know where he keeps them."

"Newspaper articles? Ones he cut from the paper?"

"Nuh-uh. Ones he wrote. He wants to be a reporter someday. He's wanted that forever." Doubt crossed her face. "I don't know if he can anymore, since he dropped out of Kent State last year. Come on! This will be fun. He's really good."

Betsie followed her to Michael's room. Today there was a single pile of dirty clothes, and the lumpy bedclothes were pulled up haphazardly.

"Here's his bookshelf. See, here's where that book was." Sheila indicated an empty slot.

Betsie ran a finger along the dusty shelf. Most of the books were thin, like the blue one. "Are these all poetry books?"

"Mostly, but this one's about grammar."

Betsie paged through that book with interest, pausing to marvel at all the rules for commas. She sat down on the lumpy bed to study it more carefully, but Sheila tugged at her sleeve.

"These are the newspaper articles Mike wrote." She thrust a tattered yellow folder into Betsie's hands. One corner crumbled between her thumb and forefinger.

"Won't Michael mind if we snoop?"

"After last night, I doubt he cares. Dad was pretty rough on him." Sheila caught the end of her ponytail and twirled it. "Mike may not like it when *I* go through his stuff, but I don't think he'd mind if *you* did."

Betsie drew out faded newspaper clippings from the two inner pockets and stacked them on the bedspread. Most of them were just words under a title, with no mention of the writer, but a few had what Sheila called a byline. That meant Michael's name was on the article.

"That one's from his high school paper, about the fire at our house." Sheila set it aside. "This one's from the Kent State paper. That's where he went to college"—she paused and bit her lip—"for a while."

Betsie glanced at the fuzzy yellow triangle on Michael's red wall. "Yes, I know."

"And oh, here's an editorial Mike wrote that ran in the Columbus paper when he turned sixteen. He was really happy when it came out on his birthday. See?" She indicated the top of the page. "June 1, 1967. Mom bought all the copies she could find at Ayers, and all the clippings are here."

Betsie read bits and pieces as they sat together on Michael's bed.

STEPHANIE REED

Near as she could make out, Michael hadn't written about much else but peace. Whether he was writing about student groups at school protests, the English war in Vietnam, or about Washington, D.C., peace was what he wanted, and he wanted it *now*.

When they reached the back of the folder, Sheila handled the papers with care. "These are about when Michael was at the Kent State massacre. Have you heard of it?"

Betsie hesitated, not sure how much Michael wanted her to divulge about what he'd shared. "The television man, Uncle Walter, talked about Kent State, didn't he? There were people killed there last year. Seems like maybe I read something in my home newspaper, now that I think on it."

"Uh-huh. There was this big protest. I don't understand what it was all about, but the governor of Ohio sent out the National Guard to keep the peace. They're kind of like soldiers, I guess," Sheila explained. "Anyway, Mike didn't like how things shaped up on the hill, rock-throwing and guns and all, so he was headed to class. That's when someone started shooting; no one knows who it was for sure. But Mike wrote this eyewitness report, and some of the national newspapers picked it up. It was a big deal."

Betsie recalled the conversation in the car outside the church. "Michael . . . he told me about it, a little."

"You're kidding! Wow, he never talks about Kent State. The only way I know what happened was from what our teacher said at school and"—she blushed—"by sneaking in here and reading his articles. But I do know one thing. When Michael came home from college, he was different." She touched a faded photograph above the article. "Here he is before the shots were fired."

Betsie's mouth dropped open. Sure enough, the young man in the picture was Michael.

218

CHAPTER 32

"Hope is the thing with feathers that perches in the soul."
—EMILY DICKINSON, QUOTED IN BETSIE'S JOURNAL

MICHAEL WORE BLUE jeans, of course, his long legs captured in mid-stride. He wore a denim jacket over a light shirt, and his hair was tossed back by the wind. Behind him grew a tree with a crooked branch, and he stood in what looked like a parking lot with many other people his age.

The most striking aspect of the picture was that Michael looked relaxed and happy as he joked with someone the camera did not see. Rarely had Betsie seen him like this.

Sheila's finger moved to the next picture. There was the same crooked tree, but now Michael looked down at a boy who was stretched out on the pavement. Betsie could easily see the insignia on Michael's shirt. He had one knee up and an elbow bent. His hair covered his eyes, but the set of his mouth made her sad. No one should have seen what Michael saw; of that much Betsie was certain.

"The one thing he told Mom was that a bullet just missed him." Sheila steadied the quiver in her voice. "Here's the students who didn't make it." She tapped four pictures, two boys and two girls: Allison, William, Jeffrey, and Sandra.

I'm still here. They died. Why? Michael's question haunted Betsie. She still didn't know the answer. They looked about Michael's age, she guessed, but they would never celebrate another birthday.

"Sheila? How would you like to help me plan a birthday dinner for Michael, complete with pie *and* cake?"

Sheila bounced to her knees. "Really?"

"*Jah*, June first is coming up fast, but we could do it easy if we work together."

"Betsie, that's so cool! I forgot all about his birthday."

"Well, we are going to change that, you and me, especially since last night didn't end so nice. Let's clean up and start planning right now."

"This will be so much fun!" Sheila enveloped Betsie in a hug that a bear would have been proud to give.

"All right, all right, you don't have to squeeze me in two," she wheezed as she slipped the Emily book in her pocket.

It did not take long to file the articles and tidy up Michael's room. Betsie decided to sort Michael's wash and water down what bleach she had left to soak the stains from the splotchy T-shirts.

In the kitchen, Sheila described Michael's favorite foods. "You take a hot dog, slit it down the middle, and you poke cheese in the slit. You know those biscuits you can buy, the ones where the tube pops open when you hit it on the edge of the counter?"

"Yes." She didn't add that waiting for the pop gave her the willies and the biscuits tasted like cardboard, besides.

"Okay, so you pull off a biscuit and roll it out like a snake. Then you wrap it around the hot dog, cheese and all, and bake them in the oven until they brown. Mom calls them pigs in a blanket." Sheila smiled at the memory.

"I guess we can make these pigs in a poke, only do you think I can use real biscuit dough?"

"Pigs in a *blanket*," Sheila corrected, "and no, it has to be the popping kind of dough. Plus, I just remembered something else. Mike always drowns them in coney sauce. Do you know how to make that? He used to eat about five pigs in a blanket smothered in coney sauce every year on his birthday."

Betsie raised her eyebrows. "Is there anything else that Michael always has on his birthday? If he has room after five of these pigs, that is."

Sheila scrunched up her face. "Um, did I say barbecue potato chips yet? And lemonade?"

Betsie jotted them down.

"Write Porch Swing brand lemonade. It's the only kind he drinks." Sheila marked the place, expression quite serious, until Betsie amended her note.

At last, the list was finished to Sheila's satisfaction. They decided on May 28, the Friday before Michael's birthday, for the party. "Mike won't be expecting you to stay and eat dinner with us, since he usually drives you home on Friday. We'll surprise him!"

"Sheila, dear heart, there's just one problem with all our plans. How are we going to get Michael to eat with us? After last night, I wouldn't be surprised if he never eats here again." She clicked the pen so the point popped in and out.

Sheila gaped. "You're kidding! That's the simplest part of all." She broke into a smile. "We'll pray that he comes."

The rest of the week, Sheila secretly signaled Betsie at odd times by folding her hands as though in prayer. Betsie winked and nodded every time because it seemed to please the girl, but truth be told, she did not have much faith it would work on Michael. Her own silent prayer went more like, "Please don't let Sheila be disappointed," meaning when Michael didn't come. Betsie lost count of how many times she had prayed that way by Friday afternoon, just one week from the big day. When Sheila hunted her down in the shop after school, they strolled arm-in-arm to the kitchen.

"I made those cookies you like this morning." Betsie reached for the lopsided purple cookie jar on top of the refrigerator. She supposed Sheila's mother had made it; it vaguely resembled an eggplant.

"The ones you make with M&Ms instead of chocolate chips? Oh, these are my favorite! Aunt Hester used to make them for me and Mike." She dug deep in the jar.

"That's funny. It was my dad's sister Lovina who used to make them for us. I guess it's the kind of thing aunts like to do." Betsie poured mugs of milk.

"You call your aunt by her first name? That's just like how Michael calls Mom by hers."

"That's right. We believe we're none of us any better than the other." Betsie dunked a cookie and let a bite crumble in her mouth. "What about Hester? When was the last time you saw her?"

"It must be . . . five years since she died." Sheila swirled cookie crumbs in her mug. "I sure miss her. But these cookies will always remind me of Aunt Hester."

Betsie reached to blot a drop of milk from Sheila's chin.

"What's this about Aunt Hester? Whoa, are those the cookies she used to make?"

Sheila jerked and hollered, "Mike!" Then she dashed to hug him.

Michael lifted the corner of his mouth in that old, endearing grin of his. "Can I have some? Pretty please?"

"Come and eat," Betsie invited. "Want some milk to drink?"

"Nah, I like 'em straight." Michael wolfed down cookie after cookie until he let out a blissful sigh and rubbed his stomach. "That hit the spot. Thanks. Hey, it's a beautiful day. Let's get out there and experience it, people."

Sheila giggled. "You sound like a disc jockey. Come on, Betsie!"

"But I have to fix dinner—"

"You always have leftovers on Friday," Sheila insisted. "How long can it take to heat 'em up?"

The lure of fresh air won her over. The three of them flopped down beneath the oak trees at the far edge of the pasture. Fledge snorted as if to say, "Keep your distance."

"Michael, thank you for the Emily book. I like her poems."

"I thought you might."

His answer was casual, but his manner was not, so Betsie changed the subject. "I didn't hear your car. Where is it? How did you get here?"

He stretched the full length of his lean frame, rumpled his hair, and leaned back to rest on his elbows. The veins on the underside of his arms stood out. "It's running again. I parked it behind the shed so *der Führer* doesn't blow a gasket if he gets home before I split."

"Aren't you going to eat dinner with us, Mike?" Sheila's limpid eyes were like pools of melted chocolate. She twirled a white clover blossom.

"Those cookies *were* my dinner," he said. "No, really, there's a peace rally out at Ohio State, and I promised the editor of this underground newspaper that I'd be there. I'm taking off in a little bit so we can slap together some posters. And chill out, Pippa. I'll drive you back to Plain City later. I'll honk when I'm ready for you."

"A 'peace rally'?" Sheila glowered. "And what's an underground newspaper?"

"Wow, Squirt, way to ask the hard-hitting questions. The answer's really pretty simple. Basically everything you read in the papers is a lie. The *Columbus Free Press* is published secretly for the protection of the truth." Michael sighed in mock exasperation. "And, yeah, technically a peace rally is a protest march. But don't worry," he said. "I know what I'm doing. No goons with guns at this demonstration." He clenched his fist and bopped Sheila on the chin. "Lighten up, Squirt. I'll be fine."

Sheila continued her level gaze, one that made Betsie uneasy. High in the oak tree, a redbird trilled, "Purty, purty, purty."

"Mike? I promise I won't worry on one condition. Wait, two conditions."

"Since when did you get to be boss around here?" he teased, but he stopped when he saw she was serious. "Shoot."

"Condition number one: you have to promise to eat dinner with us next Friday. That's the twenty-eighth," she said.

"Oh, man! That was a pretty hairy scene the other night, Squirt. Pippa may not want me coming around again, seeing as how I splattered her pie. Is there any pie left, by the way?"

"No."

"Serves me right, I guess. Okay, I promise to be here for dinner. Next Friday. May 28. Gotcha."

But apparently Sheila knew her brother's empty promises too well.

She stopped tying long-stemmed clover blossoms together to ask, "Cross your heart?"

Michael swiped a finger criss-cross on his bare chest. "Cross my heart and hope to die."

Betsie gasped. "Don't say that."

"Sorry. It's just an expression, Pippa. Nobody hopes to die." The wind briefly lifted his hair in a fluffy halo. Sheila continued to stare at him until he quirked the corner of his mouth into a half smile.

Sheila switched her gaze back to Betsie, who was in awe of how the girl had extracted the promise from Michael with such skill. "The second condition is for both of you." She took a deep breath and plunged ahead. "My church is having a revival service next Wednesday evening, and I want Mike to drive me. But you have to go in, Mike, and Betsie, too."

Michael's expression remained carefully blank. "A revival? You drive a mighty hard bargain, Squirt. How about it, Pippa? Are you game?" He grinned. "You're looking pretty thunderstruck."

Thunderstruck did not begin to describe her feelings. Betsie admired Sheila's faith. She had already gotten Michael to agree to be at the house for his surprise party next Friday. Now she had finagled a way to get Betsie into her church to hear about being saved. Clever how she had drawn Michael into the bargain, too, saying it was so she wouldn't worry about him. Suddenly Sheila seemed wise beyond her eleven years.

"Ple-e-ease, Betsie?"

Sheila's melted-chocolate gaze and her heart-shaped face were too much. Betsie had come to care for her like a little sister. "Well . . ."

"That means yes! Shake on it." She grabbed Betsie's hand, pumped it, and did the same with Michael. "That settles it." She let out a satisfied sigh.

"Wow, Squirt, you blew me away with that one. Church next Wednesday is the last thing I expected. I thought you were angling for ice cream at the Milky Way." Michael supported himself on one elbow to tug his sister's ponytail. "I think Pippa's still in shock. Maybe we should renegotiate. We wouldn't want to make her do anything that's against her religion, would we? It probably is, right, Pippa?"

Sheila gulped, hovering on the brink of joy and sorrow.

Betsie thrust out her chin. "I can do what I please in my *Rumspringa* time. I will go if Michael goes."

"Man, I don't know," Michael hedged.

"Mike, you promised!"

He relented. "Okay, okay, I guess I'm game if Pippa is. I'll be there."

Sheila grinned. She put a clover chain she'd fashioned around her own neck and held another up to Betsie, who obediently lowered her head, though she'd never worn a necklace before. After all, it was the good Lord who made the clover, she rationalized. "How do I look?"

"Purty, purty, purty," trilled the vainglorious redbird, plain as day.

Sheila giggled at Betsie's blushes, but Michael gave the cardinal a hearty thumbs-up. "I hear you, man."

C H A P T E R   3 3

"It was not death, for I stood up,
and all the dead lie down."
—EMILY DICKINSON, QUOTED IN BETSIE'S JOURNAL

MICHAEL LOADED REUBEN Hochstetler's repaired harness in the trunk of his car before he left for the peace rally. Betsie grinned when she noticed it was almost too heavy for him. Compared to Charley, Michael was a scarecrow. She was very sorry to see him go, though. It was a long while since she'd passed a more pleasant afternoon.

When Betsie and Sheila got back inside, it was high time to heat up the leftovers and set the table. "One of your conditions," Betsie needled Sheila as they worked, "should have been that Michael would drive us to Ayers next week. How am I to get what I need for the party?"

Sheila waved a hand. "Don't worry! Mike doesn't seem to mind taking you to the market. We'll ask him to stop Wednesday night after church. Just make sure to take your shopping list."

Sheila practically wriggled with excitement. Betsie had to admit she was looking forward to next week, too.

Mr. Sullivan arrived as Betsie pulled the leftover meat loaf out of the oven. He was carefully kind and courteous. Sheila even extracted a promise that he would eat dinner at home the following Friday, although he gave her a faintly puzzled look and asked, "Where else would I eat?" Of course, neither mentioned that Michael would be there.

Before she left, Betsie stopped by the sofa, where Mr. Sullivan was reading the newspaper. She glimpsed more Vietnam photos and cringed. She told Mr. Sullivan good-bye and mentioned that she had finished Hochstetler's harness repair and would pick up the payment over the weekend.

"Thank you! Wonderful doing business with the Amish. Cash on the barrelhead, every time."

She smiled. "I'm glad you are happy with my work."

"Betsie, the only thing better than your being here would be for Phyllis to come back."

The horn from the Super Bee honked. Mr. Sullivan cast a contemptuous glance out the window. "Not coming in, huh?"

Betsie tensed for more top-blowing, but Sheila smoothed things over. "We thought it would be better for you if Michael honked for Betsie. In case you had a bad day at work or something," she hurried to add.

Mr. Sullivan slumped. "I'm sorry, Sheila. I know I was way out of line the other night. When your mom is here, she can kid me out of those moods." His face reddened. "But I'm telling you what, where Betsie's safety is concerned—"

"Dad."

He put up his hands. "Okay, okay. 'Nuff said."

Betsie was amazed at the wisdom Sheila had acquired in just a few short days. She must read her *Good News* like crazy. Betsie wondered how she remembered it all.

The yellow-jacket car's engine raced. Betsie trotted out and tossed her case in the back as she plopped in the seat beside Michael.

"Hello," she shouted above the radio's blare. She glanced at him, and her mouth dropped open. Michael's right calf was scraped from knee to ankle. Blood seeped from the raw patches.

"Michael! What happened?"

He braked the car and brushed back his hair to check traffic on the passenger side. Betsie saw then that his right eye was nearly swollen shut.

"Your eye! Are you sure you can see to drive? What—"

"I'm fine." He did not sound like himself at all. "I had a run-in with some pigs, is all." His tone indicated that Betsie should drop the subject. As he twisted in his seat to see behind him before he pulled out, he caught his breath, and his face twisted.

"Michael, you're hurt."

"Don't—" He checked an outburst at Betsie's look. "Sorry. Look, don't worry. Worst-case scenario is I have a cracked rib, but I doubt it. It'll pass."

"Michael, you promised you wouldn't get into trouble."

"I didn't do anything wrong. I swear. The pigs came down heavy on us for disturbing the peace, but I'm telling you no one got rowdy, not like . . ." He shifted in his seat and sucked in his breath at the pain. "Look, they tried to make an example of us, but there was no way we were going down without a fight. We all sat on the pavement and refused to move. We even sang about peace until the cops said they were going to cite us for resisting arrest. There was a big scuffle, and then they grabbed my arms and dragged me along the street." He offered a grim smile. "That's when I kicked Mr. Pig right in the— Let's just say I kicked him, and did he ever squeal. He dropped me like a hot potato, and I took off." He cranked up the radio, making further conversation impossible.

It was easy to see who Michael took after. Anger had fizzed up inside of him until top-blowing spilled. For the rest of the ride, Betsie took her old position against the door and kept her mouth shut.

When they arrived at Betsie's house, Michael limped to unload the harness from the trunk, but she shooed him out of the way and shook him out of his bad mood by hoisting it easily.

"Who are you, Superwoman or something?" He tried to wink at her, winced, and fingered his eye tenderly.

She ignored his joke. "One thing I don't recall, Michael. This protest march, what was it for?"

He drew himself up with pride. "Peace. Catch you later, Pippa." He flashed a split-fingered wave.

Peace. She watched Michael ease into his car so as not to aggravate his battle wounds and wondered if he would ever find what he was looking for.

A familiar horse and buggy was hitched to the rail, and Betsie knew right away what *she* was looking for. Lo and behold, here he came around the corner of her house, laden with two buckets of water for her vegetable garden.

"Hi, Charley! I'm home!"

He watched the yellow car with hooded eyes before responding. "Evening, Betsie." He lowered the buckets to the ground and flexed his broad shoulders. "What's all this?" He indicated the pile of leather traces.

"*Ach*, just the harness I finished for Reuben Hochstetler. Maybe you can help me deliver it to him now?" She smiled and started to pick it up again.

"Here, you shouldn't carry that." He swung it to one shoulder like it was made of twine. "This will hold those brutes of Reuben's. *Gut* sturdy harness; should serve quite a while. I can deliver it when Sadie and I take day-old bread to Sunnyhaven."

Betsie trotted to keep up with him as he walked with purposeful strides to stow the harness in the flat wagon behind his buggy. "The children's home? *Ach*, so thoughtful, Charley, but"—she crinkled her eyebrows—"can't *I* help you deliver the harness and the bread right now? I need to collect payment from Reuben, and you know him, always anxious. He's probably watching for me."

He rubbed his chin with the back of his hand. "*Jah*, I reckon I could go right now . . . if I weren't right in the middle of chores."

Betsie studied her shoes. "I should have had Michael drive me over, I guess," she murmured, more to herself than to Charley.

He pursed his lips like he'd tasted a lemon. "Yes, maybe the Peacock should have driven you in his fancy yellow car if you're in such a hurry. He can't lift a harness, but he sure has time enough to get into trouble, looks like." He squashed a juicy mosquito against his forearm, seized the buckets, and stomped to the garden, the back of his shirt showing a river of sweat.

"I didn't mean anything, Charley! I know how hard you work," she called, and then she sighed. It was difficult, switching back and forth between English and Plain ways. Machines made work easier; there was no denying it. Poor Charley couldn't help but know that, especially since she'd pointed it out and practically rubbed his nose in it. She bit her lip and vowed to tell him how much she appreciated his help when he took her home from the singing.

Friday evening flew by, and Saturday passed in a blur. Oh, for a vacuum cleaner or a washing machine, Betsie grumbled to herself, but she knew she didn't mean it . . . really. It wasn't until Saturday bedtime that she and Sadie had a breather. "*Dat* is probably packing up now," Betsie said as she turned down her quilts. "Wouldn't it be wonderful if they went to meeting with us tomorrow?"

"There are no more trains tonight," said practical Sadie, "but that would be wonderful. *Ach*, I am tired. *Gut nacht*, Betsie."

She watched as Sadie left the room, then shrugged off the dash of cold water thrown on her pleasant thoughts, content to dream of seeing *Mem* and *Dat*.

As she drove Judith to Sol Beiler's on Sunday morning, clinging to her new knowledge of God's love and care, Betsie's faith soared. She had seen Sheila's prayer bring Michael home for a family supper, something she would not have believed possible. If the good Lord did that for Sheila, why would He not do the same for her?

A warm feeling overspread Betsie as she and Sadie waited for the People to arrive for the service. She couldn't wait to sing the hymns from the *Ausbund* with her community of friends. But when the singing began, what a disappointment! *Ausbund* 79, a mournful tune with the notes drawn out past all understanding, chilled her. She tried to translate the High German; surely the words weren't as oppressive as they seemed. However, the only phrase she managed to decipher was: "The world will hate you and drive you from wife, child, possession, and goods." The words seemed directed at *Dat*.

Betsie struggled to shut out a sense of overpowering dread. Nothing in the sermons uplifted her heart; every verse excoriated a lost soul who had gone astray, though Bishop Gingerich remained very humble and downcast as he preached. Once, Sadie's knee trembled against Betsie's, and she knew her sister felt the spirit of oppression, too.

When at last the meeting ended and it was time to prepare for the meal together, Betsie breathed a sigh of relief. She and Sadie had weathered the storm, and their secret was safe; she rejoiced inwardly.

To her chagrin, Jonas announced that the children must go outside while the rest were to remain seated for a moment while an important matter was discussed. Betsie heaved a sigh. At least it was not *Ordnung* Sunday, yet she fretted that they must sit while Jonas noted who had been caught breaking what rule. Her insides twisted as the doors closed. Who would be singled out today?

"Brothers and sisters in Christ, today a task falls very heavy on my heart," Jonas intoned.

Suddenly Betsie's attention was riveted on the bishop. This was no minor infraction.

"It has been brought to our attention that two among our number have gone astray," he continued mournfully.

Betsie felt the blood drain from her face. She saw Jonas's lips moving, but her hearing had shut off. Her toes curled inside her shoes as she fumbled for Sadie's hand.

". . . And so we must beseech our brother and sister in Christ, Noah and Fannie Troyer, to come back to the church. After a few weeks, we will then make a decision about whether to invoke the loving discipline of the *Meidung*."

Still. Must sit still, but she could not sit still. Betsie's stomach lurched, and she clapped a hand to her mouth. Sadie grabbed for her arm and missed. Betsie crashed into the bench across the way. Someone steadied her before she plunged outside. Behind a lilac bush in full bloom, she bent over and lost her breakfast.

CHAPTER 34

"I many times thought peace had come,
when peace was far away."
—EMILY DICKINSON, QUOTED IN BETSIE'S JOURNAL

As SHE BLOTTED her mouth, Betsie glimpsed Mattie Yoder and recoiled. She staggered to her feet, only to find Charley blocking her way.

"Let me by," Betsie gasped, her insides still roiling.

"Betsie, wait!"

She broke away and pushed through the crowd at a dead sprint until she was far from the house full of trouble. She entered the dappled shade of a grove of cottonwoods that bordered the Little Darby. The water twinkled over rocks. Betsie sank to rest on a fallen log while a meadowlark with a breast yellower than Charley's hair burbled a song from a nearby fence post.

After a few minutes, the roaring in her ears slowed, and she heard dry brush crackle behind her. Nerves strained to the breaking point, she rocketed to her feet and doubled her fists.

"*Ach*, Betsie. I didn't mean to startle you so."

"Charley!" She pressed one hand to her chest and flopped back on the log.

"Why in thunder did you run away like that?" Nettled but dashing in his Sunday black, he sat beside her. "Didn't you hear me?"

Betsie licked her dry lips. There was a metallic taste in her mouth.

She cupped her hands and scooped up a drink of cold creek water before answering. "I was afraid of what you would say about . . . about the shun."

He picked up a pebble and pitched it into the creek. "Betsie, there is something I have to say to you." He squared his shoulders at her protest. "I'm sorry, but I must. My *mem*, she is the one who talked to Jonas. If I had known beforehand, I would have tried to stop her, to give you time to talk some sense into your folks."

"You would have? Charley, that makes me feel some better after this awful day." Her head drooped.

"It's true. *Mem* takes too much on herself. She's had to be the master of the house for a long time, but beginning today, I am in charge. From now on in matters so important, she must speak to me first, and if it is necessary, *I* will speak to Jonas." He pitched another pebble.

Many times in the past weeks, silence had served Betsie well. She held her tongue now, though she wanted to weep with frustration and cling to Charley all at the same time.

She stole a glance at him. Yes, she could see it; he was becoming a man. He was head and shoulders above Michael, who was still a youth filled with impetuous fire—frivolous laughter one minute and explosive temper the next. Michael might come to her aid in a crisis, but then again, he might not. Charley, on the other hand, had grown solid and dependable, strong and diligent, no longer a lighthearted boy. "I'm glad you told me, Charley. It means a lot to hear you say it. And now we had better go back before I get my family into even more trouble." She paused and looked him in the eye. "I . . . I don't feel like going to the singing this evening."

He watched the water and finally nodded. "I understand. Betsie, I'm truly sorry about what happened."

She knew she was blushing. "And I am sorry for what *Dat* and *Mem* have done. They've ruined . . . everything." She dropped her gaze, but Charley lifted her chin until she faced him.

"Don't forget what I'm telling you now, Betsie. Your parents left, but you stayed, and all of the district knows it." He squeezed her hand and left her to compose herself.

When she got back to the Beiler barn, Betsie barked her shin as she climbed into the buggy. She rubbed it and clucked to Judith, who took the bit eagerly as they drove around to pick up Sadie.

Her sister, perched on the front steps away from the crowd, plucked fretfully at her apron. "Where did you go? It was horrible, everyone looking at me with sad faces." She climbed into the buggy and huddled against the side.

"I just had to get away from that Mattie Yoder. Charley found me and said he was sorry about what she did. She *was* the one who questioned Lovina and told Jonas about *Mem* and *Dat*." She transferred the reins to one hand and briefly clasped Sadie's shoulder.

Judith's hooves didn't flash near quick enough to suit Betsie once they got underway. She jiggled the reins and clucked to her horse, something she rarely did. Judith snorted and threw her weight against her collar to respond with a spurt that made Sadie catch her breath.

"Too hot to drive her so fast, Betsie. Better slow down."

Sadie was right. Dark patches slicked Judith's back. Betsie repented and reined in her mare to a slow jog. The sedate pace brought them safely home.

Once inside the barn, Betsie set the brake, unhitched her horse, and rubbed Judith's damp neck. Judith nuzzled her with slobbery forgiveness. She took care to cool her out properly, grooming her and rubbing her down while the mare cleaned her manger of every speck of feed. When she was properly cooled, Betsie pumped the watering trough full of sparkling water and let her drink to her heart's content. Judith enjoyed herself, blowing at the water and making little ripples. Betsie's heart eased yet more in appreciation of her horse's simple ways. She hugged her neck before turning her out to graze, wishing she could hug Sadie. She sighed. If she tried it, Sadie would back away in astonishment. Wish as she might, her family was not much for physical displays of affection.

When she entered the house, it was late afternoon. Worn out, Betsie slumped at the table and was surprised to spy a warm note of sympathy from Rachel Yutzy alongside one of her special glazed strawberry pies.

"'I am praying that the good Lord will bring your *mem* and *dat* home soon,'" Betsie read. "'Thinking of you.'"

"Whenever did she find time to drop up here with a pie?" Sadie marveled.

Tears smarted. "Rachel is a wonderful friend," Betsie replied staunchly. "She knows how awful it is for us, and she must have left the dinner and cut across lots to beat us here." She wiped her eyes. "We must eat, Sadie, even though we don't feel like it. Cut us a couple of pieces while I wash up."

Neither girl felt like talking after they ate Rachel's dessert, so they moved to the lonely front room to pray through the afternoon and early evening. By bedtime, Betsie was sure she felt the good Lord's presence as He reassured her that everything would come round right.

As she blew out her lamp, Betsie recalled sweet Charley's kind words. She tossed and turned and tried to sleep, knowing she needed her rest because Michael would be there to pick her up for work, first thing tomorrow.

But the next morning, Michael was late again. Betsie gritted her teeth in exasperation. He was simply not to be trusted, altogether flighty and unpredictable. Charley would never leave her in the lurch like this.

But where was he? Her anger faded as, unbidden, frightening scenes raced through her mind: Michael at a pot party; Michael at a "peace rally," kicking a pig; Michael in a terrible car accident, the Super Bee upside down and burning. Or worst of all, Michael lying on the railroad tracks, dead of his own volition.

When she heard a car turn into the driveway soon afterward, she was so relieved that she sped out to meet it. To her dismay, it was Mr. Sullivan's station wagon.

"Where is Michael?" Her voice squeaked as she pulled the door open.

"I have no clue. We haven't seen him all weekend." He smoothed the nonexistent cowlick at the crown of his crew cut. "I don't mind admitting that I'm worried this time."

She tucked up her skirts and ducked inside with her case on her lap. Mr. Sullivan backed up faster than Michael ever had.

"He will come home. He always does," Betsie said, as much to herself as to Mr. Sullivan. She kept a firm grip on the door handle. Often, Michael had poked fun at Mr. Sullivan's slow family car, but there was nothing slow about it today. The beige car sped by the fairgrounds so fast that she had to look quick to read the banner that announced the biggest horse show of the year. The last one had brought Benner to Hilliard. She shivered and hoped Michael would show up soon to keep her safe, just as he'd promised.

"I sure hope you're right, Betsie." Mr. Sullivan broke the silence as though he'd been mulling over what she said for the entire drive. "If Mike doesn't show, lock up the shop and stay in the house. Lock all the doors. I don't want you taking any chances, okay?" His eyes were troubled. "You know what? Maybe I should just take the day off."

Betsie swallowed. "No," she said. "I will be all right. You go to work, and if . . . *when* Michael comes home, I will tell him to call you because you're worried about him." And about time, too, she added to herself.

Mr. Sullivan shifted his hands on the steering wheel. "At least I'll wait until you get safely inside."

Often Betsie had thought that the capes Plain girls wore made them look square and capable. She did not feel capable as her boss's car idled in the driveway behind her. If only she had work to do! She headed for the shop and propped open the screen door with her hip. Her key popped the lock, and she wrinkled her nose as stale air greeted her; the place needed a good airing-out, but it was empty.

She turned to wave at Mr. Sullivan and stared. He was hunched over the steering wheel, his head actually resting on it. Could it be that she and Mr. Sullivan were a lot alike in that inactivity drove him crazy, too? She called and beckoned to him. "I know you're late for work, but could I ask a small favor?"

"Anything." He hopped out of the car, relief written all over his face. "Just name it."

Betsie spread out her fingers as he approached. "I know I will be fine as long as I keep busy. Could you show me how to use the embossing machine? I've been thinking maybe I can make some items to sell." And maybe she would, someday.

Mr. Sullivan exhaled and his shoulders dropped as he relaxed. "Don't know why I didn't think of it myself. The machine does most of the work." He checked his watch. "I'm not too late, so a few more minutes shouldn't matter . . . much."

Once inside, Mr. Sullivan was all efficient business. He demonstrated how the machine worked and even interchanged a couple of embossing plates to show different designs. Betsie was enchanted, even though she had no intention of actually using the machine.

"What kinds of things have you made?"

He rubbed his chin. "You've seen the book cover for the harness book. Lots of binder covers, embossed belts, even key rings. In fact," he scrabbled through a drawer, "here's where we keep the rings and snaps, and here's a finished one." He stuck his finger through a ring and dangled a rectangle embossed with a colored flower. "Pretty easy." He let it slip back into the drawer and checked his watch again.

"Go," she said. She softened her order with a smile.

Mr. Sullivan answered with one of his own, however small. "Thanks, Betsie."

He really wasn't so bad, once she'd managed to take his mind off his troubles. If only she could work out everything else so easily.

After Mr. Sullivan drove out of sight, she stowed her case under the webbed chair and opened the back window for a cross-breeze. She stood on tiptoe to search for the yellow car, but there was no sign of it. Alone again. With a shiver, she latched the screen door.

First things first; she'd been meaning to write down the dates of the local horse shows in her notebook. That way, her cousin would know when he could expect to drum up more business at the fairgrounds. She moved her case to the counter and rooted through her clean clothing, but her notebook wasn't there.

Ach, fergesslich, she chided herself, but was it any wonder she was forgetful after the weekend she'd had? Betsie scrounged for paper, came up with a blank note card, and recorded the dates before she could forget them, too.

A knock on the door interrupted her chicken scratches. She looked up. A man waited outside, his shape silhouetted by bright sunlight to shadow the screen. Betsie's heart knocked against her ribs until she realized he was not Benner, but Officer Schwartz dressed in regular clothing.

"Can you spare a minute, Miss Troyer?" he asked, meek as Moses. He seemed harmless enough, plus his job was to protect her, wasn't that right? Betsie nodded and unlatched the door.

"Sorry for the interruption, ma'am, but there's something you need to know."

Somehow, she'd suspected it all along; Michael was in terrible trouble. Betsie clutched the edge of the counter to steady her trembling fingers. "Tell me!"

"Don't be alarmed, Miss Troyer. As a matter of fact, this is good news," he continued. "I just came from the fairgrounds. I heard about an accident on the horse show circuit that concerns you."

Betsie's vivid imagination skipped ahead. Had one of her repairs gone wrong and caused a fall? A life-threatening injury? Her hands grew cold.

Schwartz droned on, oblivious to her distress. "I called Deacon the first chance I got, and the report checks out. It is my privilege to inform you that H. R. Benner, your assailant, was the victim of a riding accident. Shortly after he attacked you, he fled to Indiana, where a couple of days later the horse he was riding upon was the recipient of a sting from a yellow jacket. The horse objected strenuously, and Mr. Benner was thrown, whereupon his neck was broken." He pantomimed breaking a stick and made a cracking sound. "He was pronounced dead at the scene."

"Oh." A long, shuddery sigh escaped Betsie. She was safe.

"So needless to say, he won't be bothering you anymore. Got what he deserved, in my book," Schwartz said. "What goes around, comes around."

Relief flooded through her on two counts: that English man would bother her no more, and as yet, there was no bad news about Michael. As if in answer to her unspoken prayer of gratitude, a far-off glint caught her eye. Betsie quickly averted her gaze from the vicinity of the pony shed as the police officer preened.

"Well, Miss Troyer, I won't keep you from your work. I know news like this can be upsetting, but concentrate on the positive. Benner will never bother you again. By the way," he asked as he surveyed the shop casually, "where's your pal, Sullivan?"

In that instant, she realized the truth. Anyone who would steal milk money from a younger boy was not trustworthy, even if he was a police officer. "He is out," Betsie replied, taking care to keep her voice toneless. "What do you want with Michael?"

"Just wanted to see how he was doing. You know."

Oh, she knew. She remained silent.

Schwartz grew agitated. "Well, it's like this, Miss Troyer. That long-haired freaky friend of yours is going to get himself in big trouble one of these days. Word on the street is he's been spotted at a couple of 'peace' rallies." He rolled his eyes as he sketched quotation marks with his fingers, his true colors even more apparent. "Give him a message for me. I know what that car of his looks like, and I'm watching his every move. I'm gonna nail his hide to the wall if he so much as jaywalks."

"*Jah*, I will tell Michael to watch out, Officer. Thank you. Goodbye." She let the screen door shut behind him with a satisfying bang.

She nibbled at a hangnail and bided her time, but she knew she had to warn Michael. When she was sure Schwartz was gone, she stuck the Closed sign in the window, locked the door, and hotfooted it across the driveway for the pasture and the pony shed, where she'd noticed the glint of sunshine on glass while she stalled Officer Schwartz.

When she reached the tree where the redbird sang, she squinted at the brush behind the shed. Sure enough, there was the Super Bee.

Not for any amount of money would she disturb Fledge by crossing his domain. Instead, she crunched through the weeds that lined the rusty fence. If Michael was hiding in his car as she suspected, he surely would hear her.

He didn't appear in the window. Gingerly she cupped her hands to the glass to make sure he wasn't curled up in the back seat, but all she saw were some ripped black tennis shoes.

Where was Michael? She trotted to the house, used her key, and locked the door behind her as instructed.

"Michael?" The sunburst clock's ticking sounded unnaturally loud as she checked the living room. No one.

She slipped off her shoes and moved to the kitchen. "Michael?" The lonely green refrigerator hummed.

A faint *click* caught her ear. Betsie followed the sound, noting as she passed that the bathroom was empty. She retrieved a fuzzy pink hand towel from the rug and arranged it on the rack.

The clicking sounded louder in the hallway. Scratches and pops hissed from Michael's room. Betsie pushed open the door and peeked inside.

Michael certainly wasn't in his bed, which was covered only by the fitted sheet. The bedclothes were tumbled on the floor between the bed and the window. With a sigh, Betsie scanned the room and located the source of the sound—a black disc spun endlessly on the record player. The metal arm jerked back and forth near the colored label in the middle.

She moved to shut off the machine and stop the whispery scratches that sent nervous squiggles up her back. As she kicked aside the bed-spread, her foot nudged something warm.

"Ow," said Michael. He sat up abruptly with his back to her, shedding covers like a cocoon.

Betsie gasped and flopped on the bed, one hand to her heart. The light from the window illuminated Michael's face until he blocked the rays with his arm. His *stroobly* hair was snarled and a scraggly bronze beard sprouted from his chin. The bruises from his black eye had faded to purple and green.

"Oh, my head," he moaned.

"Michael," Betsie breathed. "You scared me."

His head jerked. "Pippa? What're you doing in my room?" He massaged his temples and moaned again.

She felt sheepish after the shock, and that made her crabby. She pursed her lips. "What are *you* doing in here when you were supposed to pick me up? It's Monday morning."

He pinched the bridge of his nose. "How did you get here?"

"Your *dat* drove me."

"My dad?" He winced at the sound of his own voice. "I bet that was a pleasant ride."

"He was worried about you, Michael. I promised him you would call. Where have you been?" she asked sharply.

He grunted and rolled over. "I slept in my car until he left. I have nothing to say to him."

"Don't you have anything to say to me? You were supposed to pick me up for work." She paused. "I was afraid . . . something had happened to you." Annoyed with herself for admitting it, Betsie grasped the metal arm of the record player to stop the clicks. A loud scratching sound issued from the speaker.

"Hey, watch it!" Michael sat up fast and turned it off before flopping back onto the piled covers. "I don't even remember turning that on."

"Michael, what's wrong with you? Are you ill?"

He opened his good eye. "No. I . . . um . . . overindulged last night. Right now what I need is some sleep; the car doesn't cut it. Really need a *lot* more sleep."

She stared at him in dismay. "You mean you were drinking alcohol? And that is why you didn't pick me up?" Betsie struggled to maintain her composure. "When you didn't come, I was worried. I thought . . . I thought maybe you were dead."

"Me? Nope. I only wish I were," he muttered.

She shot to her feet, fuming. "You think this is funny. I do not, and I am going."

"Betsie, wait," he protested feebly. She slammed his door and caught her breath.

Was there no one she could depend on? Betsie hurried to the harness shop, tears very close to the surface. She saw her note card on the counter and thought of her missing notebook. With all the trouble over *Mem* and *Dat*, she supposed it had gone clean out of her mind when she packed.

No. She couldn't think about her family. For comfort, she turned to her old standby, hard work. The shop floor could use a good sweeping, she decided, and as the minutes passed, she raised a respectable cloud of dust with the fury of righteous anger powering her efforts.

Best keep busy, Betsie thought when she finished that chore. The trouble was, until more orders came in, she was pretty well caught up. What could she do in the meantime?

The answer was simple, after all. Mr. Sullivan had shown her how to use the embossing machine. She'd merely meant to divert him from his troubles, but now . . . what if she made a present for Michael's party? Not that he deserved one, but it would please Sheila, who was staking so much on this approaching night.

The more Betsie pondered, the more she liked the idea. The present could be from all of them. She eyed the leather embossing press and sorted through the plates Mr. Sullivan had shown her. Flowers, hearts, and horses—Michael wouldn't like those, but she knew two things he did like.

In a very short time she had sketched a simple design for a key fob on an index card. There was one word in the middle: PEACE. She found the metal ring drawer and selected one. She cut a piece of scrap leather into a rectangle with a long tab at the top.

Next, she put the leather in the machine and made sure it lined up straight. She attached the embossing plate with care and gingerly started the machine. The design stamped into the leather with a *whump*.

It looked good, Betsie decided, but a rich chestnut stain would make it look even better. She rubbed it on and blotted the excess. While the leather dried, she prepared the machine that would drive in the snap to hold the doubled tab over the ring.

When the key fob was finished and dry, Betsie knew she had made something useful. She hid the key fob in her case to show Sheila when she got home.

Dear Sheila. Why not make something pretty for her? A key fob wouldn't be of any use to a girl who couldn't drive. She spent a lot of time fixing her ponytail, though.

In a flash, Betsie thought of something she'd seen English girls wear, and an idea took shape. Hastily she sketched a hair accessory. On both ends of a rectangle of leather would be small punched holes, just big enough for a whittled stick to poke through. Sheila could gather

her hair in one hand and fasten the holder to cover the elastic band she always used to make her ponytail. With the other, she could poke a stick through. Betsie had an idea Sheila would like it very much.

She took her time deciding what to emboss on the ponytail holder. At last she settled on one word again, but not PEACE. The word for Sheila would be LOVE.

When Betsie finished the leatherwork, she sought a sturdy twig, preferably of hickory. Sure enough, there was a middle-sized tree behind the shop. She chose a short branch with care and pruned it from the tree with a knife from the tool carousel. With careful strokes, she whittled it to a blunt point on one end and rounded the other one. Then she took the white peg and stained it a little darker than the leather.

Oh, how pleased Sheila would be when she saw it! Betsie imagined the girl's ponytail bouncing with excitement as she took the gift. When the peg was dry, Betsie poked it through the holes. She smiled as she pushed Sheila's ponytail cover deep in her case and hid it with a pair of clean stockings.

The shop bell dinged, and she caught her breath. Then she remembered that Benner was gone and snapped her case shut, pretty sure who had returned to pester her. "Officer Schwartz, I told you I do not know where Michael is," she huffed.

"He's right here," said Michael.

CHAPTER 35

I have a lot to learn.

—BETSIE'S JOURNAL

NOT SO LONG ago, the thought of Michael could make Betsie smile. Now the sight of him made her sad.

He paused in the doorway. "Is it okay if I come in?"

She let one shoulder rise and fall and watched him settle in the webbed chair. Several seconds passed. Her fingers itched to be working. She waited for Michael to speak, but he didn't, so she busied herself with screwing the caps tightly on the jars of stain. She hung the used rags on a peg. Then she brushed up the odds and ends of leather from the table.

As she stacked the embossing plates and put them away, she stole a glance at Michael; he was watching her. Hastily she looked away, but in that short glance she noticed that he was clean-shaven, his hair damp.

"Pippa, I'm sorry." He had folded his hands in his lap, but he worked one thumb over a big knuckle. The veins in his scrawny arms stood out, and his bare toes squirmed. He reminded Betsie of a puppy who had chewed something he knew he shouldn't.

"I forgive you, Michael." She studied the oozy, raw patches on his leg. "How are you feeling?"

"Awful."

"Serves you right, then, ain't so?"

His grin was lopsided. "That's what's so cool about you, Pippa. You tell it like it is."

"What other way is there?"

"You'd be surprised. But that isn't the only thing that's different about you. We talked about it before. You have such peace. I feel it whenever I'm around you. Life doesn't affect you like it does me."

"That's not true."

"How did you get to that place? I really need to know. If I can't get a grip pretty soon, I'm going to go crazy. Does your peace come from being Amish? Because if that's what it is, then maybe that's what I need."

Two thoughts occurred simultaneously. The first was that Michael didn't really know her way of life at all. She'd let him see behind the veil briefly on the way home from the devastating trip to Belle Center. Her life since then had been the opposite of peaceful.

The second thought was harder to pin down. Her father and mother—they'd lived, to all appearances, the peace-filled life that Michael coveted, yet they'd found something they wanted so much that they'd sacrificed everything, severed all ties with their community. But how it hurt the family they'd left behind. Michael had lost his mother to her painful personal search, but now he thought he was ready to desert his father and sister to seek peace among the Amish.

Michael noticed Betsie's hesitation. "What's wrong, Pippa?"

"I was wondering why people can't be content with what they have," she said slowly.

"Are you? Content, I mean?" He searched her face.

Well, was she? Modern appliances, riding in cars with English men—and lying about it, making friends with the English, waiting on customers, being upset and anxious over her parents, and yearning after Charley had occupied her for quite some time. No, she certainly didn't *feel* content, but if she was now experiencing trouble because her parents left the church, was it not God's will?

The solution was easy: be in submission to the Amish church and thereby to God. She could no longer be expected to submit to her parents since they had left the Amish; in fact, she was discouraged from doing so, insofar as they tried to influence her to join them. Perhaps her lot in life had grown simpler than she knew. Now fewer barriers came between her and God. Surely that was good.

Michael watched her hungrily. She nodded. "I am."

This seemed to satisfy him. Betsie was glad to leave the serious talk behind, except for one detail. "Have you seen my notebook?"

He gave her a blank look. "Your notebook? You don't have it?"

"I've looked for it all over the shop."

"Bummer. Do you think you left it at your house? You're always forgetting it."

Betsie frowned; it was what she'd been wondering herself.

"Hope you find it soon," he added. "That notebook is a work of art. No, really," he insisted at her exasperated sigh. "You have a gift, Pippa. People write for years without finding their voice. Apparently you were born with yours."

"Well, of course." She stroked her throat. "Where else would your voice come from, if you weren't born with it?"

Michael grinned. "The kind of voice I'm talking about is something different. Look, how about I give you a few pointers?" He spread his hands. "I used to be a pretty good writer."

"I know."

He was startled, she noted. That made two unguarded feelings in the last few minutes. "How?"

"Sheila showed me your folder of newspaper articles," she said as she smoothed a piece of paper.

"She found those, huh? What a snoop," he said, but Betsie thought he looked pleased.

"She said it was a big deal to get your name in the paper that way."

"Too bad four people had to die for me to get a byline," he deadpanned. "Ready? Take this down. To be a good writer, you need to revise, revise, revise." When Betsie's pencil stilled, he added, "You might say a rough draft is your best friend."

"Draft?" He was speaking a language more foreign than English slang.

Patiently, Michael explained that writing something down one time wasn't good enough. Whether she wrote instructions, a letter, or even a poem, he said Betsie should read it again and use words that made her writing more clear. She thought of the hasty, crossed-out passages in her journal and resolved to make it better.

"Keep your first draft, okay?" Michael was saying. "Like, don't ever get rid of that notebook when you find it—it's a classic. Buy another one for your second and third drafts. It may be painful to cut and polish what you wrote, but your writing will improve, for sure." He seemed almost like a teacher, a good one who made his students wish to learn. "Have you ever heard of Samuel Clemens? He wrote *Tom Sawyer*."

Betsie grinned at the memory of the lawn mower. "It's one of my favorite books."

"Good old Mark Twain. Anyway, he has a famous quote about the right word. He said, 'The difference between the right word and the almost right word is the difference between lightning and the lightning bug.'"

Betsie stopped writing to ponder. "I guess fixing what you write is like what *Dat* always says about trouble. 'The gem cannot be polished without friction, nor the man perfected without trials.' Ain't so?"

"Exactly so." Michael looked everywhere but at her. "Listen, Betsie—"

"Hi, Betsie! I'm home!" Sheila charged into the shop, happier than Betsie had ever seen her. "Mike, you're here, too! Guess what? Betsie got a letter, and we got one from Mom." She waved a pink envelope with round loopy writing on the front and a white one. "Dibs on reading it first," she taunted her brother as she hoisted up on the stool, kicked off her shoes, and peeled off her socks.

"A letter?" Michael asked, disconcerted. "From Phyllis?"

Sheila slit the envelope and laid it on her lap with the other one to dig out the flowered stationery. "She starts out, 'Dear family—'" She choked up and struggled to continue. Michael gently took the letter and began to read aloud.

"'Dear family, I hope you've all been taking your vitamins. I found the coolest supplement at a shop out here in Idaho—'"

STEPHANIE REED

"She's in Idaho?" Sheila squeaked, forlorn.

Michael touched his sister's arm briefly before continuing. "'I miss you all like crazy, but I know you're making out just fine without little ol' me. Your stomachs are probably in better shape than they were when I was there, since you don't have to digest any of my burnt offerings. Ha! Ha!'" Michael exchanged rueful glances with Sheila, and she laughed through her tears.

"Maybe I should not listen to your family letter." Betsie stacked her cards and rose to go.

"Please stay," Michael said.

"You're family, Betsie!" Sheila chimed in.

Family. She swallowed and stayed put.

"'Wanted to drop a line to let you know I got a bit part, just a walk-on really, in the Boise production of *Hair*. Can you believe it, guys? I'm only one curtain call away from being Sunshine Sullivan, star of stage and screen! My big debut is Friday, May 28.'"

Sheila nudged Betsie. Friday was a doubly special day for the girl, what with Michael's birthday dinner and now her mother's debut.

"'Well, that about wraps it up,'" Michael read. "'I have to get back. There's fittings, rehearsals, hair and makeup—the works! It's everything I ever dreamed of. Except I wish I could have my two kiddos here to see me go on. Well, Mikey, anyway. The production is a little mature for Sheila, I guess. But I gotta start somewhere. Take care of yourselves. Love and kisses, Mom. P.S. Tell Gerald I said hello.'"

"Oh, wow. I'm really happy for her." Michael passed the letter back to Sheila with a cautious look. "How about you, Squirt?"

"Yeah, I guess I am," Sheila mused.

Michael pretend-staggered backward. "Whoa, I can barely wrap my head around that. I thought you'd be devastated that she's not coming back. What gives?"

"I dunno." Sheila stuck the letter in her math book. "It's weird. I've been praying and praying for a letter from Mom. I hoped she'd say she's coming home, and I thought if she didn't I'd be really sad. But I'm not, Mike. It's like I know God will send her home when it's the right time."

"Must be nice. I wish I knew what God had in mind," he muttered.

"That's great, Mike!" Sheila said. "You have questions, and we're going to the revival together on Wednesday. Debbie and I are so excited that you're both going to be there."

"Oh, the revival, right." Michael drew out the last word and looked at Betsie in alarm.

"We did agree," she reminded him abstractedly. A feeling that something had slipped her mind nagged at her, but she shrugged it off. "Exactly what happens at a revival?"

"I dunno, I've never been to one, but Debbie says there's even more singing than usual. And it's fun because the service is outside in a tent."

"Pray for rain," Michael stage-whispered.

"Stop kidding around, Mike. It will be so much fun to have you and Betsie there." Her smile grew almost as sly as Mattie Yoder's. "Besides, most of the kids go with their whole families, but I can't do that." She sighed heavily and studied her bare toes.

"I know someone who's as dramatic as Sunshine Sullivan, star of stage and screen, if not more so." Michael bopped his sister's arm. "Cool it, Squirt. We told you we're coming. It's a date, right, Pippa? Be there or be square."

"It's a date," Betsie affirmed. She fervently hoped the good Lord would forgive her for showing up in an English church.

CHAPTER 36

"When we dread something, it comes to pass quicker."
—FANNIE TROYER, QUOTED IN BETSIE'S JOURNAL

BEFORE BETSIE KNEW it, it was Wednesday evening, and they were riding in Michael's car to the tent revival at the Amity Church of God.

Sheila smoothed her white blouse and a very short plaid skirt. She wore socks that came all the way up to her knees, though the socks bagged around her ankles at odd times.

"This elastic's shot." She gave one sock a vicious yank. "I wish I had a couple of rubber bands to hold my socks up. They look awful."

Betsie patted her hand where it rested on the seat back. "It's all right. No one will notice."

She wasn't as stoic when she wondered how the church people would react to her Plain dress. She prayed without much hope that they wouldn't notice her.

She glanced sideways at Michael. He wore a pair of jeans that she had mended for him, and also the green button-up shirt he'd worn when they first met, only with the frayed edges snipped from the cuffs. He was not too *stroobly-Haar*, and he had shaved again. He smelled good, too.

Soon he pulled up at a pretty white church with a steeple. A huge tent stood to one side near an oak grove. Yellow light shone from where the tent flaps were pushed open in a shape like a letter A.

Michael parked in the grass and stuck his hand out the window. "What are you doing, Mike?"

"I said a prayer. I'm checking for rain."

"That's so funny I forgot to laugh." Sheila punched his arm. "Hey, there's Debbie!"

Sheila jogged to join a girl in a skirt shorter than Sheila's. The girls held onto their hemlines as they jumped up and down and hugged each other with squeals of joy. A woman smiled fondly at their antics and Betsie recognized Mrs. Keith, the customer from the harness shop who was also Debbie's mother. She gave Betsie a friendly wave and entered the tent with Debbie. Sheila paused to search for Michael and Betsie in the crowd and crooked her elbow to make a hurry-up motion.

Michael took a deep breath. "Here goes nothing."

Betsie took a couple of steps and balked. "I'm not sure I can do this, Michael."

Michael smirked until he got a good look at her expression. "Oh, hey, you don't look too good. Wait, does this have to do with your religion? Like, what happens if your Amish L'il Abner finds out you came here?" He winked. "With me, worse yet? I don't want to get you into trouble at home. Look, Sheila can hitch a ride with Debbie's mom. Let's split."

Betsie drew a deep breath and shook her head. "I can't do that to Sheila."

He thought a moment. "How about this? If it gets too bad in there, like against what you believe"—he pressed his keys into her hand—"wait for us in my car."

"*Denki*, Michael." Her hands were shaking as she placed the keys in her pocket. Michael seemed to know exactly when she needed him most. Despite the fact that he didn't want to be at the revival, Betsie was glad for his company.

They found seats in the rows upon rows of brown metal chairs that faced the front of the tent. Betsie picked up a yellow booklet from her seat. On the cover was a drawing of English-dressed men and women with their mouths open. She rested the booklet on her lap and enjoyed the novelty of a seatback. Such a luxury compared to the backless benches at home; the English sure liked comfort in church.

It was certainly a novelty to see men and women sitting together, too. She envisioned sitting next to Charley during church the way she was sitting next to Michael and immediately fanned herself with the booklet. A bald man walking down the center aisle noticed and handed Betsie a paper fan with the words "Compliments Schiller's Funeral Parlor" stamped across the front in block letters.

"Hot in here," he said with a sympathetic smile.

A crash of noise made her jump and drop the fan. Up front on a platform, a woman in a pleated blue skirt sat at a piano and moved her hands fast in a crashing swell of chords. By the time she'd retrieved the fan, Betsie's ears had adjusted. The tune was prettier than anything she'd heard on the radio, though it was *veesht* to sing with or play a musical instrument in church. Sheila and Debbie did not appear to feel wicked, though. They opened their yellow booklets and their mouths and sang along.

Now the woman played slow music that rippled like water over rocks. A man seated near her stood to remove his dark speckled jacket, which he draped over the back of his metal chair. He rolled up the sleeves of his white, button-up shirt. His face was pale under black glasses. He had thin dark hair, a graying mustache, and he wore a skinny black tie and dark trousers like Mr. Sullivan wore to work every day. He wasn't physically imposing, yet he seemed important.

The man held a black book that Betsie recognized as a Bible. When he reached the wooden stand in the middle of the platform, he spread the Bible open in front of him. The crowd rustled expectantly. A baby fussed.

Sheila whispered, "That's Brother Burchett."

Betsie turned and held a finger to her lips to show Sheila she must be quiet while the minister spoke. As she faced front, Michael cracked his knuckles. The pops were explosive; the lady ahead of them turned in a huff to stare. Michael winked and plunked his shoes on the bottom rung of the lady's folding chair.

"Good evening. We're glad you're with us." Brother Burchett spoke into a silver pole attached to the wooden stand. His voice echoed slightly. "Would you please stand and open your hymnals to number fifteen? Let's worship the Lord together."

Betsie heard more rustles as people opened their yellow booklets. The piano-playing lady raised her hands, and *crash!* Her fingers came down on the keys and plunked out music. Voices blended and sang along ten times faster than Betsie had ever sung before about goodness and mercy. Before she knew it, that song ended and another one began, this one about flying on a morning that was glad, by and by. The piano set a dizzy pace for this hymn. Betsie counted six hymns in the time it would take the People to sing just one hymn from the *Ausbund*.

Michael surprised Betsie. He riffled through the pages to find the right hymn and stood close so she could follow along. His singing voice was better than many she'd heard on the radio, and he made Betsie smile when he rose slightly on his toes to hit high notes.

Sheila and Debbie took pains that neither Michael nor Betsie would suspect they were being watched. They failed, but Betsie pretended not to notice. In fact, no one noticed her Plain clothes, either, or Michael's long hair. Couldn't people see that her dress and manner were different, or were they so intent on God that nothing else mattered?

At last the giddy singing ended, and several men passed baskets up and down the rows. As they worked, Brother Burchett talked about a *love offering*. Betsie watched with interest as people cast coins and crumpled bills into the baskets. It was much like when the People gave alms for the poor after their worship meetings.

Michael surprised her yet again by digging his wallet out in plenty of time to put a dollar in the basket. Sheila and Debbie offered shiny quarters as more ripply music flowed from the piano.

Betsie waved the funeral fan to move the stuffy air. Outside a faint rumble echoed, far off. Michael shifted and darted anxious glances around the tent, but Betsie thought a thundershower would certainly cool things off. The smell of sun-scorched canvas threatened to choke her.

Brother Burchett took his place in front of the congregation again.

When he picked up his Bible, Michael slouched next to her with arms crossed and jaw set.

To Betsie's surprise, the preacher read Bible verses in much the same way that *Dat* always did, like he was reading stories about his good friend Jesus. He flipped through the pages with breathless speed; the Bible nestled into his hand like it belonged.

He shared verse after verse. Betsie bit her lip to keep from missing her *dat* so much. Unshed tears welled as the snarls and rumples in her soul smoothed.

"My friends, doesn't it seem as though the world is constantly crying, 'Peace'? 'Peace, peace, when there is no peace.'"

Michael straightened a fraction, his head to one side like a dog trying its best to understand.

"That's what it says in Jeremiah 6:14." Brother Burchett raised the Bible above his head. "Matthew 11:28 says, 'Come unto me, all ye that labor and are heavy laden, and I will give you rest.' That's a sure promise, friends." He put the Bible down and rested his forearms on the wooden stand. "There may be some of you here tonight who are seeking that kind of peace."

Thunder rumbled again, nearer this time, and Betsie saw Michael glance uneasily at the roof of the tent. Fans waved and paused, waved and paused as people in the congregation sought relief from the terrific heat.

Brother Burchett paused, too, and scanned the congregation until his attention seemed to fix on Michael and Betsie. Michael met Brother Burchett's unflinching gaze with an almost defiant glare. Betsie's gaze dropped. When she looked up again, Brother Burchett shared his attention equally with each person in the congregation, to her relief.

"Oh, there's many like you who seek peace, my friends," the preacher continued. "Less than a month ago, more than two hundred thousand young people marched at a peace rally in Washington, D.C. April 24, that was. Did you see the report, mothers and dads? Did you see the young people gathered at the National Mall, restless and hurting and longing for peace? Did you hear their voices raised in songs about peace?"

His voice dropped to a whisper, though it was still audible because of the microphone, and that was a marvel to Betsie.

He pointed at someone near the front, and Betsie shivered. "Were you secretly relieved that it wasn't *your* wayward daughter photographed for all to see at that demonstration? That it wasn't *your* son who was arrested because he wanted real peace but didn't know how to find it?"

Betsie dared not look at Michael.

"Or, my dear friends, maybe it's not really the longing for peace that consumes you. Maybe it's fear of death." The microphone bounced the word off the ceiling. Brother Burchett took a sip from a glass of water and continued. "Whether it's here at home facing crazy men like the Hilliard Stalker or across the seas in Vietnam, there is danger and fear. I saw the latest body count in the paper. Forty-five thousand men have lost their lives in Vietnam . . . including my only son." Brother Burchett's voice broke. He gripped the pulpit and bowed his head before resuming. "But I have good news for you, friends. You will never have to fear death again when you're saved by the blood of the Lamb."

"A-men," drawled many in the congregation, including Sheila and Debbie.

"Romans 10, verse 9, says, 'If thou shalt confess with thy mouth the Lord Jesus, and shalt believe in thine heart that God hath raised him from the dead, thou shalt be saved.' It's simple and straightforward, friends, and that's what the good news is all about."

Saved. Betsie thought of all her *ferhoodled* choices over the last few weeks and shivered despite the sweat dripping down her back. This man! Has he been at my house, watching us down through the years as *Dat* read his favorite *Biewel* verse to us? Has he been in my broken home as Sadie and I wept for our wayward parents and wondered whether we would ever find peace for our broken hearts?

"That's all you have to do, friends. Whether it's eternal life, or real love, or true peace that you're seeking, accept Jesus Christ as your Lord and Savior. Believe that He was crucified for your sins and He has risen from the dead and lives today, right now." Brother Burchett pounded the wooden stand. "And what happens next? Why, my friends, it's all right here in Philippians chapter 4, verses 6 and 7. 'Be careful for nothing; but in everything by prayer and supplication with thanksgiving let your requests be made known unto God. And the peace of God, which passeth all understanding, shall keep your hearts and minds through Christ Jesus.' It's that simple. The peace that passes understanding can be yours. King David said, 'Surely goodness and mercy shall follow me all the days of my life: and I will dwell in the house of the Lord forever.' Forever. That's a sure promise from the Word of God."

Brother Burchett seemed to shrink as he finished speaking. Wearily, he took his seat. Another man stood and offered a prayer spoken aloud. A second man expressed hope that those who had been moved by the sermon would come forward during the final song to accept Jesus into their hearts. Betsie realized that this was what Sheila must have done the other day.

Outside thunder cracked again, the report sharp like a gun, and Betsie flinched. Michael started and jostled her elbow. Uneasily she thought of the oak trees that sheltered the tent, but the revival continued.

After the prayer, they sang a song that talked about the Lamb of God and bade everyone to come. A wayward breeze lifted one tent flap slightly and meandered through the congregation as the hymn ended.

Betsie watched in amazement as first a trickle, then a flood of people shuffled into the aisle and proceeded toward the front of the tent. As more seats emptied, she feared that the four of them would be the only ones left in the congregation. By craning slightly, she could see scores of people who knelt at the foot of the platform, heads bowed in prayer.

Alarmed, Betsie gripped the seat in front of her and gritted her teeth to keep from joining them if her feet should betray her. She couldn't deny that Brother Burchett had a gift for speaking, and he sincerely seemed to care about people. The Bible reading Betsie had enjoyed, but that was all. Well, the Bible reading and the lively singing and the lovely ripples of music, but no more. One day soon she would join the Amish church, and shortly thereafter, she hoped to marry Charley, now more than ever.

For Michael's sake, however, she was glad they had come to the revival. During the sermon, she'd seen his attitude go from scornful to rapt to wistful, and better yet, although he'd certainly been aware of the thunderclaps, he hadn't weirded out. Maybe this revival was just what he needed to shake him up and help him get a grip. Betsie certainly had no illusions about his going forward to be saved, although Sheila and Debbie held hands and watched him like a pair of hawks.

The man up front raised a hand to stop the singing. The piano-playing lady cut off in the midst of a ripple, curved fingers poised above the keys.

"If there's someone who's been waiting for the right moment to come forward, now is the time. Come," he entreated.

Betsie trembled. She sneaked another glance to make doubly sure every head was bowed and every eye was closed. Then she stood up, careful not to jostle Michael, and slipped past Sheila and Debbie into the middle aisle for the exit.

Once outside, she trotted against the rising wind to locate the yellow-jacket car, her hand on the keys in her pocket. She found the car, her hiding place and refuge, and wished for a light as she fumbled to find the right key.

A split second later, blinding light flashed. The boom of thunder was simultaneous and Betsie nearly jumped out of her skin as bark sizzled and popped. Splinters of wood pelted her head and arms. The ground shuddered and somewhere high above her head, dead wood creaked and moaned.

CHAPTER 37

I never realized that misconceptions could be so painful.
—BETSIE'S JOURNAL

BETSIE RAISED HER arm to shield her eyes. The next instant, something slammed into her. She tumbled to the ground. As she fought for breath, a massive dead branch speared the earth a few inches away. The vibrations from the fall seemed to last forever.

Dazed, she tried to make sense of what had happened. Somebody shook her and shouted, "Are you all right?"

Another peal of thunder unleashed sideways sheets of rain. The car door creaked open. Strong arms hauled her to her feet. She struggled to make her rag-doll legs obey her brain. She sat down abruptly in the seat and the door shut out the rain. The car jostled as someone plopped in the other seat.

"Whew. That . . . was close." Michael breathed hard, one hand to his chest.

Betsie moved gingerly to peer in his direction. "Where did you come from?"

"Followed you out," he said. He gulped air. "Lucky I did. That branch missed you by—" He held his thumb and forefinger a couple of inches apart. "When I saw lightning strike that oak, I took off running. Barely had time to tackle you. Sorry I tackled you, by the way."

Betsie gulped, too. What if he hadn't been there? Michael might not be the most dependable person, but when real trouble reared its ugly head . . .

A burst of hammering startled her. "Mike, help! Let me in!" Sheila squinted through his window.

"Hold your horses." He hopped out of the car and popped the seat down for his sister.

She squealed and scrambled into the back. Her legs squeaked against the vinyl. "I'm soaked," she moaned. She squeezed out her ponytail and leaned between the bucket seats. "Wasn't that a great service? What happened to you guys, anyway? Betsie, why are you so pale?"

"I . . . I didn't feel so well, so I came to the car. Lightning hit the tree, and Michael—"

"Good grief!" He sliced off her explanation like a surgeon and glared at Sheila. "What is with you, Motor Mouth? Take it easy. You don't have to answer every question she asks, Pippa." From his wry expression, Betsie guessed he knew exactly why she'd left the revival.

He didn't say so, but Betsie also inferred that Michael, for whatever reason, didn't want to talk about saving her for the second time. No matter. The birthday dinner and key ring would serve as thanks. As for his habit of popping up when she was in trouble, she'd have to be more careful, that was all. Charley was always telling her so. He would have pushed her out of the way, too, if only he'd known she was in danger. Betsie was sure of it.

The storm soon wore itself out. She rolled down her window a crack to enjoy the rain-cooled breezes.

Sheila's ponytail hung in wet straggles. "That was pretty smart, Betsie, to run for the car before the storm hit. You still got pretty wet, though, and you didn't even get to stay for the end." She brightened. "Hey, I know! There's one more night for the revival meeting, and I don't think it's supposed to rain tomorrow. We could come back—"

"No," Michael and Betsie said simultaneously.

"Tomorrow is your last day of school, ain't so, Sheila?" Betsie went on. "That's pretty much excitement for one day, so we won't go to the revival again. But see here, aren't you forgetting that we need a few things at the store? *For Friday.*"

"Wha—? Ohhh." Sheila grew more artful than Tom Sawyer with a bucket of whitewash. She sized up her big brother. "Betsie and I have some shopping to do at Ayers Market, Mike. Can you drive us there before we go home?"

"The market?" He frowned. "It's pretty late. They're not on summer hours until June first." If he realized he'd named his birthday, he didn't show it. "That means they close at nine tonight." He raised his wrist to check the mouse's hands, which glowed in the dark. "That's less than forty minutes."

Betsie nodded. "Plenty of time. I have a list, and I brought house-keeping money, so I am ready."

He raised his eyebrows but cranked the car key. "All right, ladies. Would this trip by any chance have to do with Friday's mysterious dinner invitation?"

Sheila frowned. "No fair, Mike! How did you guess Betsie and I want to have a cookout to celebrate Memorial Day weekend? We need to have it Friday because she won't be here this weekend."

Michael flipped on the car's heater. He sighed. "Okay, I'll take you, but I'm not going in. I don't want to see—I mean I don't want to get soaked. I'd rather wait in the car."

"Oh, that's okay, Mike. You don't have to go in. We won't be long." Betsie felt Sheila's conspiratorial kick underneath her car seat as she reassured her brother.

There were only two cars parked in front of the market when Michael pulled up. He said he'd leave the car running so the heater could dry them out when they came back. He drummed his fingers slowly on the wood wheel to some inner tune of his own as Sheila squelched out of the car to Betsie's side.

The butcher whistled as he redded up the meat counter. Sheila had insisted that frankfurters would be better than plain old hot dogs, so Betsie put in her order, and the butcher smiled as he wrapped them up. "Thank you, Archie."

He winked and made a fist. "Power to the people." Betsie nodded with dignity. It was hard to believe now that she'd fallen for Michael's tricks on how to speak at the market that day.

"Napier," a man barked.

Archie straightened. "Yes, sir, Mr. Ayers?"

A harried gentleman appeared, the one who'd once called Archie a boy. "Here's the store keys. My wife called—her dad suffered a stroke. Lock up for me, will you? I've gotta meet her at the hospital."

"I'm sorry to hear that, sir. I'll take care of things."

Mr. Ayers grimaced. "I hope I can be back to open up tomorrow. I guess there's not too much damage you can do. Peggy's too flighty, so you get the job."

"Don't worry, sir. I can handle things here. Hope your father-in-law comes out of this okay."

But Mr. Ayers was already striding down the aisle for the front of the store. Archie jingled the keys and stuck them in his pocket. He stood a little straighter. "Anything else, Miss?"

"No, thank you."

By the time Betsie ticked off everything on her list, the store lights had already flickered twice. A decidedly damp Sheila manned the squeaky cart while Betsie fished out a twenty-dollar bill. As the pair entered the only open line, the lights at the very back of the market went off. Startled, Betsie let the shopping list flutter to the floor and stooped to retrieve it. When she straightened, Peggy was glaring at her. Sheila had expertly unloaded the cart onto the moving belt, but the cashier had not yet started to ring up the order.

"Can you check us out, please?" Sheila asked.

Peggy curled her fingers to examine her nails and buffed them on her uniform. "We're closed. You'll have to put everything back on the shelf."

She started to say more, but happy whistling interrupted her. Archie emerged from the aisle behind them with a push broom, his white butcher's apron swiped with bloody smears and fingerprints.

"These here are my friends, Peg," he said. "I know it's past closing time, but go ahead and ring 'em up. You have a good evening, ladies." He whistled and resumed sweeping.

The second he was out of sight, Peggy savagely punched buttons on the cash register. The groceries slid down the belt, but she made no move to bag them, and it was perfectly obvious to Betsie that she was somehow to blame. A biscuit can revolved against the Porch Swing Lemonade tin like a log in deep water.

Peggy eyed Sheila. "You're Michael Sullivan's kid sister, right?"

Sheila smiled like all her problems had been solved. "Yeah, do you know him?"

"Oh, yeah, I know Michael, and I know what he likes to eat." She winked. "Betcha this stuff is for his birthday, huh, sweetie?" Peggy's words dripped honey, but they hid a sting.

"Yes, please don't tell him! It's a surprise," Sheila begged.

"You don't have to worry about that. Why would I want to ruin Michael Sullivan's birthday surprise?"

Betsie knew why, but she said nothing. The quicker they got out of there, the better.

Sheila chattered happily on, oblivious. "The surprise is from me and Betsie."

"Betsie, huh?" Peggy raked her with contempt. "Gee, that's a really cute outfit you got on there, honey. You must really love it; you wear it all the time." She smiled like Mattie Yoder. "I guess they don't allow too much baggage on the *Mayflower*, huh?"

Sheila gaped. "Betsie's not a Pilgrim. She's Amish."

Peggy's eyes glittered like a snake's. "Oh, honey. I know what Betsie is, believe you me. She's a dirty, rotten, low-down boyfriend stealer," she hissed. The cashier's hand flashed and slapped Betsie's cheek.

Stunned, Betsie staggered into the rack behind her. Candy bars slithered to the floor.

"You can't do that to Betsie!" Sheila hollered. She lunged, her blouse coming untucked from her short skirt. Betsie grabbed the tail of her shirt and yanked Sheila from the moving belt before she could slap Peggy back.

Peggy hadn't even flinched. "Got what she deserved, sis, coming in here dressed in those snooty clothes, trying to show me up. I've got news for you, Miss Betsie Holier-Than-Thou. You're no better than me, even though you think you are."

Flabbergasted at Peggy's outburst, Betsie managed to keep hold of Sheila as she lunged again like a terrier after a rat. "Betsie's a hundred times better than you any day of the week! Don't you touch her!"

"What in the world is going on up here?" Archie sprinted up, hair bobbing.

Sheila pointed at Peggy, eyes blazing. "She slapped Betsie! You can see her handprint on Betsie's cheek!"

Archie stared. "Have you lost your mind, Peg? How dare you strike a customer?"

"She stole my boyfriend!" Peggy shrilled.

Archie winced. "I'll have to speak to Mr. Ayers about your conduct. Until then, beat it. Get your stuff and clear out of here."

"Where do *you* get off, telling me what to do, Napier? I'll leave because it's quitting time." She shot Betsie a look of pure evil. "I'll tell you what—that slap was worth it." She ripped off her apron and stomped to the door.

Sorrow showed in Archie's dark eyes. "Nothing like this has ever happened in our store. Please accept my profound apologies." He bagged their groceries and popped up all zeroes on the cash register. "This order is on the house. Listen, are you sure you're okay?" he asked.

Betsie's cheek throbbed. She nodded, but the truth was, she was not okay. Thoughts spun in her head like a mill wheel. Had Peggy been yelling about *Betsie* the day she left Michael in the driveway? Did Peggy think Michael was Betsie's boyfriend? He was undeniably a friend. Betsie enjoyed talking with him when he wasn't too weirded out, but that state was standard lately. How absurd. Charley was her special friend, not Michael.

What about the other thing Peggy said?

Betsie started, yet the thought was insistent and painful as she mulled it over. Is that what my Plain clothes mean to Peggy, that I think I am better than her? But that would mean I am proud, an attitude my Amish clothes are meant to ward off.

Betsie realized Archie was speaking again, but she was too *ferhoodled* to answer. Sheila came to her rescue again, charming as she reassured Archie that no, it was not necessary to help them to the car with the groceries, but gracious as she thanked him nicely when he said he was going to, all the same.

Betsie was glad of his assistance when she spotted Peggy lurking in the vestibule. When the cashier saw Archie, she stormed outside with a vicious glance at Michael's car.

Michael, parked in the car and apparently oblivious to the drama, had the trunk open already. Archie unloaded the groceries, apologizing the whole time for the trouble. Confused but game, Michael thanked Archie and tipped him a dollar as rain showers resumed.

"What's the deal?" He started the car. "Peg left in a heck of a hurry."

Betsie cupped her cheek. "It's nothing."

But Sheila gripped the sides of the bucket seats and scooted forward until she was practically up front. "Peggy slapped Betsie: that's what the deal is. And Archie kicked her out!"

Michael tromped hard on the brakes. "*What?* Spill it, Squirt."

Betsie groaned inwardly and watched the windshield wipers splips-splop as Sheila related the miserable tale. She shifted uneasily as Sheila neared the end.

"Then Peggy said Betsie was a dirty, rotten, lowdown—"

"Don't say it, Sheila," Betsie pleaded.

"But, Betsie, I'm almost to the worst part!"

"Can it, Squirt," Michael said. "Pippa doesn't want to hash it over anymore."

Sheila scowled and flopped into her seat to sulk. As Michael twisted to back up, his fingertips grazed Betsie's forearm, and he jerked his hand away like he'd been shocked. Betsie was fairly certain that he'd already guessed what Peggy said.

CHAPTER 38

The wounds that hurt the most are those
which are allowed to fester.
—BETSIE'S JOURNAL

BETSIE WAS GRATEFUL for the quiet ride home—that is, until the siren whined. Red flashing lights reflected on Michael's wary face from the rearview mirror.

"Oh, great. Hilliard's finest." He pulled over and glowered.

Sheila knelt on the seat and peeked out the back while Michael rolled his window down. Raindrops splattered and cool air washed over Betsie's hot cheek.

"Here he comes, Mike," Sheila stage-whispered.

Betsie ducked to see who it was and sucked in her breath. Officer Schwartz—he'd said that he'd be watching for Michael's car. If only she'd remembered to warn him! The officer shone a flashlight in her face and Sheila's before he played the beam over Michael.

"Would you mind telling me what this is all about . . . Officer?" Michael asked in an oily tone.

"I'll ask the questions here." The officer glanced toward the rear of the car. "Know you have a taillight out?"

"Oh, for—is that why you stopped me? I thought you were on probation."

"Not that it's any of your business," Schwartz retorted, "but I came off probation yesterday."

"Got a fresh batch of tickets to write, huh? Why don't you concentrate on real criminals?"

Schwartz eyed Michael. "Have anyone special in mind?"

Michael spread his hands to show his innocence while every muscle in Betsie's body quivered. If only he wouldn't blow his top . . .

"I need to see your license and registration."

With a resigned sigh, Michael dug out his wallet. While Schwartz examined his license, Michael reached past Betsie to snap open the glove box. He extracted a paper, slapped the box shut, and handed the paper to Schwartz.

"Looks like you have an important birthday coming up, Mr. Sullivan."

Sheila kicked underneath Betsie's seat.

Schwartz smiled thinly at Michael, who didn't reply. "Uncle Sam is going to be mighty happy to whip a hippie like you into shape. He'll send you to Nam so fast you won't know what hit you."

Michael went white, but he mustered a sarcastic smile. "You're older than me. Why hasn't Uncle Sam sent you to Nam, Petey?"

"Again, not that it's any of your business, Sullivan, but I'm classified 4-F. Medical reasons." He tapped an area near his heart. "If not for that, you better bet I'd go in a red-hot minute."

"There's just one problem." Michael's smile was grim. "Uncle Sam wouldn't touch you with a ten-foot pole."

Sheila's troubled gasp caught Betsie's ear as the war of words escalated. Betsie touched his arm. "Michael."

"No, ma'am, let him shoot off his mouth," Schwartz sneered. "Why don't you think they'd take me, freak?"

Michael looked him straight in the eye. "Because I hear the army doesn't like the smell of pigs."

Schwartz trembled with rage. "When you get to Nam and they blow your commie head off, then we'll see who's laughing." He opened a pad and scribbled rapidly, ripped the paper across the top, and flung it at Michael. "See you in court, if you live that long." He thumped the car's roof and strode away.

The minute Schwartz drove out of sight, Michael shredded the ticket and scattered the tiny pieces to the wind. "What a boor."

Contrary to Sheila's hopes, the revival had done Michael no good at all. Betsie folded her hands and stared at her lap. The image of Brother Burchett's anguish as he spoke of his dead son returned unbidden to torment her.

"I don't want you to get your head blown off! Are you going to get drafted, Mike?" Sheila's voice was thick with tears.

"Not if I can help it, Squirt."

"But he said . . ."

"Hey, that guy is a clod. Nothing's going to happen to me, all right? Tell you what, let's see if we can find your favorite song on the radio." Michael clicked the selectors until he found a song that soothed Sheila not at all. He drove fast, with one hand on the wheel. With the other he patted the armrest in time with the music. He didn't talk.

It didn't take long until they pulled into the driveway, but Betsie was exhausted. Michael popped the trunk and started to help with the groceries.

Sheila recovered some of her spunk and pushed him away. "You can't! You'll ruin the surprise."

She and Betsie gathered up the bags as Michael headed to the house. He checked when he saw his father's car and started to get back in his own. Instead he headed for the mailbox, although surely, Betsie thought, they'd gotten the mail already.

Sheila managed to ring the doorbell with her elbow. While they waited for Mr. Sullivan, Betsie kept an eye on Michael. He reached in the box and slid out a long, brown envelope. He stared at it for a long time.

"Back from church?" Mr. Sullivan said through the screen. "Where's Michael? Did he chicken out on the revival?"

"No, he went, and he even drove us to the store." Sheila gestured with her head. "He's getting the mail. C'mon, Dad, this stuff is heavy!" She clambered inside with many dramatic moans and groans.

Betsie propped the door with a hip and hitched the heavy bags. She watched the indistinct shape that was Michael approach the Super Bee. "Come on in," she called to him.

He ignored her and flicked the letter into the back seat. With a vicious yank, he opened the door and slid behind the wheel. The engine revved, and the car raced into the night.

"What is all this, ladies?" Mr. Sullivan inquired as Betsie deposited her heavy load. "Are we gearing up for a holiday barbecue?" He pitched in to help.

"No, we're planning a surprise dinner for Michael," Sheila informed him.

Betsie put the parcel of frankfurters in the green refrigerator. "For his birthday. We're celebrating it on Friday."

Mr. Sullivan's happy smile slipped. "Michael's birthday?"

"I know, I know, it's not his birthday yet, but we wanted this to be a surprise. He would be too suspicious if we had it on the actual day, so we're having it Friday." Sheila's voice was muffled as she rearranged the milk and orange juice to make room for party groceries. "Dad, can you hand me that package of cheese?" She stuck out her hand. "Dad?"

But her father was lost in his thoughts. "His twentieth birthday," he muttered as he sat heavily in the kitchen chair.

Betsie handed the package of cheese to Sheila. Mr. Sullivan looked sadder and lonelier than she'd ever seen him, and she thought she knew why. "Mr. Sullivan, did you see the letter from your wife?"

"What? A letter from Phyllis?"

Sheila blushed. "I guess I forgot to give it to you, Dad. Hang on a sec and let me get it."

When the girl was out of earshot, Betsie confided, "I know it is a disappointment that your wife won't be here Friday, but don't worry, Mr. Sullivan. Michael promised to be here and you can make everything right between you then."

Mr. Sullivan held his forehead and closed his eyes. "It's too late, Betsie. We've lost Michael. And in a way, it's mostly my fault. I just can't keep my fat mouth shut. Michael dropped out of Kent State after . . . what happened. He quit his job at the Milky Way and lives off his bank account, near as I can tell. Now he's eligible to be called up." He stared at her. "He's a dreamer. He writes a few articles for that radical *Columbus Free Press*, a monthly rag that will set you back fifteen cents, and he thinks he's a journalist. What kind of job security is *that?*" He realized what he'd said and winced. "He's nothing like me, and maybe that's a good thing."

Betsie sought to comfort him, but he headed for the living room and collapsed on the white sofa. "He and his mother are two of a kind. She dropped out of our lives to follow her dreams. Michael dropped out of college to get away from his nightmares." He met her gaze. "Has he told you about the shootings?"

"Yes."

"I know it was a terrible thing to see, but he should have gotten right back up on that horse and enrolled here at Ohio State when the time came. Why can't he move on like a normal person?" He checked himself, his expression bitter. "And there I go again. But the truth is, if only he had gone back to school somewhere, anywhere, we wouldn't have this problem and he'd be safe."

"Don't worry. Everything will be all right."

"You're fooling yourself, Betsie. Almost the last thing Phyllis and I argued about before she left was that I was too hard on Michael. She says he's very sensitive, that he takes life's normal ups and downs much harder than I do. I wish I had done a better job of relating to him, but he'll soon leave for good."

"Please don't say that," Betsie said sharply. "Michael will come back, Mr. Sullivan."

"I wish I could believe that." He rubbed the back of his neck and changed the subject. "I have to go out of town on business tomorrow, Betsie. I won't be back until Friday, but I'll be home fairly early because it's the start of Memorial Day weekend. Can you keep everything going for me in the meantime? I think you and Sheila will be all right if Mike comes back like you say he will."

"*Jah*, sure," she said, relieved. The break would be good for Michael and his dad.

Sheila hurried into the room. "Sorry it took me so long. I found Mom's letter in my math book! I'm sorry I didn't remember sooner. I guess I got excited about the revival and the last day of school and Michael's birthday dinner . . ."

Betsie took her hand and led her gently away from her dad and his regrets. "Why don't we pick out something to wear to school tomorrow while your dad reads it?"

"Really, Betsie?" Her eyes were twin stars. "I wanted to call Debbie and ask her because it's our last day of sixth grade and elementary school and I want to wear something special, but I already used up my thirty minutes of phone time today and I don't want Dad to blow his top. I really need your help because no matter what I wear, that jerk Kevin who sits next to me—you know, the one who gave me a hard time about the Mother's Day poem?"

Betsie nodded as they passed Michael's empty room.

"Like I was saying, that jerk Kevin is always on my case. He's always like, 'Nice threads, Sullivan,' but I can tell he doesn't mean it, not really. The good news is, after tomorrow I won't have to put up with him for the whole summer." She grew thoughtful. "Although I might run into him at the pool, I guess."

Betsie plumped down on the ruffled white bedspread and studied the horse pictures on Sheila's wall—horses trotting, horses galloping, manes fluttering, nostrils flared. The picture above the headboard hung askew, and she pressed the yellowed corner back into place while Sheila scooted hangers in her closet and rained clothes on her bed. Noncommittal replies satisfied the girl as she chattered and displayed outfit after outfit for Betsie's approval. Meanwhile her mind raced faster than Sheila's tongue.

So much had happened this evening. Impressions of the revival swirled. Brother Burchett—he was so filled up with the Bible, just like *Dat*. Both of them believed that knowing Jesus made everything so simple and peaceful. Betsie tried to imagine her parents' lives now. No Plain dress. No horses. No *Ordnung*. No heaven.

Betsie pushed the thought away. Her cheek smarted where Peggy had slapped her; she hoped it wouldn't bruise. She had no idea how she would explain that to Charley and Sadie.

"How's this look, Betsie?"

She gave a vague nod. "Yes, that looks good."

Sheila glanced from the purple-striped top in her right hand to the orange flowered pants in her left. "*This* looks good together? Really? But we're not allowed to wear pants to school until junior high." Her eyes glittered. "It would be so cool to wear pants *anyway*, even though we're not supposed to. What could Hosket do about it on the last day of elementary?" She gurgled. "What a fry!"

Three rebels in one house were too many. "*Ach*, Sheila, that's maybe not such a good idea. I don't know what I was thinking. I guess I'm still pretty muddled after what happened in the store."

Sheila threw down the clothing and clenched her fists. "I was so mad when Peggy slapped you! I don't care if she *does* think you stole my brother." She winked. "I mean, you *do* like Mike, don't you?"

CHAPTER 39

The People know many ways to show love, but the
English are one up on us.
—BETSIE'S JOURNAL

"WAS IN DER WELT?" Betsie's voice shot up three notches. "I—"

The telephone bell shrilled, and Sheila clapped her hands. "There's the phone! Maybe Dad won't care how long I talk since Debbie called me this time!" She answered before the phone rang a second time. Giggles spilled into the hall from Mr. Sullivan's room.

Slowly, Betsie tidied the whirlwind of blouses, skirts, and dresses and arranged them in the closet. She smoothed the sat-upon place on the bed, but then she plumped right back down on it and chewed her lip.

She hadn't dreamed it was possible to feel so *ferhoodled.* No longer did she want to prepare a family birthday dinner for Michael. She did not want to see him at all. She wanted to go home to Plain City, pour out her troubles to Charley, and have him reassure her that everything would be all right once they were married.

She reached for Sheila's math book, flung helter-skelter on the bed. The shiny cover slipped from her grasp and landed on the spine, the pages open. Betsie stooped to pick the book up and stared. A white envelope addressed to her in care of the Sullivans slithered to rest at Betsie's feet.

Mem's handwriting. Betsie's pulse pounded. Sheila had forgotten all about Betsie's letter in the excitement over her own.

She hurried to her room and locked the door. In a flash she undid her *Kapp* and fished a hairpin from her heavy twist of hair. With shaking fingers she slit the envelope and pulled out the letter. Surely this was the good news she'd been waiting for. *Mem* and *Dat* were coming home! Her cheeks hurt from her wide smile as she began to read:

My dear Betsie,

I take the opportunity to write to you at Mr. Sullivan's address so we do not cause trouble at home. Your dat had the numbers still from Nelson. Well, though we were happy to see you, still we wish you had stayed to visit more. Betsie you don't know how we miss you. It would be such a comfort . . .

Overcome with longing to work at her mother's side once more, Betsie sniffled and dropped into the ladder-back chair. She composed herself and read on:

It would be such a comfort to have you and Sadie with us, and your brother Abijah, too, where you can learn of the good Lord and His bountiful grace in providing a Savior, Jesus Christ . . .

Growing horror brushed up the hairs on the back of her neck.

. . . who takes away our sins so we can be saved.

No. The letter they'd written, the prayer, *Lovina* . . .

Dat is watching over my shoulder as I write this. He urges you to bring Sadie so we can share the good news with you. There is some good news that I can share in this letter, and that is your dat's sister Lovina is also now saved. She sends her love. Don't wait, Betsie, please come soon. Remember Isaiah 26:3, "Thou wilt keep him in perfect peace, whose mind is stayed on thee, because he trusteth in thee."

Your loving mother and father,
Fannie and Noah Troyer

"Why can't You leave my family in peace?" Betsie whispered to the good Lord. She threw herself across the bed, the letter crumpled in one hand, and cried into her pillow until she fell asleep.

On Thursday, the sun rose in a clear sky and quickly dried the early morning raindrops that sparkled on the lilac's heart-shaped leaves. Beauty was all around, and unaccountably, Betsie's heart lifted. She made up her mind that today she would tend the harness shop; it was sure to be busy with the county fair visitors. If no customers came, she planned to scrub the house to get it ready for the party.

A steady stream of horse show customers, many of whom said they were referred to the shop by Mrs. Keith, kept Betsie busy all morning, but the fixes they required were relatively simple. By eleven thirty the rush slowed, and she locked up.

After eating, Betsie dusted the lumpy vases and the wooden TV. She refused to tackle the persnickety vacuum cleaner, preferring to leave that job to Sheila. Mopping could wait until after she finished making the red velvet cake that Sheila insisted was Michael's favorite. Sheila had located her aunt Hester's secret recipe, and Betsie had purchased the necessary cocoa, red food coloring, and buttermilk.

Baking cakes was messy but satisfying, with clouds of flour flying. She rolled up her sleeves and made such a *Hutsch* as she sifted flour and measured sugar that it would take a *gut* long time to clean up the floor. At last three layer-cake pans went into the oven, each filled with blood-red batter. She shivered and whipped up the white icing.

While the cakes baked, Betsie set to work on another banana cream pie, vaguely annoyed that she'd promised to make both. The thought of Michael nudged at her again as she trimmed the crust and set it aside until she could brown it in the oven. He hadn't slept in the harness shop, nor had Betsie encountered him snoring on the floor when she put away his folded wash. A worried feeling gnawed.

To Betsie's consternation, she heard children singing. Surely it was not yet time for Sheila to get home, but one look at the clock told her it was so. She hurried toward the road, where kids of all ages stuck their heads out of the bus windows and bellowed at the tops of their lungs while the bus driver hollered for everyone to sit down. With difficulty, Betsie made out the words. "School's out, school's out, Teacher let the monkeys out!" And that was exactly what the children resembled—long-armed monkeys clamoring for attention.

One older boy in the front window kept a wistful gaze glued to Sheila as she yelled her good-byes from the bus steps. Betsie hid a smile and wondered if he was Kevin. If he wanted to court Sheila, he was going to have to do better than teasing and mooning over her from afar. Sometime soon, she hoped Charley Yoder would come to her window in the dead of night and wake her by tossing a handful of pebbles to tap the glass. Then there would be no doubt about his intentions.

She laughed at herself. Pebble tossing was a silly old custom. No one did that nowadays.

"No more school! Wheee!" Sheila tackled Betsie, her face bright with hopes for the summer, her body blinding in purple-striped shirt and orange-flowered pants. Betsie pretended to cringe, and Sheila laughed.

"I will be glad to have you at home every day. That is, when you are not at the pool with Debbie. And Kevin," she ribbed.

"Betsie! Kevin is the last person I want to see this summer." She blushed and changed the subject. "Wow, Mike finally mowed the lawn? Boy, oh boy, was the grass ever long."

"*Schnickelfritz!* Do you think only boys can mow?"

"*You* mowed it?"

"Yes, days ago." She didn't add that Sheila probably hadn't noticed because of the police officers' visit after Benner's assault. "You are not too observant, ain't so? Anyway, driving a tractor is not so hard."

275

"Well, if the lawn is done, I guess we're all ready for the party tomorrow night."

Betsie scoffed. "We are not ready at all! We have plenty of work left to do. And now that you have no more school, you can help. I've already done a lot of the cleaning by myself, and I have a cake and a pie to finish."

"But when you're Amish, work is fun," Sheila said.

"Oh, so you *are* observant when it behooves you to be. I have news for you. Work *is* fun, and *you* are going to have lots of fun right now. Race you to the house!"

"You got a head start, no fair!" Sheila yelled, but she quickly passed Betsie and sprinted up the steps to tag the house. "I win!" She stuck out her tongue.

Betsie shoved her aside, but Sheila shoved back as each tried to squeeze through the door first. They burst into the house together, practically fell down the steps into the sunken living room, and collapsed on the white sofa, hugging each other until they were breathless with laughter. Tears sprang to Betsie's eyes. If only this happiness, this freedom to love and show it, could last for always.

CHAPTER 40

I think people would be better off if their stories had
happy endings, like Joe's in *Lassie Come-Home*.
—Betsie's journal

FRIDAY MORNING DAWNED fair and hot. Betsie hoped the indoor
weather would remain calm after Mr. Sullivan and Michael arrived.

She and Sheila had taken care of themselves with no trouble at
all. Noise was not a problem since Mr. Sullivan was gone, so the pair
worked into the night on Thursday. Michael had not returned, but
Sheila stayed chipper as a chipmunk.

Betsie tried to remain positive. Luckily it was difficult to brood
while Sheila swept and mopped the floor. She flicked water on Betsie
when her back was turned and snickered as she passed the dirty mop
over her toes.

When they finished on Friday afternoon, the girls took turns getting ready in the pink bathroom. Pigs in a poke, as Betsie persisted
in calling the dish, did not involve much preparation. Pop the cookie
sheet in the oven when Michael, the guest of honor, showed up: that
was all that was left to do. The cake had taken forever—Betsie did not
enjoy frosting layer cakes—but finally it glistened white on the green
glass cake plate that Sheila scrounged out of the cupboard.

Together they watched anxiously for Michael. Betsie cringed every
time Sheila declared she heard Michael's car and raced to the door to

distract him before he entered the house too early. As the afternoon progressed, Betsie chewed her lip and brooded. As quickly as she banished worries of Michael behind bars after kicking another policeman at a peace rally, more gruesome thoughts of Michael in a car wreck took shape. *Ach,* he was so exasperating! If only she didn't feel like a mother hen, always mindful of her helpless chick.

At five o'clock, the beige station wagon with wooden sides rolled into the driveway. Betsie stirred the simmering coney sauce and dashed to join Sheila behind the curtains. An exhausted Mr. Sullivan opened the big door at the back of the wagon and removed his luggage. He checked for the missing Super Bee. Pain flickered in his eyes.

"Welcome home, Dad!" Sheila shouted. "I'll take your suitcase." She lugged it valiantly to her dad's room.

"Michael hasn't been here, Mr. Sullivan," Betsie warned in a low voice.

"Not at all?" The air seemed to go out of him.

"Don't worry, Dad!" Sheila scurried into the room. "Mike hasn't been back, but he promised he would be here for dinner tonight. We shook on it."

Her simple faith moved Betsie, but a gleam came into Mr. Sullivan's eye. "Are you sure he hasn't been staying in the harness shop, ladies?"

"Why do you ask?" Betsie's conscience pricked.

He chuckled. "I'll let you two in on a little secret. I know perfectly well that Michael sleeps in the harness shop when I kick him out of the house. I figure it won't hurt him to spend a night out there once in a while. Betcha that's where he is. Run out there, Sheila, and bring Mike in for his party."

She was gone before Betsie could stop her. "I know he's not there, Mr. Sullivan," she insisted. "I'm awful worried about Michael. Where can he be?"

"Hmph. Most likely with what's-her-name, Peggy, from the market."

"No." Betsie cupped her cheek. "She doesn't like him anymore."

"That's right, she doesn't." Sheila shook her head to show she hadn't found her brother and twined the end of her ponytail around her finger. "Don't you think we should start on the pigs in a blanket, Betsie?"

Mr. Sullivan and Betsie exchanged troubled glances before Betsie made a determined effort to smile. "That's a good idea. Time to see if frankfurters taste better than plain old hot dogs, ain't so?"

Betsie coerced Sheila into striking the dreaded tube of biscuit dough against the sharp edge of the countertop. When Sheila gave up after several thumps, Betsie unplugged her ears and reached for the can. As she touched it, the tube flexed. *Crack!* It sounded like a gunshot. Beige dough welled out of the split tube, and Betsie managed a shaky laugh at the state of her nerves.

Sheila slit the frankfurters and tucked the cheese inside. Betsie rolled and wrapped the strips of greasy biscuit dough around each frankfurter, but she found it difficult to get the dough to stick without it snapping back to the original shape. Finally she anchored the ends with toothpicks and lined the pigs up in rows on a cookie sheet. She set the oven to preheat.

"Everything looks great." Sheila lifted the lid of the coney sauce and sniffed. Her stomach growled, and Betsie laughed.

"Sure smells good, girls."

Mr. Sullivan had changed out of his suit and wore what Sheila called his weekend clothes, namely old blue jeans and a plaid, short-sleeved shirt. He glanced at the sunburst clock. It was 5:35, with no sign of the Super Bee.

"I'll put the potato chips in a bowl, okay, Betsie?"

Betsie didn't have the heart to answer. Sheila dumped the whole bag of chips and nibbled a couple. "Just to make sure they're the right kind." Her eyes widened. "Oh, no!"

She knows Michael isn't coming. Betsie braced for a storm of disappointed tears. "What is it, dear heart?"

"We forgot to make the Porch Swing Lemonade! I have to hurry before he gets here!" She banged around in the cabinets with great energy until she found a glass pitcher.

"Do you need any help?"

"Nope. If there's one thing I know how to make by myself, it's Porch Swing Lemonade. We drink it by the gallon all summer long." She busied herself with the plastic measuring cup that came in the package. Sheila was so happy that Betsie didn't care when some of the powdered mix sifted onto the spotless floor and crunched under Sheila's sandals as she added water and stirred up a lemony tornado.

Betsie's nerves twanged. She paced to the living room where Mr. Sullivan sat reading the newspaper.

"I wish things had turned out better tonight, Betsie," he said over the lowered page. "You do realize Michael's not coming?"

"It's just now six," Betsie protested. "He may come yet."

His smile didn't reach his eyes. "You girls have gone to a lot of trouble. I hate to see you disappointed."

"Disappointed about what, Dad?" Sheila skipped the two steps and landed in the living room with a thump. She looked at the clock, and her eyes got bigger than a begging puppy's.

"Disappointed if frankfurters aren't as good as hot dogs," Betsie broke in. "Michael's a bit late, so what do you say we put those pigs in a poke in the oven now? I'm hungry."

"I guess we can." Sheila plodded to the kitchen as though living in the grownup world of weak faith exhausted her.

"That's my girl!" Betsie followed her. "The oven is good and hot now, and maybe Michael will be here by the time they're done. Want to slide them in?"

Sheila perked up as she watched the pop-out rolls puff and brown around the sizzling franks and melty cheese. At a quarter after, Betsie set the table and matter-of-factly put a ladle in the coney sauce while Sheila clinked ice and poured lemonade. Mr. Sullivan sat down and Sheila asked the blessing. Nobody mentioned Michael.

The pigs in a blanket were delicious, especially when smothered with coney sauce. The barbecue potato chips made them thirsty for lemonade with lots of ice. Plenty of food was left after supper, though. Betsie cut and served the banana cream pie and each of them had a slice. They didn't have the heart to cut the snowy birthday cake that waited on the green glass cake stand.

When the last bite of pie disappeared, a subdued Sheila cleared the table while Mr. Sullivan took out the trash.

"Sheila honey," he said when he returned, "we need to take Betsie home for the weekend. Grab your shoes and—"

"Dad, can I please stay? I want to be here when Michael comes home."

Mr. Sullivan's eyes widened until Betsie thought they would get stuck. He searched for words. "I don't think that's a good idea."

"You won't be gone very long, and I'm not a baby. I'm done with elementary school and I'll be fine until you get back. Please?"

Mr. Sullivan smoothed his nonexistent cowlick. "How about this? Call Debbie and ask if it's okay to drop you off at her house on the way. Leave Michael a note so he can come and pick you up when he gets home."

"That would be keen! Thanks, Dad! I'll call and write the note and be ready in a jiffy." She dashed to her brother's bedroom and emerged a few seconds later. "I'm so excited that I can't find any paper!"

"Dear heart." Betsie chuckled. "I will do it." She tousled Sheila's hair as she passed.

She nipped into Michael's room, which was uncharacteristically neat. She rummaged for a pencil from the coffee mug and scrabbled through the desk drawer for a scrap of paper. When she finished the note, she fumbled in her pocket and drew out the key ring. She laid it gently beside the paper and wrote, "For your birthday, from Betsie." Then she rejoined the family.

When Sheila was safe at Debbie's, Betsie and Mr. Sullivan headed for Plain City. Mr. Sullivan drove fast. The back seat was one long bench, and Betsie had a hard time sticking to one spot. She thanked the good Lord when they reached her driveway in one piece.

"Betsie."

"Yes?"

Mr. Sullivan removed his glasses to polish them. When he put them back on, tears sparkled. "I'm so sorry."

"It's all right," she repeated.

"No," he said. "It's my fault. First Phyllis and now Michael; I've driven them away."

She tried to interrupt, but he kept talking as the motor sputtered gently.

"I'm nothing but a postscript to my wife. 'Tell Gerald I said hello,' like I'm some casual acquaintance instead of her husband." He laughed without mirth. "I know I'm just as big of a joke to Michael."

"That's not true. Michael loves you." Betsie thought a moment. "You are just very different from each other."

"That's the understatement of the century. Look, maybe you're right, but I have to find out for myself. I'll do my best to help Michael through whatever is eating him before he's drafted. The minute we get that worked out, I'm going after Phyllis. I've made up my mind to find her and bring her home where she belongs, and I'm not coming back until I succeed."

Far from reassuring her, his single-mindedness frightened Betsie. "What about Sheila and Michael?"

"Don't worry; I know I can't go right away. First things first. Michael and I need to do some serious talking when he gets back. I need to find out where his head is at, as the kids today say. I just hope I'm not too late."

Betsie watched his taillights as she wished for the peace she'd once had here at home, but it was no use. She lived in two worlds now, and both of them were in a *Hutsch*. Only one thing would make her feel better.

In a couple of minutes she was swinging open the big barn door. She dropped her satchel in the loose straw underfoot and felt her way to Judith's stall as her eyes adjusted to the gloomy barn. Her horse snorted a welcome, neck arched low and ears tipped forward. Betsie reached up to scratch Judith's poll, pressed her cheek against her satiny neck, and let the hot tears flow. When her tears dried, utterly spent, she curled up in the straw.

Betsie sat up with a start. Judith snorted, and Betsie realized that she'd fallen fast asleep. She stroked her mare's nose and soothed her with soft words before she fumbled for her satchel and stumbled groggily out of the barn.

Thankfully, the house was dark. She had no desire to explain her red eyes or to share *Mem*'s letter this evening.

As she groped her way to the stairs, something twined around her ankles. She gasped. "Amelia! Such a turn you gave me." She scooped up the calico kitten and listened to her purrs. "Come with me while I light the lamp. I bet that cranky old Sadie didn't pet you once today." Her breath ruffled Amelia's fur, and Betsie sighed with contentment, grateful beyond words for the precious gift Charley had given her.

A few minutes later, as a smug Amelia licked her whiskers after a snack, Betsie made a fruitless search for her notebook. Distraught, she prepared for bed and turned in, nose to nose with Amelia.

Hours later, a rumble like thunder brought Betsie out of a deep sleep. She sensed that it was not yet morning and groaned. Amelia batted playfully at Betsie's hair as she tossed and turned.

A short while later, her eyes popped open again. What had awoken her this time when she wished to sleep for a whole week? There it was again. Was she imagining things or had someone thrown pebbles at her window? Her heart hammered. Had Charley Yoder come courting her in such an old-fashioned way?

Betsie sat bolt upright and clapped her hand to her mouth. She dressed lickety-split and shut up Amelia firmly in her room. For the second time, her heart filled to bursting with gratitude to Charley.

Betsie marveled at her presence of mind as she avoided the creaky parts of the staircase. This special sitting up with Charley should be their own time, so she tiptoed through the dark house to avoid waking Sadie, heart quivering with happiness at the thought of the young man who waited patiently on the other side of the door.

She detoured to the kitchen, where with shaking fingers she attempted to light the lamp wick; it took four tries. At last, Betsie set the lamp on the hall table and smoothed her front hair. After a couple of shaky breaths and a final pat to her *Kapp*, she yanked open the door.

"Charley! Come—"

She stopped in confusion; no broad-shouldered Amishman stood there with his straw hat in hand. Betsie giggled; he was playing a trick on her. She stuck her head out the door.

"Charley, this is no time for hide-and-seek," she pretended to scold. "I know you are here."

He didn't answer. Betsie heard the rattle again, only now it sounded more like a snarl. Nightmare images of the Hilliard Stalker resurrected panicked her. She snatched up the lamp.

The light fell on a prone figure. At Betsie's gasp, the figure stirred. Michael Sullivan was curled up on Betsie's front porch like *Lassie Come-Home*, fast asleep.

CHAPTER 41

Better days are coming.

—BETSIE'S JOURNAL

"MICHAEL!" BETSIE STEPPED outside and shut the door. She knelt and shook him. "Michael, wake up! You can't sleep here."

He snored again and adjusted his arms to cradle his head, out cold. Something slipped from his hand and clinked on the worn boards— his car keys, on the key ring she'd made for him.

Betsie bit her lip. Through the gloom she glimpsed the telltale yellow-jacket car parked at the end of the driveway. Come daylight, the bright English car would be visible for the world to see. Even Charley couldn't keep Mattie Yoder from having a banner day with this news.

The sweet smell of Joe Miller's new-mown grass tickled Betsie's nostrils and sparked her memory. She tucked Michael's keys in her pocket and raced for the barn. Judith whickered a question as Betsie dragged both doors wide open. She marched to the yellow car before she lost her nerve and slid behind the wheel. She scooted the keys around the ring to find the driving one, pushed it into the ignition, and tried to dredge up memories of Michael starting the car. What came next?

An image of a triumphant Mattie Yoder taunted her instead, the sly cat smile evident as Mattie spread the story of the English boy's late-night visit to Betsie Troyer's house all over Plain City—it would be a disaster.

She gritted her teeth and cranked the key. The roar of the motor nearly stopped her heart. She prayed that Sadie wouldn't wake up. What next? Oh, yes, the gas. She held onto the wood wheel, felt for the pedal, and mashed it with her shoe. The car responded with another roar, but still it didn't move. Desperate, Betsie craned to see if her foot was in the right place. Her elbow brushed the silver stick in the middle. *Ach!* She found the letter D and popped the stick to rest beside it. Then she pressed the gas pedal again.

She was driving! Only problem was, she wasn't driving near fast enough. The car hesitated and roared. She'd never experienced this when Michael was behind the wheel; she must have forgotten a part of the procedure, but she didn't have time to figure it out. She kept the pedal depressed and turned the wheel toward the barn. The car inched over the bumpy grass.

By the time she drove through the barn doors, Betsie was sweating. It was hard to see inside the dark barn, but she couldn't recollect how to turn on the car lights, either. She pulled alongside the buggy and guided the car as far ahead as she dared before she pressed the brake with all her strength. She moved the silver stick back to P with a long, drawn-out sigh and twisted the key toward her. Mercifully, the engine shut off.

Every muscle ached, but she had done it. She opened the door and eased into the narrow space between the car and the buggy. Even in the dim light, she made out white rings around Judith's brown eyes. The mare pinned her ears flat to her skull with an indignant snort. Betsie hurried to console her and made a mental promise that she would never again drive a car.

One problem was solved, but another one still snored away when Betsie returned to the porch. She sidestepped Michael, miffed. If Charley Yoder *did* come courting tonight, wouldn't this be a fine kettle of fish? How would she explain away the English boy asleep on her porch? Her stomach bubbled uneasily. If Charley saw Michael here, it would be all over between them forever, especially in view of his newfound maturity.

She had to move Michael, all six odd feet of him, and fast. If only he wasn't such a sound sleeper. Betsie licked her dry lips and hurried to the kitchen. She dipped a cup of water from the bucket. Oh, how cool and refreshing! She started to replace the dipper, but instead she laid it on the counter thoughtfully. She picked up the bucket and the remaining water made a satisfying slosh.

Bucket in hand, she plunged through the sitting room and shoved open the door. With the frustration of the past days to lend her strength, Betsie pitched the water at Michael.

The silvery arc made a satisfying splash as it hit him full in the face. He inhaled enough of the water to make him snort worse than Judith. He spluttered and scrambled to his feet.

"What was that for?" He coughed and choked. Water streamed from his eyes and nose.

Betsie set down the bucket and grabbed his arm. "Be quiet! *Was in der welt* do you mean by coming here to sleep?" As she scolded, she ushered him off the front porch and toward the barn.

"Hey, where's my car?" He winced, wide awake now, as the gravel dug into his bare feet.

"Shh!" Betsie clapped a hand to his mouth and didn't let go until they crossed the driveway. When he saw where they were headed, he nodded. His wet hair brushed Betsie's arm as she removed her hand and they ran together into the darkness.

Once inside the barn, Michael pulled one door shut while Betsie pulled the other. A strip of starlight filtered through the crack; by its light, Michael looked almost happy, though a bruise outlined his jaw.

"What is the matter with you?" Betsie flashed. "Don't you know how much trouble I would be in if anyone found you here?"

"Well, hello to you, too." He reached up and tucked a stray hair away from her eyes. Betsie flinched.

"Michael. I haven't talked with you since Wednesday, when Peggy slapped me, in case you forgot." She windmilled her arms. "You promised you would eat with us, but you didn't come. Sheila and I worked on your surprise birthday dinner for *days*. What did you do, go to a . . . a *peace* rally and get beaten to a pulp? You scared us all to death, and now you are drunk again, sleeping it off on my front porch. I am sorry, but I don't feel like saying hello."

He winced and caught her hand before Betsie could stomp out of the barn. "I haven't been drinking! I've been up for two days and I'm beat—you know what a sound sleeper I am. Look, Pippa, I know I say this a lot, but I'm sorry. Please give me a chance to explain."

Betsie jerked her hand away. "No. Just go home, Michael. I will talk to you on Monday. No, wait, that's Memorial Day and I am not coming. Explain on Tuesday, your birthday." She tried to wither him with a glance.

Suddenly Michael looked pale and sick. Betsie's heart melted a little. "What's wrong? Do you need to sit down?"

"No. Listen, I deserved what you said, every word." He took a deep breath. "I'm kind of fuzzy-headed from a lack of sleep, but I have to say this tonight. I finally have a plan, Pippa. So, please, just give me a chance—"

"Shh!" Betsie held up a hand and watched as Judith tossed her head and perked her ears. Out of the still night came the sound of hoofbeats fast-stepping down the road. Betsie was positive she recognized them.

"It's Charley. He's coming!" She tried to slip outside, but Michael caught her sleeve.

"Pippa, please don't go to him."

"I will come back later to talk. I promise." She left him in the barn and skipped to meet Charley Yoder.

Sure enough, Charley's buggy topped the rise. Betsie kept to the shadows and sprinted for the lilac hedge at the corner of the house. She crouched behind the hedge. Through a gap in the leaves, she watched Charley step out of the buggy.

But what was this? Charley crossed to the other side of the buggy and offered his hand . . . to Sadie.

A roaring filled Betsie's ears. She stared as her sister and her Charley strolled into the house. Then she pressed one hand to her mouth and stumbled to the barn, where Michael eased the door open just wide enough to let her slip through. She sank to her knees on the dirt floor, buried her face in her hands, and wept.

After an eternity, she felt Michael's hand on her shoulder. "Hey, I saw. Tough break, Pippa."

Distraught, she curled around the pain in her heart. To lose Charley to her own sister was too much. "Do you think . . . Michael, do you think he loves her? And n-not me?" Betsie breathed in painful, short jerks as she waited for his answer. She was surprised to find herself seated on a scattering of straw, propped against the car. Michael sat next to her, his presence solid and warm.

Very gently he brushed away her tears. "I don't see how he could love anyone but you."

Oddly comforted, Betsie blushed and struggled to regain her composure. At last she faced him again. "You are sweet to say so. But you wanted to tell me something, *jah?*"

Michael shrugged and stared at his feet. "It really doesn't matter so much now." He let out a gusty breath. "You already know what happened to me at Kent State last May. The shooting just missed me, and it was awful to see them—regular students like me—dead."

"Horrible," Betsie shuddered.

He sighed again. "Less than a month after Kent State, I turned nineteen. A month later, on July first, the government held the draft lottery for everyone born in 1951, which included yours truly. I guess you know about the draft, like with your cousin and the harness shop."

"And like Schwartz talked about when he gave you a ticket. You told Sheila not to worry," she accused.

"That's right, I'm a liar—I worry about it all the time. Seemed like I'd barely make it through one rough emotional patch, and I'd hit another one, *bam.* By the time July 1 rolled around, though, I was pretty sure my luck was gonna change. Me and my other buddies who were born in 1951 got together to watch the draft lottery on TV—we made it into kind of a sick party. The military types on the tube drew capsules out of a big bowl, and each one had a date of the year inside. The first birth date drawn out was the first to go, #001. So the later my birth date was drawn, the better. If it were one of the first ones, I'd probably have to go, you get me?"

She nodded.

"Every time the guy on TV drew a number, we all got quiet. It was like having a gun pointed at your head. Some of the guys were drinking." He sat up, suddenly tense. "Listen. I don't blame you if you don't believe me, but I really don't like alcohol. You need to know that. I don't handle it well, and it doesn't help me forget like I thought it would. I'm through with it forever."

"That's good, Michael." She shivered.

"You're cold." Chagrined, he retrieved his denim jacket from the back seat of the car. Betsie drew it under her chin as Michael draped it over her shoulders. Betsie smiled. The jacket smelled like him.

"So, wouldn't you know it? They draw *my* birthday out of the jar, and I'm number sixty-five. Out of 365, I get sixty-five!" He shook his head, bemused. "My number would have been 365 if I'd been born on July 7."

Betsie sucked in her breath. "That's Charley's birthday!" she blurted, sorry and relieved at the same time. "I mean . . ."

Michael's smile was bittersweet. "It figures. My buddies' birth dates didn't get drawn until near the end, either, so they're home free. They all avoided me like I'd just received the death sentence. I've been drafted, Pippa. So many times I marched for peace, protested for peace, wrote about peace, but what good did it do? Real peace—I can't find it."

Amidst Betsie's jumbled thoughts, one became crystal clear. "And the peace of God, which passeth all understanding, shall keep your hearts and minds through Christ Jesus," she murmured.

Michael started. "What?"

"The *Biewel* verse, at the tent revival, the one about peace." She shrugged.

He sat up and peered at her intently. "Pippa, do *you* believe that's where true peace comes from? Is that what the Amish believe?"

She hedged. "I know Sheila believes it, and the tent revival pastor believed it, too. He talked a lot about peace. That last letter from my *mem*, she quoted a verse like it. Wait, I have it here." She drew the crumpled letter she'd meant to share with Sadie from her pocket and found the place. "'Thou wilt keep him in perfect peace, whose mind is stayed on thee, because he trusteth in thee.'"

Michael nodded slowly. "It's so unreal that just when I'm about to discover what real peace means, it's all taken out of my hands. I feel like I'm being sent to die, you know? And Pippa, I'm not ready to die yet." He looked at Betsie, shamefaced. "I have something for you." Betsie watched as he went back to his car again and returned with her notebook. "I'm really sorry, but I read the parts at the back when I was having such a rough time, the parts where you told what it was like to live with us, because it made me laugh." He paused. "That white poem about the laundry on the line . . ."

Betsie clutched the notebook. "Please don't, Michael."

His shoulders slumped. "Yeah, you're right. Bad timing. Sorry." He drew the key ring from his pocket, and rubbed his thumb slowly over the single word. "Pippa, I trust you. I'm not telling anyone else this. I'm supposed to report to the draft board so I can be inducted, and the minute I complete basic training, that's it. I'll be shipped to Vietnam so fast it'll make your head spin. But get this; I'm not going. I'm headed for the Farm, that commune down in Tennessee, and you're the only one who knows. It's the closest I can get to being Amish. No government, no laws, no wars." He smiled faintly and held out his hand. "Want to come with me? You can teach me everything you know about living off the land."

Her heart sank. "My place is here with my people, where it's safe, where the good Lord wants me to be." With Charley. "Besides the army warned Nelson not to try to get out of his time of service," Betsie reminded. "They said he shouldn't dodge the draft."

He shrugged and dropped his hand to his side. "What's the worst they can do if they catch me—kill me? They're already sending me to die, so it's six of one, half a dozen of the other." He laughed, but it wasn't a happy sound.

"Michael, your family—how can you leave them?" She thought of Sheila and winced.

"I'll be leaving them either way. What's the difference?" His tone was almost brusque.

A tear rolled down Betsie's cheek. "I will miss you. Will I see you again before you go?"

He cleared his throat and gave her *Kapp* string a gentle tug. "You're the only one who understands what I need." He held up the key ring and in the dim light the word *peace* barely showed. "As hard as it will be, I think . . . I think it would be better if I split now. I'm always getting you into trouble. I don't fit your way of life, you know? And I'm just making life harder for Sheila, too. Can't seem to do anything right these days."

In a daze, Betsie slowly drew off his jacket and folded it over on the seat. As Michael slid into the seat and backed his car out of the barn, she stayed at his side. He drove slowly to the road, hesitating before he reached out the window for her hand. His fingers intertwined with hers and lingered for a moment. "Good-bye, Betsie."

He was out of sight before she realized he'd called her by her real name. She stared at her hand. Though it was still warm from his touch, she was alone.

You are not alone It was almost as though Betsie had heard the words spoken aloud.

Faces came to mind. She saw her dear friend Rachel Yutzy. Lovina, *dat*'s sweet sister, had stood by her in a time of great trouble. Ellie and Sol Beiler, too—there were many good friends who loved her very much.

New faces intruded from the English world. Archie, the gallant butcher at Ayers Market. The good policeman, Deacon, diligent to protect her; the postman who'd helped her after the accident; and even Mr. Sullivan as he taught Betsie how to use unfamiliar machines—each had been kind as she struggled to fit into the English world.

She thought of Sheila. The image of her dear face, so loving as she accepted a stranger into her home, was a balm to Betsie's broken heart. At first, she had been just a funny little girl, but she had grown into a good friend when Betsie sorely needed one. And of course, there was—

"Why was the Peacock here?"

She whirled and slipped the hand Michael had touched into her pocket. Charley Yoder sat on the porch steps. She'd completely forgotten that he was here.

"Charley! You nearly scared me out of my wits!"

"I've been waiting for you, Betsie," he said. "I was worried."

"Waiting . . . for me? But you came home with Sadie. I saw you." Betsie's lower lip trembled.

Charley was very solemn, star-lit blond hair framing his angel face. "*Mem* is sick with what Miriam Bontrager had. Sadie stayed late to help care for her, and when I brought her home, I asked her to wake you. When she told me you weren't in your bed, I didn't know what to think. How can I watch out for you when I don't know where you are, Betsie? It's not good for you to spend so much time with the English, especially alone with that boy so late, ain't so?"

"*Ach.* I thought—never mind." A quick fire of shame blazed across her cheeks, and she rushed to explain. "Michael is my friend only." Her conscience pricked like a needle through a thimble. "He's very troubled, and I was trying to help him. But don't worry, Charley. He's leaving. And he won't be back." The words caught in her throat.

Charley ducked his head. "*Ach*, that's so good, Betsie. Come here and sit by me, why don't you?" He patted the step.

She'd waited forever to be near him again, and she did not hesitate.

"Betsie, I have another question to ask you."

Her heart pounded. "What question?"

But now Charley hemmed and hawed. "*Ach*, maybe I'm no good with fancy words, but I do know where you need to be and what is best for you." He stopped to ponder, searching for a better way to put it. His face lit up with a thought. "You know it is true that you will never get to heaven if you stay with the English."

Betsie felt a quick stab of fear. "But Charley! *Mem* and *Dat*—"

"*Ach*, no." Charley groaned and cradled his face in his hands. "I told you I am a *Nixnootzich* when it comes to words. Of course I pray that your *mem* and *dat* will return soon." He raised his head. "I am trying to say that I want you to stay here. I want you for my special friend." He added, very low, "I hope one day we will have a home together. What do you say, Betsie?"

She nodded, a lump in her throat. "I . . . I'd like that more than anything."

"Then kiss me once, Betsie," he said.

Excitement fluttered through her; she'd waited a long time for this. She raised her lips and closed her eyes. His kiss brushed her mouth like a moth's wing, tentative and chaste.

He drew back and smiled, visibly relieved. "Well, it's awful late. I'd better get back to *Mem*. She needs me."

Betsie bobbed her head. "All right, Charley. See you soon." For the second time, she waved good-bye. She touched her lips as she watched Charley unhitch the horses and drive away into the darkness.

So that was a kiss, she mused as she stepped inside the door. She turned up the lamp and sat down at the scarred oak table in the kitchen. Now, now she was free to think of Charley and all the wonderful times that awaited the two of them.

After a couple of minutes, she stirred restlessly and stoked the fire in the cookstove. She searched for the bucket and remembered she'd heaved the contents at Michael. She grinned. My, hadn't she surprised him!

But it was time to dream of Charley, she reminded herself. She emptied the pitcher of cold water from the ice box into the tea kettle and put it on to boil. While she waited, she measured tea leaves and tamped them into the tea ball. Carefully she took out a twin of the cup she'd broken at the beginning of the month. She suspended the tea ball by the hook and filled the cup brimful once the kettle boiled. Then she left the tea to steep while she sorted out her life.

Much of her future was uncertain, she knew. Things would be changing at the Sullivan household if Mr. Sullivan chased after his wife. Betsie would miss Sheila something awful, for she would, of course, go with her dad. There would be nobody left to help Betsie tend the harness shop since Michael had left for the Farm, so that part of her life was over for now. At least she would no longer have to figure out how to live with the English and stay out of trouble.

She cherished no hopes of *Dat*, *Mem*, and Lovina returning to Plain City any time soon, not when *Dat* felt so strongly about their new life. Whatever it was that had taken her family away from their Amish beliefs was mighty powerful, surely.

And what of Abijah, staying with their brother Eli in Missouri? Neither he nor their other siblings knew about *Mem* and *Dat*'s decision. If Sadie and Betsie were to write to them, surely they could help persuade *Dat* to return home with *Mem* and Lovina.

Then there was Sadie. Betsie swallowed. She and her sister would need to grow closer, she realized. They must be everything to each other now; well, almost everything, now that Betsie had Charley.

Only one loose end remained—Michael. She had the oddest feeling that she'd let her friend down, but suddenly she brightened. Mr. Sullivan had said he needed to make amends with Michael, too. If only his father could bump into him at home before they each went their separate ways, maybe things would turn out right for Michael at last.

Betsie sugared her tea and blew to cool it. The most important thing was that Charley, *her* Charley now, made up for all the uncertainty in her life. She sipped from her cup and smiled as the sun made a quiet pink glow beyond the dark fields. The day promised to be beautiful—a beautiful new day for a new beginning.

AUTHOR'S NOTE

While *The Bargain* is a work of fiction, Betsie Troyer's story is loosely based on that of a real-life Plain City, Ohio, Amish woman who took over a harness shop after her nephew was drafted. I interviewed "Betsie" in 2006, when only nine members of the once-large Plain City Amish population remained. What happened to the rest? Rapid sprawl of the Columbus metropolitan area doubled and tripled land prices over the course of fifteen years. Since Amish families are traditionally large, there were simply not enough affordable farm sites left for the sons. As a result, many Plain City Amish patriarchs sold their farms at a premium and sought cheaper, more plentiful land in Ohio and Missouri.

Land prices are only part of the story, however. The Plain City Amish who remained found it increasingly difficult to host traditional worship services when the burden fell more frequently to the same aging families. Eventually, services were held in "Betsie's" own outbuilding once a month, with traveling bishops from Holmes County presiding. As time passed, most of the former Plain City Amish embraced other beliefs, mostly those of the Mennonite faith. Today, although only five of the original Plain City Amish still live in town, plenty of Troyers, Gingeriches, Millers, Yutzys, and Yoders can be found at the helm of area shops, restaurants, and farm markets.

I am grateful to all the fine folk who generously answered my questions in the process of writing this book: Saloma F., Martha Yoder

Garrett, Lovina G., Minerva G., Mary Ann K., and Rachel M., as well as Misstion to Amish People and Brenda Nixon.

Author Brenda Nixon (http://www.brendanixononamish.blogspot .com/) aids former Amish after they leave their homes and families, with the help of Mission to Amish People (www.mapministry.org/). You can read some of the heart-wrenching testimonies of former Amish at their website; many profess to never having realized the good news of the gospel of Jesus Christ. Brenda knows firsthand that Amish who desire to leave the church, like Betsie's parents Noah and Fannie Troyer, face intense pressure to remain and discipline if they leave. She also states that Amish women in Betsie's shoes, having been assaulted, would have little reason to report the attack, whether to their churches or to the authorities, the consensus being that the women "brought it upon themselves" by throwing in their lot with the outside world.

I am also grateful to many others: to family and friends for prayers and support; to Kregel Publications, where the nicest people in publishing are found; to agent Greg Johnson, president of WordServe Literary; to Susan K. Marlow, author, editor, and friend; and to other fellow authors, Janet Eckles, Miralee Ferrell, Ellen Kennedy, and Kevin Williams.

BOOK CLUB DISCUSSION QUESTIONS

1. In the early 1970s, the military draft lottery was still in effect in the United States. Setting aside your views on military service to our country, what are your thoughts about a lottery system with the luck of the draw and one's birth date determining which young men served during the Vietnam War?

2. The Amish are well-known pacifists. Nevertheless, eligible young Amish men were drafted to serve alongside eligible "English" men as early as the World War I era. Most if not all Amish declined to serve, citing conscientious objector status. As a result, they were ridiculed or even physically abused by others who did not share their beliefs. In later years, alternate methods of service were established for conscientious objectors. Amish author David Kline tells of his Vietnam War alternative service at a Cleveland hospital in his book *Great Possessions*. How would you react if the draft were reinstated today and conscientious objectors were allowed to remain stateside doing community service? What if women were drafted, but not Amish women of the same age?

3. The Amish speak a unique language, but so did the people of the 1970s! What are some favorite expressions from that era or from your own teen years that Betsie may have found strange? Now brainstorm "church speak" phrases that may make perfect sense to believers but may confuse others. (See http://www.youtube.com/watch?v=rjBbRb78SfI.) Discuss clearer ways to talk about Jesus Christ with a nonbeliever.

4. Tragic memories of the May 4, 1970, Kent State massacre are

strong in Ohio. Over forty years later, emotional scars are still evident; adults who were students at that time report PTSD as a result. Given that PTSD is at the very least emotionally taxing for everyone involved, do you identify with Gerald Sullivan's get-on-with-it response to Michael's problems, or would you respond more like Betsie, willing to listen?

5. Readers of a certain age may feel they were "raised Amish" when they compare their own growing-up years with those of their children. Remember when having a phone in the car seemed the epitome of luxury? Name other modern-day marvels that have rendered everyday items from your childhood obsolete. What simple pleasures do you miss the most? (See www.youtube.com/watch?v=LQqyDj7RX6Y for a 1970s Faygo advertisement that resurrects nostalgia.)

6. Recently, there has been a proliferation of reality TV shows about the Amish. Sadly, many Amish youth are portrayed as running away from rather than toward a saving faith in Jesus Christ, choosing freedom to make their own choices for better or worse (usually worse, if the programs are any indication). How is Noah and Fannie Troyer's choice different? Do they have anything in common with their television counterparts?

7. Mrs. Sullivan leaves her family in an attempt to accomplish a goal of her own. Discuss her situation and feelings that would lead her to such an extreme decision. How would that decision be met in our culture today? How would you advise a friend whose family was asking things of her that she didn't feel capable of—like Phyllis's incompetence in putting dinner on the table?

8. Betsie greatly desires to splice the broken Sullivan family back together. Her method is very practical: to gather the family around the table for a wonderful meal, a tradition that occurs daily in an Amish family. How often does your family eat together in a typical week? Do you serve homemade meals, or is takeout as good as a feast at your house? What difference can

sharing a meal make, and why? If family mealtime is impossible, share your family traditions.

9. Sometimes it's difficult to separate the '70s from the drug culture that was so prevalent at the time, running the gamut from popular music lyrics to sharing a high school restroom with drug users (tobacco, alcohol, or otherwise). Have you, like Betsie, ever found yourself in unwelcome contact with drug users/dealers, such as at a party or a concert? How did you handle the situation? Do you have a story to share about former drug use and how God helped you "go straight"?

10. One holdover from the turbulent '70s is demonstrating in a public place to make a point. Have you ever participated in a protest/demonstration? For what cause? Name some times/causes when demonstrations witnessed on TV or in person turned violent. Do you feel that followers of Jesus Christ should put themselves in harm's way to make a point?

11. At the revival/camp meeting, an uncomfortable Betsie slips out during the altar call. If you have attended a church that issues an invitation to publicly come forward, kneel, pray, and accept Jesus Christ as personal Savior, how did the invitation affect you? What was/would be your response? What do you believe happened when you accepted Jesus Christ? Can salvation be assured? Share Bible verses to support your answers.

12. According to 1 Peter 3:3–4, what makes us beautiful in the sight of the Lord? Do you think Betsie's Amish dress matters in God's eyes? Why or why not?

13. When her world turns upside down, Sheila Sullivan longs for Betsie to be her friend. Though Betsie is resistant at first, she agrees. Their friendship is sweet, yet Sheila needs more. Is there a danger when we depend on humans to fill a "God-shaped hole" in our hearts?

14. Sadie and Betsie spend a lot of time in the kitchen. The sisters have their favorite family recipes, like so many English families. The recipe for Banana Cream Pie that follows comes from the author's husband's talented Grandma Reed. Share a

favorite recipe or kitchen tip with the group. Do you associate a special memory with a recipe?

15. The people of the '70s, like the people of today, long for peace. Why do you think peace is so elusive? Do you long for peace, or does "peace" equal "boring" for you? What Scripture verses about the subject of peace bring you the most comfort or encouragement?

16. How different the young men in Betsie's life are! Charley Yoder and Michael Sullivan each bring different qualities and sensibilities; and each has disappointed Betsie. Which man would you choose, and why?

MASHED POTATO DOUGHNUTS

2 cups warm mashed potatoes (without added butter or milk)
2½ cups sugar
2 cups buttermilk
2 eggs, slightly beaten
2 tablespoons butter or margarine, melted
2 teaspoons baking powder
2 teaspoons baking soda
1 teaspoon ground nutmeg
½ teaspoon salt
6 to 7 cups flour

In a large bowl, combine the first four ingredients. Stir in butter, baking powder, baking soda, nutmeg, salt, and about half the flour. Continue adding flour until it forms a soft dough.

On a floured surface, pat dough to ¾-inch thick. Cut with floured doughnut cutter.

Heat oil to 350 degrees in skillet. Fry doughnuts, a few at a time, for two minutes on each side or until golden brown, turning with a fork. Drain on paper towels. Dip tops of warm doughnuts in fudge frosting or roll in cinnamon-sugar mixture.

for fudge frosting:
4 cups confectioners' sugar
½ cup cocoa
¼ teaspoon salt
½ cup boiling water
⅓ cup butter or margarine, melted
1 teaspoon vanilla

Combine dry ingredients and set aside. Mix water, butter, and vanilla. Stir in dry ingredients and beat until smooth.

for cinnamon-sugar topping:
1 cup sugar
½ teaspoon ground cinnamon

BANANA CREAM PIE WITH
OIL-BASED PIE CRUST

for the crust:
   1¼ cups flour
   ⅓ cup canola oil
   2 tablespoons *cold* water
   1 teaspoon cinammon

Preheat oven to 350 degrees. Mix ingredients well with fork until dough forms a ball. Pat dough into bottom and sides of a 9-inch pie plate. With a fork, poke holes in the bottom of the crust. Bake for 10–15 minutes or until pie crust looks dry but not brown. Cool, then fill.

for the filling:
   ⅓ cup sugar
   2 tablespoons cornstarch
   2 egg yolks, beaten
   2 cups milk
   2 tablespoons butter
   2 teaspoons vanilla
   2 medium bananas

Mix sugar and corn starch well in a saucepan. Add the beaten egg yolks and milk and bring mixture to a boil over medium heat, stirring constantly. Let boil one minute. Remove from heat. Add butter and vanilla and stir until the butter is melted.

Slice bananas into cooled pie shell; pour pudding over. Chill.

Decorate with whipped cream if desired.